The Gift

The young man stood, transfixed, in the ring of stones.

The woman before him was regal, but no longer beautiful. She reached out to touch his cheek and her fingers scorched his skin. "Do you know who I am?" she asked.

"You are the mother of us all," he said. "The *darlai* of the land."

She smiled. "I am Celi herself, and my gift will be with you always. I promise you service but not happiness. Happiness is for lesser souls."

He stepped forward and reached out. "Lady . . . " but there was nothing around him except silent stones, megaliths reaching upward. Even the moon was gone.

Books by Ann Marston

The Rune Blade Trilogy

Kingmaker's Sword
The Western King
The Broken Blade*

Published by from HarperPrism

*coming soon

ATTENTION: ORGANIZATIONS AND CORPORATIONS

Most HarperPaperbacks are available at special quantity discounts
for bulk purchases for sales promotions, premiums, or fund-raising.
For information, please call or write:
**Special Markets Department, HarperCollins*Publishers*,
10 East 53rd Street, New York, N.Y. 10022.
Telephone: (212) 207-7528. Fax: (212) 207-7222.**

The Second Book of the Rune Blade Trilogy

THE
WESTERN
KING

Ann Marston

HarperPrism
An Imprint of HarperPaperbacks

HarperPaperbacks
A Division of HarperCollins*Publishers*
10 East 53rd Street, New York, N.Y. 10022-5299

This is a work of fiction. The characters, incidents, and dialogues are products of the author's imagination and are not to be construed as real. Any resemblance to actual events or persons, living or dead, is entirely coincidental.

ISBN: 0-06-105628-6

HarperPrism is an imprint of HarperPaperbacks.

HarperCollins®, ®, HarperPaperbacks™, and HarperPrism® are trademarks of HarperCollins*Publishers* Inc.

Cover illustration by Yvonne Gilbert
Map by Barbara Galler-Smith

First printing: October 1996

Printed in the United States of America

Visit HarperPaperbacks on the World Wide Web at
http://www.harpercollins.com/paperbacks

❖ 10 9 8 7 6 5 4 3 2 1

This book is dedicated to some very special IMPs:
Lyn D. Nichols, Louise Rowder, and, of course, David
Bollinger and Barb Galler-Smith.

Notes

The year is divided into eight seasons:

Late Winter:	Imbolc to Vernal Equinox (February 2 to March 21)
Early Spring:	Vernal Equinox to Beltane (March 22 to May 1)
Late Spring:	Beltane to Midsummer Solstice (May 2 to June 21)
Early Summer:	Midsummer Solstice to Lammas (June 22 to August 1)
Late Summer:	Lammas to Autumnal Equinox (August 2 to September 21)
Early Autumn:	Autumnal Equinox to Samhain (September 22 to October 31)
Late Autumn:	Samhain to Midwinter Solstice (November 1 to December 21)
Early Winter:	Midwinter Solstice to Imbolc (December 22 to February 1)

The four sun feasts are Midwinter Solstice, Vernal Equinox, Midsummer Solstice, and Autumnal Equinox.

The four fire feasts are Imbolc, Beltane, Lammas, and Samhain.

Pronunciation Guide

The "C" in Celi is the hard Celtic "C," so Celi is pronounced "Kay-lee"

The "dd" is the Welsh "th" sound, as in then, thus Jorddyn is pronounced "Jorthun."

Book Two of the
Rune Blade Trilogy

THE
WESTERN
KING

Prologue

Dun Eidon, ancestral home of the Prince of Skai, sat like a jewel at the head of the deep inlet where the River Eidon emptied into the sea. Built of white stone, the graceful colonnades and soaring towers glistened against the background of winter-bare trees and mountains. A small village nestled close to the walls, the neatly thatched roofs of the buildings golden in the sun against the layer of snow still lying thick on the ground. At the foot of the track leading down from the west gate of the palace, a stone jetty thrust out into the clear, blue water of the Ceg. Two tall-masted ships rocked, sedate and stately, at anchor at the end of the pier amid a cluster of small fishing boats, like two swans among a flock of ducks.

On the side of the mountain rising above the palace, surrounded by twelve oaks hung with leafless strands of ivy, the shrine of the Duality serenely overlooked the village and the harbor. Beyond the shrine stood a small stone circle, a dance of seven menhirs, each three times the height of a man, one for each of the gods and goddesses.

Below the palace, in a large field between the village and the pier, men and boys trained with swords, spears, and bows. Despite the late winter chill, some of them were bare to the waist and sweating with exertion. The voices of the weapons-masters rang clear and sharp in the still air. Near the barracks separating the practice field from the village, a young woman worked with three girls, leading them through the sword drill. Two of the girls were ten or eleven years old, already showing the promise of great skill. The youngest was a child of only six.

Two men stood at the edge of the trampled snow that defined the practice field, watching the training. Red Kian of

Skai, father and Regent to the Prince of Skai, stood taller and broader than the man beside him. His red hair glowed in the early afternoon sun and hung free to his shoulders except for the thick braid by his left temple. A topaz on a fine gold chain dangled from his left earlobe and sparked gold flashes onto the skin of his throat as the sun caught it. Jorddyn ap Tiernyn, Captain of the Company, watched the boys critically, but Kian's attention was riveted on the three young girls.

"Jorddyn," he said, not taking his eyes off the girls, "whom is Alys training besides Ylana and Torey?" As he spoke, the young woman went to one knee beside the smallest girl, taking great care to position the child's body correctly to perform the thrust and sweep maneuver she had been demonstrating.

"What?" Jorddyn looked across the field. "The little one? That's Letessa, Morfyn's daughter. He brought her down from Dun Llewen the other day. The High Priest and Priestess of their shrine say she has a calling."

Kian frowned. "A calling? How very odd."

Jorddyn nodded thoughtfully. "That's true," he said. "It's rare to have two bheancoran in training at the same time. Three is highly unusual."

"Alys, Ylana, and now this little one," Kian murmured, more to himself than to Jorddyn. "Whom will she serve?"

Alys was pledged to serve Keylan, Kian's eldest son, the Prince of Skai, when she finished her training in three years. Tradition said that only the Prince of Skai was served by a bheancoran, a warrior-maid who acted as personal guard, confidante, friend, and companion, a deep and abiding bond between them. Kian and his wife Kerridwen shared that bond, but even after fifteen years, he was not sure he could define it. Indefinable as the bond might be, it had no difficulty making its presence known.

Kian watched the girls, trying to recall all the stories Kerridwen had told him about bheancoran. It had happened before that a bheancoran served a man not the prince. Kerri herself was bheancoran, sworn to serve Kian, yet Kian was not prince. He had abdicated his rights to the coronet and torc of Skai in favor of Keylan. Although his daughter Torey had no calling and would not be bheancoran, she trained with Alys because her friend Ylana trained, and the pair were all but inseparable.

"Whom will she serve?" Jorddyn repeated. "Perhaps Donaugh? Ylana has already pledged to serve Tiernyn." He glanced across the field to a group of young men. "Having a bheancoran pledged to serve him proves Tiernyn is destined to be a truly great Captain of the Company."

Kian turned to watch his sons, who were working with a group of younger boys. Keylan, tall and red-haired like his father, worked with a young boy, teaching him the first of the advanced exercises, both of them using wooden practice swords. Keylan patiently led the boy through the same movement again and again, coaching him until it was perfect. The twins, Tiernyn and Donaugh, nearly five years younger at thirteen, sparred against each other under the critical eye of the Swordmaster.

"I doubt Donaugh will need a bheancoran," Kian said. "He'll have his magic."

Amusement glinted in Jorddyn's eye. "You have magic, too," he said. "And you have Kerri."

Kian laughed. "Your daughter constantly reminds me that I don't deserve her."

"Kerri's much like her mother. The two of you were made for each other." Jorddyn grinned. "And that could be counted as blessing or curse."

"I'll count it as blessing," Kian said. "Kerri raised Keylan as her own." He still felt a twinge of mild guilt when he thought of Keylan's mother, who had died in childbed. It had been an arranged marriage, and he had felt nothing but a mild fondness for her. Her death had stirred only a vague sadness, but no real grief.

He watched the twins for a moment, then Torey, who was sparring with Ylana. "And I certainly couldn't ask for finer children than the twins and Torey." He shook his head. "No, Donaugh won't need a bheancoran. His magic will be stronger than mine ever was or could be. I hope he'll be the one to find a way to use it against our enemies."

"Celae magic comes from Tyadda magic," Jorddyn said. "It can't be used to kill."

"I know. But I found a way to make it help me fight an enemy. A limited way, granted. Donaugh will find a better way." He frowned. "This means something, Jorddyn. I hope it doesn't mean the time we won to solve our problems with the Saesnesi is almost up."

Jorddyn glanced at Kian, startled. "Surely not," he said. "It's only been fifteen years. You said we had a lifetime . . . "

Kian shrugged. "Who's to say fifteen years isn't a lifetime, or isn't all the time we get. The news from Tyra wasn't good."

"No news from the continent is good these days," Jorddyn said.

Kian's attention went back to the three girls. Alys led them through the elegant, stylized exercises designed to train young muscles into conditioned reflexes. The graceful movements always reminded him of a dance.

"I don't like this," he said. "I wish I knew what it meant."

The fire burned low on the hearth in the solar. Light and shadow danced across the large room, flickering softly on the glow of burnished wood and polished tile. Kian sat in a deeply cushioned chair, wrapped in a bedgown of rich, dark green velvet. He pressed his tented fingers to his lips in an attitude of deep thought as he watched the crescent moon toss among a thin layer of high clouds outside the tall windows. Even when Kerri slipped into the room behind him and placed her hand on his shoulder, he didn't move.

"I can't hide anything from you, can I?" he said in wry amusement.

"Even without the bond, I'd know when you were troubled," she said.

He reached up to cover her hand with his. "I didn't mean to disturb you."

She moved to the side of his chair and sat on the arm, putting her hand against his cheek to turn his head toward her. "You," she said severely, "are still as stubborn as ever."

"Aye, well, I was born with it," he said. "I come by it honestly enough."

"You do," she said. "Kian, have you started dreaming true again?"

He shook his head. "No. Not since we came back to Celi."

"Then are you worried about the news from Tyra?"

"Partly," he said. "The continent has the Maedun at its throat. We have the Saesnesi raiders, and we're no closer now to uniting all the provinces of Celi against them than we were fifteen years ago."

"You know that's not yours to do."

"I know," he said tiredly. "But how can I say to one of our sons that it's his problem, and I can't help?"

"You've helped a lot already, you know."

"But not enough. The only other prince or duke in all of Celi who even halfway agrees with me on the need to unite is Ryvern of Wenydd, and he only because Skai and Wenydd have always been strong allies. We've so little time."

"Keylan turns eighteen next summer," she said. "The law says a regent can step aside when the prince turns eighteen, but if the prince agrees, the regent can corule until the prince is twenty-five."

One corner of Kian's mouth curled in amusement. "You needn't quote the law at me," he said mildly. "I know it as well as you do. I've been thinking of it a lot lately."

"What are you going to do?"

"I don't know."

She slipped to the floor beside his chair, laced her fingers across his knee, and rested her chin on the back of her hands. He reached out and put his hand to her head, letting his fingers tangle in the soft hair above her ear.

"You're Prince of Skai in everything but name," she said quietly. "It is, after all, your birthright. You could let the High Priest and Priestess instate you."

"And Keylan?"

"Keylan would be the first to cheer, and you know it."

"We've been through this a hundred times," he said.

"More like a thousand," she said with practiced equanimity.

He laughed. "You're right." He ran his finger down her cheek in a tender gesture. "I haven't changed my mind, *sheyala*. My mother was yrSkai, but I was born in Tyra, raised to be a Tyran clansman. I love this island, but Tyra is my home. Not Skai. Not Celi. This is a beautiful island, and Skai is its most beautiful province. But Tyra is home. I swore only to stand regent for Keylan. I'm not a prince, and I never was."

Without conscious volition, his hand went to the braid at his left temple. He had forgone the kilt and plaid of a Tyran clansman, but he was unable to give up the braid, or the topaz in his left ear. The tradition was too deeply ingrained. A clansman's braid was his strength; he gave it up only in death.

Unfazed, Kerri smiled. "Being the grandson of both Prince Kyffen of Skai and the Clan Laird of Broche Rhuidh in Tyra doesn't count?"

"The son of a daughter in the first case," he said. "And the son of a younger son in the second. No, Kerri. Keylan is Prince, and I'm going to have to step down soon. It's almost time to go home."

"But that's not what's troubling you now."

He shook his head. "Not entirely." He hesitated. "Alys is training another bheancoran. Letessa al Morfyn."

Startled, she looked up at him. "What does that mean?"

"I don't know. I wish I did."

"Kian?"

He raised one red-gold eyebrow in inquiry.

"I think you should talk with Rhegar."

"I think you're right."

Kian's house shoes made no sound on the polished wooden floor of the corridor, but the door to Rhegar's chambers opened before he could lift his hand to knock. The old man himself stood framed in the doorway, the light from the hall torches giving back some of the youthful color to the white of his hair and beard. Well over eighty, he still carried himself with the erect bearing of a man half his age. He was Tyadda, one of the strange, fey race that had inhabited the Isle of Celi since long before the Celae came, when the island was called Nemeara.

When the Celae came to the island, the Tyadda were a fading race, their once-strong magic slowly dying away. Intermarriage between the Tyadda and the Celae strengthened the magic, but it would never be as powerful as it had once been.

The Celae didn't conquer the Tyadda; they married them. It was a gentle conquest in that regard. There were very few true-born Tyadda left, and those few for the most part lived in hidden fastnesses deep in the mountains of Skai. Their dark gold hair and startlingly dark brown eyes tended to show up in the descendants of the Celae who intermarried with them. Kian had inherited his mother's Tyadda brown eyes along with his Tyran father's red hair and build.

"I've been expecting you, my lord Regent," Rhegar said, holding the door wide. "Please come in."

Kian smiled. "You've been looking into the fire again, Rhegar," he said.

The old man went to an ornately carved chest in the corner and poured two goblets of wine. He handed one to Kian and gestured toward two comfortable chairs drawn up in front of the hearth.

"Please be seated," he said. "The fire is only for warmth, my lord. These old bones need the comfort on a winter's night."

Kian sat with his legs stretched out before him, the goblet of wine cradled against his chest. "You heard that a messenger came from Tyra the other day?" he said.

"I saw him ride into the courtyard," Rhegar said. "I take it the news was bad?"

"When is news from the continent good these days? Sion says the Maedun are pressing Isgard and Saesnes hard. Laringras fell shortly before Midwinter and there's a Maedun sorcerer sitting on the throne as Lord Protector. That makes two—one in Falinor, and now this one in Laringras."

Rhegar sipped his wine, then nodded thoughtfully. "If the continent falls, the Maedun will look to Celi next."

"Exactly. And no two provinces will stand together against them, just as no two provinces will stand together against the Saesnesi raiders."

"And how fares Tyra?"

"Tyra has its own protection against the Maedun. At least against Maedun sorcery." Kian smiled grimly. "Tyran clansmen also tend to fight more fiercely than Maedun. Isgard is holding, but Saesnes is suffering."

The old man nodded again. "And when Saesnes suffers, it drives more longships across the Cold Sea to the east coast of Celi. Does Elesan welcome them?"

"I would think he had little choice. He calls himself High Prince of the Saesnesi in Celi. They're his countrymen and kinsmen, after all. That means there will be more Saesnesi raids on the provinces of Celi this spring."

Rhegar got up to place another log on the fire. He stood with his hands outstretched toward the flame, warming them, a frown drawing his silver eyebrows together above his dark eyes. "Dorian and Mercia will suffer the worst, being right beside the Saesnesi Shore."

"Skai will suffer, too. As will Wenydd. The Saesnesi won't

come through the mountains. The Spine of Celi has always served as good protection from the eastern provinces. But we've got so many miles of seacoast and thousands of inlets where a Saesnesi raiding party can land."

"How comes work on the watchtowers?"

"Nearly finished. With luck, this summer, we'll have several hours' warning before a raid."

Rhegar went to the chest. He refilled his goblet, brought the flask of wine back to his chair, and held it out to Kian. Kian put his hand over the top of the goblet and shook his head.

Rhegar placed the flask within easy reach on the small marble table between the chairs. "I don't think that's what brought you to me in the middle of the night, my friend."

Kian drained his wine and looked down into the empty goblet. The dark red dregs clung to the sides, making a random pattern. A fortune-telling hedge witch might make something out of the pattern, but Kian couldn't. Finally, he reached for the flask and refilled the goblet, shattering the pattern.

"No, you're right," he said. "It isn't." He was silent for a few moments, watching the flames leap among the logs on the hearth. "You know Alys al Rhan is training another bheancoran."

"Yes."

"I need to know what it means, Rhegar. Does it mean something will happen to Alys?"

"Or to Keylan?" Rhegar asked shrewdly. "A bheancoran seldom survives her prince if he dies in battle. Is that what you're worried about?"

Kian let out a long breath. "Yes," he said. "It's not just that Keylan's my son, and I love him and don't want anything to happen to him. It's Skai. Skai needs a strong prince. If something happens to Keylan, I don't think Tiernyn could be that prince. He has the fire and the spirit, but he's not focused on Skai as Keylan is."

Rhegar rose from his chair in a swift, fluid motion and went to a small table by the window. A wide, shallow bowl of polished copper sat in the middle of the table, gleaming in the light of the two candles in copper candlesticks beside it. Rhegar filled it with water from a glazed earthenware pitcher and beckoned to Kian.

The firelight glimmered in the glass of the window. Kian's reflection approached him like a pale ghost as he crossed the room and sat down across the table from Rhegar. Rhegar placed both hands around the bowl and leaned forward to peer down into the water. Lines of strain appeared around his eyes, and his brows drew together in a frown of concentration.

"When you first came to Celi from the continent, you carried a Rune Blade forged in Skai," he said, his voice taut and attenuated, as if he spoke from a great distance. "It was crafted by Wyfydd the Smith, one of the blades made with music and magic to defend this island."

"Kingmaker," Kian said softly. "I carried it in trust for the man who would unite Celi against the Saesnesi. It was Seen that my son would be that man." He leaned forward intently. "But which one, Rhegar? I have three sons."

Rhegar peered down into the bowl, frowning. "It may be Tiernyn," he said. He passed his hand over the softly glowing, misty surface of the water. "I see the sword shining here. And I think it's Tiernyn carrying it, with Donaugh at his side. I see two shadows only."

"But what of Keylan?"

"Keylan carries Bane, Kyffen's sword. He will be Prince. I see the torc at his throat, and the coronet binds his brow." Rhegar frowned again, the skin around his eyes taut with the strain of Seeing. "There's nothing clear, my lord Regent. All I can see ahead are troubled times."

"Will we have time enough to defeat the Saesnesi before we have to deal with Maedun invaders?"

"I can't tell you that. There's nothing of that here."

"Then can you tell me if my sons will be safe?"

Rhegar's face, already pale, took on the color and texture of old parchment. His eyes swam amid unshed tears. "My lord Regent, I see blood staining the walls of Dun Eidon. I see three stone cairns, hung with the ivy hoops of mourning, and I see a man weeping at his loss."

Kian gripped the edge of the table and leaned forward intensely. "Who weeps, Rhegar?" he asked hoarsely.

Rhegar shook his head. He passed his hands over the copper bowl as if trying to brush away mist. "I cannot tell. It may be you, my lord. It may be Keylan. I cannot tell."

"Rhegar . . ." Kian had to clear his throat before he could continue. "Who lies beneath the cairns? *Who?*"

Rhegar bent over the bowl, peering down intently, his mouth pinched and bloodless. He frowned. "I don't know," he whispered. "It is not here." He looked up and smiled. It cost him an effort. "But I can tell you that you and Kerri will return safely to Tyra when the time comes."

Kian forcibly calmed his racing heart and let one corner of his mouth lift in an answering smile. "Well, that's something, anyway," he said. "Thank you, Rhegar."

Rhegar passed his hand over the bowl again, but Kian reached out and caught his wrist gently. There was more he wanted to ask, but Rhegar had used up most of his strength already. "That's enough, old friend," he said. "It's late, and you're tired. Please get some rest now."

In his dreams that night, Kian walked a blighted landscape of ash and cinder. Under a colorless, gray sky, drifts of ash blew in the wind like swirls of mist. Only Maedun blood sorcery could produce a wasteland like this. At first, he thought it was the same dreamscape he had walked fifteen years ago, before he came to Celi. But it was different, and he could not at first say how.

Gradually, he began to recognize landmarks and knew the land he walked was the Isle of Celi. He turned and saw behind

him three stone cairns, the mourning wreaths adorning them
sere and burnt and dead.

He awoke with his heart pounding in his chest and tears of
rage and sorrow flooding down his cheeks.

"Who weeps?" he whispered into the silent darkness. "Oh,
gods, who weeps? And how long do we have left?"

PART

1

The Regency

1

Donaugh twisted in his saddle to watch as Tiernyn nocked the arrow and swept the tip around, leading the goose. Even as Tiernyn loosed the arrow, Donaugh knew it was a true shot. Pride in his twin brother stretched his mouth into a wide grin. At fifteen, Tiernyn's skill in archery was equal to any grown man's.

"You got it!" Eryth ap Morfyn yelled.

The goose tumbled out of the sky like a falling leaf, Tiernyn's arrow piercing its breast. It splashed into the still water of the loch fifty paces from the shore, and the little gold-and-white spaniel bounded joyfully after it.

"Good shot!" Donaugh cried.

Tiernyn grinned at him, flushed with excitement and pleasure. Heedless of the loose stones on the shingle, he set his horse leaping toward the water, yelping with delighted laughter. Even as he dismounted, the dog lunged forward to take the goose between his teeth and turned toward shore. Tiernyn went to one knee as the spaniel brought the bird from the water and laid it gently on the gravel before him. Tiernyn caressed the dog's ears with rough affection, then got to his feet and held the goose up in triumph.

"A good fat one," he shouted. "Bigger than yours, Donaugh."

Donaugh guided his horse to the rough gravel of the shore, more careful than Tiernyn of the treacherous footing. "Aye," he said. "The biggest one today, I think."

Eryth leaned forward across the horn of his saddle and peered down at the goose. "Big enough," he said. He grinned. "You may have got the biggest, but I got more."

"Three fine ones," Tiernyn agreed. He laughed. "I'll bet Keylan wishes he were with us rather than back at the landhold, discussing the rent with your father."

Donaugh grinned. He'd glimpsed Keylan through the door of Morfyn of Dun Llewen's workroom as they were leaving on their hunt. His eldest brother looked as if he were glazed over with boredom and trying desperately not to show it. They had arrived at Dun Llewen Landhold late in the afternoon of the day before, Donaugh's parents Kian and Kerri, and his brother Keylan, leading an entourage of twenty armed soldiers, while the twins, Donaugh and Tiernyn, and their sister Torey, raced madly ahead. Shortly after fast-breaking this morning, Kerri and Torey took themselves out of the way of boredom with Morfyn's wife. Keylan and Kian had closeted themselves with Morfyn. The accounting was likely to consume most of the day. The annual Rent Taking Progress through the province was always a grand adventure, but the stultifying details Keylan had to endure as he spoke with the landholders were definite drawbacks to being Prince of Skai.

"Be glad it's Keylan and not you," he said. "Being Prince isn't always just fun and glory."

Tiernyn lashed the goose to the back of his saddle and swung up onto the horse. He reached out and cuffed Eryth's shoulder. "Your father is probably boring Keylan silly right now," he said. "Recounting every lamentable detail of the Rent Taking."

Eryth sighed. "He can get that way sometimes," he said. "He's a careful man, is my father."

Donaugh grinned. Kian often said that Thane Morfyn of Dun Llewen Landhold knew the worth of every tenant, subtenant, and cotter on his considerable lands. And he was fully capable of itemizing every last sheaf of grain, basket of fruit, pig, goat, sheep, horse, cow, chicken, and pledge of manpower for the army that accrued to the lands, one-tenth of which he himself received from his tenants as rent, all of it calculated down to the last copper coin. One-tenth of all he collected, he paid to the Prince of Skai as rent, and itemized those, too, in painstaking detail.

"Your father's a good man, Eryth," Donaugh said. "My father says there's no one he'd trust more to hold the north of Skai against the raids of the Saesnesi."

Eryth shot him a grateful glance, then grinned. "I'll lay bets that the Regent wishes he were here instead, too."

"Father's more practiced at hiding his boredom than is Keylan," Tiernyn said. "He can make any man believe that his day would never have been complete without the encounter."

Eryth laughed, then glanced over his shoulder as his younger brother, Llan, guided his pony down to the shore. "It's just about time to go home," he said. "We said we'd be back by noon. We've less than an hour to go."

"But I haven't got a goose yet," Llan protested.

"You can have one of mine," Donaugh said. "I've got two."

"But I want one of my own!"

"I'm tired of hunting," Tiernyn said. He grinned. "We could cross the river and see if we can find any Brigani cattle to raid. I've never been on a cattle raid."

"Splendid idea," Eryth cried enthusiastically. "I can show you how it's done."

Donaugh pulled his horse around to look at Eryth. "Are you serious?" he asked in dismay.

"Of course I am," Eryth said indignantly. "Those thrice-cursed Brigani stole over a hundred head of cattle from us this last summer. It would serve them right if we went out and took some of theirs."

Even though Kian had strictly forbidden the practice in Skai, cattle raids were common all over Celi. In most provinces, they were regarded as great sport and a good way for young men to gain fighting experience without having to face the deadly serious axes and swords of the Saesnesi. But inevitably each year, some of those young men were killed. Blood feuds were not uncommon. Donaugh knew of several cross-border blood feuds that had existed for generations. He had no desire to see one arise between the south Brigani and the men of Dun Llewen because the impetuous young heir to

Dun Llewen managed to get himself killed. It didn't occur to him that he and Tiernyn might also be killed. The thought of incurring the wrath of his father when Kian found out they had participated in an impromptu cattle raid was by far the greater deterrent.

"No," he said finally. "My father says that raiding your neighbor's cattle is no way to persuade him to become your ally."

"Gods in the circle, Donaugh, don't be such a treacle-foot," Tiernyn said. "Cattle raids are nothing but good fun."

"Father's forbidden them, and you know it," Donaugh said. "Remember what happened the last time we tried one of your brilliant ideas? You spent a fortnight mucking out the stables, and I spent it scouring pots. It was another fortnight before I got the sting of that lye soap out of my hands, and you *still* stink of the stables sometimes."

Tiernyn shot him a disgusted look, but he turned his horse back toward the forest. He didn't often listen to Donaugh's counsel, but he had grudgingly given up the notion of a cattle raid. Donaugh hid his sigh of relief.

"Well, let's get these geese to the cook back at the castle, then," Tiernyn said. "They'll make a fine dinner."

A man stumbled out of the trees between the loch and the track. Blood matted his gray hair, and he clutched a bleeding wound on his arm. Struggling for breath, he flung himself to one knee beside Eryth's horse.

"Patro!" Eryth cried. "Are you hurt?"

The man shook his head. "Only a scratch, Master Eryth," he gasped. "It's the Brigani. They've taken the cattle we had penned at Llewenford."

Tiernyn swung his horse around, making the animal dance nervously. "Cattle thieves?" he said. "Which way did they go?"

"North, my lord," Patro said. "Back to Brigland."

Excitement flared in Tiernyn's eyes. "We'll go after them," he cried. "We'll get the cattle back."

Apprehension made a sudden, cold knot in Donaugh's chest. It was bad enough to think of raiding cattle guarded by only unarmed herders. Chasing after a band of armed thieves was quite another thing. "No, Tiernyn—"

Even Eryth saw the wisdom in Donaugh's protest. "We have no weapons," he said doubtfully.

"Blather and nonsense," Tiernyn said. "We may not be old enough to carry swords, but we have our bows, and we have our daggers." He curbed his horse sharply as it pranced in a quick circle. "How many raiders were there?"

"A few more than a dozen," Patro said. "They were armed with swords and daggers, my lord."

"Was anyone else hurt?" Donaugh asked.

"I was alone with the cattle, my lord," the man said. "My son was fetching our dinner. He's tracking the raiders now."

"How long ago, Patro?" Eryth asked.

"An hour, Master Eryth. Perhaps an hour and a half. No more."

"We should go back and tell Father and Thane Morfyn," Donaugh said.

"If we wait for them, the raiders will be long gone," Tiernyn said. "We have to go after them now. What say you, Eryth?"

Eryth hesitated only a moment. "Aye, we should go now if we're to have a chance to catch them before they get back to Brigland." He turned to his brother. "Llan, go back to the castle. Tell Father what's happened, and tell him to come quickly."

Llan glared at him. "I want to go, too."

"You can't come. You're only twelve . . . "

Llan's mouth lengthened into a stubborn, sullen line. "You're only fifteen, and so are the twins. I'm nearly as old as you are."

"Llan, really, someone has to tell Father," Eryth said in exasperation.

"Someone has to tell my father, too," Tiernyn said.

Llan glowered. "I want to come with you."

"You're the lightest, Llan," Tiernyn said. "Your horse can go the fastest. You can bring help sooner than Donaugh or I could."

Llan brightened. "Aye, I could," he said. "My horse is pretty fast."

"Good man," Tiernyn said. "Hurry, then."

Llan set his heels to his pony's flanks and turned toward the track leading back to Dun Llewen, bent low across the saddle.

Tiernyn hardly waited until Llan gained the track. "Come on, Eryth. Let's go. Are you coming, Donaugh?"

Donaugh knew very well his father would disapprove, but he couldn't let Tiernyn go haring off on his own. Against his better judgment, he nodded. "I'm coming," he said reluctantly.

Tiernyn whooped with delight. "Let's go then."

Lather spraying from its heaving chest and sides, Tiernyn's horse burst out of the trees at the top of a hill. With a sharp exclamation of dismay, Tiernyn reined to a stop, nearly setting the blowing horse down on its haunches, and flung himself to the ground. Donaugh and Eryth brought their mounts to a tumultuous halt beside him as he stared down into the glen below.

"Oh, sweet Deity," Donaugh said softly. He dismounted and moved to stand beside Tiernyn.

A pall of black smoke lay thick over the ruins of the Brigani village huddled at the foot of the gray castle walls, blending with the gray of the overcast. A gentle breeze blew the smoke east up the glen, away from the hilltop where the three boys stood. In places, flames still licked at the nearly ripened grain in fields at the edge of the village.

Only the shells of the stone-built houses remained. Broken pieces of household furnishings lay scattered through the spaces between the houses. Hacked corpses of men, women, and children lay among the strewn wreckage and slaughtered animals.

More bodies lay tangled together near the foot of the castle wall. Even from the top of the hill, Donaugh saw flaxen hair on many of the corpses riffling in the wind. At the edge of the village, the stolen cattle milled unattended, restless and nervous at the smell of smoke and death.

"Saesnesi." Tiernyn spit out the word like a curse.

The Brigani raiders, their stolen cattle forgotten, wandered through the village, their movements wooden and halting. They looked like walking wounded themselves as they searched for friends and family among the dead.

Donaugh caught a flash of movement in the trees on the other side of the village. His first thought was of returning Saesnesi. Automatically, his hand went to the hilt of his dagger.

A woman carrying a child stumbled out into the ruins of a grainfield. One of the young men paused in his search through the bodies and gave a loud cry, then sprinted across the field to the woman. Moments later, a few more people made their way out of the trees. The castle gates opened. A handful of men and women moved out into the village to begin an anguished search for survivors. The heartbreaking cry of a child broke the unnatural silence.

Donaugh reached for the reins of his horse. Leading it, he walked slowly down the hill. Tiernyn hesitated only a moment, then followed him.

"Where are you going?" Eryth demanded.

Donaugh turned to look up at him, his face grim and set. "To help," he said.

"But they're Brigani," Eryth said indignantly. "They're cattle thieves."

Donaugh glanced at his brother. Tiernyn stiffened. A muscle jumped in anger, bunching at the corner of his jaw.

"They're Celae," Tiernyn said.

Eryth made a disgusted noise in the back of his throat, but he followed Donaugh and Tiernyn down the hill.

Donaugh had to swallow several times before he could enter the village. There had been Saesnesi raids on Dun Eidon, but he had never seen anything like this. These people could not have had any warning at all of the approach of the Saesnesi. Skai—no, his father—had shown the foresight to build watchtowers along the coast. Why hadn't the Brigani? Surely Kian had spoken with Duke Morand to share the idea. Why were the Brigani so unprepared and unprotected?

Donaugh looked away quickly from the corpse of a small girl and stared into the eyes of a man whose head had been nearly severed from his body. A cold, shivery lump knotted in his belly.

A young man knelt in the dirt, holding the body of a young woman in his arms, rocking back and forth. He looked up as Donaugh approached, his face a blank mask of grief and shock. Black-haired and blue-eyed, he could have been from the village around Dun Eidon.

"Can I help?" Donaugh asked.

The young Brigani's face cleared. Donaugh saw the moment when he recognized the Tyadda influence of dark gold hair and brown eyes. Slowly, the Brigani struggled to his feet, still carrying the dead woman. Her long, black hair spilled down his shoulder and across his arm. He spit into the dirt at Donaugh's feet.

"I need no help from an yrSkai mongrel," he snarled. He brushed past Donaugh and walked toward the walls of the castle.

Helplessly, Donaugh turned away, shivering with shock, a deep ache in his chest. More survivors trickled into the village from the forest. A woman fell to her knees beside the body of a man, her cry of anguish sharp and clear. She didn't look up as he approached. He went to one knee beside her.

"I'll help you take him to the castle," he said gently.

The woman looked at him vacantly. Dried blood smeared her face and throat from a wound in her cheek. "Go away," she muttered. "We take care of our own here. We ask no help from yrSkai curs."

Donaugh flinched as if she'd hit him. He got to his feet in time to see Tiernyn bend to take an infant from the dead arms of a woman. Tiny fists waved feebly as Tiernyn held the child close against his chest. A man in the uniform of a castle guard snatched the child without a word and hurried toward the castle. Tears formed in Tiernyn's eyes.

Twice more, Donaugh's offer of help was rebuffed. He stood amid the sprawled dead, anger churning in his chest. Anger at himself for not knowing how to make these people let him help. Anger at the Brigani thane for not being able to defend his people better than this. Anger at the Saesnesi for the senseless murder and slaughter.

A raven alighted on the body of a child and began pecking at the hacked throat. Rage exploded within Donaugh. He ran toward the bird, waving his arms and shouting incoherently. The bird merely eyed him warily for a moment, then set again to pecking the dead child's throat. Donaugh stumbled and snatched up a stone. He threw it, and the bird fluttered out of range. Moments later, two more ravens landed beside the small body. Donaugh kicked at them, then flung his cloak over the body. It was all he could do.

Tiernyn sat on a low stone wall beside a charred grainfield, his hands and face smudged with soot and smoke, tracks of tears plain on his cheeks. Beside him, Eryth sat with his elbows on his knees, chin in his hands, staring at the ground between his feet. Defeated, Donaugh trudged across the track to sit beside them. He clenched his hands between his knees to control their trembling.

"It won't live," Tiernyn said softly. "The child I found? It won't live. It was wounded in the belly."

Donaugh swallowed bile and felt tears, hot and stinging, fill his eyes—tears of helpless rage and frustration. He couldn't speak.

"They won't even let us help," Tiernyn said hoarsely. "Dear gods, they won't even let us help."

Donaugh looked at him, his eyes still bright with tears.

Helpless rage flooded visibly across Tiernyn's face, forcing out the shuddering shock. "But we're all Celae," he said. "We're all Celae. We shouldn't be enemies like this. We should stand together against the Saesnesi. It's not right. If we all stood together, we could push the Hellas-birthed Saesnesi back into the sea . . . "

Donaugh made a helpless gesture. "They're Celae," he said. "We're a stubborn race."

"We're stupid," Tiernyn said fiercely. "Father is right. We need to stand together."

Donaugh started to say something, but was interrupted by the sound of approaching horses. He looked over his shoulder to see his parents and Keylan ride into the village, followed by a column of men.

A troop of armed Brigani spilled from the open castle gates to confront them. The leader of the Brigani, a thane by his dress, pulled his horse warily to a halt before Kian. "Leave here," he said. "You have no business here in Brigland."

"We've come to help," Kian said.

"We need no help—"

"Don't be a fool," Kerri said. She pointed to a child who cradled a bleeding arm against her chest. "She needs help. You have people here who will die unless someone helps them very quickly." She dismounted and went to the child. She smiled at the girl, then put her hands to the wounded arm. When she removed them, the wound was gone. The child's face broke out into a grin of amazement.

"My wife is a Healer," Kian said to the Brigani leader. "As am I. Unless you want to spend the winter starving because you lack the men to work the fields—men we could have saved—you need our help."

The Brigani leader's mouth lengthened into an uncertain line. Finally, he nodded. Kian dismounted and motioned to the men behind him. In moments, the yrSkai and the Brigani were working side by side to collect the dead and wounded.

Donaugh left the Great Hall of the Brigani lord, the stench of smoke, vomit, and death thick in his throat. It wasn't much better in the courtyard. Beyond the gates, wan moonlight augmented by flickering torches illuminated the burial parties filling the last of the graves. All the fires in the village were out, but the scorched smell of burning still hung heavy in the air.

The darkness vaguely surprised him. He had completely lost track of time as he worked shoulder to shoulder with Brigani and yrSkai to gather in the wounded while other mixed parties collected the dead for burial. He couldn't remember when he had stopped noticing if the accent of the man working next to him was Brigani or yrSkai. Certainly something that had never happened to him before.

He sat on the bottom step and scrubbed his hands wearily across his face. The skin of his cheeks felt crusty and vaguely oily beneath his fingers. He leaned back against the granite balustrade and closed his eyes, resting his head against the cool stone. When someone left the Great Hall, he didn't bother to look up.

Keylan sat on the other side of the steps, clearly as weary as Donaugh felt. He slumped forward in silence, his elbows resting on his knees. Moments later, someone else came out of the Great Hall.

"Keylan?" It was Tiernyn's voice.

"M-m-m-m?"

"Back there—In the Great Hall, I mean. Everybody's working together as if it doesn't matter who's yrSkai and who's Brigani."

Keylan nodded toward the fields beyond the gates. Too

tired to speak, Donaugh looked out across the still-smoking ruins to where the last of the burial parties were dispersing. He closed his eyes to shut out the sight of the devastated fields. It hurt to look at them.

"And out there, too," Keylan said. "Something new."

"New, indeed," Tiernyn said. "Father was right."

Light from the distant torches faintly limned Keylan's face. The corners of his mouth curled in a brief smile. "Father usually is," he said.

"We *can* work together." A note of excitement crept into Tiernyn's voice. "And if yrSkai and Brigani can work together, why not all of us, yrSkai, yrWenydd, Brigani, Mercians, Doriani, and even Veniani? All of us, Keylan. All of Celi. If we could bring everyone together, we could beat back the Saesnesi and rid Celi of them forever."

"That's what Father's been saying for years," Keylan said.

"I know. But I never thought it could work before this." Tiernyn got to his feet and paced restlessly back and forth along the step. Donaugh opened his eyes and watched him. In the faint light spilling from the open door behind him, Tiernyn's face glowed with excited animation, the fire of crusade in his eyes. He paused in the middle of the step and swung around to face Keylan.

"Take the fight back to the Saesnesi," he said. "Right out to the Saesnesi Shore and fight them there, before they raid us again. If you take the army there, others will join you, Keylan. Everyone would come to your banner. Think of it. Skai would lead all of Celi against the Saesnesi."

"Aye, and who'd be in Skai to protect our people should the Saesnesi send a raiding party there?" Keylan asked. He gestured to the ruins beyond the gate. "Then our villages would look like that. I can't let that happen to Skai."

"But it has to be you, Keylan," Tiernyn cried. "You're Prince of Skai. Men would follow you because you're Prince."

"Aye, mayhaps," he said. "Mayhaps. Time enough to think of that later. I'm too weary to argue with you now."

Tiernyn said nothing, but the spark in his eyes had kindled. Donaugh knew with sudden concrete certainty nothing or no man would ever quench it. Given Keylan's protective attitude toward Skai, and Tiernyn's newfound fervor, Donaugh thought the next few years might prove to be very interesting.

Forever after when he looked back, Donaugh remembered that evening as the first turning point in his life, and in Tiernyn's. The second came three years later. They celebrated their eighteenth Name Day at Imbolc, the Feast of New Fire. Less than a season later, shortly before Vernal Equinox, they fought in their first major engagement against nearly two hundred Saesnesi raiders, who sailed up the blue waters of the Ceg in six longships. Warned by the watchtowers Kian had ordered built along the rugged, indented coasts of Skai, the yrSkai of Dun Eidon were ready when the raiders landed. They were outnumbered nearly two to one, but they were fighting to protect their homes. That gave them strength.

The battle was brief and bloody. Donaugh would never forget the battle and its aftermath. That day, his life—and Tiernyn's—changed forever.

2

Donaugh spent the first hour after the battle helping to gather in the wounded. He left the collection of the dead, both their own and the Saesnesi raiders, to parties of soldiers and went to the Great Hall of Dun Eidon to give what assistance he could. He had no Gift of Healing as his parents had, and as his sister Torey had. Her Gift was stronger even than their father's. The magic he did have was of little use to the wounded in the Great Hall. But he knew well the value of the comfort his presence and concern might bring them.

He knelt by the side of one of the men, murmuring words of comfort. The soldier's hand gripped his hard enough to hurt, but he made no attempt to dislodge it. The young priestess had given the man poppy before she began, but it was a long time before the hand gripping Donaugh's relaxed into sleep. His hand still showed the white imprint of the soldier's fingers as he climbed stiffly to his feet while she finished stitching the wound in the soldier's side.

The air of the Great Hall was thick with the smell of blood and vomit, woodsmoke and medicinal decoctions. Beneath the moans and cries of the wounded, the quiet, soothing voices of the priests and priestesses of the shrine throbbed in a soft undercurrent like the sound of waves on the shore as they comforted the wounded and gave orders to assistants.

On the other side of the smoky room, Torey knee-walked from one sleeping patient to the side of another. She bent over him, her hands moving gently on his shoulder, her face pale and drawn as she looked down at him. Donaugh grimaced as he watched her. She was only just turned fifteen. Far too young to be thrust into the aftermath of a hard-fought and bloody battle.

Not far from her, Kian knelt by another wounded man,

working quickly and deftly over him. Holding a tray of surgical knives, Keylan worked with a priestess on the dais below the great banner of Skai, and Tiernyn crouched beside a priest near the hearth, passing bandages, his face grim and set. He looked far older than eighteen. But Donaugh had no doubt that he himself also looked too old for his years right now. The fight itself had not etched that bleakness into Tiernyn's face. It was the aftermath that tore at the guts and shredded the spirit.

Kerri touched Donaugh's shoulder. "Does this one need a Healer?" she asked. She was pale, her face showing the strain of Healing. Lines of fatigue creased the skin around her eyes and created a deep furrow between her golden eyebrows. She should have been resting. She had fought as hard as any man, riding at Kian's side, but they had only three Healers, and she was needed.

The priestess was nearly finished. She looked up and smiled wearily. "No, my lady," she said before Donaugh could reply. "Save your strength. There are others more in need. The wound isn't deep. He merely needs rest now."

Kerri nodded. She squeezed Donaugh's hand briefly before moving on. She paused for a moment to speak with Tiernyn, then knelt by another wounded soldier.

So many wounded, Donaugh thought bleakly. Too many. Far too many. And far too many dead lying in the courtyard outside, awaiting the final attentions of the priests and priestesses. But the living came first. The dead would wait with infinite patience.

He moved quietly among the wounded, pausing here and there to speak with any man still conscious, offering what assistance he could to the priests and priestesses. Healing extracted a heavy toll from the Healer. Kian, Kerri, and Torey could help only the most severely wounded. The others had to rely on the skill of the priests and priestesses, and their potions and decoctions. There wasn't much Donaugh could do, but even passing bandages was some help.

Over the quiet uproar, he heard a woman cry out. He turned to see Torey kneeling stiffly by the side of a young soldier, her hand pressed to her lips. The priest, his face a mask of helpless resignation, leaned forward and drew the sign of the Unbroken Circle on the soldier's forehead. Donaugh swallowed hard as the significance of the quiet gesture hit him. Another death, then. A mortal wound even Torey's powerful gift couldn't Heal.

Torey knelt unmoving for a moment longer, then suddenly leapt to her feet and stumbled out of the Great Hall, her fist still pressed tightly against her mouth. Donaugh put down the bandages he held and slipped out quietly behind her.

He found her huddled beneath an ornamental tree near the massive balustrade of the steps leading to the Great Hall, clinging to the slender trunk as if it was all she had to support herself. She stared at the thick, black smoke boiling into the air from the pyre on the other side of the village, where the Saesnesi dead burned along with the four longships that had not managed to escape. He knelt beside her and touched her shoulder. She turned to him, tears streaking her face, her eyes wide and unseeing.

"Are you all right?" he asked.

"Oh, Donaugh." She threw herself into his arms, sobs wracking her body. "It happened three times. Three times . . . "

"What happened, Littlest?" he asked, stroking her hair back gently.

"They died. They died, and I couldn't help them. I touched them and I could feel the life flowing out of them, like water out of a broken ewer."

"You can't help everyone, Torey. Nobody has a Gift that strong. No Healer can Heal a mortal wound. Not you, not Father or Mother. Nobody can."

"But it's not fair," she cried. "It's not fair. I knew that soldier. He always used to smile at me when he saw me. Oh, gods, Donaugh. The life went out of him as I touched him. Oh gods, I couldn't prevent it. I touched him, and I felt him

just—stop. It's not fair. And I can't even remember his name!"
She broke down into a storm of grief, clinging blindly to him
as sobs wracked her body.

He held her as he would a child, murmuring to her, knowing for the moment she had no idea who he was, had no idea
who she herself was. She was too young for this, he thought
again. Helplessly, he wished there were some way he could
protect her from the ravages of her Gift. But there was no way;
they needed her Gift too much.

Torey drew away and stared up at him, her eyes wide, an
odd listening expression on her face. "Oh, gods, Donaugh,"
she said in a very small voice. "I'm going to be sick."

She turned away from him. He held her forehead as she
vomited into the young spring grass beneath the tree, supporting her as spasm after spasm wracked her body. Finally, she
straightened up and wiped her mouth on the hem of her gown.

"Better now?" he asked.

She nodded and drew in several deep breaths. He rose and
helped her up as she got unsteadily to her feet. Sweat beaded
her forehead, but her color was nearly back to normal.

"I've got to get back," she said. "They still need me in
there."

"I'll go with you. Come on."

Hours later, Donaugh knew there was nothing more he could
do. Keylan had left to make sure the burial parties came in for
hot food, and Tiernyn was gone. Kian, Kerri, and Torey still
worked with the wounded, all three drooping wearily, but
there was nothing Donaugh could do to help them. Right now,
he wanted a bath to wash away the stink of blood and sweat,
and he wanted wine to take the taste of the foul air from his
throat. If he was lucky, the wine might erase the images of the
dead men's faces swirling in his head. He left the Great Hall
and climbed the stairway to the family quarters.

Tiernyn was already in the solar. He sat on a low stool, his dark gold hair hanging over his forehead, matted and filthy, his hands clenched between his knees. He looked up as Donaugh entered.

"They'll keep coming, you know," he said softly. "The Saesnesi will keep on coming back until we go out there to the Saesnesi Shore and smash them where they live. Until we throw them back into the sea."

Donaugh went to the tall chest against the wall beneath a hanging depicting Cernos of the Forest standing with his hand resting on the shoulder of a stag. The tapestry was old and had been repaired several times. Either by accident or design, Cernos had acquired an unbecoming squint. It usually made Donaugh smile, but not today. He poured a goblet of wine and went to stand by the window.

Ravens circled above the gravel shingle of the beach, like flakes of soot in the twilight. Below, outside the walls of the palace, men of the village dragged the bodies of the last dead Saesnesi raiders to the huge funeral pyre burning beyond a small rise at the end of the shingle. The pitch-soaked longships blazed fiercely in the heart of the flames. Black, oily smoke rose in thick, twisting ropes high into the air. The stench would hang heavy over the Ceg for days.

"Did you hear them?" Tiernyn pounded one fist into the open palm of his other hand. "Did you hear them cheering Keylan after the battle?"

"He earned it," Donaugh said, not turning from the window. "He fought well."

"Aye, he fought well," Tiernyn said bitterly. "He always fights well. If he led his men through the portals of Annwn into the Pit of Hellas, they'd follow. But he won't lead them against the Saesnesi in the east."

Donaugh said nothing. He'd heard this rant too many times during the last three years. And he'd heard Keylan's impassioned reply too many times. He had taken no part in the argument, but he'd stood at Tiernyn's shoulder, a silent show of solidarity he knew Keylan resented. He had no answer for

Tiernyn. Keylan was Prince of Skai even though Kian still held the Regency. The army of Skai followed its Prince. Donaugh understood Keylan's position. If he led the army out of Skai, who'd be left to guard Skai from the raiders? Yet Donaugh could also see Tiernyn's point of view. Raids like the one today cost too many lives. So he said nothing, but ached to see his brothers constantly at each other's throats.

"Were I Prince, it would be different." Tiernyn's voice, low and fierce, was hoarse with anger. "The wrong brother was born first."

"We can't change our birth order," Donaugh said mildly enough.

"Why can't he see what has to be done, then do it?" Tiernyn brought his clenched fist down onto his knee hard enough that it surely must leave a bruise. "Sometimes, Donaugh," he said very softly, "sometimes, I hate him." He brought both hands up to cover his eyes. "And I hate myself for hating him. He's my brother. How can I hate him when I love him, too? How—" He broke off abruptly as Keylan entered the room.

Blood stained Keylan's clothing, some of it his own from a wound in his forehead, now neatly bandaged. His bright red-gold hair hung in strings around his pale face. He paused for a moment, looking first at Tiernyn, then at Donaugh, then went to the chest to pour himself wine. He leaned against the chest and raised the goblet to his mouth, draining it in one long swallow before pouring more.

"It's early for them," he said. "Not even Vernal Equinox yet. Six longships . . . Gods!"

"Nearly two hundred of them, Keylan," Tiernyn said, his voice taut with strain. "It grows worse every year."

"This was the worst raid yet," Keylan agreed tiredly.

"Twenty-one dead," Donaugh said without turning. "And more than fifty wounded. We won't be able to fight off another attack like that without calling men back from the plowing and planting."

"And without the plowing and planting, there'll be no harvest to feed us come winter," Tiernyn said. He scrubbed his hands wearily over his face, then went to the chest to pour wine.

"We can probably count ourselves lucky the Saesnesi on the continent are busy fighting the Maedun," Donaugh said. "Mayhaps there will be no longships crossing the Cold Sea from Saesnes this summer."

"It's never stopped them before," Keylan said. "The harder the Maedun press them, the more longships come to the Saesnesi Shore."

Tiernyn's knuckles whitened around the stem of his goblet. "There should be no safe landing for them on the east coast of Celi," he said hoarsely. "I told you. Last summer, you should have taken the army east and driven the Saesnesi back into the sea."

Keylan raised his hand to rub his eyes. "We won't go through that again, Tiernyn. We've skinned that particular wolf too many times already."

"We've not," Tiernyn said fiercely. "Look what happened today. If you had taken the army—"

Keylan slammed his goblet down on the chest hard enough to splash wine onto the inlaid and polished surface. "If we had taken the army out of Skai last autumn, we would have returned to find nothing but smoking ruins and corpses of farmers and their families."

"If you had taken the fight to the Saesnesi, they would not have sent raiders."

"My first responsibility is Skai." Keylan clutched the goblet stem, his knuckles white, as if the stem were his temper and only by a firm grip could he hold it in check.

"You could have asked the men of Wenydd to help."

"Ryvern would have given the same answer I did. His responsibility is Wenydd, as Blais's is Dorian and Gemedd's is Mercia—"

"You should be thinking first of Celi," Tiernyn cried. "It's Celi who has to be strong."

"I know that," Keylan said. "Don't you think I know that? But what man of Skai would fight beside a man of Mercia, and what man of Mercia would fight beside a man of Dorian? And who would fight beside a Brigani? Would you?"

Tiernyn remained silent.

Keylan shook his head tiredly. "We've all been feuding for centuries. You know that. No one can mend that overnight, and certainly not I."

"But it's up to you to try," Tiernyn said. "They have to see that we've got to band together. You have to be first, Keylan. You know Father would listen to you if you approached him about it. You could make him see how important it is. You're Prince. It has to be you who does it. Take the army east—"

"We will *not* leave Skai undefended, or even weakened." Keylan's words rasped like a file across Tiernyn's voice. "We cannot. She'd have Saesnesi pillaging her coasts and Mercians ravaging her east border. And only the gods know what the Brigani would do in the north."

"You care nothing for Celi," Tiernyn cried, his face flushed with anger. "You don't care anything for Celi, as long as you get to play the role of heir to the torc and coronet of Skai."

Keylan went white. "How dare you accuse me—"

"It's true, though," Tiernyn interrupted hotly. "Celi can get raped or bludgeoned to death by the Saesnesi as long as you get your own way."

Keylan raised a clenched fist and took a step toward Tiernyn.

"That is quite enough."

Kian's voice cracked like a lightning strike through the charged air of the solar. Keylan let his hand fall to his side, fist still clenched, as he turned to face his father. Kian stood with Kerri in the doorway, one arm supporting Torey, who looked perilously close to collapse. Kian gently handed her over to Kerri, then advanced to confront his sons.

Donaugh had never before seen his father so angry. The skin around his mouth was taut and pale, the mouth itself drawn into a grim and bloodless line. His eyes, cold as winter stones, flicked back and forth between Keylan and Tiernyn.

"I will not have my sons arguing like children in a nursery while good men of Skai lie wounded or dead below," he said softly. "Even if you two have no respect for their pain and sacrifice, you owe them the dignity of your own restraint."

Keylan dropped his gaze, not meeting the cold eyes, so like his own. Still crackling with anger, Tiernyn glared for a heartbeat longer, then looked away, dusky color suffusing his throat and cheeks.

"You will all three of you present yourselves before me in the Council Room two hours after sunrise tomorrow. I've had more than enough of this. Get out of here. Go to your chambers and clean up. You look disgraceful."

Even Tiernyn knew better than to argue. Keylan flung down his goblet and stalked from the room. Donaugh paused, looking at the misery and distress on Torey's face. He managed a reassuring smile before he left the solar beside Tiernyn.

Torey awoke in the dark, not knowing what had wakened her. The air of her bedchamber felt strangely charged, as if the last echoes of a chime had only just faded away.

She threw back the quilts and sat up, wincing at the unexpected stiffness and aches of her body. She felt as if she had spent two days on the practice field being pummeled by the merciless training blade of the Swordmaster. Healing had never before left her so sore, but then, she had never before had to draw so deeply on the Gift.

The air around her vibrated softly. She listened for a moment before thrusting her feet into fur slippers and reaching for her bed robe. Her maid, Minna, slept soundly, curled like a kitten into the quilts on her bed near the door. Whatever had awakened Torey, it had not disturbed Minna, who was usually a light sleeper.

Wrapping the thick, blue velvet robe firmly around her,

Torey went to the small door that opened out onto the terrace. She groped beneath the heavy draperies for the latch, then stepped out onto the wet flagstones.

Mist swirled thickly around the palace, but the moon glowed like a hazy lantern directly overhead. The tall pots containing rosebushes and ornamental trees made darker shadows against the night.

One of the tall shadows moved by the parapet. Even as Torey realized it was one of the twins, she knew it was Donaugh. She wondered if he had come out because he had heard or felt the same thing she had.

People said of Tiernyn and Donaugh that they were one soul born into two bodies, and that Tiernyn had all the vitality, charm, and sparkle of two men, while Donaugh was only a pale shadow of his twin. Torey knew this was untrue. But Donaugh let everyone believe it. Even Tiernyn. Donaugh knew his twin better than Tiernyn knew himself, and certainly better than Tiernyn knew Donaugh.

She thought she knew Donaugh better than any of the others did. Her favorite brother was gentle and kind with her always, and never teased her as Tiernyn often did. There was something about Donaugh she could never quite define, an aura of latent power, a sense of fires banked and stilled until need called them forth. He handled a sword as well as any man, even Keylan or Tiernyn, but without Keylan's massive strength or Tiernyn's brilliant dazzle. Always, he stepped back and let Tiernyn have first place, but not because he was self-effacing or suffered from any sense of inferiority. No one had more quiet confidence in himself than Donaugh had. He stepped back because that was how he wanted the world to see him. And to see Tiernyn.

As she watched, Donaugh cupped his hands and let the nebulous moonlight flow into them. The light firmed until it was an opalescent globe. Even though she had seen it before, Torey shivered slightly.

As each of his sons turned sixteen, Kian took him to the

Dance of Nemeara, that magnificent triple-ringed stone circle erected in the shadow of Cloudbearer, the highest peak on the Isle of Celi. Keylan returned with the Rune Blade called Bane, once carried by Kyffen, Prince of Skai, Kian's grandfather. Tiernyn returned with a pair of daggers, the hilts traced with an intricately woven pattern in silver and gold wire.

Donaugh had returned with magic.

It came to him from both parents. Tyadda blood was strong in both their father and their mother. With the chance addition of Tyran blood through Kian, it produced in Donaugh a wild magic indeed. Tiernyn had none. If he had inherited the bright flame of both twins, Donaugh received all the magic.

The globe of moonlight shimmered in Donaugh's hands. He gazed down into it as if it held answers to all the questions, if he but realized what to ask.

Torey was certain she made no sound, but Donaugh looked up and turned toward her. The globe in his hands melted and spilled like water through his fingers, splashing on the wet tile and vanishing into the mist. Torey came quietly across the dew-damp flagstones to stand beside him.

"Were you looking to see what Father will say in the morning?" she asked.

He smiled. "No. I have a pretty good idea."

Torey shivered in the chill air. "Why do Keylan and Tiernyn have to argue all the time?" she said irritably. "Why can't they get along as brothers are supposed to?"

Donaugh laughed softly. "Because both of them are stubborn as rocks," he said. "A trait they come by honestly, it seems."

Torey smiled. "I agree Keylan's stubbornness can be truly awe-inspiring at times," she said. "Remember what Mother used to say?"

"Three parts Tyran obstinacy and one part Celae tenacity," Donaugh said. "An impressive mixture. But he's our half brother. That means the rest of us have only one part Tyran mule-headedness. More than enough to outstubborn any man living. With the notable exception of our father."

Torey sighed. "And Keylan."

Donaugh smiled. "And Keylan," he agreed.

"Father was very angry, wasn't he?" Torey said. "What do you suppose he's going to do?"

"He's not going to banish us, if that's what you're thinking," Donaugh said.

Torey did not miss his pronoun. It was a given that where Tiernyn went, Donaugh went, too.

"I'm frightened, Donaugh," she said quietly. "Everything is changing. I can feel it."

"Change isn't necessarily bad, *cariad*."

"I know, but this is too fast."

"It will be all right," he said. "Go back to bed now. You're cold, and this is no night to be wandering the parapets."

"Are you going to bed?"

"Yes." He hugged her. "Whatever happens in the morning, it will be all right. Remember that."

"If you say so."

"I say so. Now go to bed and get warm again."

3

The waters of Lake Vayle lay still and quiet beyond the glazed windows of the stronghouse. Dawn tinted the smooth surface of the lake shades of pale pink and yellow, but Hakkar of Maedun hardly noticed. He stood with preternatural stillness, hands behind his back, waiting for word from the birthing chamber. Three times in three years, he had been disappointed. Twice, the woman had produced sons, but stillborn, and once a daughter who had lived for only a few days.

He raised his eyes and looked west—west toward Celi. Isgard and the Cold Sea lay between Maedun and Celi, but one day he would lead the Maedun army across Isgard, and from the port of Honandun, take ship to invade that accursed isle.

But first, he must have a son. He had been cheated out of his inheritance from his father nearly twenty years ago. Hakkar the Elder had been unable to pass his magic on to his eldest son—his only son—in the traditional way as he died.

"Kian dav Leydon ti'Cullin." Hakkar whispered the name of his enemy aloud, the name of the man who had killed his father. Because of the Tyr, the cycle had been broken. Hakkar had inherited his father's name. The instant his father died, he was no longer Horbad. But having his father's name implied he also owned his father's power. Without that power, he was effectively yet only Horbad, the son. It was a secret he kept well.

He had been born with the potential for magic as strong as his father's magic. Over the years he had augmented that potential with magic stolen from others by means of his father's secret ritual. But it was fragmented, difficult to control, unreliable. Because he had been unable to complete the link when his father died, he was unable to mold the magic to his own use. There was only one way to gain control of his power—forging a bond with his own son. Even then, his magic would be nowhere near as powerful as his father's was when he died. But it would be a start, and by judicious use of his father's blood rite, he could further augment his power until it surpassed his father's, as his father's had surpassed *his* father's. He would be more powerful than Weigar, who ruled as Lord Protector of Falinor, or Tamid in Laringras. He would rule in Celi, and bring that accursed isle to its knees before him.

But it would take time. Years. Perhaps half a lifetime.

"One day, I will kill you, Tyr," Hakkar said softly, still staring westward. "One day I will kill you and take *your* magic, too. And I will kill your sons. For what you've done to me, you and all your line will die."

Half a lifetime . . .

He could wait. Victory was sweetest when long anticipated.

Hakkar's hands made fists by his sides. But if he held his father's power right now . . .

Even as he killed Hakkar's father, the man now known as Red Kian of Skai had used some unexpected magic of his own to prevent the transference of power at the moment of death. Hakkar the Younger, only a child at the time, had not enough of his own magic to stop the Tyr from destroying the black sword, the receptacle of his father's power. He looked at the thin scar on the side of his palm and shuddered as the scene rose again in his memory.

The general, his father, lay crumpled on the grass. As he watched, a dark mist rose from the body and slowly dissipated in the moving air above the grass circle. The body withered and shriveled until it was little more than a husk, frail enough for the gentle breeze to shred and fray.

The Tyr straightened slowly as Hakkar in his assumed

adult form stepped up to the circle, cloaked in shadow, a dark-
ness of his own making swirling around him. The Tyr's eyes
widened as he recognized him.

"That is mine," Hakkar said, his voice a rustling whisper in
the mist surrounding him. He pointed to the black sword rest-
ing in the grass an armspan beyond his father's clawed fin-
gers.

Still breathing unevenly, the Tyr raised his sword and
moved to stand between Hakkar and the general's sword.

"Then come and claim it, but you'll have to go through
me."

Hakkar glanced at the black sword, then back at the Tyr.
"You cannot touch it," he said. "Remember how it burned you
the last time you tried to take it?"

"I don't want it."

"Then you have no objection if I take it."

The Tyr bared his teeth in a feral grin. "Come and try."

Hakkar held up both empty hands. "I have no weapon."

"But I do."

Even as Hakkar tensed himself to dive for his father's
sword, the Tyr lifted his own sword and slammed the brightly
glowing blade down on the obsidian sword. The glaring explo-
sion nearly blinded and deafened Hakkar. The black sword
shattered.

Hakkar howled with rage and scrambled away from the
dark splinters on the grass, a long shard embedded in the flesh
of his palm. He rolled to the edge of the circle and staggered
to his feet, cradling his injured hand to his chest.

"It was mine!" he shouted. "It was mine!"

The Tyr made no reply. He merely stood there, drooping
with exhaustion.

The dark mist swirled around Hakkar again, but it was
thinner, more tenuous. He glared at the Tyr, black eyes glitter-
ing with rage.

"You have won for now," he said quietly.

"I have gained time."

*"Put it to good use," Hakkar said. "You should have killed
me, too, when you could." He stepped out of the circle and
drew the mist close around himself. The circle, the Tyr, and
his father's shriveled corpse vanished, together with the brittle
shards of the sword that should have been his.*

Hakkar traced the thin, white line of the scar. He had neither
his father's sword nor his power, but he had his father's secret.
And when he had sired a strong son, another sword could be
forged and imbued with his own magic. The time would come.

The sun rose. He hardly noticed, his gaze fixed on the far
horizon. The woman had been taken to the birthing chamber at
dusk. Word would come soon enough.

He stood unmoving for another hour before he heard a foot-
fall on the polished tile floor behind him.

"The woman is dead," Francia said, her voice flat and without inflection.

Hakkar did not turn. "She is unimportant. The child?"

"A son."

He hid the leaping joy in his heart, not moving.

"Stillborn." Malice tinged Francia's voice.

"So." He would not allow his bitter disappointment to
show, neither in his voice, nor in his stance.

She came to stand beside him, her scarlet silk gown a flam-
boyant contrast to his black trews and shirt. Both had the tar
black hair typical of the Maedun, their eyes only a shade or
two lighter, and they bore a strong family resemblance to each
other. Where he was a handsome man, her femininity had soft-
ened the same features to striking beauty. She was six years
older than her brother, but appeared much younger. And, all
but unique in Maedun women, she had inherited some of their
father's magic. It made her arrogant, and he hated her for it.

"You will need another woman to sire a son on if you are to
bring Celi to its knees." Her voice was carefully neutral.

It startled him that she should discern so easily the path of his early dawn musings. "There is time yet," he said blandly enough. "Only one of the Tyr's get in Skai has magic, and he is not the enchanter of the prophecy."

"The one who will destroy Maedun?" Francia smiled sardonically. "Surely you don't believe that. Ravings of a half-mad old fool, that's all that is."

He looked at her. "It matters little whether I believe it or not. It's the excuse Vanizen, our very noble uncle and king, will use to invade Celi once the continent is ours."

She made a derisive noise. "In nearly twenty years, he hasn't been able to subdue Isgard. Or Tyra. Or even Saesnes. Only Falinor and Laringras belong to us. There are not enough sorcerers left in Maedun to subdue Isgard." She raised an eyebrow. "What would Vanizen, our very noble uncle and king, as you say, do if he knew what happened to those sorcerers?"

He smiled, a cruel parody of affection. "He will not find out, will he, dear sister?"

"How unfortunate for you that taking their magic didn't help."

He shrugged. "When I have my son, you will see that it did, and Isgard will be ours. And Saesnes, too."

"And Tyra?"

He shrugged again. "All those mountains? We need them not. The Tyrs are only barbarians and will be contained and harmless."

She went to the table on the far side of the room and poured herself a goblet of wine. "Weigar would give you his daughter to bear your son," she said. "A strong woman, Mora."

He glanced at her. "And in return?"

"Our father's secret."

He laughed softly. "He will not give up, will he? For fifty years, he's been trying. The answer is still the same. My father refused him. I also refuse him."

"*Our* father, Hakkar," she said sharply. "He was my father, too, not just yours. I bear his blood just as you do. And I bear some of his magic."

"You are only a woman."

Anger flared in her eyes. Her knuckles whitened around the stem of the goblet. "Only a woman," she said in a dangerously soft voice. "Yet I could bring the Prince of Skai to his knees at my leisure and with ease."

He met her gaze, mockery in his face. "And what price would you demand for such a service, dear sister?"

"Father's secret."

He laughed. "Father's secret given to a woman? Ridiculous and impossible."

She set the goblet down too carefully on the table, her face white and set. "Some day you will beg for my help, Horbad," she whispered.

His face flushed angry red. "I am Hakkar," he snarled. "Not Horbad. Hakkar."

"You are still Horbad and only a boy until you gain full power," she said icily. "A boy until you prove man enough to get a living son." She turned away and swept out of the room.

Donaugh sat quietly on one of the cushioned benches opposite the tall, arched windows of the Council Chamber, watching Tiernyn pace and prowl like a caged mountain cat. Above and behind him, the blue banner with the white falcon of Skai hung motionless in the still air.

Tiernyn paused in his restless pacing as Keylan entered, then stepped forward to meet his elder brother. For a moment, they stood watching each other warily. Then Tiernyn smiled ruefully.

"I apologize," he said quietly. "I shouldn't have said half the things I said last night. I had no right. Will you forgive me, Keylan?"

Donaugh made sure he was studiously engaged in arranging the folds of his short cloak. One corner of Keylan's mouth tried to curl as he looked again at Tiernyn. The two had spent three years fighting over this one issue like two dogs over a bone, but in spite of it, they both loved each other, and Keylan had never been able to hold his anger at anything very long. After the unaccustomed bitterness of the quarrel the night before, Donaugh breathed easier to see that Keylan apparently held no grudge.

"We were both overwrought," Keylan said.

"Mayhaps," Tiernyn replied. "But you'll be Prince of Skai someday. Your first thoughts must be for Skai."

"You were right in much of what you said." The eager light flared again in Tiernyn's eyes, and Keylan raised his hand to forestall the torrent of words. "But you were wrong about the Skai army going east."

"But we—"

"Tiernyn, this is what got us into this mess in the first place," Keylan said acidly. "We will *not* discuss this now."

Before Tiernyn could launch into a fierce rebuttal, Kian entered the room through the small door behind the High Chair on the dais. Donaugh blinked in surprise. Kian wore the kilt and plaid of a Tyran clansman. As always, his copper gold hair hung free to his shoulders except for the single braid by his left temple, and the large topaz on its fine gold chain dangled from his left earlobe.

Kian stood behind the High Chair, beneath the white falcon banner. "Keylan, fetch your sword," he said. "We're going to need it."

"Need Bane?" Keylan asked, perplexed. "Why?"

"Please. Just fetch it."

Keylan hurried out. Kian said nothing while Keylan was gone. He merely stood quietly, letting the silence stretch out uncomfortably. He was, Donaugh realized, still disturbed by the quarrel Tiernyn and Keylan now chose to ignore.

When Keylan returned with his sword, Kian had still not moved. Keylan caught Donaugh's eye. Donaugh raised one eyebrow slightly, indicating he knew as little as Keylan about what Kian planned to do.

Kian raised his hand and beckoned his sons to stand in

front of him. He looked first at Keylan, who was made in his image, then at the twins, who resembled their mother. For a long moment, he simply looked at them, as if measuring their worth as men. When he finally spoke, his voice was oddly flat and hoarse.

"I have a twofold purpose for calling you here," he said, glancing back and forth between Keylan and Tiernyn. "The first is, I will tolerate no more of this constant bickering between you two. And I intend to see it stopped immediately." He looked first at Keylan, then at Tiernyn. "Is that clearly understood?"

"Yes, Father," Keylan muttered.

Tiernyn nodded.

Kian looked at Donaugh. "I include you, Donaugh," he said quietly. "You have never taken part in any argument, but you of all my sons should understand who's right and who's wrong. You should have stopped this nonsense yourself long ago."

Heat climbed in Donaugh's cheeks. "Yes, Father," he murmured.

"Tell me, then. Who is right?"

Donaugh glanced at Tiernyn, then at Keylan. "Keylan is," he said. Then, as Tiernyn's face began to flush with outrage, he said, "And Tiernyn is also right."

Kian smiled sardonically. "And do you have a solution to this conundrum?"

"No," Donaugh said helplessly. "Had I a solution, I would have said so before Keylan and Tiernyn nearly came to blows, and you ran out of patience with all of us."

"I believe it came to me." Kian turned his attention back to Keylan and Tiernyn. "Mayhaps if you two weren't so busy going for each other's throats, you might have also seen this solution."

"There is only one solution," Tiernyn cried in frustration. "But Keylan won't do it. He must take the army east and bring the battle home to the Saesnesi. He's prince. Only he can do it." He turned to Keylan. "Gather an army of all Celae—"

The muscle in the corner of Keylan's jaw bulged as he clenched his teeth. "Confound you, Tiernyn," he cried. "If you know it must be done, then why don't you simply do it yourself!"

Tiernyn's eyes widened. Thunderstruck, he stared blankly at Keylan. "Do it myself?" he repeated. "But I will never be prince."

The idea burst like a seedpod in Donaugh's mind, spilling so many possibilities he couldn't keep track of all of them. He stared at Keylan in shock as the ideas spun and tumbled through his head. He turned to Tiernyn, excitement quickening his breath. He saw that same excitement kindle in Tiernyn's eyes, then in Keylan's. The very air around them seemed to crackle with it.

"A Brigani won't follow a yrSkai prince," Keylan said. "Nor would a Mercian or a Doriani. But they might follow a man who proclaimed himself to be Celae first and foremost."

"In Tyra, we call such a man a *corrach*," Kian said. "A War Leader. A man who can lead all the clans."

Keylan glanced at his father, then back to Tiernyn. "You've always said the Celae have to band together to defeat the Saesnesi," he said. "And I've always said we can't strip Skai of her army to fight the Saesnesi in the east."

"Someone has to bring together an army made up of all Celae," Tiernyn said slowly. "Men of Skai and Wenydd, men of Mercia, Dorian, and Brigland. Even Venia."

"And none of them would ever follow one prince or duke," Keylan said.

Tiernyn bit his lip. "But as Father says, they might follow a War Leader, a *corrach*."

"My responsibility is Skai," Keylan said. "That's why I've always told you I'm not that man."

"But I might be," Tiernyn said softly. The idea visibly caught fire in him. His face flushed with excitement, he stared at Keylan as the implications flashed through his mind. He began pacing restlessly as he thought, blind to all but the vision Keylan's outburst kindled.

"The men of Celae have a deep capacity for loyalty to a good leader," Donaugh said. "A persuasive man might convince them of the necessity of banding together to fight the Saesnesi. Such an army would be formidable."

"Such an army would need the support of every prince and duke in Celi," Keylan said.

Tiernyn paused in his pacing, his head cocked to one side. "I could do it," he said, more to himself than the others. He nodded, frowning thoughtfully, then looked at his father. "Skai would support this combined army?"

Kian shrugged. "Ask Keylan. He's Prince of Skai. I'm but Regent."

"Keylan?"

"Fifty men from Dun Eidon, well trained and armed, including officers," Keylan said instantly. "And horses for them, as well as food and goods to support them in the winter. In return, I'd expect your army to assist Skai when she was attacked."

"A hundred men," Tiernyn said.

"Fifty," Keylan said firmly. "The thanes of Skai will give you more men. If you recruit others who are not soldiers, you'll have to see to training them yourself. I'll assist with arming them."

"Done."

"You can take the first fifty volunteers once the men return from spring planting. If you can persuade the thanes to give you men, and support for them, you may do it."

"Fair enough," Tiernyn said. "I can recruit men from other provinces, and ask support of their lords." He looked at Kian. "When may I start?"

"Immediately after Beltane," Kian said.

"Why Beltane?" Tiernyn asked. "Why not now?"

"That's the second reason I called you here," Kian said. "The Regency is ended."

Donaugh stared. Beside him, he heard Tiernyn's quick intake of breath.

"Does that mean you're finally going to take your rightful place as Prince of Skai?" Keylan asked, visibly startled. "You should have done it nearly twenty years ago now—"

"No," Kian said. "It means you are."

"But you are Prince of Skai," Keylan said blankly. "You always have been, even if you call yourself Regent."

"No, Keylan," Kian said gently. "I am not Prince of Skai, nor have I ever been. I never carried Bane. The sword declared you, not me. Kyffen himself named you his heir. I took no vows, save only the vow to hold safe the throne of Skai for you until you became a man."

"The men of Skai follow you as Prince," Keylan said. "You're Prince in everything but name."

"Then it's time I stepped aside so the men of Skai might follow their rightful Prince," Kian said. "I've sent out messengers to all the thanes and lords of the outlying districts. You will be proclaimed officially the day after Beltane."

"So soon?" Keylan asked. "But why now?"

Kian smiled. "Is it that ye dinna wish to be Prince, Keylan?" he asked, the Tyran burr in his speech suddenly stronger.

"Of course I do. But—"

"The men of Skai will follow you, Keylan," Donaugh said.

"Of course they will," Keylan said impatiently. "But I always thought I'd have more time to prepare." He looked up at Kian. "You're still a young man, Father. I really thought—"

"They won't follow me anymore, nor would I ask them to." Kian held up his left hand. The last two fingers were entirely missing, the newly healed stumps still pink and shiny with new scar tissue.

Donaugh's breath caught in his throat. All the stories about maimed princes and maimed lands flashed through his mind as he stared at his father's mutilated hand. He remembered seeing Kian fighting against the Saesnesi raiders, his hand wrapped in a bloody bandage. Even with the wound raw and bleeding, it hadn't impaired his ability to wield that great Tyran sword. But Kian was right. The men of Skai would be hesitant to follow a maimed man. The belief that the Prince was intimately tied to the land was too deeply ingrained.

"Kerri and I will return to Tyra," Kian went on. "We plan on taking ship the day after the Investiture ceremony. Torey will come with us."

"But you can't—" Tiernyn said quickly.

"I can and I will," Kian said. "I'm going home, Tiernyn. I love Skai, and I love Celi, but Tyra's my home, and I love it more. I'm going home to Broche Rhuidh. I have a duty there, as well." He held out his right hand to Keylan. "Give Bane to me."

Keylan stared at the sword for a moment as if he'd never seen it before, then slowly placed the sheathed blade in Kian's outstretched hand. Kian drew the sword and held it up before him.

"Read the runes inscribed on the blade," he said softly.

Keylan looked at the deeply etched runes. They glittered in the light like facets cut on a gemstone. "**Courage Dies With Honor,**" he said, his voice quiet but firm.

"Now tell me what it means," Kian said.

"Two meanings," Keylan said. "A man who has courage will die with honor. And, when honor dies, courage dies with it."

"You'll do well to remember that," Kian said. "You will swear to me as Regent you shall not dishonor the sword or the title of Prince of Skai while you live."

Keylan reached out and put his hand on Bane's hilt below Kian's hand. "I so swear by the Duality, by all the seven gods and goddesses, and by the sword Bane. If I break this vow, may the sky fall upon me, may the earth open to swallow me up, and may the sea rise to sweep me away."

Kian sheathed the sword and handed it back. "You'd best go now and speak with the High Priest and Priestess at the shrine. I believe they'll have much they want to tell you in the next two fortnights."

Keylan made a wry face. "I'm sure they will," he said in resignation. "I take my leave of you, my lord Regent. And may I say I heartily wish it was you on his way to the shrine rather than I."

Kian grinned. "You may wish, of course," he said, unperturbed. "But it will do you little good."

Keylan inclined his head to Kian, then turned to Donaugh. "As my youngest brother, will you do me the honor of acting as First Sword for the coronation?"

Donaugh glanced at the great sword Bane, now sheathed safely in Keylan's hands. Should the *darlai* indicate Keylan was not worthy of the coronet and torc of Skai, it was the duty of the First Sword to execute the rejected prince with his own sword. It had happened only once in the history of Skai, but the thought startled and frightened Donaugh.

Keylan waited patiently for an answer. Donaugh cleared his throat. "I will," he said at last. "You honor me."

Keylan sketched a brief bow to his father. Kian waited until Keylan had left, then turned to Tiernyn and Donaugh. "Tomorrow, you two will come with me. There's only one more task I have to perform before I'm free to return home."

"Go with you?" Tiernyn said. "Where?"

"The Dance of Nemeara."

4

They came alone, without escort and without guards. Kian rode slightly ahead, Tiernyn and Donaugh flanking him, riding hard. The track leading north along the coast was level and wide, well traveled, and they made good time.

They reached the plain at the foot of Cloudbearer on the evening of the third day in that mystic, transitional time between sunset and dusk when the sky was still streaked with light and color. Bands of red and orange flamed in the west, illuminating the triple ring of standing stones set in the center of the flat plain. The imposing menhirs of the outer ring stood starkly black against the luminescent sky, crowned in pairs by massive lintels to form trilithons. The middle ring of stones bulked slightly smaller, gracefully joined all around by capstones, polished like jet to reflect the incandescent glow of the sky. The inner ring, standing alone without lintels, was not really a ring at all, but a horseshoe of seven menhirs enclosing a low altar stone that reflected the burning sky like a mirror. It reminded Donaugh of a jewel cradled safe in cupped and loving hands.

His attention was on the Dance as he dismounted. He was barely conscious of Kian and Tiernyn coming to stand beside him. Silhouetted against the sunset, the Dance was a place of immense power. The energy of the place tingled along Donaugh's nerves, vibrating like a plucked harp string. Music and magic, the very soul of the Dance, thrummed in his body and quickened his breath.

It was more than two years since he had last been here, since the night Rhianna of the Air bestowed her gift of strong magic. That night, the stars ran like water across the sky, and the air rang like crystal. Then she came to him across the frost-whitened grass, her moon silver hair floating mistily around her. In her hands she held a nebulous globe, glowing like a cabochon gem. As she placed it in his hands, the globe dissolved into smoke. The mist wrapped his body, seeping into skin and muscle, nerve and tendon, until it was part of him. It sang like music in his veins, beat within him with the rhythm of his heart and the cadence of his breath.

That aura of power still surrounded the Dance. It tingled and rippled along his skin like a breeze moving across a field of ripe grain.

"I don't like this place," Tiernyn murmured. "There's too much magic here. It gives me the shivers."

Kian watched the Dance, a faint smile lifting one corner of his mouth. "I agree," he said.

The sky behind the Dance faded. The menhirs stood black against the gold sky. Shadows wrapped the inner horseshoe and crept toward the outer rings until only the tops of the lintel stones showed bright in the gathering dusk. Donaugh thought he saw something move in the inner horseshoe. He glanced at his father, suddenly aware that Kian watched something or someone near the polished altar stone. It was just as obvious that Tiernyn saw nothing but an empty circle. When Donaugh looked back, there was nothing there.

"Who was it?" Donaugh whispered, afraid to speak louder.

Kian shook his head. "I don't know," he said quietly. "For years I dreamed of a Watcher in a stone Dance like this one. But on a hill." His hand made a sweeping gesture to include the Dance and the plain. "Not a flat plain like this. I called him only the Watcher on the Hill."

Tiernyn looked at him inquisitively. "Before you met Mother?" he asked. "When you were a merchant train guard on the continent?"

Kian smiled. "Yes," he said. "I hated magic then."

"But you *had* magic," Donaugh said.

"Aye, I did. But I hardly knew it then." The smile widened

and he laughed softly. "Your mother was rather annoyed with me in those days. Almost continuously it seemed."

Tiernyn grinned. "Mother can get that way."

Donaugh looked at the Dance again. "Why are we here?"

Kian paused a long moment before answering, his gaze fixed on the Dance. Finally he said, "Because I have to know if the magic was true—that I dreamed true."

"We—Tiernyn and I—have to go in there again?"

"Aye. You do."

Tiernyn visibly shivered. "Surely not," he said. "Father, the last time was bad enough."

Kian turned to look at him. "What do you remember of the last time?"

Tiernyn shook his head. "Not much. Just an eerie feeling of being watched. And strange dreams of people moving all around me, saying things I couldn't understand. Then that pair of daggers beside me when I woke up."

"They belonged once to my foster father," Kian said. "Cullin dav Medroch. He meant you to have them."

Tiernyn frowned in sudden suspicion. "Did you put them there beside me?"

A hint of a smile touched Kian's mouth. "No. I put them on the altar stone shortly after you were born. And I did it in broad daylight." The last of the light faded from the sky, leaving only a pale azure glow in the west. "It's time. I'll wait here for you."

Tiernyn swallowed hard. "You won't come in with us?"

Kian shook his head. "It's not for me tonight," he said. "There's no place for me in there. I'll be here. With the horses."

Donaugh fell into step with Tiernyn. It seemed a very long way to the outer ring of trilithons. He was conscious of the fresh scent of young grass rising in a fragrant cloud around them as their feet crushed the springing blades. A soft breeze flowed toward the cliffs above the sea at the edge of the plain, ruffling his hair. Something small scuttled through the grass, disturbed by their feet. Overhead, the muted beating of wings broke the silence as a late hawk glided through the twilight in hushed grandeur.

They approached the Dance together, side by side. Tiernyn paused between two of the menhirs and glanced up at the massive lintel capping them. He shook his head in awed reverence.

"Surely the hand of no man put these stones here," he said.

Donaugh looked up. "They were carved and fitted by the hands of men," he said. "And raised by men and music and magic."

"Magic." Tiernyn shivered again. "I don't mind the simple magics, the everyday ones. But this smacks too much of the gods and goddesses. I'd soonest keep my contact with them more distant."

"You honor them."

"Aye," said Tiernyn. "I honor them, but I don't like sleeping with them." He straightened his shoulders resolutely. "But if we must, then we must." He stepped into the circle.

The moon rose, full and clear. The Dance became a place of hard, black shadows and pale, washed silver. Donaugh sat cross-legged, his back against the residual warmth of the polished black altar stone. As the moon lifted behind the shoulder of Cloudbearer and climbed into the black, star-dazzled sky, he watched it, envying its serenity. A dreamy lethargy crept through his body. He was barely aware of Tiernyn's soft breathing beside him, where his twin sat with his legs drawn up, forearms propped on his knees. They had been quiet for a long time now. Donaugh had no idea how long, but there was no sense of strain in the easy silence.

The moon cast a strange pattern of light and shadow on the seven pillars of the inner horseshoe. Donaugh studied them with renewed curiosity. How had he failed to notice the deep carving in the stones before this? It looked as if the figures of men and women had been cut in bas-relief into the stone. They appeared queerly alive.

As he watched with growing interest, he suddenly realized they *were* men and women. They stood quietly, still as stones, but relaxed and at ease in the moon-shot night. One by one, he recognized them.

They were all there. Rhianna of the Air, her long, moon-silvered hair floating like a veil about her body. Cernos of the Forest, with the tall rack of stately antlers rising from his brow. Adriel of the Waters, carrying her enchanted ewer. Gerieg of the Crags, with his mighty hammer that smote the peaks and shook the ground, spilling great land-slips down the crags. Beodun of the Fires, carrying in one hand the lamp of benevolent fire and in the other, the lightning bolt of wildfire. Sandor of the Plain, his hair blowing like prairie grass around his face. And the *darlai*, the Spirit of the Land, the Mother of All, smiling in compassion and tenderness.

They waited in companionable silence. Donaugh felt a mild amazement because he wasn't startled or frightened. But Rhianna of the Air had claimed him as her own when he was sixteen. Although she never so much as glanced at him, he was aware of her radiant warmth near him. He was under her protection.

Something not quite audible broke the silence, something just under the threshold of hearing. A new shadow spilled across the silvered grass. The tall figure of a man stood framed by the gateway trilithon. Silently as a shadow, he moved to stand between the capped menhirs of the second ring of standing stones. Tiernyn scrambled to his feet as the man stepped between the stones and approached the altar. Donaugh rose more slowly, staring as hard as Tiernyn.

The man wore a long robe, pale in the moonlight, girdled by something that glinted like gold. His hair and beard, silver as the moon itself, framed a face carved into austere planes and hollows, the eyes shadowed by silver eyebrows. In his hands, he carried something long and narrow, and the flash and sparkle of stars blazed at one end.

Quietly, the man crossed the grass toward the altar, his feet making no disturbance among the young, green blades. He gave the impression of vast age and wisdom, but moved with the lithe grace of a youth.

Donaugh's muscles tightened convulsively. The Watcher on the Hill. This was the man who spoke with Kian long ago in dreams. *Do I dream now*, he wondered in surprise. *Does Tiernyn dream with me?*

The robed man stopped, facing Tiernyn, close enough to reach out and touch him. "Tiernyn Firstborn," he said, his voice akin to the whisper of the breeze in reeds.

"Aye, my lord?" Tiernyn's reply came hoarse and raw from his dry throat.

A smile caused a ripple to shimmer through the white cascade of the man's beard. "I am called Myrddyn, and I am the guardian of this place. I have a gift for you, Tiernyn ap Kian."

"I have no need of gifts, my lord," Tiernyn said.

"You have need of this." Myrddyn stepped forward, the long bundle held before him. "Hold out your hands, Tiernyn Firstborn. Accept the sword of Wyfydd Smith."

Tiernyn held out his hands. Myrddyn placed the bundle across his palms. It was a sword in a worn leather scabbard. The hilt, bound in stained leather, was unadorned except for a faceted crystal gem on the pommel.

"Draw the sword," Myrddyn said.

Tiernyn grasped the scabbard in his left hand and drew the sword with his right. Runes glinted along the blade, flashing shards of light like the points of a gem.

"Can you read the runes?" Myrddyn asked.

Tiernyn held the blade closer to his face. He dropped the scabbard and reached up to trace the carved figures. "**Take up the Strength of Celi,**" he murmured.

Myrddyn turned the blade in Tiernyn's hands. "And these?"

Tiernyn traced them, frowning, then shook his head. "No," he said at last. "These I can't read."

Myrddyn smiled. "You will when it's time," he said. "Do you know its name?"

"It's the Rune Blade my father carried when he first came to Skai," Tiernyn said. "I've heard men call it Kingmaker."

"Aye, that's Kingmaker. Your father carried it until he was informed that it was time to lay it aside. He gave it then to me to hold in trust. It will tell you when it's time to pass it on." He turned to Donaugh. "I have no sword for you, Donaugh Secondborn, but I believe you will find your own gift."

"If I need more than the blade I carry now," Donaugh said, "I think it will come to me."

"It will." The pale figure stepped backward into a shadow and was gone.

Tiernyn held the sword up to the light of the moon and stars. Donaugh had the strangest sensation of merging with Tiernyn, becoming one with his twin. Tiernyn's awe quivered in Donaugh's chest, and he saw the sword through Tiernyn's eyes, felt the ridged leather wrappings of the hilt against his own palms.

The sword began to resonate in Tiernyn's hands. Softly at first, then faster and faster until Donaugh swore it was alive. He became aware of a high, clear, sweet tone singing in the air around them, like a note plucked from a harp string in the highest register. At the same time, the blade began to shimmer, then to glow. At first, like the musical note, softly and gently. Tiernyn's hands on the hilt trembled and his whole body quivered like the air just before a lightning strike as the vibration traveled from the sword into him, but it was Donaugh whose skin shivered with it.

The musical note increased in pitch and volume, wild and keen, sharp and distinct as shards of crystal in the circle of the

Dance. Overtones of triumphant jubilation sang in the note, with shades and subtle nuances of burgeoning power. As the harmonic tone increased in pitch and intensity, so did the gleam of the blade. It moved swiftly through red to orange, then to yellow until it was incandescent white, burning with a radiance to rival the sun, too painful to look at directly. The whole spectrum of the rainbow swirled and spun in wild patterns, edging the looming standing stones in flashing patterns of coruscating color. The joyous chord rang wildly in the air. Donaugh had the distinct impression of something awakening and stretching after a long sleep.

The runes blazed bright and clear, flashing silver fire back to the gibbous moon. The words ran like liquid flame along the length of the blade with a life of their own, searing their eyes with unbearable brilliance.

Surrounded by a brilliant corona of light and color, Tiernyn spread his arms wide, brandishing the sword with a flourish around the inner horseshoe. He cried out in a strange mixture of elation, triumph, and fear.

Tiernyn stood transfixed, staring at the sword he held. A faint twinge of envy pricked at Donaugh's belly. Even if Tiernyn was not yet aware of what the gift of the sword meant, Donaugh knew. He wanted desperately to know Celi needed him as much as it needed Tiernyn.

A woman's soft laughter behind him spun him around, startled and breathless. She had stepped from her place in the center of the horseshoe, tall, graceful, but obviously no longer young. Her dark hair, streaked with silver, hung down across her shoulders and framed a face more kind than beautiful. She reached out to touch his cheek, and a rich, quiet sense of peace filled Donaugh's heart.

"Why do you long for a destiny not yours, Donaugh Secondborn?" she asked, her tone whimsical. "Do you hunger after glory and fame?"

The heat of shame climbed in Donaugh's cheeks. "No, Lady," he said. "I know whose is the glory. I've always known."

"Yes, you have. Do you know who I am?"

"You are the Mother of All," he said. "The *darlai* of the land."

She smiled. "I am the living spirit of Celi, Donaugh Secondborn," she said. "I am Celi herself, and my gift to you is not tangible as is the gift given to your brother. You are mine now, and my gift will be with you always. Do you hear the song of the sword, Donaugh Secondborn?"

Donaugh heard it clearly, a high, sweet harmony that sounded like the melody of flute, harp, and bell combined, chiming in the night. He had thought it the magic of the Dance, but its note was too fierce, too warlike to be the voice of the gentle Tyadda magic contained within the stone circle.

"Do you hear it?"

"Aye, Lady. I hear it well."

"The sword sings in Tiernyn's hand, Donaugh Secondborn, but only you can hear its song. You must act as guide to your brother, as interpreter for the sword."

"I? But I have not the wisdom, Lady . . . "

"Wisdom I cannot grant you, my child. But you will know the path Tiernyn and the sword must take. Search your soul and you will know." She touched his cheek once more, and her fingers scorched his skin with a stab of pain hardly distinguishable from ecstasy. "Never fear, my child. You are needed as much as your brother. I promise you that, but I cannot promise you happiness."

"If there is service, I shall be content."

"Contentment, at least, shall be yours, child. And your son will sire kings."

"My son, Lady? Surely Tiernyn's son . . . "

"Three sons for you, Donaugh Secondborn. One son your bitterest enemy. One your staunchest ally. And one to seed a line of kings forward into the time when these stones will crumble back to dust."

She stepped back. Donaugh stumbled forward and reached out to her. "Lady . . . "

But there was nothing around him but silent megaliths, thrusting upward from the spring carpet of grass. Even the moon was gone, and the first pale hint of dawn stained the eastern sky.

"Did you see him, Donaugh?" Tiernyn's breathless whisper sounded loud in the hushed circle. "Did you see him?"

Donaugh jerked around, slipping in the dew-wet grass. Tiernyn stood holding the glowing sword before him, his lips parted, his eyes shining.

"This is Kingmaker," Tiernyn said, his voice tinged with awe. "It's Kingmaker, the sword Father brought home to Celi. Did you see him?"

"Myrddyn?" Donaugh said. "Yes, I saw him. The sword was built for you. It will serve you well as long as you serve it."

"Kingmaker," Tiernyn said again. "By the seven gods and goddesses, Donaugh. Do you realize what this means?"

Donaugh smiled. "None better than I," he said. "Look. It's dawn. Father will be waiting."

"He knew this would happen, didn't he?"

Donaugh looked around at the silent menhirs. "I believe he hoped it would," he said.

Tiernyn reverently sheathed the shining blade. He unclipped the scabbard on his back and handed it to Donaugh while he fastened Kingmaker in its place. Taking the old sword and scabbard from Donaugh, he placed it squarely in the center of the altar stone, then turned to walk between the stones. Donaugh made a small obeisance to the center stone of the horseshoe, then followed his twin. When he looked back, the altar lay bare and shining in the morning sun. Tiernyn's sword had vanished.

In the brightening dawn, Tiernyn glanced at Donaugh and frowned. "Whatever have you done to your cheek?" he asked. "How did you burn yourself?"

Donaugh raised his hand to his face. The blister beneath his cheekbone was hard and smooth, slightly smaller than the pad of his finger. It would very likely leave a scar.

"I burned myself in the bright fire of your triumph," he said. Then, when Tiernyn stared blankly at him, he smiled and shook his head. "It was nothing."

Beltane Eve saw Dun Eidon filled to overflowing with the lords of the outlying districts, their families and their retinues. People from all over the province camped in the area around the village, come for the double festival. The guest wing housed emissaries from the royal houses of Wenydd, Dorian, Mercia, and Brigland. Servants scurried back and forth in the corridors as last-minute preparations required one unexpected item or another. The whole palace hummed with cheerful uproar and tumult.

High on the flank of the mountain above the shrine, the wood for the Beltane Fire lay ready in the glade amid the oak grove. Excitement ran like needfire through the valley as men and women prepared to celebrate the only night of the year when the Duality separated into its male and female aspects and coupled as man and woman to assure the fertility of field and herd, sea and forest. This night every woman represented the goddess and every man the god.

The further celebrations in the morning as Keylan ap Kian was invested as Prince of Skai promised more excuse for revelry and feasting. Skai had not invested a prince for over sixty years. Not since Kyffen had the torc and coronet been worn. The people of Skai were determined to make the most of the celebrations.

Donaugh dodged through the crowd surrounding the shrine as he sought Tiernyn. He could never remember so many people assembled for a Beltane procession before. The air all but fizzed with the sense of anticipation, tangible as mist under the oaks. Even the curtains of ivy trailing from the twelve oak trees seemed to quiver with it. The eleven pipers had already taken their places at the foot of the path leading to the clearing higher up the mountain, waiting for the procession to begin. Kian and Kerri stood near the pipers, surrounded by people, nobles and commoners alike. On this night, there was no difference in rank among the people of Skai. At the Beltane fire, a princess could offer mead to a stableboy, or a kitchen girl to a lord.

Donaugh stopped and looked around. There was no sign of Tiernyn among the crowd. The procession would begin soon. If he didn't find Tiernyn before it started, he would have to wait until after the celebration around the fire, and by then, it might be too late.

The last of the villagers and visitors approached the shrine along the path from the village. Donaugh saw Keylan and Torey among them. Keylan looked nervous, and Torey wore an expression of wide-eyed expectancy.

But where was Tiernyn?

Donaugh finally spotted him standing alone near the far pillar of the shrine. He cut through the throng and grabbed Tiernyn's arm, pulling him into a protected corner behind the shrine, away from the swirling crowd.

"Have you lost your mind?" he demanded without preamble.

Tiernyn pulled his arm from Donaugh's grasp. "What are you talking about?"

"You know very well what I'm talking about. The hundred and twenty men you're planning on taking out of here first thing tomorrow morning. That's what I'm talking about."

"The hundred and twenty—?"

Donaugh cut him short. "Are you mad?"

Tiernyn rubbed his arm, scowling. "They all want to come with us," he said. "All of them volunteered."

Donaugh ran a hand through his hair. "I've no doubt they did," he said with a harsh laugh. "You could persuade a sparrow to sit on a cat's ear if you set your mind to it. But Keylan promised you fifty men, not a hundred and twenty."

"They want to come," Tiernyn repeated. "They want to take the fight to the Saesnesi. They're tired of Celi being fragmented and helpless to stop them."

"Keylan promised you arms and upkeep for fifty men. What in the name of mercy do you think he's going to do when he finds out you've gone with a hundred and twenty of his best men? That's nearly half his army! What do you think he'll do? Bless your name and send more provisions and arms? Or horses?"

"They want to come," Tiernyn insisted.

"Stubborn," Donaugh muttered. "Both of you. Stubborn as rocks. Even now—"

"They came to me," Tiernyn said. "I didn't recruit them."

"Tiernyn, for Annwn's sake—"

"What was I supposed to do?" Tiernyn kicked at a pebble. "Was I supposed to tell more than half of them they had no place with me?"

"Yes. That's exactly what you were supposed to do."

"How do I tell seventy men they won't be allowed to serve Celi?"

Donaugh slammed his fist against the pillar hard enough to raise a bruise on his knuckles. "By the horns of Cernos, Tiernyn," he said softly, "I knew you were stubborn and willful. But I didn't realize you were stupid, as well."

Tiernyn turned on him fiercely. "Don't you dare call me stupid," he said, his voice quiet and dangerous.

"And who better to point out your folly?" Donaugh demanded. "Tiernyn, you carry Kingmaker. You will be High King of Celi. But only if you serve the sword and Celi truly."

Tiernyn stared at him. His mouth fell open for a startled moment, then he closed it, swallowed hard, and bit his lip. "High King?" he repeated. "I?"

Donaugh made an exasperated noise with teeth and tongue. "Why else do you suppose Myrddyn gave you the sword?"

"I thought it was so I could unite all Celi against the Saesnesi. That's what the legend says . . . "

"Yes, that, too," Donaugh said impatiently. "But how do you suppose you're going to do it? Who will men follow? The younger brother of a prince? Or a king?"

"But High King? Are you sure?"

"As sure as I can be without seeing the crown on your head right now. Look . . . "

He reached out and grasped a thread of power flowing through the earth beneath him. He let the magic build slowly. He felt light and airy as a bubble in a wineglass. The music sang in his blood, and crackled along his nerves. Behind Tiernyn on the wall of the shrine, their shadows wavered and shimmered like water sheeting down the sheer rock face of a cliff. As the shadows re-formed, they built a picture of a man wearing a crown, standing tall and straight as one of the twelve sacred oaks, the sword in his raised hand glowing with a radiance that lit the trees. But where Donaugh stood, there was nothing—only a slim wisp, smoke or mist in the moonlight.

"There," Donaugh whispered, his voice rough and hoarse. "Do you see?"

The king-shadow stood sharp and clear as letters painted on parchment. Wordlessly, Tiernyn nodded.

"This is your destiny," Donaugh said. "But it won't happen if you don't listen to me now. How are you going to persuade all the princes and dukes of Celi to trust you and support you with men and provisions and arms if they know you played your own brother false? Are they going to trust you if the Prince of Skai says you betrayed him?"

Tiernyn started to say something, then let out his breath in a long hiss instead. Donaugh released the thread of power. The magic dissipated and fled in a rush. The shadows melted, then blew away like mist, until only the memory was left. Behind them, the first tentative droning of the pipes sounded as the pipers fine-tuned their instruments. Donaugh looked over his shoulder, then back to Tiernyn.

"Pick fifty men," he said. "Only fifty. And don't leave before Keylan is invested. He'll never forgive you if you strip him of a hundred and twenty of his best men. You know that. And he'll have a hard time forgetting the insult if you vanish before the investiture ceremonies."

Four people, two men and two women, came down the steps from the door of the shrine. Each carried a decorated and carved pole supporting one corner of a green silk canopy. They stood waiting at the foot of the wide steps as the pipers made ready. The young man and woman chosen to represent the god and goddess ran lightly down the steps, arm in arm, and took their place beneath the embroidered green silk. The first skirl of the pipes sounded as the sun dipped below the horizon. Torchbearers hurried to take their places to guide the god and goddess to the glade in the oak grove. Rippling flags of flame streamed back from the torches as the people of Skai fell in behind the pipers. An excited murmur of laughter shimmered through the crowd as the procession began to move.

"We'd best go," Tiernyn said.

Donaugh caught his arm. "First your promise," he said.

Tiernyn met Donaugh's eyes. "I will be High King?" he asked softly.

"I promise you. High King of all Celi."

"But only if I do as you say."

"No. Only if you don't play the sword false."

"You speak for the sword?"

"In that much, I do. Your promise?"

Tiernyn smiled crookedly. "It seems I have no choice," he said. "You have it."

"Fifty men."

"Aye. Fifty men."

Donaugh nodded. "Very well." He laughed. "We should hurry. This is Ylana's first Beltane, as well as Torey's. She'd never forgive you if she thought you forgot and came late."

5

It was still dark when Donaugh slipped through the silent, deserted corridors of the palace to Keylan's room. He wasn't surprised to find Keylan awake and standing at the window, dressed only in his smallclothes. As Donaugh entered, Keylan nodded silently and pointed to where Bane lay on a chest by the bed. Donaugh buckled the baldric around him and unsheathed the sword. In the pale glow of the setting moon, the runes along the blade glimmered softly. First Sword of Skai. He shivered as he thought for a moment of his duty should the *darlai* indicate disfavor. Would he have the courage to kill his brother, as that long-ago Nemedd had been called upon to kill Llewen? He ran his finger along the deeply etched runes.

"*Courage dies with honor,*" Keylan quoted, his voice sounding strained.

Donaugh shivered again. "Surely it won't come to that," he said. "Bane has already accepted you. How could the *darlai* find fault?"

"With gods and goddesses, who can tell?" Keylan laughed shortly without humor. "I keep wondering what would happen if Lameth and Shena came to the door to ask if I was ready, and I yelled *No!* and slammed the door in their faces."

The image of the stunned expressions on the faces of the High Priest and Priestess was too much for Donaugh. Laughter bubbled up in his chest, and he couldn't prevent it from spilling out of him. He sat on the bed and tried to muffle his laughter. "We shouldn't be taking this so lightly," he said, but couldn't stop laughing.

"Lightly?" Keylan repeated. "I'm dead serious!" Then he grinned. "Well, almost anyway."

Donaugh's laughter died as someone tapped softly on the door. Keylan went to open the door. No servants would attend him today until after the ceremony at the shrine. It was symbolic of his servitude to Skai and to her people.

Lameth and Shena stood side by side in the corridor, bound together at ankle, hip, and chest. They wore one robe, allowing Lameth to use his right arm and Shena her left. They looked grotesquely wide, a two-headed being not of this earth. Together, they represented the twinned aspect of the Duality, neither male nor female, but both.

Lameth carried a robe of coarsely woven brown wool folded over his arm. Shena carried a hempen rope to use as a girdle. They stepped into the room as Keylan opened the door for them. Donaugh rose from the bed and held Bane before him like a banner pole.

"Donaugh ap Kian," Lameth and Shena intoned in practiced unison. "Are you ready to take up the duty this day placed on you as First Sword of Skai."

Donaugh glanced at Keylan. He nodded. "I am."

Lameth and Shena turned to Keylan. "And you, Keylan ap Kian, Scion of the Royal House of Skai, are you ready to take up the yoke of servitude to Skai in the sight of the Duality and all the seven gods and goddesses?"

Donaugh couldn't look at Keylan. He was afraid he'd burst into laughter. He heard Keylan's deep, indrawn breath.

"I am ready," Keylan said.

Lameth proffered the brown robe and Shena held forth the hempen cord. "Then dress yourself and come with us."

Keylan pulled the robe over his head and belted it. He folded his hands into his sleeves and bowed his head. "Lead me," he said. As he passed Donaugh to follow Lameth and Shena from the room, he whispered, "Curse this thing. It itches."

Donaugh thought that would be the least of Keylan's discomfort this day. He fell in behind Keylan, his knuckles white on the hilt of the sword.

———

Dawn was little more than a pale hint behind the shoulder of the mountain as Lameth and Shena led Keylan and Donaugh out of the palace and up the track to the Dance of standing stones above the shrine. Keylan flinched visibly as sharp stones bit into the soles of his bare feet as he walked with his head bowed.

Lameth and Shena stopped at the entrance to the Dance. They stepped aside and beckoned Donaugh to enter.

Donaugh stepped to the center of the circle and raised Bane high before him.

"*Darlai* of Skai, guide me in this endeavor," he said quietly. "As First Sword of Skai, I beg your favor for Keylan ap Kian, but should you deny this, I ask for strength to carry out the solemn duty imposed on me." He bowed deeply to the *darlai* stone, then turned to the entrance of the circle.

His fists clenched by his sides, Keylan straightened his shoulders, raised his head, and stepped resolutely into the circle. He knew what was expected of him. He had rehearsed this every day for two fortnights. Slowly, he walked to the center, then did a slow turn, bowing to each of the standing stones, leaving the stone representing the *darlai* to the last. Donaugh moved silently to stand behind him.

Stepping forward, Keylan went to one knee before the stone representing Rhianna of the Air and raised both hands, palms up in supplication.

"Rhianna, Mistress of the Air, help me from this day forward until the number of my days are counted and totaled by the Counter at the Scroll. May the breath of my body be spent in service of Skai and her people, and in service to you and all the seven gods and goddesses, and to the Duality who sits above all." He went to his belly and reached out to touch the base of the stone.

Something flickered between the stone and the tips of Keylan's fingers. Donaugh had not realized how wrought up he was until the tension drained from him as he realized what the glimmering flicker meant. Surprise registered briefly on Keylan's face, then an expression of peace took its place.

Keylan rose and bowed deeply to the stone, his breathing uneven. Stepping sideways, he went to one knee before the stone representing Beodun of the Fires.

"Beodun, Master of the Benevolent Fire of the Hearth, and the Wildfire of the Skies, help me from this day forward until the number of my days are counted and totaled by the Counter at the Scroll. May the fire of my soul be spent in the service of Skai and her people, and in service to you and all the seven gods and goddesses, and to the Duality who sits above all." Again, when he reached out to touch the base of the stone pillar, the same glinting shimmer flowed from the stone to Keylan's fingers.

From one stone to the next Keylan went, pledging the rock of his will to Gerieg of the Crags, the rich soil of his heart to Sandor of the Plains, the strong branch of his sword arm to Cernos of the Forest, and the living water of his blood to Adriel of the Waters.

When at last he came to the center stone, he went to both knees, then prostrated himself at the foot of the stone before raising himself to his knees again.

"*Darlai* of Skai, Mother of All, giver of the gift of life and bringer of the peace of death, help me from this day forth. May the whole of my being be spent in the service of Skai and her people, and may I prove a worthy son to you and to Skai. To you, to Skai, and to her people, I give my service. This I pledge by the Duality, and by all the seven gods and goddesses, and by the sword Bane. If I break this vow, may the sky fall upon me, may the earth open up to swallow me, and may the sea rise up to sweep me away."

As he said the last words, the sun rose and a shaft of pure, golden light spilled into the circle. The stone before Keylan shone like silver. The reflected glow bathed him, a benediction and acceptance. His face transformed by the soft radiance of the mirrored light, he turned to Donaugh.

"I have been accepted," he said clearly. "You have fulfilled your duty. There is no further need for your services as First Sword."

Donaugh lowered Bane, letting his tense muscles relax. The knot in his belly loosened. He felt light and free as a puff of thistledown on the breeze, washed clean as a forest after a spring rain. He bowed to the *darlai* and turned to face Lameth and Shena as they stepped into the circle.

"Are you ready, Keylan ap Kian?" the High Priest and Priestess intoned in chorus.

Keylan inclined his head in acceptance. "I am."

Torey stood on the dais before the altar, dressed in a simple white gown trimmed with gold. Her rose-gold hair tumbled about her shoulders and down her back, held by a plain circlet of gold around her brow.

The torc she held felt too heavy in her hands. Fashioned of gold to resemble a twisted rope, it was thicker than two of her fingers. At each end, the finials of gold and enamel made falcons' heads, each with brilliant sapphires as eyes. It was as old as the Royal House of Skai, and the gold had taken on a soft luster that made it gleam softly, more like silk than metal, in the rich light of the sun.

Torey was mortally afraid she would drop it when she lifted it to place it around Keylan's neck, and she was terrified she would giggle and spoil the whole ceremony. But as Keylan's closest female relative, it was her duty and her privilege to bind him to the service of Skai. She sent up a small, fervent prayer to the Duality that she do this well, with all the dignity and solemnity the occasion demanded.

The broad doors of the shrine stood open, flung wide to the early summer sunshine. Inside, bright silken ribbons in green and gold and blue festooned the walls among riotous cascades of spring blossoms. On the altar, the wide stone bowl was filled with clear water, petals of violets and crocuses floating serenely on the surface. A hoop of ivy hung with ribbons and flowers, representing the Unbroken Circle of the cycle of birth, life, death, and rebirth, stood beside the bowl.

Between the hoop and the bowl, the coronet of Skai sat gleaming in the sun. Only a thumblength in thickness, flaring to a shallow point in the front, it glowed in the brilliant light, the gems encrusting it flashing back sparks into the sun.

There was room inside the shrine for the twelve priests and priestesses, the royal family, and the visiting nobility. The rest of the people assembled outside, crowding around the open doors. The breathy trill of dozens of twin flutes sang sweetly in the air as musicians wove their way through the crowd.

Torey glanced at her parents, standing to the right of the dais. Kerri also wore white, her hair done in braids and drawn back into a netting of gold. Poised and calm, she smiled assurance at Torey.

Beside her, Kian, resplendent in the kilt and plaid of a Tyran clansman, looked magnificent. He wore the kilt to remind the people of Skai why he had agreed to stand as Regent but not be invested as Prince. Today, he was not only Regent, he represented the Royal House of Tyra and his uncle, Rhodri dav Medroch, the Clan Laird, at the investiture of the Prince of Skai.

Donaugh had slipped almost unnoticed into the shrine, his duty as First Sword complete. Torey had not missed the slight relaxing of the stiffness in Kian's shoulders, or the quick smile he and Donaugh had exchanged. The twins now stood together behind Kerri and Kian, both of them dressed in light blue. In repose, both faces were so alike, for a moment Torey couldn't tell which was Tiernyn and which was Donaugh. Then Donaugh smiled and gave her a barely perceptible wink. She smiled back and most of her nervousness fled with the confidence the shared smile instilled.

A murmur like the sound of a swelling sea drifted from outside the shrine. Torey looked up to see Lameth and Shena leading Keylan down the track from the Dance of standing stones. He towered a full head above the chunky figure of the twinned High Priest and Priestess, his hair glowing copper gold. Even dressed in the rough brown robe, he moved with a lithe grace that was both regal and confident. A serene smile touched Keylan's lips, and the lines of strain were no longer apparent around his eyes and between his eyebrows.

As he stepped into the shrine, he looked up and met Torey's eyes. The smile widened, turning up the corners of his mouth. He walked to the base of the dais, then stood quietly as the six priests came forward and stripped the brown robe from him. The six priestesses stepped forward with a robe of white and a surplice of dark blue, the white falcon of Skai embroidered on the left shoulder. They dressed him, then went back to stand behind the dais.

Shena and Lameth mounted the dais beside Torey and turned to face Keylan. They made the sign of the Unbroken Circle in the air and Keylan came forward to kneel on the dais at their feet.

"Keylan ap Kian, will you take up the torc of Skai, representing the yoke of servitude to all the people of Skai?" The pleasant harmony of their voices filled the shrine.

"I will." Keylan's voice was quiet and even, strong enough to all corners of the shrine.

"Will you pledge your sword and your life to the protection of Skai and her people?"

"I will."

"Will you swear before the Duality and this assembly of the people of Skai that your service to them will be first in your life, from now until the number of your days are counted and totaled before the Counter at the Scroll?"

"I swear."

Torey glanced at Shena and Lameth. Shena gave her a subtle nod and smile.

Torey took a deep breath and stepped forward, lifting the torc. "I represent the people of Skai, Keylan ap Kian," she said, her voice clear and sweet, carrying to fill the shrine. "To you I give the torc, yours to carry through your life. May its burden be light and may your service be joyous."

She slipped it around his neck and stepped back. He raised a hand to settle it more comfortably at his throat. The falcons' heads fitted well into the hollows above his collarbone. He looked up at her. Torey saw his eyes shining with unshed tears, and her own eyes filled as she smiled at him.

"I accept this torc and the attendant responsibilities and privileges," he said.

Lameth and Shena, turning gracefully together, picked up the gold circlet that lay on the altar stone. Each holding one side of it, they crossed the dais to stand in front of Keylan and raised the coronet above his head.

"Here, the Unbroken Circle," they intoned. "Here, the symbol of birth, life, death, and rebirth. Yours, Keylan ap Kian, Prince of Skai, to mark your place in the circle of life. Let it grace your brow, knowing the Duality blesses your wearing of it."

As they placed it on Keylan's head, the sun caught the gemstones, splashing rainbows of color among the ribbons and flowers adorning the pristine white walls. Keylan seemed to kneel a little taller, a little straighter, as the coronet settled into place, gleaming in his red-gold hair.

Lameth and Shena held out their hands. "Rise, Keylan, Prince of Skai, and accept the loyalty of your people."

Keylan climbed to his feet and stepped onto the dais to stand between Torey and the High Priest and Priestess, turning to face the crowded shrine.

Torey went to one knee before Keylan and held up both hands to him. She looked up at him. His eyes were bright as he smiled at her and took both her hands in his.

"Inasmuch as you have pledged your service to Skai, Keylan ap Kian," she said, "as representative of the people of Skai, I offer you the loyalty and support of all the people. May your will be ours, and may your honor and courage always be a beacon to light our way through all the days and nights of your reign."

Keylan raised her to her feet, then bent to kiss both her cheeks. "As you say, so will I do," he said gravely, but his eyes shone.

Torey stepped back to her place behind him on the dais.

Kian came forward and went to one knee on the dais. He raised his hands and placed them into Keylan's. Torey saw Keylan stiffen. He would have drawn his hands back, but Kian held them tightly.

"You don't kneel before me, Father," Keylan said softly. "Not you."

"I kneel before the Prince of Skai like any other man," Kian said firmly. One corner of his mouth turned up in amusement and he remained on one knee. "I pledge you my loyalty and my service, my lord Prince," he said. "And I bring the pledge of friendship and support from Rhodri dav Medroch dav Kian, Twelfth Clan Laird of Broche Rhuidh of Tyra, First Laird of the Council of Clans, Protector of the Sunset Shore, Laird of the Misty Isles, Master of the Western Crags and Laird of Glenborden." The titles rolled effortlessly from his tongue.

"I accept your service, my lord Father," Keylan said quietly. "And I accept the friendship of Tyra. You may return my thanks and my pledge of support to your kinsman Rhodri, Clan Laird of Broche Rhuidh and First Laird of the Council of Clans."

Tiernyn and Donaugh came forward next, pledging their loyalty and service. One by one, the rest of the nobility of Skai came to the dais. As the last stepped aside, a long line of the people of Skai approached the dais.

By the time the last had left the shrine, Keylan was gray with fatigue, and the sun stood high in the sky. Torey put her hand on her brother's arm and smiled at him.

"Will you escort me to the feast, my lord Prince?" she asked.

"I shall be delighted," Keylan said. He bent forward and put his lips by her ear so only she could hear. "If I don't eat soon, I'm going to faint dead away and disgrace myself forever!"

After the feasting came the games. In the demonstrations of swordplay and horsemanship, the young men vied noisily with each other for prizes of gold or wonderfully crafted weapons. No one was much surprised when Alys al Rhan roundly defeated Eryth ap Morfyn on the archery range. She left him plaintively demanding consolation in the form of a kiss as she danced away, laughing, with the prize of a yew bow inlaid with precious ivory.

The shouts and laughter of the contestants in the swordplay contests mingled with the music of flute, pipe, and harp. An ever-changing mosaic of swirling color revolved across the practice field, the village, and the palace courtyard as guests in their finery strolled around, trying not to miss anything. Gems, gold and silver, gleamed and sparkled in the warm spring sunshine. Children whooped and yelped, planning and executing raids on the kitchens, where the scent of baking sweet breads and roasting meat stirred in the air, thick as fog, tempting and irresistible.

On the village green, young women danced to the wild skirling of the pipes of Celi, weaving bright ribbons about the Beltane Pole and flirting outrageously with the young men who gathered to watch them. Old men and women gossiped on benches at the edge of the green, shaded by overhanging silverleaf maple, chestnut, and oak trees. They kept the young people scurrying to fetch food or chilled cider.

Connor of Wenydd caught up to Tiernyn at the edge of the track where the green flags marked the finish line of the horse racing course. Tiernyn, flushed and laughing, stroked the sweat-stained neck of a fine-boned gray mare. The horse snorted and pranced sideways as Connor cut through the crowd to Tiernyn's side.

"She's a beauty," Connor said. The horse warily submitted to his stroking hand. "What do you call her?"

"Cloud," Tiernyn replied. "She nearly won today. She'll be

more canny about staying away from that thumping great gelding of Donaugh's next time. He threw her off stride when he cut her off back at the turn by the willows."

Connor's dark blue eyes filled with laughter. "The gelding won't take her measure next time," he said.

Donaugh appeared, leading the gelding in question. The mare skittered sideways. Her head went up, nearly jerking the hackamore rope from Tiernyn's hands.

"Steady, my lady." Tiernyn stroked the mare's neck. "He'll behave himself now. Donaugh will keep him honest."

"You owe me a silver," Donaugh said, grinning. "We beat you."

Tiernyn shrugged. "Aye, you did. But neither of us could beat Deyr and his sorrel."

"I need to talk to you," Connor said. "Both of you. Somewhere quiet."

Tiernyn caught Donaugh's eye. Donaugh nodded.

"The stables," Tiernyn said. "They should be quiet enough, and we have to see to the horses anyway."

The stables were empty except for a handful of grooms and stableboys tending horses sweating from the races. Tiernyn waved away a stableboy and took Cloud to a stall himself. Connor perched on the rail of the stall as Donaugh put the gelding into an adjoining box. Tiernyn picked up a brush and set to work on the mare's withers.

"What did you want to talk about, Connor?" he asked.

Connor hesitated. "Is it true?" he asked at last. "Is it true you have Kingmaker?"

"Aye, true enough." Tiernyn reached up to untangle the mare's black mane.

"Then it's also true you're raising an army to go after the Saesnesi," Connor said.

"Aye, that's true, too."

"I want to come with you," Connor said.

"Why?" Donaugh asked.

Connor turned on the rail. Donaugh stood with both arms

resting on the withers of the gelding, watching him closely. "What do you mean, why?" Connor asked.

"Why do you want to come?" Donaugh repeated.

One of Connor's hands made a fist. "Because I've seen what the Saesnesi do when they come raiding," he said quietly. "Because I think Tiernyn's right in thinking we have to take the fight to them. Because I can see the logic my father uses when he says our first duty is to protect Wenydd. If we can stop some of the raids before they begin, we're protecting all of Celi, not just Wenydd or Skai." He looked at Tiernyn. "You and I, Tiernyn. We're second sons. Your brother is Prince of Skai. My brother will be Duke of Wenydd. What we have is what we can make for ourselves. I'd rather carve a place for myself by the side of the man who'll unite all Celi against the Saesnesi than sit in Wenydd as a useless second son."

"What can you offer us?" Donaugh asked.

Connor laughed. "Not a lot," he admitted. "Myself, my sword arm, and my skill. But I've also thirty-five men who follow me and would welcome an opportunity to fight the Saesnesi in the territory they've stolen from Celi."

"Thirty-five men," Tiernyn repeated. "With arms, horses, and provisions for the winter?"

Connor nodded. "Yes. Wenydd and Skai have always been allies. My father might be persuaded to give you more men. And he might provide arms and grain for wintering. The thanes of Wenydd will surely give you men and support, too."

Donaugh returned to grooming the gelding. "It seems a good start," he said.

"A good start?" Tiernyn repeated. He laughed breathlessly. "It's an excellent start. Keylan's given us fifty men. We can recruit more men from the thanes. Eryth wants to join us, and he can bring twenty men. Oh, Donaugh, we'll have an army of a thousand men—*two* thousand men!—by the end of summer." He dropped the grooming brush and held out his hand to Connor. "You'll be the first Companion of the *Corrach*," he said. "I'll make a fine War Leader with Companions like Donaugh of Skai and Connor of Wenydd by my side."

Connor leapt nimbly down from the rail and grasped Tiernyn's hand. "A fine *corrach*, indeed," he said.

Donaugh finished with his gelding and came around the dividing wall to lean a shoulder against the supporting pillar. "Best to wait until after we've spoken with the men of Mercia, and Dorian, and Brigland before you count your army," he said dryly.

"But he carries Kingmaker . . ." Connor began.

"Aye, he does," Donaugh said. He grinned. "And he has a silver tongue. Mayhaps we'll have an army of five thousand before next Beltane."

Torey slipped away from the celebrations and found a quiet spot on the far side of the practice field. She spread her shawl beneath a chestnut tree in full, riotous bloom and sat down, careful of her white gown. Minna would undoubtedly scold her if the gown were grass-stained. She rested her back against the broad trunk and closed her eyes.

She had spent most of the day eluding Eryth ap Morfyn's pursuit and avoiding Connor of Wenydd. Eryth, a brash young braggart, bored her to tears, and his arrogant assurance that she found him irresistible set her teeth on edge.

She had overheard two of Eryth's men discussing his intention to have his father speak with her father about arranging a marriage. She highly doubted that ridiculous notion would get past Kian, but should her father broach the subject, her answer would be a resounding no! She could not imagine a lifetime spent with Eryth ap Morfyn. That would cross her eyes and glaze her over in deadly tedium.

Connor of Wenydd on the other hand . . . No man should be that good-looking. That black hair—black enough to send blue sparks back into the sun—made her want to touch it to assure herself it was real. And he had the bluest eyes she had ever

seen on any man. His elder brother, Ralf, was handsome, but
Connor was beautiful, if she could apply such a term to a man.
Nearly as tall as Tiernyn and Donaugh, he was lithe and supple, his broad shoulders narrowing to slender hips. Definitely a
man to entice a woman's eye, Torey thought.

The problem was—he knew it. He was accustomed to having besotted young women clustering around him, sighing and
waiting for a smile. Torey was not about to join an army of
female admirers. But those dark blue eyes were definitely
stunning. There was no denying it. And there was no denying
the fact that Connor had spent an inordinate amount of time
during the five days past smiling at her, or that the smile
caused the most charming crinkles to appear at the corners of
those devastatingly blue eyes.

Even as she sat thinking about him, she saw him walking
toward the stables with the twins, all three of them laughing.
Almost as if he felt her gaze, he looked over his shoulder and
met her eyes. He smiled, and heat rose in her cheeks. She
deliberately looked away toward the barracks beyond the
hedge.

Ylana al Finn crept out of the side door of the barracks.
Tiernyn's newly declared bheancoran looked both ways, hanging back in the shadows, before darting into the shelter of a
flowering thornbush. Torey was about to wave and call out
when she realized Ylana's posture was oddly furtive. Torey
frowned as Ylana slipped behind the hedge of hollies, to reap-
pear moments later as if she were returning from watching the
horse racing on the far end of the practice field. She saw
Torey, waved, and changed direction, running across the grass
to fling herself down beside Torey.

"Where have you kept yourself all day?" Ylana asked,
laughing. "Eryth's been wandering around like a lost puppy
looking for you."

"I've been keeping myself out of his way," Torey replied.

Ylana grinned. "You'll break his little calcified heart."

"I'm utterly devastated," Torey said.

"No, he is." Ylana made a face and cuffed the side of Torey's head lightly. "And so, may I say, is Connor of Wenydd."

"Ylana . . ."

Ylana laughed again. "I saw you last night at the Fire. Those two were nearly at each other's throats, each of them falling all over the other trying to attract your attention."

"Ylana . . ."

Ylana hugged her knees to her chest, watching Torey's face closely. "You did, didn't you?" she said at last. "You *did* offer your mead to Connor."

Torey blushed scarlet. "I only did it to make Eryth leave me alone," she said.

"You can't fool me, Torey al Kian," Ylana said. "You like him, don't you?"

Torey took a deep breath and kited off on another track, one less dangerous. "What were you doing in the barracks just now?" she asked. To her surprise, Ylana blushed.

"Nothing," Ylana said. "I was just talking to one of the officers. He wanted to go with Tiernyn, and I—"

"What are you up to?" Torey demanded, sitting straighter. She reached out to grasp Ylana's arm. "You looked like a thief in the night coming out of the barracks. You're up to something, aren't you?"

"I'm not! I just wanted to talk to Lluddor about—"

"Tiernyn told Lluddor he couldn't go with him. What did *you* tell Lluddor?" Lluddor's company consisted of forty men. All of them had volunteered to go with Tiernyn. None of them were among the men Tiernyn had picked to accompany him.

"Nothing." Ylana pulled her arm away. "I just said it was too bad he couldn't go because he wants so much to go with Tiernyn." She rubbed her arm. "Lluddor won't go with Tiernyn. He said he wouldn't. He swore allegiance to Keylan this morning, didn't he?"

"Yes," Torey said. "He did swear. I saw him myself."

"You're leaving tomorrow on the morning tide, aren't you?" Ylana said, changing the subject herself this time.

Torey nodded. She had almost forgotten it in the hectic preparations for Keylan's investiture. It was only after the ceremony that she suddenly realized she would be leaving Skai, and all her friends. Tears came unbidden to her eyes and she brushed them impatiently away.

"I shall miss you," Ylana said. "Oh, Torey, I shall miss you desperately."

"You're going with Tiernyn," Torey said, trying to smile. "You won't have time to miss me."

"I will. Oh, but I will."

The two young women both burst into tears and hugged each other. But Torey couldn't stop thinking about how furtive Ylana looked as she left the barracks.

6

The moon slipped low on the horizon above the rippled waters of the Ceg, pursued by the relentless Huntress Star. Donaugh stood on the garden terrace outside the solar, his hands resting on the crenellated wall, and watched the silver moon-path running the length of the inlet. It led straight and true from the moon to the ship lying at anchor by the jetty.

Even now, in this hour before dawn, lights bobbed and darted across the deck and in the rigging of the ship as the crew made final preparations to leave for Tyra with the morning tide. By midmorning, the *Skai Seeker* would be rounding the south coast of Celi and well on its way to the west coast of Tyra on the continent.

By midafternoon, Tiernyn with his picked men would be ready to leave Dun Eidon.

Donaugh suppressed a sigh. The change that Torey had feared so much was well and truly upon them with a vengeance. After tomorrow, nothing would ever be the same again. He had told Torey that change wasn't always bad. He still believed it. Change wasn't a bad thing—just different, and difference took becoming accustomed to.

"I thought I might find you here."

Donaugh turned at the sound of the voice. Rhegar moved like a tall wraith across the tiled surface of the terrace, moonlight caught in his beard and hair. He approached the wall and leaned his forearms on it, looking out over the water at the gently rocking ship.

"It's strange to think my father will be leaving on that ship in the morning," Donaugh said. "Stranger yet to stop thinking of him as Red Kian of Skai."

"Your father has completed his work for Skai," Rhegar said. "It's time for him to go home and take up his work there."

"Will he be safe?" Donaugh asked. "He and Mother? And Torey, too?"

"I assure you," Rhegar said. "Torey will return. And Kian ap Leydon will remain one of Skai's greatest friends."

Donaugh laughed softly. "I didn't doubt that for a moment," he said.

"I watched Tiernyn today," Rhegar said. "He certainly took full advantage of the opportunity to speak with this great assemblage of the nobility of Skai."

"He did that," Donaugh said. "His powers of persuasion haven't failed him yet. He's extracted promises of men and support from each thane here."

Rhegar grinned boyishly. "And you carry those pledges, signed and sealed, I expect."

Donaugh laughed. "I do. In my writing case. The least number of men pledged was ten, the most, fifty from Keylan. We've nearly five hundred men pledged from Skai alone. All that needs to be done is gather them. It's a good start."

"A very good start," Rhegar agreed.

"Duke Ryvern has given his permission for Tiernyn to speak with the thanes of Wenydd. Blais of Dorian has agreed to help. Morand of Brigland was a little more skeptical. He won't exactly offer support, but he won't object if any Brigani want to join our army."

"Tiernyn will build the greatest army ever seen in Celi, Donaugh," Rhegar said quietly. "He carries Kingmaker. All of Celi knows the legend."

"Persuading the Mercians will be difficult," Donaugh said. He smiled and tapped his finger against his temple. "Mercians are even more mule-headed than yrSkai, if that's possible." He watched as the moon dipped below the horizon. Now alone, the Huntress blazed white as she hastened in pursuit.

"They will follow," Rhegar said. "They will all follow as surely as the Huntress follows the moon. Farmers, merchants, fishermen, cobblers, the sons of nobles and commoners alike—all will flock to Tiernyn's banner."

"This seems too easy, Rhegar," Donaugh said. "It troubles me."

"It shouldn't," Rhegar said. "Raising the army is not the difficult part. The difficult part will be persuading the princes and dukes of Celi to support the army. Stubborn men, all of them. That will be almost as arduous as defeating the Saesnesi. They grow stronger every year as more and more cross the Cold Sea from the continent."

"They flee the Maedun," Donaugh said. "If we can't stop them, they'll take all of Celi."

"The Celae will follow Tiernyn," Rhegar said. "He has the words to inspire men and make them willing to follow him anywhere. Tiernyn will be the heart and the strong sword arm of the army. But you, Donaugh. You will be its soul, its spirit."

"I?" Donaugh asked. "I'm not sure I understand that."

"You will," Rhegar said. "One day soon. Why else your magic?"

Donaugh laughed bitterly. "Aye, why else," he said. He turned to the old man, impulsively reaching out to grasp his arm. "Rhegar, I'm afraid. You say I will be the spirit and soul of the army. I've been told also I must be the conscience of the sword. How can I do this? What right have I to dictate to Tiernyn what he must do?"

"Do you not believe in the power of your magic, my child?" Rhegar asked quietly.

Donaugh dropped his arm and turned away. Beneath his hands, the stone of the parapet was cold and rough. The glimmering moon-path had gone with the moon. Only the lights on its decks illuminated the ship secured to the stone jetty. Above the ship, the sky had already begun to pale toward dawn.

"How can I doubt my magic?" he whispered. "The *darlai* herself came to me the night Tiernyn received Kingmaker. But Rhegar, had I your wisdom, it would make more sense."

Rhegar laughed. "Wisdom comes to a man with time," he said.

Donaugh smiled, then bowed his head. "Can the sword wait—can Celi wait until I have achieved this nebulous wisdom? Rhegar, what if I make a mistake? I cannot use my magic properly yet. I'm still learning, and probably will have to learn a lot more before I can use it properly. What if I make a mistake? What if I misinterpret what the sword is trying to tell me?"

"Do you think your magic might let you down that way?"

Donaugh shook his head. "No, I don't. But I might let the magic down. There's a difference."

"When you need it, it will be there," Rhegar said. "Celi needs you as she needs Tiernyn. Together you will build a formidable force to use against the Saesnesi."

"Will we succeed, Rhegar?" Donaugh asked. "Have you Seen this?"

"I've Seen enough," Rhegar said. "The future is not set in stone, my young friend. What I See in the bowl is what might be. And even then, I See only glimpses. But yes, I believe you will succeed. But Donaugh . . . "

Donaugh turned to face Rhegar. The old man stood watching the Huntress as she dived below the horizon still in pursuit of the moon. His silver eyebrows drew together above the bridge of his nose, and his mouth made a level line.

"You must never let Tiernyn betray the sword." Rhegar's voice was like the wind whispering in dry reeds. "The expedients of politics are many and attractive, and not all are good, although they seem they are for the best at the time. Tiernyn will be sorely tempted. But if he betrays the sword, it will let him down when his need of it is greatest. At all costs, he must not betray the sword."

Donaugh clenched his hands on the parapet. The rough stone bit into his knuckles. For a moment, he looked up at the shoulder of the mountain where the stone circle stood above the shrine. Could he bear the burden placed upon his shoulders? And what would happen to Celi if he could not?

Keylan, Kian, and Kerri were already on the pier with Jorddyn when Donaugh and Tiernyn walked down with Torey, Ylana, and Connor of Wenydd. Traces of recent tears stained the faces of both girls. Donaugh realized with a pang of sorrow that he was going to miss his little sister. When next he saw her, she would be a woman grown.

The boxes and bales were already stowed aboard the ship. The crew stood ready to weigh anchor and raise the sails. Combined with the current of the Eidon as it flowed into the Ceg, the ebbing tide would quickly carry the *Skai Seeker* out of the inlet to the open sea. Everything was ready. All that remained was for Kerri, Kian, and Torey to climb down to the coracle bobbing at the end of the jetty and go aboard the ship.

Kerri hugged her father, then turned to embrace Keylan. "We'll be back to see you and Alys wed," she said. She kissed him, tears springing to her eyes. "Oh, Keylan, you were magnificent yesterday. I was so very proud of you."

He held her tightly for a moment, then let her go. "Thank you," he murmured. "I'll miss you, Mother."

"We'll send messengers regularly," Kian said. "You'll want all the information we can gather about the Maedun."

One of the sailors in the coracle stood up. "Begging your pardon, my lord Regent," he said. "If we're to catch the tide, we'd best be going now."

Kian reached out, caught Keylan's shoulders in both his hands. For a moment, father and son looked at each other, neither knowing quite what to say. Then Kian pulled Keylan to him and embraced him.

"You're a son any man would be proud to call his," Kian said, a rough edge to his voice. "Always remember. Celi needs Tiernyn and Donaugh, but she needs you, too. And Skai needs you. Give Tiernyn all the support you can, but never forget Skai must come first with you."

Before Keylan could reply, Kian turned away to speak with the twins. He embraced Tiernyn, then turned to Donaugh.

"Keep him out of trouble, Donaugh," Kian said, smiling.

An unexpected curl of resentment flared in Donaugh's belly. Even his father presumed wisdom in him that he himself could not find. He swallowed the irritation and smiled. The smile felt tight and unnatural, as if it didn't quite fit his face.

"I'll try," he said.

Kian glanced over his shoulder at Tiernyn, who was talking with Torey. "I know it's a lot to expect," he said quietly. "But all your lives, it's been Tiernyn who got the both of you into trouble, and as often as not, it's been you who got you out of it." He embraced Donaugh again, then took Kerri's arm to help her down into the coracle.

Torey hugged Tiernyn and Donaugh, then she and Ylana cried for a moment in each other's arms. Finally, she ran across the jetty and flung her arms around Keylan's neck.

"I'll be back one day, Keylan," she said through her tears. "I'll be back. Don't ever forget me."

Keylan kissed her forehead. "How could I forget you?" He brushed a tear from her cheek with a fingertip. "You'll always have a place here. You know that."

She gave him a tremulous smile, then turned to climb down to the coracle. Before she could step down onto the stone-cut stairs, Connor caught her hand, pulled her into his arms, and kissed her. Donaugh bit his lip to stop his smile at the astonished expression on Torey's face before she began to kiss him back.

Finally Connor released her and stepped back. "I'll be here when you return, Torey al Kian," he said. "You remember that, too." He walked away before she could gather her wits to reply.

Tiernyn and Donaugh came to stand beside Keylan. Ylana now stood to Tiernyn's left. Donaugh had moved to stand half a step behind Tiernyn's right side, giving up his place to Ylana as Tiernyn's declared bheancoran. Connor of Wenydd stood firmly shoulder to shoulder with Donaugh.

They watched as the sailors raised the sails. The anchor came up ponderously, spilling seawater in a bright cascade down the wooden planking of the hull. As the ship gathered speed, Torey appeared at the stern, leaning far out over the taffrail, waving a bright blue scarf.

Tiernyn and Donaugh left that afternoon with little fanfare, riding at the head of a column of fifty men of Skai and thirty-five men of Wenydd. Ylana rode to Tiernyn's left, her shoulders back, her head up, as if daring anyone to challenge her right to be there. Donaugh, with Connor of Wenydd at his right shoulder, rode to Tiernyn's right. Behind them, a standard bearer carried the new banner of the *Corrach* of Celi, a leaping red stag on a field of green.

As they rode away from the village on the track leading east and south, only Donaugh turned and raised a hand in farewell to Keylan, who stood on the battlement walk above the wide-flung gates to the palace.

For the first fortnight after his parents left, the day-to-day running of the palace kept Keylan busy and frustrated as he began to realize how much his father and mother had taken off his hands in the ordinary little daily chores necessary to keep the palace running. Finally, in a flash of inspiration, he called his grandfather Jorddyn and turned the running of the household over to him.

"You've been promoted," Keylan told him. "You're now Seneschal of Skai. You served Skai well as Captain of the Company for forty years. Will you serve me in this capacity, Grandfather?"

Amusement glinted in Jorddyn's eyes. "I doubt I've forty more years left in me, my lord Prince," he said gravely. "But what years I have are yours to command." He cleared his throat. "Don't look so relieved, lad. Sometimes it's not a good idea to let men know how big the favor they've granted is."

"Sage advice, Grandfather," Keylan said. He left Jorddyn calling for the clerks and settling in to examine the account books, and made his escape.

The palace seemed empty and deserted. The solar where the family had gathered for meals, talk, and laughter, or just relaxation, all but echoed as Keylan entered. Yet nothing in the room had changed. Cernos of the Forest still squinted above the ornate chest. The cushioned couches and chairs were the same. Only the family was gone.

With a hollow feeling in his chest that wasn't quite loneliness, Keylan went to the window. Now that the guests were gone home and the village stripped of tents and wagons, normality had returned to Dun Eidon. After the interruption of Beltane and the Investiture, the people of the village took a deep breath of relief and picked up life again where they left off. Very practical of them, Keylan was sure. But he was left with an oddly breathless sensation of being left twisting in the wind, waiting for something he couldn't name.

On the practice field, the weaponsmasters supervised recurrent training of men returning to service after the hiatus of spring plowing and planting. The new trainees, boys of twelve and thirteen, sweated at the rigorous exercises designed to accustom them to using weapons rather than farm implements.

The unnatural silence of the solar pricked against Keylan's skin like needles of freezing rain. Flexing his shoulders to ease the tight muscles, he left the solar and went to the practice field, taking Bane with him.

It was so easy to lose himself in the exacting rhythm of the kata. This was something he knew he excelled at, something he had been trained for since he was a child barely hip high to his father, something familiar and comfortable. While he

danced with the sword, he could forget the weight of account-
ability on his back and become merely one more man testing
his skill on the practice field.

He was barely aware of the moment the Swordmaster
stepped aside and Alys became his partner in the exercise. The
clang and slither of blade meeting blade rang like music
around him. Thrust and parry, slice and riposte. It was a dance,
graceful and purposeful as the movement of a gull's wing.
While performing it, Keylan had no responsibilities beyond
the concentration required to keep each movement, each foot-
step, precise and unerring.

"My lord Prince?"

The voice broke Keylan's concentration and he stumbled,
snapped back to the present without warning. Alys stepped
aside, lowering her sword. Annoyed at the major breach of
etiquette, Keylan wiped the sweat from his forehead and
cheek with his left sleeve. He lowered the sword and turned
to find Lluddor ap Vershad standing a respectful distance
away.

"A moment of your time, my lord Prince," Lluddor said.

Keylan took a deep breath and calmed himself with an
effort. "Certainly, Lluddor," he said. He sheathed Bane and
beckoned Lluddor to follow him to the shade of the chestnut
trees lining the field. "What may I do for you?"

Lluddor bit his lip and color rushed into his face. "My lord
Prince, I've come to ask that you release me from service," he
said, the words tumbling out of his mouth in his hurry to say
them. "I know it was but the fortnight past that I pledged fealty
and service, but I've since received word that my father wishes
me back at the landholding. I wish your consent to leave, and
my men with me."

Keylan folded his arms across his chest and leaned one
shoulder against the broad trunk of a chestnut tree. Lluddor's
face was flushed, his breathing much quicker than normal.
Keylan kept his face carefully expressionless. During the fortnight since Tiernyn and Donaugh departed, Lluddor had

become increasingly restive. The request for permission to leave did not surprise Keylan overly much.

"Vershad said nothing of this to me before he left here a fortnight ago," Keylan said mildly. "Is he ill, then?"

Lluddor stared at him blankly. "Ill?" he said. "Oh, no. Not ill." He looked away. "Not ill, my lord Prince. But he wishes me home."

Keylan remained silent for a moment. Lluddor dropped his gaze to his boots, his shoulders hunching uncomfortably. The color drained from his face, leaving his skin pale and clammy.

"Very well," Keylan said at last. "You may leave as soon as your replacements arrive."

Lluddor glanced up quickly, his eyes widening. "My—my replacements, my lord?"

"Surely you know one of the conditions under which your father holds High Meadow is the provision of forty trained soldiers per year, together with their officer," Keylan said smoothly. "That Vershad chose to send me his son honors me, but I will accept a lesser officer."

"But—but my lord Prince," Lluddor stammered. "My father can ill afford to send another forty men."

Keylan smiled without warmth, without humor. "Surely he'll have you and your men at High Meadow, will he not?"

For a moment, Lluddor's face went blank again, then he nodded. "Oh, of course. Yes, of course. My father will send my cousin Jerym with the replacements, my lord Prince."

Keylan inclined his head. "Very well, then. You have my leave to go." As Lluddor broke out in a relieved smile, he added, "As soon as your cousin arrives with the replacements. I don't want to be left short-handed if there's another raid on Dun Eidon."

Lluddor's face shuttered again. Two bright pink spots appeared on his cheeks. "Thank you, my lord Prince," he said. "Jerym and the replacements should be here within the fortnight." He bowed, then turned and hurried across the practice field for the barracks.

Keylan watched him go, frowning thoughtfully. He raised one hand to rub his chin. It took no gift for Truth-Seeing to recognize a lie in someone like Lluddor ap Vershad. He wondered how soon a messenger would leave at the gallop for High Meadow.

Lluddor had been one of the first to volunteer to go with Tiernyn. His disappointment at not being chosen was obvious to all. That his father would call him home within a fortnight of the day Tiernyn left was too much of a coincidence to be credited.

Keylan could not call him a liar, not without proof. He had no doubt that Lluddor's cousin Jerym would arrive in due course with a replacement company, repeating the same lie. But Lluddor would not be at High Meadow Landhold. He would be with Tiernyn.

Keylan clenched his fists. "Damn you, Tiernyn," he whispered. "Is this how you repay me? With deceit?"

Alys's hand on his arm startled him. He turned quickly.

"So Lluddor deserts to Tiernyn," she said.

"So it would seem," Keylan said. "I can't prove desertion. His father will back his story as, no doubt, will his cousin Jerym."

"What are you going to do about it?"

"What can I do? I can't prove Lluddor's desertion is Tiernyn's work. Oh, it was. I've no doubt it was."

"But without proof . . . "

"Without proof, I can do nothing," Keylan said bitterly. "Celi needs Tiernyn. Skai needs the protection he promised. If I denounce him for deceit, what happens then?"

"He'll lose the support of all the thanes of Skai."

"Aye. And mayhaps the support of Wenydd and all the rest of the provinces. Then what happens to Celi?" He raised his hand, making a solid fist. "I will say nothing, Alys. But it will be a long time before I forgive him—if ever."

7

Two fortnights after leaving Dun Eidon, Tiernyn rode out of the mountains of Skai and Wenydd—the Spine of Celi men called them. He rode into Mercia with only Donaugh, Ylana, Connor of Wenydd, and the eighty-five men who had been with him at Dun Eidon. Behind him, camped in a valley in the eastern foothills, were nearly eight hundred men pledged by the thanes and lords of Skai and Wenydd, together with the servants, cooks, hostlers, armorers, and artisans necessary to keep a highly mobile army on the move. That many armed and mounted men entering Mercia might too easily be construed as an invading force by Gemedd, Duke of Mercia. Besides, the wagons of the van kept the pace far too slow for Tiernyn's liking, and he wanted to make all haste to speak with Gemedd.

"I want to build our headquarters on the River Camus," Tiernyn told Connor. "Close to the Saesnesi Shore, but out of easy striking distance for them on foot."

"You'll need Gemedd's permission to build in Mercia," Connor said. He grinned. "But after the way you handled my father, Gemedd should offer little challenge."

"There's a bluff of land overlooking a bend in the river about five or six leagues upstream from Clendonan on the Tiderace," Tiernyn said. "It would be perfect for a stronghold. There's a tower keep with a small bailey and a curtain wall there now. We can expand it easily to house an army."

Donaugh listened with only half his attention. He had said little as he watched Tiernyn speak with the people of Skai and Wenydd. Thanes and soldiers, farmers and nobles alike, wore expressions of rapt and spellbound attention. Those who said Tiernyn had no magic had never listened to him speak to a crowd. The living flame of his enthusiasm and conviction kindled an answering spark in men's eyes and set their hearts ablaze with the same fire. Rhegar was right. Men followed Tiernyn. They followed him, and he followed a dream.

Ryvern of Wenydd had been skeptical at first. Donaugh thought the Duke surprised himself by pledging another twenty-five men besides those who followed Connor. It hadn't surprised Donaugh at all. Tiernyn's unique magic swept all around him up into the excitement of his dream.

"What's that?"

Ylana's voice brought Donaugh out of his reverie with a start. She sat straight in her saddle, pointing east. Donaugh followed the direction of her finger. A dark smudge of smoke stained the sky behind a low hill less than half a league away. Even as he watched, it grew until it was a billowing black tower against the blue of the sky.

Connor reined in, controlling his prancing horse with unconscious ease. "Looks like a whole village afire behind that hill," he said.

"Saesnesi raiders," Tiernyn said. "What else can it be?" He stood in his stirrups, wheeling to face the column of soldiers. The men reined in, spreading in a loose semicircle around him. Tiernyn waited until he had their full attention.

"Men of Celi," he cried. "We came out of the Mountains of the West, down from the Spine of Celi, to fight Saesnesi. Do you wish to start now?"

The answer thundered from eighty-five throats. "Yes! Death to the Saesnesi!"

Tiernyn drew Kingmaker and raised it with a flourish. The silvery blade flashed in the sun. "Then follow!" he shouted. "Follow Kingmaker and follow me!"

Ylana beside him, Tiernyn wheeled his horse and kicked it to a canter. Donaugh and Connor fell into place at his right. The men of Skai and Wenydd, well trained and well disciplined, formed into ranks of ten and fanned out behind.

Tiernyn called a halt at the brow of the hill, leaning forward in his saddle as he rapidly assessed the situation in the valley.

A hard, savage light glittered in his eyes, and his mouth curved back in a grin that had nothing whatsoever to do with amusement. The sword in his hand sang eagerly with a clear, vibrant tone, like harp and bell combined. The music echoed in Donaugh's head, and it surprised him that Tiernyn didn't appear to hear it.

In the valley below, the village burned fiercely. Blond-bearded raiders swarmed through the green fields of crops, ax blades and swords flashing as they hacked at fleeing women and children. Flames leapt from thatched roofs and boiled out of heaps of household furnishings piled outside the burning cottages. Corpses of slaughtered villagers lay strewn like broken dolls among the debris. The crackle of flames nearly drowned out the triumphant shouts of the raiders and the terrified screams of the wounded villagers. Donaugh's stomach knotted as the stench of charred flesh carried by the breeze reached him.

"There are hundreds of them down there," Connor said. "Hundreds of Saesnesi."

"And eighty-nine of us," Tiernyn said. He bared his teeth again in that primitive grin. "But we have the advantage of surprise."

Donaugh raised his hand to shade his eyes. The only resistance appeared to be coming from a small knot of fifteen or twenty men barricaded behind a hastily constructed breastwork of debris and overturned wagons. They fought desperately against the tide of Saesnesi. Dead men and horses littered the ground around the breastwork. Near the center of the defenders, one man still held aloft a stained banner, a black boar on a field of red. The Mercians fought well, but it was clear they couldn't hold out much longer against the screaming horde of raiders.

"That's Gemedd's banner down there," Donaugh said. "Look."

"It won't hurt our chances with Gemedd if we rescue him, will it?" Tiernyn grinned, then stood in his stirrups. "Connor, take your men and come in from the right," he said. "We'll come down on them from the left. When you're ready. Go!" He raised Kingmaker, sweeping it in a broad arc around his head.

"For Celi!" he shouted. "For Celi!"

The answering shout from eight-five men reverberated like thunder down the valley. "For Celi and the *Corrach*!"

They poured down the slope into the village like an avalanche, howling the wild, ululating war cries of the mountains. Caught unawares, the Saesnesi barely had time to turn before the soldiers of Skai and Wenydd were upon them.

Time slowed for Donaugh. Guiding his horse with his knees alone, he leaned far to the right. A startled face, blue-eyed, blond-bearded, swept into his field of vision, then vanished in a spray of blood as he swung his sword.

The gelding reared and spun around as a Saesnesi roared and charged at Donaugh's back. Donaugh swayed to one side. The huge blade of the war ax whirled past his head, missing his left eye by inches.

A shout went up from the hard-pressed Mercians behind the breastwork as the Saesnesi raiders turned to face the new threat. The Mercians spilled over and around the breastwork and plunged forward in renewed fervor. They fell upon the startled Saesnesi, swords and daggers flashing in the sun.

Donaugh caught a glimpse of Tiernyn, his horse plunging and rearing as Kingmaker rose and fell, red with blood, in a deadly rhythm. Beside him, Ylana twisted in her saddle to strike at a blond giant lunging at him. Her sword took the raider's hand off at the wrist, and the man disappeared beneath the hooves of her horse.

"Donaugh! Your back!"

Connor's voice sounded high and clear over the tumult. Donaugh wheeled his horse. The gelding reared, and his hooves cut into the forehead of a Saesnesi brandishing a longsword. The man's face disappeared in a splash of blood and brains.

Donaugh whirled to meet another raider. Connor's horse sprang over a huddle of Saesnesi corpses, fighting to Donaugh's left side. Donaugh lashed out with his foot as a shrieking raider tried to pull him off his horse. The man fell back, and Connor's sword bit into his side.

"There are too many of them," Connor shouted. "We'll have to pull back and regroup."

Ylana screamed in anger and outrage. Donaugh turned to see a raider leap onto Tiernyn's horse behind the saddle. Even as the raider raised his hand to plunge a dagger into Tiernyn's throat, Ylana drove forward. The tip of her sword thrust into the raider's armpit. Tiernyn flung his free hand back, sweeping the dead raider from the back of the horse. He raised Kingmaker high.

"To me!" he shouted. "Men of Celi! To me!"

Huge hands closed around Donaugh's throat. He dropped his sword as the Saesnesi dragged him backward off the horse. They hit the ground together. Donaugh reached for his dagger even as they fell. The impact knocked the wind from his body.

The grip on his throat tightened inexorably. Donaugh's vision blurred and darkened. Bright lights exploded behind his eyelids. He tried to raise his dagger but his hand and arm felt big and soft and clumsy as a feather pillow. He brought the dagger down in a short arc. He couldn't tell if he had hit the Saesnesi, but his hand felt sticky and wet.

The raider's weight disappeared suddenly. Gasping for breath, Donaugh rolled facedown into the blood-mired dirt. He tried to get to his feet, but his legs had no strength.

A hand caught his and pulled him up. He staggered to his feet to find Connor grinning fiercely at him. Blood smeared Connor's face, some of it his own from a deep slash across his cheek.

"You might want this." Connor grinned again and tossed Donaugh the sword he had dropped.

Somebody shouted. Donaugh and Connor turned to see a troop of horsemen sweeping down the hill into the valley. In the lead, Lluddor ap Vershad swung his sword in a broad arc, urging his men faster, a manic grin of anticipation on his face.

The Saesnesi broke under the second surprise attack. Even as Lluddor brought his forty soldiers into the fray, the battle turned to a rout. The Saesnesi turned and fled. Lluddor's men cut them down as they scrambled through the ripening grain in the fields surrounding the village.

Tiernyn, with Ylana hard by his side, dismounted to meet the leader of the surviving Mercian soldiers. Donaugh recognized Eachern, Gemedd of Mercia's eldest son. He bled from several wounds, but needed no assistance from his men to run toward Tiernyn. Tiernyn bled, too, from a wound in his thigh. His eyes glittered, and he grinned widely. Eachern threw his arms around Tiernyn, both of them laughing and pounding each other on the back. Donaugh turned back to Connor.

"We had better see to that cut on your face," he said.

The rooms Gemedd assigned to them were large, airy, and comfortable. Tiernyn limped slightly from the wound in his thigh, but the doctor had pronounced it minor when he bound it with a poultice of medicinal herbs. His hair was still damp from the bath he had taken to wash away the blood and dirt. Donaugh, his throat bruised and sore, stood quietly by the window, watching as Tiernyn paced like a caged mountain cat.

Ylana sat curled on a cushioned bench beneath an elaborate wall hanging, idly drawing an ivory comb through her freshly washed hair. She was pale, but unscathed. The barest hint of a smile played around her mouth as she watched Tiernyn and occasionally glanced at Donaugh.

"I won't send him back." Tiernyn whirled to face Donaugh. "Not after he saved our lives like that."

Donaugh said nothing. He folded his arms across his chest.

"You heard him," Tiernyn said. "He said Keylan released him. Keylan gave him leave to go."

"He lied," Donaugh said.

"Are you saying he deserted?"

Donaugh didn't move. "I've no doubt that Keylan released him," he said. "But Lluddor lied to him to get that release. Send him back."

"How do you know he lied?" Tiernyn persisted. "How can you tell?"

Donaugh said nothing. He unfolded his arms and held one fist out in front of him. When he opened his hand, a small blue flame danced over the palm of his hand. He lowered his hand. The flame remained, wavering and flickering, unsupported, in the air before him.

"I've not a lot of the Truth-Seer's art," he said. "But I've enough to know a lie when I hear it from one such as Lluddor. Whatever excuse he gave to make Keylan let him go, it was not the truth. Send him back, Tiernyn. You can't base the finest army Celi has ever known on deceit."

Tiernyn's mouth tightened. "No," he said flatly. "I can't send him back after he saved our lives. It would look as if I were punishing him. What would the other men say? Gemedd has given me permission to speak with his soldiers. He's pledged fifty men because we saved Eachern's life. What's he going to think if I send Lluddor back?"

"That's your final word?" Donaugh asked.

"It is." Tiernyn picked up Kingmaker and slipped into the harness, settling the scabbard comfortably against his back. "Lluddor stays. They're waiting for me out in the courtyard. Will you come?"

Ylana rose to follow Tiernyn out of the room, the tiny, smug smile still on her lips. Donaugh caught her arm as she walked past him.

"You put Lluddor up to this," he said.

Ylana met his eyes defiantly. "So what if I did?" She yanked her arm free of his grip. "He wanted to come. Tiernyn deserves the best men. Lluddor proved his worth, didn't he? He saved all our lives."

"It was deceit," Donaugh said.

"Keylan said Tiernyn could take fifty men with him," she said. "He took only fifty. It's not his fault Lluddor followed later. Lluddor wanted to come."

"And he came with a lie in his heart."

"Will you announce it publicly, Donaugh?" Ylana said fiercely. "Will you denounce your brother in front of the men of Celi? You've always stood beside him, no matter what. Will you stop now when he needs you most?"

Donaugh took a deep breath. "You know I won't."

She smiled, triumph bright in her eyes. "Then we had best go out to listen to him speak, hadn't we? So you can take your place beside him and show the men of Celi your support."

Donaugh seized her arms. Her eyes widened with the sudden pain as his fingers bit into her flesh. He gripped tighter. She had to realize the gravity of what she'd done.

"Ylana, I swear by all I hold dear that, if you've hurt Tiernyn's chances of succeeding in this endeavor because you've been stupid and manipulative—I swear I'll see you pay for it. Do you understand me?"

"You're hurting me," she whimpered.

"I meant to. Do you understand me?"

She nodded.

"And realize this, too. By your own action, you may be the one to cause Tiernyn's death."

She paled. "His—death?"

"If he dishonors the sword, it will fail him when he needs it most."

"Because Lluddor came to us? That will cause his death?"

"Because Lluddor came to us through treachery and deceit. It might."

"But I didn't think . . . "

He released her. She rubbed her arms, still pale, her underlip trembling.

"No," he said. "You didn't think. He's waiting for us. We'd best go."

———

Donaugh stood to one side in the courtyard. Tiernyn leapt nimbly onto a bench and placed one hand on the trunk of an overhanging beech tree. He seemed to glow. His contagious energy and drive radiated from him in tangible waves to engulf his listeners. As he spoke, Donaugh watched the magic ignite in the eyes of the men crowded around him. Whatever the gods and goddesses thought of Lluddor's deceit and Tiernyn's acceptance of it, it didn't affect Tiernyn's ability to arouse the flames of fervor in the hearts of the men who listened to him.

"Together," Tiernyn cried. "Together, the men of Mercia and the men of Skai and Wenydd, the men of Brigland and Dorian—all Celae. Together we can beat back the Saesnesi tide and reclaim the stolen lands." He drew Kingmaker and held it high above his head. "Who is with me? Who will fight with me for Celi?"

The roar of approval in reply reverberated against the walls of the courtyard. But Donaugh hardly heard. His whole attention was on Kingmaker. The sword flashed and glittered in the sun, the runes along the blade etched deep and sharp. But a small stain marred the gleaming blade near the hilt. Smaller than the fingernail of Donaugh's little finger, it was distinct and obvious.

Donaugh moistened his dry lips and wondered what it meant.

PART

2

Corrach

8

Donaugh pulled his cloak closer around him as he left the Great Hall of Dun Camus in the predawn chill. As Midwinter Solstice swiftly approached, sunrise came perceptibly later, and sunset earlier, with each passing day. The churned mud of the yard stuck to his boots, and the air was still damp from the recent rains. Clouds hung threateningly low above the buildings, reflecting the light of the torches in sconces along the inner bailey walls. Above the massive gatehouse, the Red Hart banner of the *Corrach* snapped and cracked in the stiff breeze.

It still amazed Donaugh when he looked at Dun Camus. The castle was a living testament to what enthusiasm and belief in a cause could do. In two years, it had grown from a scattered handful of tents and rude wooden huts surrounding a crumbling keep and curtain wall to a well-ordered fortress behind thick stone walls, and a fair-sized town. Built on a wedge-shaped promontory in the curve of the river and surrounded on three sides by deep, swift water, the castle had a wealth of natural defenses. No trace remained of the original tower and wall. The stones they had been built of were now incorporated into the new gatehouse and in the foundations of the main house. Most of the wooden buildings had been replaced by stone structures.

Outside the gates, the town was as neatly ordered as the fortress. An army of five thousand men quickly attracted all the people needed to support it, the blacksmiths and weapons crafters, innkeepers and merchant vendors, weavers and leather workers, carpenters and wheelwrights, and the women and children of the soldiers. Even this early in the morning, the streets hummed with the sound of commerce, punctuated by the ringing clang of a blacksmith's hammer in the forge just beyond the gate.

Within the walls, the main house, the stables, and the kitchens blazed with light and activity as the new day began. Singly or in small groups, soldiers still rubbing the sleep from their eyes made their way from the barracks built into the east wall by the gatehouse to the kitchens that formed the west wing of the main house. The scent of baking bread and roasting meat hung heavy in the damp air. The army of the *Corrach* ate well because well-fed men had more strength and endurance in battle.

The moist wind carried the scent of snow. Donaugh pulled his cloak tighter around his throat as he walked. He missed the smell of the sea in the air. And somehow, the winters seemed colder here near the center of the Isle of Celi than they had at Dun Eidon.

The shouts of weaponsmasters drifted through the open gates, and the first sounds of sword practice rang out as the new arrivals began their day's training. When fully trained, they would swell the ranks of the army to over six thousand men, a figure beyond all expectations two years ago, when they had left Dun Eidon with eighty-five men and the pledge of nearly five hundred more.

Rhegar had been right. Men flocked to Tiernyn's banner—men of Skai and Wenydd, Brigland and Mercia and Dorian. Even the men of Venia in the north had come. Surprisingly, they made some of the best soldiers in the army. Mostly fisherfolk and sheepherders, the Veniani recognized no man as prince or duke. They lived in small, nomadic tribal groups under their separate chieftains. The Saesnesi had never bothered the Veniani much. They had little worth plundering and tended to melt away into their thickly forested mountains at the first sign of a raid. They came for the promise of good and plentiful food, warm and comfortable homes, and good pay. They made fierce and canny fighters, and were deadly with their small, recurved bows. Tiernyn often wished aloud that he had ten companies of them.

As Rhegar had predicted, they all came, the sons of nobles

and commoners alike. They came partly because, in the first summer, Tiernyn won every encounter with the Saesnesi. Donaugh could not call them battles. They were little more than skirmishes against undisciplined bands of raiders. But they proved what a well-disciplined and trained army could do against the Saesnesi when led by a brilliant and determined man.

In the second summer just past, the Saesnesi had become more organized. Their leader Elesan, who called himself Celwalda, or High Prince in Celi, was a canny and capable man. Under him, the Saesnesi developed an army with a semblance of order and control. Tiernyn had still won all the encounters between the two forces, but the victories had been harder fought and dearer in the cost of men.

Tiernyn had demonstrated more than just an ability to lead. Following Donaugh's subtle suggestion, he had sent troops of five to eight hundred men to Skai, Wenydd, and Brigland, and a thousand men into Dorian, with orders to patrol the coastline near villages and towns. When that tactic cut the Saesnesi raids by half, he sent Connor of Wenydd to each of the princes and dukes to request a tithe to support the army. Only one duke, Morand of Brigland, refused. Tiernyn withdrew his detachment of troops. Two fortnights later, as bands of Saesnesi raiders swarmed through Brigland, Morand sent a messenger to Dun Camus agreeing to the tithe.

Donaugh shivered as a cold draft found its way under his collar. This year, the coming of winter didn't signal a time to rest and regain strength. The Saesnesi were not winter warriors. They preferred to retire to their strongholds and villages on the Saesnesi Shore, warm and safe around their hearths, until spring brought better weather. This year, Tiernyn was not going to allow them that luxury. The winter campaign began this morning when Donaugh took a small party of men on a scouting mission to estimate the strength of one of the major Saesnesi settlements.

Walking with his head down against the wind, deep in his

reverie, Donaugh didn't see Connor until he nearly bumped into him. Connor stood in the shelter of the roof overhang by the stables, supervising the stableboys as they exercised a group of yearlings. The wind blew his dark hair about his forehead and reddened his cheeks. The high color made the long scar running from his left eye to the corner of his mouth livid white in contrast. He turned and raised his hand in greeting as Donaugh came to stand beside him.

"They look quick and canny," Donaugh said, watching the horses critically.

"Aye, they do, don't they?" Connor said, pleased. "And strong, too. Stamina like rocks. Bred for it. They'll make good warhorses. Most of them should breed true."

"You've done well with them."

Connor grinned. The scar tipped the corner of his mouth up at a rakish angle. "My father always said I was good for only two things. Fighting and breeding horses." He broke off as one of the horses pranced sideways, nudging against another. He stepped forward. "Here!" he shouted at the stableboys. "Untangle those two before they do each other harm! Look lively there, or I'll have your ears."

One of the stableboys stared at Connor in alarm, but the other grinned widely. Deftly, they separated the two horses, and Connor relaxed and stepped back into the shelter of the stable roof.

The stableboys led the horses back into the stables. Connor nodded in approval, then turned to Donaugh again. "I'm still not sure I like the idea of a winter campaign. It's going to be hard on the horses."

Donaugh laughed. "And how about the men?"

"Well, us, too," Connor said. He glanced up at the main house behind them. "I can understand Tiernyn's reasoning, though. I don't have to like it, but I understand it. Well, the horses are strong."

"And Tiernyn's star is bright," Donaugh said.

The nine men of Donaugh's scouting party entered the

courtyard and went into the stables, nodding at Donaugh and Connor as they passed. One of the stableboys led out Donaugh's bay gelding, saddled and ready to ride.

Donaugh took the reins of the horse and thanked the boy with a smile, receiving a wide grin in return. The gelding tossed its head, restive with inactivity. Donaugh spoke a few soothing words to it, stroking its neck. He swung up into the saddle. The bay pranced sideways, eager to be off.

"We should be back by this evening," Donaugh said. "With luck, we'll have the information Tiernyn needs."

Connor stepped back. "Good luck," he said.

The chamber was small and plainly furnished and the fire in the hearth provided enough heat to banish the damp chill. Maps of all the provinces hung on the walls. Behind the simple worktable was a larger map showing all of Celi and the western part of the continent, including Saesnes, Tyra, Isgard, Falinor, western Maedun, and Laringras. Plain wooden chairs and benches stood against the walls, but could easily be moved to provide seating around the table when needed for a conference.

Tiernyn left the letter from his father on the table and went to stand by the window. The room was a small one on the second floor of the main house above the Great Hall. From the window, Tiernyn had a good view of the courtyard and the town beyond the curtain wall. In the practice field outside the walls, men and boys trained with swords and bows under the relentless and watchful eye of the weapons-masters.

He raised his hand wearily to rub the bridge of his nose, turning his thoughts back to the letter on the table. His father had an excellent network of spies scattered all over the continent. He also had a knack of putting together wildly disparate snippets of information and drawing uncannily accurate conclusions from them. Tiernyn had read the letter on the table a dozen times. Each time, he could see only one course of action as a result of the disturbing news the letter contained.

Below in the courtyard, Donaugh and Connor stood together, watching some of the horses being exercised. Tiernyn watched idly as he tried to sort through the information from Kian. Finally, he turned and went back to his chair at the worktable and picked up the letter.

"All signs indicate the Maedun will attack Saesnes in force once spring has come," Kian wrote. "Information from within Maedun itself is difficult to come by, but Sion tells me there are rumors about the disappearance of two more sorcerers. He believes that there can be no more than three or four left, excluding the two in Falinor and Laringras. My old enemy Hakkar apparently still refuses to leave his stronghold on Lake Vayle. Sion believes he is holding himself in reserve for the attempted invasion of Celi once Isgard and Saesnes have fallen.

"The Maedun might not need a sorcerer to defeat Saesnes. The new Saesnesi king, Baniff, is not the king his father was, nor is he the leader Elesan on the Saesnesi Shore is, and the country is torn by internal squabbling and power struggles. Baniff's favorites change daily, it would seem, and some of his best people have died in bids for favor. Sion thinks they are ripe to fall to Maedun. If Saesnes falls, you must be prepared for an influx of longships. There will be hundreds of them heading for the safety of the Saesnesi Shore. Mayhaps if Baniff escapes, there will be a struggle among the Saesnesi to determine who will call himself Celwalda. It's my belief that Elesan will win any such contest, but the internal quarrel may be something you can take full advantage of and turn to your own benefit. I will provide you with more information as I obtain it."

Tiernyn rubbed his temple. Hundreds of longships. Two to four thousand Saesnesi coming to Celi. It wasn't a pleasant or encouraging thought. If Baniff didn't escape, all those Saesnesi would make a formidable addition to Elesan's army, disciplined soldiers or not. No one could deny the Saesnesi were savage and ferocious warriors. Even a well-trained army would be hard put to stop them.

He picked up the letter again.

"Isgard continues to hold strong against the Maedun. As yet, there seems to be no sorcerer powerful enough to use against them, and Vanizen's warlocks are loath to go into Isgard. The Ephir of Isgard appears to have an unending supply of ill-trained foot soldiers to throw against the warlocks and burn them out trying to deflect the mass of weapons. Even their magic can turn only so many arrows and pikestaffs back against the men who wield them.

"Tyra has a thousand men in Isgard fighting as necessary beside the Isgardians. Rhodri trusts the Ephir as little as did my grandfather, but Tyra itself is in no immediate danger. There has always been a feeling here that Maedun blood sorcery will not work in the high country. This has never been proved or disproved, but it is something you may want to keep in mind as it might affect anything untoward happening in Skai or Wenydd.

"Your mother and Torey are well and send their love to both you and Donaugh . . . "

Tiernyn rolled the letter and put it aside. Where was he going to get the men to fight an additional three thousand Saesnesi? He could see only one answer. Every battle he had won so far was more of a skirmish than a real battle. It was time for a decisive victory. If they could catch the Saesnesi unprepared in their winter refuges, perhaps they could achieve that decisive victory.

By midday, the wind died down and the air felt a little warmer on the exposed skin of cheek and brow. As the wind abated, a mist slowly began to form, growing thicker as they moved eastward. The gray, shadowless light made it difficult to discern the contours of the land around them.

Donaugh was cold, but all his senses were pricklingly alert for danger as they followed the narrow valley cut by a small burn through the downs. Behind him, the nine soldiers rode in silence, scanning the misty low hills around them.

Donaugh studied the mist-shrouded hills. They were close to the ill-defined area that marked the border between Mercia and the Saesnesi Shore, which the Saesnesi called the Summer Run. This was downsland, hilly and rolling, covered with grass, gorse bushes, and heather in the summer, striped with occasional areas of thick forest. Good land for grazing but poor tillage. Kian had described Saesnes on the continent as a barren, rocky land where the winters were long and bitter and the summers wet and stormy. All scrub pine, coarse grass, and salt marsh, Kian said. Little wonder the Saesnesi came looking for better land and called the east coast of Celi the Summer Run. By contrast to their homeland, Celi was paradise.

The Saesnesi Shore had once been part of Mercia, but sparsely populated. The Mercians were mostly farmers more than sheepherders or cattle herders. The Saesnesi Shore offered little to a farmer except in isolated areas in the delta of rivers, where the soil was richer. This country was a stark contrast to the green mountains and glens of Skai. Bleak and windswept, it seemed to be worth little to anything but the hardiest grazing animals.

The valley curved gently. As they rounded the bend, they came upon the burned-out shell of a farmstead. Small wisps of smoke still curled from the charred ruins, but there were no bodies or slaughtered livestock apparent in the debris.

Donaugh called a halt. Lemil ap Carryn drew his horse up beside him, frowning as he surveyed the wreckage.

"Deserted," he said. "Probably was long before the Saesnesi got here."

Donaugh nodded his agreement. "Quite likely," he said. "It's late for them to be out raiding."

Lemil dismounted and tossed the reins of his horse to

Donaugh. "Let me see if I can find anything." He began rang-
ing back and forth along the bank of the stream, head bent,
body stooped, looking for signs.

Donaugh watched, smiling to himself. Lemil was the best
tracker of all the Companions, and he always reminded
Donaugh of nothing more than a hunting dog, nose to the
ground, searching for the spoor of deer or boar.

Lemil straightened and shouted, lifting his arm and waving.
Donaugh kicked the flanks of his bay and trotted to where
Lemil stood looking east.

"Eight of them," Lemil said. "On foot and traveling single
file. In something of a hurry, too. They went that way." He
gestured to a narrow valley between two hills. A small burn
wound its sluggish way out of the valley to join the river half a
league downstream.

"How long ago?" Donaugh asked.

"Not more than two or three hours."

Donaugh handed Lemil the reins of the horse. Lemil
vaulted into the saddle. "Do we follow them, my lord
Donaugh?" he asked.

Donaugh reached for a strand of power in the ground
beneath him. There were fewer here than in the mountains.
Cautiously, he sent a thread of awareness ahead into the valley. They were too close to the Saesnesi-held territories to
plunge recklessly into what could be a trap. But he found no
sense of danger in the valley.

"We'll follow them to see where they're going," he said.
"They might lead us to a stronghold we didn't know about."

They had gone less than a league up the narrow valley
when the sudden awareness of danger hit Donaugh like a fist
in the belly. Every hair on the back of his neck prickled erect
as he wheeled his horse and drew his sword.

"Back!" he shouted. "Ambush! Get back!"

Even as he shouted, a horde of screaming Saesnesi poured
out of the mist over the brows of the hills on both sides of the
valley in front of them and behind. Donaugh couldn't count

them, but there were more than two dozen, all of them swinging heavy, deadly war axes or longswords.

The Companions paired off, Lemil spinning his horse to cover Donaugh's left. Donaugh was only subliminally conscious of his presence as he swept his sword down into the mass of Saesnesi warriors surrounding him.

He felt the blade of his sword bite into flesh and bone, then swung back in his saddle as another Saesnesi leapt at him from behind. The ax in the blond giant's hands whistled, gleaming dully in the gray light. Donaugh swept his sword backhand. The blade caught on the handle of the ax. The shock of the impact shivered all the way up his arm to his shoulder. The ax spun out of the Saesnesi's hand. Roaring like a bear, the Saesnesi launched himself at Donaugh's throat, both hands outstretched.

Donaugh kneed his horse sideways. There was no room to use his sword. He yanked his dagger from his belt with his left hand and stabbed. The blade entered the side of the Saesnesi's throat and caught on his collarbone. Blood gushed out over Donaugh's hand. The Saesnesi fell, wrenching the hilt of the dagger from Donaugh's fingers as he tumbled beneath the hooves of the horse.

Something tugged at Donaugh's cloak. He caught a glimpse of the blade of the war ax as it tore through the fabric. Wild blue eyes stared into his as the Saesnesi struggled to free the ax from the folds of the cloak. Donaugh swept his sword sideways. The shoulder of the blade just beneath the hilt caught the Saesnesi on the temple, splitting through skin and bone and spraying blood and brains over the saddle cloth.

"Donaugh, beside you!"

Lemil's voice choked off into a bubbling gurgle. Out of the corner of his eye, Donaugh saw him slump over the saddle, then tumble to the ground. Blood flowed thickly from his belly, where the Saesnesi ax bit deep.

Donaugh's horse floundered beneath him, its throat torn open by an ax blade. He barely had time to kick his feet from the stirrups and leap to the ground before the horse fell. Beneath his feet, the ground was slick and slippery with blood. He stumbled as he tried to spring backward, out of the way of the Saesnesi who vaulted over the dead horse toward him.

The Saesnesi bellowed and swung the ax again. Donaugh staggered back, slipped in a pool of blood, and went to one knee. The edge of the ax blade sliced through his sleeve, into the muscle of his arm. Blood, hot and sticky, flooded down his arm and across his wrist and hand. His fingers slipped on the sword hilt. Ax drawn back to swing again, the Saesnesi lunged at him.

Donaugh snatched his sword with his left hand and brought it up with the same motion. He thrust it into the Saesnesi's side even as the warrior plunged into him. Donaugh twisted sideways, rolled away, and came to his knees.

Another Saesnesi loomed up out of the mist, screaming. Donaugh yanked his sword from the dead Saesnesi's belly. But even as he brought it up, he knew it was too late. The war ax swung in a deadly arc at his throat. He lunged forward desperately. His blade drove deep into the raider's belly. At the same instant, the ax slammed into the side of his head. The world exploded in a vast sheet of white flame.

9

Snow fell from the dark gray clouds. Thick, lazy flakes in no rush to reach the ground floated past the rippled glass of the window as Tiernyn watched. Already, the stable roof was a smooth expanse of white. Thin drifts of smoke rose from the chimneys beyond the walls to blend with the uniform gray-white of the falling snow and the sky. A single dark figure hurried from the stable toward the main house, cloak pulled around him tightly against the wet snow.

The uneasy tension knotted in Tiernyn's belly relaxed its grip a little as he watched the snow fall. Memories of first snowfalls in Skai darted through his mind. Preparing the Yule Log, searching for the perfect gift for his parents, hunting with his father for the venison to feed a palace brimful of guests. Those days of innocence and simple happiness seemed a lifetime ago.

The troubled certainty that somewhere, something was dreadfully wrong came back with a rush. He quelled the urge to pace restlessly and forced himself to stand still as he tried to understand what was bothering him. He was sure he had not left something important undone. But something was wrong. It was almost as if he could hear a small voice muttering in the back of his mind.

Without knowing why he did it, he crossed the room and picked up his sword. Slowly, he drew it from the scabbard and looked at it. In the flickering light of lamp and candle flame, the blade gleamed softly, the runes spilling along it making deeply etched shadows. He rubbed the ball of his thumb against the tiny stain on the shoulder of the blade.

The sword had magic. The stories and songs of the bards told of its magic resonating with Kian's. Tiernyn had no magic to answer the sword's, but he felt *something* when he held it—a sense of rightness, or belonging. Something.

The blade felt warm in his hands, yet Tiernyn shivered as he ran his fingers along the sharply defined runes. The cold ball of foreboding in his chest intensified.

The door behind him opened. He turned, the sword still in his hands, as Ylana entered, carrying a tray holding fresh, new bread, slices of venison, cheese, dried fruit, and two mugs of brown ale. With one hand, she pushed aside a pile of papers on the worktable to make room for the tray and set it down quickly. The crockery on the tray rattled, and the sound grated on Tiernyn's raw nerves like a file on metal.

"By the gods, Ylana," he snapped, "why must you be so clumsy?"

Ylana turned on him. "If you would remember mealtimes, I wouldn't have to chase after you like the mother of a two-year-old."

He looked down at his hands, his knuckles whitened with the firmness of his grip on the scabbard, then looked back at her. His own tension reflected back to him in the level line of her mouth and the taut skin about her eyes. Snarling at Ylana served no purpose. He took a deep breath, then another to calm himself.

"I'm sorry," he said at last. "I had no call to snap at you."

"What's wrong?" she asked. She crossed the room and took his arm as he shook his head. "Don't try to tell me nothing's wrong, Tiernyn. I've been jumpy and restless for the past hour, and it's worse now we're in the same room. I know it's coming from you." She gripped his arm tighter. "We're bonded, remember? I know what you're feeling, just as you know what I'm feeling."

"I don't know what it is," he said. "I feel as if I've forgotten something important. Or that something terrible is going to happen. But I don't know what."

"The sword?" she asked.

He looked down at it. "It seems to intensify the feeling," he said. "But I haven't the magic to understand what it's trying to tell me."

"Ask Donaugh," she said. "He'll know. Where is he?"

"With Connor, in the stables, I think," he said. "I sent him out on a scouting expedition this morning. He said he'd be back before the evening meal, and Connor said something about showing him the new studs he just got from Dorian."

"I'll send someone for him," Ylana said.

Before she could reach the door, it opened and Connor entered, shaking the snow from his black hair.

"We'll have a foot or two of this before it's finished," he said cheerfully. "I hope—"

"Have you seen Donaugh?" Tiernyn interrupted.

Connor lost his smile. "No," he said. "I thought he was with you. Isn't he back yet?"

The sword in Tiernyn's hands felt like a long shard of ice. It trembled in his hands and he shivered. He knew now what caused the nebulous urgency. The knowledge quivered along the link forged between himself and his twin in the shared womb. His knuckles whitened on the hilt of the sword as he gripped it.

"Something's happened to him," he said. "Something's happened to Donaugh." He thrust the sword back into its scabbard. "Tell them to get my horse ready. I'm going to look for him."

Connor glanced at the window. The snow fell so thickly, it obscured the stable. The town was visible only as faint, hazy shadows beyond the walls.

"You'll never find anything in this," he said. "And it will be dark in less than an hour."

Tiernyn fixed Kingmaker to his back and snatched up his cloak. "I'll take twenty men," he said. "We can start now. If we have to, we'll camp for the night . . . "

Ylana caught his arm. "No, Tiernyn," she said. "You can't go until morning. The horses will kill themselves in the dark if they slip in the snow. Donaugh has his magic."

"I'll have a troop of men ready to go at dawn," Connor said. "We'll start as soon as it's light enough to see."

They were right, both of them. Tiernyn knew it, but the churning anxiety in his belly screamed to start *now*, to sprint to the stable and hurl himself into the gathering darkness in search of Donaugh. The sword on his back quivered with tension and urgency, almost impossible to ignore. He looked at the window. Snow fell more thickly, and the ominous moan of a rising wind echoed under the eaves.

Slowly, Tiernyn unbuckled the sword and hung it on the wall again. "First light tomorrow," he said softly. "See to it, Connor. First light tomorrow."

The cold, wet touch of snow on his cheek woke him. For a long time, Donaugh merely lay there, aware only that his head ached abominably, and he was horribly uncomfortable. A crushing weight pressed down across his chest and belly, and one leg was folded awkwardly beneath his body. It hurt to breathe.

He opened his eyes and stared directly into the lifeless, icy blue eyes of a Saesnesi warrior, the dead face contorted into an astonished rictus.

Donaugh cried out, startled and horrified. He scrambled out from beneath the body, coming to his feet, crouched, in a single convulsive heave. Nausea flooded through him. He fell to his knees, retching, doubled over by the pain in his head and the cramping in his belly. When, finally, he could raise his head and look around, his blurred vision brought on a renewed spasm of nausea. He put his hands over his eyes and breathed deeply, trying to will strength back into his trembling body.

All about him, the sprawled bodies of his own men and the Saesnesi who had ambushed them lay, stiff and motionless, under a thickening blanket of snow.

Donaugh closed his eyes, swaying as pain and dizziness engulfed him. Just a reconnaissance patrol, he had told Tiernyn. Just a quick foray out from Dun Camus to scout the

terrain for Saesnesi enclaves, or the Saesnesi army. We'll be
back in time for the evening meal, he told Tiernyn.

He put his hand to his aching head, looking around in horror and dismay. "What have I done?" he whispered. "Oh,
gods. What have I done?" He rose slowly to his feet and
looked around.

Dusk approached swiftly, but the heavy, lowering cloud
gave away no sign of the sinking sun. The snow fell more
heavily, obscuring the shapeless bundles on the ground.
Donaugh could not distinguish friend from foe in the wan
light.

The scabbard on his back was empty. Dully, he searched
the area, kicking at the snow. He finally found his sword, still
thrust through the belly of the Saesnesi warrior who had fallen
across him. He vaguely remembered the desperate thrust that
was not quite in time to prevent the Saesnesi war ax colliding
with his skull.

He raised a hand and covered his eyes. His forehead felt
cold and clammy. But without the blurred, overlapping images
before him, he felt a little steadier. The ax must have turned in
the dead hand before it hit his head, or only the handle had hit
him; otherwise, it surely would have taken his head from his
shoulders.

Blood had frozen and dried along the blade of his sword.
Donaugh fell to his knees and used the Saesnesi's cloak to
scrub the blade, working with slow determination. He had difficulty concentrating, and his right hand was slow and clumsy.
It wouldn't work properly. His ears buzzed, and his vision
kept blurring out of focus. He knew only that it was important
that the blade be gleaming clean, but he couldn't remember
why.

His wasn't a sword of power like Tiernyn's. Tiernyn's
blade was legend, containing its own intrinsic magic.
Donaugh's sword was not a Rune Blade and carried none of its
own magic. He had never needed more magic. His own had
always been enough.

Until now . . .

Why had he not sensed the danger before it was too late? Where was his magic when his need was greatest?

He pulled the scabbard from its harness on his back and tried to thrust the cleaned blade home, but the tip of the sword refused to find the mouth of the scabbard. His vision blurred again; he saw two scabbards and two blades. He lowered the scabbard to his knee and closed his eyes. By touch alone, he brought the sword tip to the opening and slid it home.

He lifted a hand to his head again and discovered a lump the size of an apple just above his left ear, the center split and ragged. His fingers came away sticky with clotted blood. Then he saw that the right sleeve of his shirt was stiff with blood. The torn edges of a wound in his arm showed through the rent in the fabric, but there was no pain—just a cold numbness.

For some reason, it seemed important to count the dead. Ten of them had ridden away from Dun Camus. Donaugh lost count after thirty snow-covered lumps. So they had acquitted themselves well even though they were outnumbered. It was little comfort. Nine of those white heaps had been good friends.

Or had one of them escaped and gone back to Dun Camus to bring help? Was Tiernyn even now on his way here?

He had no idea how many Saesnesi ambushed them. He wondered if all were dead but him. The Saesnesi did not usually leave their dead on the battlefield, but took them home for cremation if they were able to.

Climbing to his feet made him dizzy again. He swayed for a moment until he regained his balance, then slowly began walking from corpse to corpse. Patiently, doggedly, he brushed the snow from cold faces until he found them all. Nethyn, who had sung like a lark with his gittern. Artus, huge and black-bearded, fierce and strong as the bear he was named for, surrounded by the bodies of the Saesnesi he had taken with him to Annwn. Maddis, who had the smooth, unbearded face of a child yet fought with the savagery of a mountain cat.

Weymund, Gerrod, and Bors, as close in death as they had been in life. Llyr and Cadwyn, who would play no more practical jokes. And finally, Lemil, good friend and companion, his quiet voice and ready laughter stilled forever.

No help would be forthcoming from Dun Camus. Donaugh had nothing to rely upon but himself.

He went to his knees and traced the sign of the Unbroken Circle on Lemil's forehead. "May your soul be brightly shining, Lemil ap Carryn, so the Duality may find you quickly," he whispered. "And may the Counter at the Scroll find you not wanting as you stand before him."

A wave of dizziness and nausea swept over him as he knelt there, snow collecting on his head and shoulders. He had lost his heavy cloak and fur-lined gauntlets during the fighting. It would be impossible to find them again under the rapidly thickening cover of snow.

He pulled the cloak from Lemil's body and wrapped it around himself. Lemil had no further use for it, and would not begrudge his taking it. It was woven of good wool and would help keep him warm.

There were no living horses in sight. Donaugh tried to count the slaughtered horses, but lost track as his vision blurred. The gray light obscured everything and made him dizzy again.

If he was to get back to Dun Camus, it appeared he must walk.

He looked around. In the gloom, everything looked the same. He had no clues to give him a sense of direction, not even a glow in the sky to indicate west. All the hills looked alike. He could not tell which end of the narrow valley was which.

Still on his knees, he closed his eyes and concentrated, searching vainly for the lines of power that flowed in the earth beneath him and shimmered in the air around him. But there was nothing. His head ached abominably, spoiling his focus. He could not even find the deep well of power within himself.

When he searched, he found only a barren emptiness where his magic should be.

Muttering a prayer to all the seven gods and goddesses, he climbed stiffly to his feet and looked around again. He thought the shape of the hill to his left looked familiar. That must be west, leading back to the River Camus.

He felt remote and detached, as if he were in a dream, or watching a vision in a fire that had nothing to do with him. Again, he lifted a hand to his head and brushed away the wet snow. For a moment, he couldn't remember why it was so urgent that he find his way back to Dun Camus.

It wasn't until he tripped over a fallen branch lying beneath the thick blanket of new snow that Donaugh realized he was lost. Still dazed and detached from himself, he struggled to his knees and looked about. He had wandered away from the downs and into a forest. He had no idea which way lay Dun Camus. He looked behind him, but the heavy snowfall had already begun to fill in his footprints, leaving only faint dimples in the thick, white carpet.

He raised his hand to his face and wiped away the heavy, wet flakes clinging to his eyebrows and lashes. Night had come while he wandered unaware of his surroundings. He knelt amid a hushed stillness, in the preternatural quiet of a bare forest under an evening snowfall. Not a breath of wind stirred the stripped branches. The snow fell in large, wet flakes, drifting soundlessly in the motionless air. Melted snow ran down his face and soaked into his cloak and tunic, glazing the fabric with ice.

Numbly, he realized he was in danger. His cloak was soaked, as were his tunic and shirt, and his boots. He couldn't remember what happened to his own heavy, woolen cloak with its fur lining. Without it, he was in immediate peril of freezing to death.

He struggled to his feet, shivering in his wet clothing, and looked around. It was full dark now, but even without moon or stars, the new snow gleamed faintly, making the dark, skeletal trees show plainly as stiff, black shadows against the glow.

Behind him lay the downs. Leagues and leagues of open, rolling grasslands, offering no shelter from the snow. In the forest, he might find a thicket of hazel or a shaw of hollies where he could build a fire to warm himself. If, he thought bitterly, the blow to his head had not stripped him of the ability to make fire. He remembered the empty, barren place he had found where his magic should have been when he had tried earlier. He shuddered.

He stumbled on the uneven ground and nearly fell again. The weight of the snow collecting on his shoulders began to be oppressive. He tried to brush it away, but discovered he was shivering so violently, he could not control his hands, and he could not feel his right arm.

He staggered past a tangled thicket of hazel, blindly aware only of the need to keep moving, to warm his sluggish blood with exercise. The air grew colder as night deepened. He could no longer feel his feet in his sodden, half-frozen boots. A wind sprang up, driving the snow before it like needles and rattling the barren branches of the oak and alder.

His numb foot caught in a tangle of ivy and he fell sprawling into the snow. It felt warm and soft as a feather bed beneath the stiff flesh of his cheek. He wanted to sink down into its comforting depths and sleep. He closed his eyes wearily, grateful for the sudden warmth spreading through his body. He could rest just for a moment. Just until he felt stronger . . .

Someone whispered his name, a murmur only barely louder than the moan of the wind. A gentle hand touched his shoulder. Irritably, he pushed it away.

"Let me rest," he muttered.

"Donaugh, you must get up," the voice said. A woman's voice, soft and musical, but with an unmistakable tone of command in it.

He rolled over in the snow. Ice crusted on his eyelashes. He tried to blink it away to see properly. A woman stood before him, naked in the silver chill of the falling snow. Her hair fell to her knees in a floating mantle around her the color of moonlight. Her eyes glowed a clear turquoise-green, the same shade as the glacier-fed waters of the Eidon in Skai. Her pale skin glowed faintly pink and warm in the night.

For a long moment, he merely lay staring at her. Her lips, redder than holly berries on Midwinter Night, curved back in a gentle smile.

"We've met before, Donaugh ap Kian," she said softly. "Don't you know me?"

"Rhianna of the Air," he whispered, his stiff lips forming the words clumsily. "Giver of the gift of magic."

"You must get up, Donaugh," she said again. "If my gift isn't to be wasted, you must get up now." She extended her hand to him. "If you do not get up, you will surely perish here."

He reached out reluctantly and grasped her hand. It was warm as summer air, soft as a child's hand. He allowed himself to be drawn to his feet. The pleasant sensation of warmth vanished, leaving him too cold even to shiver. The woman pointed, her bare arm smoothly rounded and delicate, draped by clinging strands of silver-gilt hair.

"That way," she said quietly. "There is shelter for you. That way. Hurry."

He stumbled forward a few steps. When he looked back over his shoulder, she was gone. The only marks in the snow were the imprint of his own body and his dragging footprints. He forced himself to move again, first one foot, then the other in slow, painful progression through the deep, hampering snow.

Then suddenly ahead through the swirling snowfall, he thought he saw the gleam of warm, yellow lantern light. The trees thinned to a clearing. The light shone mistily from the center of the glade, welcoming and beckoning. It drew him forward as the Nail Star drew lodestone.

He tripped at the edge of the clearing. Again, the snow received his body with the deep, welcoming softness of a fine mattress. He closed his eyes as the warmth of it seeped into his body. In a moment, he would get up and go to the small lodge in the clearing. He would rest only for a few minutes. Only a few minutes to gather his strength . . .

10

Nothing remained of the farmstead but a few charred sticks glazed over with ice. His breath misting whitely in the cold air, Tiernyn reached forward to stroke the neck of his horse. It didn't like the scorched scent left in the air by the long-dead fire, and pranced nervously as Tiernyn waited for Connor to finish his survey.

Muffled in his cloak and hood, Connor led a troop of twelve men on foot in a widening circle around the ruin. A fine drift of snow that was almost frozen mist fell from the gray sky. Not a breath of wind stirred.

Ylana stood in the snow beside Tiernyn's horse, holding the reins of her own horse and Connor's. Her weight resting against Tiernyn's calf and thigh was warm. Beneath the hood of her cloak, her cheeks glowed red from the cold. Frost formed around the edges of the hood as the steam of her breath condensed and froze on the thick woolen fabric. Impatiently, she reached up and brushed it away.

Tiernyn looked away from the blurred figures circling the farmstead, out over the white, barren hills. The sword on his back throbbed softly with the same energy he had felt in it the evening before. Even before Connor returned, Tiernyn knew they had found nothing.

"No bodies, no dead livestock," Connor said. He took the reins of his horse back from Ylana. "Probably long deserted. It's my guess the Saesnesi burned it out of sheer spite."

"Donaugh and his men were here, though," Tiernyn said. He pointed up the narrow valley leading east. "They probably went that way. It looks like the best chance."

"That leads into Saesnesi territory," Ylana said.

"Send five men ahead to scout," Tiernyn said. "Tell them

to use caution. There may be Saesnesi raiders still in the area."

"He's not dead, Tiernyn," Ylana said. "There's a strong bond between you. You'd know if he were dead. We both would."

Tiernyn nodded without speaking.

Strewn haphazardly across the floor of the narrow valley, the corpses lay in grotesque attitudes of death. Some lay openly under the gray sky, stripped of the protective blanket of snow by the capricious wind; others lay buried deep so that they looked like nothing more than logs or small hummocks.

Tiernyn reined to a stop and sat for a moment, slowly scanning the battle scene. His face pale beneath the hood of his cloak, he dismounted and dropped the reins to the ground. The sword on his back vibrated gently against his spine. Reaching behind his shoulder to touch the hilt, he began walking toward the scattered bodies.

He had taken no more than four steps when Ylana recovered from her shock and slid from her horse.

"Tiernyn, no," she cried, running after him. She caught his arm. "Please. Let us look."

"If he's here, I have to find him," Tiernyn said.

Connor urged his horse forward. He dismounted quickly and stood in front of Tiernyn. "If he's here, my lord *Corrach*," he said formally, "we'll find him. It would be better if you waited here."

Vibration from the sword shivered against Tiernyn's spine. "I know what you're trying to do, Connor," he said. "And I appreciate it. But I have to look. I won't ask any man to take an unpleasant task that is mine upon his own shoulders. Set your soldiers to finding our men. We'll take them home for burial with honor."

With Ylana at his side, he walked into the midst of the frozen corpses.

It was Connor who found Donaugh's cloak. Tiernyn straightened as Connor approached him and wordlessly held out the tattered and bloodstained cloak. The fabric, stiff and frozen, crackled in Tiernyn's hands as he took it.

"Did you find him?" he asked.

Connor shook his head. "No. Just the cloak."

Again, the sword on Tiernyn's back vibrated softly. "He's not here," he said. He gestured at the corpse at his feet. "This is the last of them. Donaugh is not here."

"No, he's not here," Connor said. "We found all of the others, but Donaugh's not here."

"Then he either wandered away, or they took him with them," Tiernyn said. "Send scouts out. I want this whole area searched." He looked down at the cloak, turning it over in his hands. Blood had frozen thickly on the fabric. "He was wounded. He can't have gone far. Find him."

"How can we track him through this?" Luddor ap Vershad asked. "Look around you. The snow is a foot deep and still falling. If he's buried under it, we'll never find him."

"We have to try," Ylana said.

Connor nodded, pain in his face. "Aye, we have to try," he said.

Tiernyn raised his hand and clasped the hilt of the sword. "He's alive, Connor," he said. "The sword tells me he's alive."

"He was hurt," Ylana said, reaching out to touch the cloak. She looked around at the bleak landscape. "If he wandered away . . . "

"He has his magic," Tiernyn said softly. "We'll look until we find him."

"In this?" Luddor swept his hand out in an eloquent gesture. "My lord *Corrach*, this is Saesnesi territory. And we can't even track him because of the snow."

"We'll look," Tiernyn said again. His eyes glittered fiercely as he clutched the cloak in both hands. "We'll bring the army out, and if we have to tear apart every Saesnesi settlement in this forsaken land, we will find him."

———

At first, Donaugh was aware only that he was warm. He remembered being told that the last thing a man freezing to death felt was a delicious sense of false warmth. He decided that, if this was death, it was much preferable to the cold, numbing misery of the snowstorm. Death came to him as a friend to be welcomed, not as a grim enemy to be feared, and he was content to let it take him. He closed his eyes and let himself drift into the comforting warmth.

He awoke again to a firelit darkness, hazed with color and drowned in shadows, threaded through with the sweet smell of burning applewood. He discovered he lay between thick, soft blankets, a pillow covered in fine linen beneath his cheek. He moved his legs and his foot encountered a pair of hot stones wrapped in woolly cloth. To either side of the bed, braziers shed blessed heat, reviving his frozen body. Beyond them, a fire blazed high on a hearth. For a while, he lay bemused, pondering the vividness of this strange dream—for dream it had to be. Reality was swirling snow and the fatal chill of wet boots and clothing.

He moved again, burrowing deeper into the dream-given blankets and realized suddenly that something warm and soft pressed tightly against his bare back. He lifted a leaden, reluctant hand and found an arm clutched around his chest. The warmth behind him, radiating life-giving heat like a massed bank of torches, was another body. His exploring hand encountered a rich swelling of hip flowing into a deep incurve of waist. Vaguely amused, he pondered the wonder of being with a woman when he was certain he should be dead. Did the joys of Annwn include satin-skinned women to warm a man?

His mind refused to function, his thoughts moving as sluggishly and murkily as muddy, weed-choked water, and he abandoned the effort of trying to puzzle out what had happened to him. He was warm, he was comfortable, and he seemed to be alive. For the moment, it was enough. He closed his eyes and slept.

———

His hands and feet itched and burned at the same time, and his face felt raw and sore. Donaugh moved restlessly on the bed, trying to find a position to ease his discomfort, then sat up, shockingly wide-awake, aware of his strange surroundings. The sudden movement caused a wave of dizziness and weakness to flood through him. He fell back against soft pillows and closed his eyes, breathing deeply to control the nausea that threatened to choke him.

His right arm ached, the pain bone deep and sharp. Someone had bandaged it with clean, white linen. The thick padding would not allow his arm to bend. He discovered another bandage around his head when he lifted a hand to try to ease the pain throbbing behind his eyes with each pulsebeat. He lay for a moment, waiting for the dizziness to abate, then rubbed his eyes with his left hand and sat up slowly to look around the room.

A young woman sat on a chair by the bed, head bent over a pile of fabric in her lap while she carefully stitched a design in soft colors along the hem. Her unbound hair fell in a gleaming spill of cream and gold across her shoulders, pinned back from her face by a pair of gold combs that were darker than her hair. She wore a pale brown woolen gown cut high at the throat for warmth, a shawl in a deeper shade of brown around her shoulders. As Donaugh stared in surprise, she looked up at him. Her eyes were a shade of gray that was nearly lavender, fringed with startlingly dark lashes. She smiled at him, a smile so full of tenderness and warmth that something squeezed at his heart.

"Where am I?" he blurted. "Who are you? What happened?"

She smiled again, then put aside her needlework and stood up. Lifting one slim hand in a graceful gesture implying *Wait*, she went to the door of the chamber.

"No," he cried. "Come back. Who are you? Where am I? How did I get here?"

But if she heard him, she gave no sign. The door closed firmly behind her.

He stared at the closed door, a hundred questions clamoring in his head. He was in the act of throwing back the bedclothes to scramble out of bed when she returned, carrying a steaming bowl of broth and a goblet of hot, mulled wine. The aroma of the broth filled his nose and made his mouth water as she offered it to him, still without speaking, but smiling. She paid no attention to the fact that he was naked and the bedclothes thrown to one side.

He reached for the broth, then grabbed the bedclothes instead and pulled them up to his waist. Her smile widened as he blushed. She pushed the bowl into his hands. When he had drained the last rich drop from the bowl, she took it back and handed him the goblet. It was of a design he had never seen before, made of beaten silver and worked with an unfamiliar pattern of scrolls and geometric shapes. But the wine was good Doriani red, and spread a deep, warm glow through his body as it radiated out from his belly, despite an odd, lingering aftertaste.

The woman nodded in approval as he finished the wine. She took both the bowl and the goblet, and left the room. He stared after her in wonder. She had not said one word.

His clothing was nowhere in sight, nor were his sword and dagger. He swung his feet over the edge of the bed to the floor, then had to sit, head down, taking deep breaths, as he waited for the dizziness to abate. He staggered to his feet and stumbled across the room to a tall wardrobe closet, intricately carved with a design similar to the one incised on the goblet. Each movement sent fresh bursts of pain shivering through his arm and bright lights exploding behind his eyes.

The wardrobe contained only a few gowns and several pairs of women's slippers. It seemed a long way back to the bed. He collapsed against the pillow and lay gasping for breath.

He raised his hand to his face. Beneath the pads of his fingers, the skin of his cheeks and forehead felt rough and chapped. He shivered as he contemplated how close he had come to death in the swirling snow. He could vaguely remember finding the small clearing and seeing the light in the window of the lodge. Someone must have discovered him lying in the snow and brought him into the house before it was too late. He wondered if it was the strangely silent woman.

The bedchamber had one window glazed with thick, rippled glass. It let in the wan light of early evening. A leaden gray sky hung low above the tracery of bare branches, but he thought it had stopped snowing. On the sill outside the window, the snow lay two handspans deep, mounded like heavy cream on a pastry.

A strange lethargy swept over him. He sank back onto the pillows, suddenly recognizing the aftertaste in the wine as poppy. His eyelids were too heavy to keep open. Before he could feel the first stirrings of alarm, he was asleep.

When next he woke, it was dawn. The young woman once again sat by the bed, intent on her needlework. Donaugh lay quietly against the pillows and watched her. He remembered waking once with the pliant heat of a woman pressed to his back. For warmth, he realized. Bestowing her own life-giving body heat to him to pull him back from the edge of cold death.

As if sensing his gaze on her, she raised her head and turned to look at him. Her eyes, gray as smoke, gray as the sea in a misty dawn, looked deep into his. She smiled and something twisted in his chest. There wasn't enough air in the room to fill his lungs. His heart pounded wildly against his ribs.

He knew her. He had always known her.

The air between them shimmered and sparked. Images of her flashed in the midst of the fizzing air. He saw her running through thigh-deep grass in a summer meadow, a wreath of wildflowers trailing from her hair, laughing as he pursued her joyfully. They stood side by side in a large room, fingers interlaced, as flutes and pipes played in celebration of their joining. She held an infant tenderly in her arms, the curve of the child's head in her cupped hand echoing the rich curve of her breast. She sat on a cushioned chair, holding a child, while a ray of sun slanted through a high window and turned her hair to molten gold. And she stood beside him as a tall young man turned away from them to mount a warhorse while a troop of men waited.

He knew her, and she knew him. He had no idea if the images he saw came from past or future, or both, but he knew her. Their souls were bound, had always been bound, and always would be. They were two with one soul between them, perfectly joined, perfectly fitted.

Bound souls. He had always thought the stories of men and women bound throughout all eternity by the strength of passion, either love or hate, were but pleasant tales for a long winter's night. Bound souls, two sides of the same counter, together through all the lives of the souls, and forever before and afterward. But he recognized the woman just as surely as she recognized him, and he knew the tales were true.

The vision dissolved, and the shimmer faded until the air between them was once more merely ordinary air. She smiled again, then rose and left the room. Moments later, she returned with bread, cheese, cold meat, and hot tea.

He glanced suspiciously at the tea. "More poppy?" he asked.

She shook her head. She wore pale willow green this morning. It made her eyes look gray as autumn mist.

He took the food, discovered he was ravenously hungry. She made sure he was comfortable, and left him to his meal. He had not quite finished when the chamber door opened. The girl came in, then stepped aside to let a man enter.

Donaugh's heart gave one hard kick against his ribs, then settled into a swift, tense rhythm. The man who stood by the door was tall and broad, his white-blond hair bound in two plaits to either side of his jaw. His long mustache lifted into carefully waxed curls upward along his cheeks, and his full beard bushed like a halo, leaving lips and nose as islands among the pale hair. His eyes were the same color as the girl's eyes, but infinitely colder and more hostile. He was obviously Saesnesi, and Donaugh wondered how he had failed to see it in the woman.

"So I have fallen among enemies," Donaugh said softly. He glanced at the woman, who smiled again in reassurance.

"So it would seem." The Saesnesi's accent was heavy, but his Celae was fluent. "I am Elesan, Celwalda of the Saesnesi. You have already become acquainted with my daughter Eliade."

Donaugh lay back against the stacked pillows and folded his hands across his belly to hide the trembling which would belie the outwardly calm expression on his face.

"So, not just the enemy," he said quietly. "But the chief of enemies."

Elesan smiled, but there was neither warmth nor humor in the expression. "I have heard of your bravery, young firebrand," he said. "It would appear the reports are not exaggerated. You face me without quailing."

Donaugh met the shrewd gray eyes levelly. "Perhaps I'm not afraid because I know my own end, and it isn't by your hand, Celwalda of the Saesnesi."

Unexpectedly, Elesan threw back his head and laughed. "So," he said at last. "I have not in my hands the man who would be King of all Celi. The enchanter, then. The younger brother."

"As much as I dislike to disappoint you, I'm afraid that's true."

"I admire your confidence in the truth of your Seeing," Elesan said. "Had I found you in the trees instead of Eliade, your blood would be bright against the snow now."

"Your daughter is most kind," Donaugh murmured. He glanced at her. She still stood by the door behind her father, watching him carefully, her eyes strangely intent upon his face.

All traces of amusement faded from Elesan's face. "My

daughter is a fool," he said harshly. "And more fool I for the love I bear her. I cannot deny her plea for your life."

Donaugh looked at Eliade. She met his glance, her face grave but unworried. Again, he felt the tug of the threads that bound them together. "You have my thanks, my lady," he said.

"I will live to regret not slitting your throat the instant I discovered you in my daughter's bed," Elesan said grimly. "But you have eaten of my bread and salt, and by all the laws of the gods and of hospitality, I cannot kill you beneath my roof if I would maintain my honor."

"And when I leave the shelter of your roof?" Donaugh asked.

Elesan smiled sardonically. "By my promise to Eliade, I cannot kill you then, either." He turned and made a series of quick, deft movements with his fingers. Eliade smiled, then nodded and left the room.

Understanding burst upon Donaugh like a flash of summer lightning. Eliade neither heard nor spoke. He had seen others use the language of the hands, and he cursed himself for a fool because he had not recognized the fact of the girl's deafness before this.

"Was she born without hearing?" he asked gently.

Elesan glanced at him in surprise. "No," he said. "A fever left her unable to hear when she was three. Now she'll never leave my hearth."

"She is very beautiful," Donaugh said.

A bitter smile twisted Elesan's mouth. "No man will marry a flawed woman," he said. "She's lost the ability to hear and speak, and I've lost any grandchildren she might have gifted me with. But I've gained the company of the child I love more than life, and I'll never lose her to another man's hearth. It's some compensation."

"The gods and goddesses wield a capricious sword," Donaugh said. "Their gifts have barbs, but occasionally their cruelties contain compassion." He pushed himself up in the bed, leaning forward stiffly. "When may I leave here?"

Elesan waved toward the window. "The snow is nearly a man-height deep on the windward side of the lodge. You will not be able to get through even if you were fit to travel."

Donaugh inclined his head. "Then I am your grateful guest, my lord Elesan."

"Make no mistake, Donaugh ap Kian," Elesan said softly. "I would see both your head and your brother's nailed to my gates, as I'm sure you would see mine on yours. I trust your fragile Celae honor not to betray my hospitality, however grudgingly I must give it."

Donaugh lay back against the pillows, folding his hands across his belly. "My honor demands that one day I repay your kindness, my lord Elesan," he said. "I won't begrudge it. Your daughter saved my life."

Elesan grunted. He turned to go, then looked back at Donaugh. "You might pray to your gods your brother thinks enough of you to ransom you sufficiently." He smiled sardonically. "And if you should wish to relieve me of the responsibility of hospitality toward you, let me assure you that there are guards here who do not consider themselves bound by my promise to my daughter."

11

Donaugh stood on a high mound under a sky that glowed *with a light that was neither dawn nor dusk, but some mystic, transitional interval out of time. At the foot of the hill, a vast plain stretched westward until it met the sea. Around him loomed a forest of standing stones thrusting up in stark silhouette against the luminous sky. He waited as he had been waiting ever since he could remember, patiently yet oddly incurious about what he awaited. He had never before dreamed true, but understood that he had never before needed to come to this dream place.*

The energy of the Dance flowed around him, filling him with its magic, replenishing the deep well of power within him. He welcomed it with quiet relief. All traces of pain drained from his wounded arm; the headache faded until it was less than a memory. Donaugh looked down at his arm. A thin white scar marred the taut smoothness of the skin, all that remained of the deep wound cut by the war ax.

Something moved behind him. He turned as the figure of a man stepped between the standing stones of a trilithon. Myrddyn looked exactly as he had the last time Donaugh had seen him.

"You are well come here, Donaugh Secondborn," Myrddyn said gravely.

"How did I come here?" Donaugh asked.

"Does it matter?" Amusement tinged Myrddyn's voice. *"You are here, and you are welcome."*

"Is this why you called me here?" Donaugh asked, indicating his healed arm.

Quiet laughter lit Myrddyn's face. "You're very like your father, Donaugh Secondborn," he said. *"He would never believe that he came here without my summons, either."*

"This is his dreamscape, then?"

Amusement brimmed up in Myrddyn's eyes and spilled over into a smile. "Aye, it is. But it's yours, too." He came forward and reached out to touch Donaugh's wounded arm. "This no longer pains you?"

"Not now," Donaugh said.

"It is healed well now," Myrddyn said. "As is the head wound. Your magic will not desert you again."

"You called me here to tell me this?"

Myrddyn laughed. "I did not call you here," he said. He gestured to the standing stones behind Donaugh. "Look, if you will."

Donaugh turned.

She came to him through the menhirs, her hair gleaming in the fey light. Her feet passed so lightly over the tender young grass that the blades seemed hardly to bend. Her gown of pale green flowed about her body, clinging briefly to breasts and thighs, then rippling sinuously to outline hips and waist. She was so lovely, the back of his throat ached with his need and love for her.

"I called you here, beloved," she said. "As you called me."

The sound of her voice startled him, strange yet familiar at the same time. His astonishment must have showed on his face because she laughed.

"I speak here," she said. "And I hear you well, beloved. Awake, I have no magic. Not in this body. But in this dream place, I have all I need to be with you."

"Eliade . . ." He took both her hands and pressed them to his lips.

"Do you remember this? Look."

The standing stones had disappeared. They stood at the edge of a clearing in a grove of mixed oak and ash. Two huge fires burned brightly in the warm night, flaring brilliantly in the center of the clearing. Laughing men and women dressed in simple white tunics danced around and between the fires to the wild keening of pipes, meeting and parting in a swirling

*pattern of light and shadow. Donaugh had just time enough to
wonder why two fires before familiarity swept over him. The
empty goblet he held in his hand still retained the warmth of
her fingers; the taste of the Tyran heather ale it had contained
tingled on his tongue.*

*Donaugh laughed and flung the goblet high into the air.
The silver chasing on the cup flashed and sparked in the firelight, then disappeared into the dark as the goblet fell
unheeded to the ground. Donaugh reached to take Eliade's
outstretched hands and pulled her close to him. She came to
him joyously and led him through the stylized steps until he
caught her up in his arms and carried her between the trees,
away from the fires to a secluded place beneath an overhanging ash tree.*

*As they sank down together onto the deep grass, he cradled
her face between his hands. "My soul is cupped in the palm of
your hand," he said softly.*

*"Ah, beloved," she whispered. "Your soul has always been
sheltered safe within my hands and my heart."*

*The bond they shared drew them together, one soul in
two bodies. Donaugh lost track of where he ended and she
began. The wild music of the pipes of Tyra sang in his
blood the same way the rapturous magic of her love played
like music along his skin and nerves. The world shattered
and spun for them, and as it subsided into sweet lethargy,
he held her close against him, her head cradled on his
shoulder. He closed his eyes and breathed in the fragrance
of her hair. She smelled of apple blossoms and clean, crisp
herbs.*

*After a long time, she kissed his throat, then pulled reluc-
tantly away and sat up. When he opened his eyes to look at
her, she sat cross-legged beside him, once again dressed in the
pale green gown. They rested in a small alcove in a formal
garden, a high wall of sun-warmed stone behind them. A narrow herb border ran along the foot of the wall, the scent of
savory, mint, and thyme rising like heat waves in the air.*

Overhead, the boughs of an apple tree, heavily laden with blossoms, stooped low above them. A few petals fell and caught in her hair like pearls. She reached up to brush them away, but he caught her hand.

"Leave them," he said. "They suit you well."

"My grandmother planted that apple tree on her fifth Name Day," she said. "When my father was only a child, he fell out of it while he was stealing apples. He still carries the scar on his elbow where he cut it on that stone wall."

He sat up and rested his back against the thick trunk of the tree, watching her. Their knees were only inches apart. She didn't look at him, but glanced up at the tree instead.

"The fruit makes marvelous cider," she said. "Every year since I can remember, we've gathered the apples and pressed them."

She looked at him then. Her eyes reminded him of the color of the tightly folded gray-bells that grew so thickly along the lower slopes of the mountains in Skai. She reached up and plucked one of the gleaming red fruits from the tree and handed it to him. He bit into it. The tart flavor of the juice burst on his tongue like a flash of sunlight.

"Do you know what I'm saying, beloved?" she asked.

He nodded. "I know," he said.

"Your people are blood and bone and heart of this island," she said. "The Celae have been here for generation upon generation. But Donaugh, I was born here, too, as was my brother Aelric. And our father and mother before us, and their people before them." She dug her hand into the rich, dark earth of the herb garden. The crumbly soil stained her fingers as she lifted them to show him. "This is part of me, just as surely as I'm part of it. This island has always been my home. Your people would kill me and let my blood enrich this soil, but they will not allow that perhaps I might love this island as much as they do."

"Eliade, I—"

"I can see your pain, beloved," she said. "In this life, we

might not be allowed to be together, even though our lives are intertwined like the ivy and oak in your sacred groves. But must our people continue to be such bitter enemies? Is there no way there can be peace between us?"

He closed his eyes, seeing before him images of raiders and dead and wounded yrSkai soldiers, and the blood of women and children soaking into the charred ground. The smoke of burning villages drowned out the scent of herbs and crisp, ripe apples.

"Ever since I can remember," he said, his voice hoarse and raw in his throat. "Ever since I can remember, Eliade, the raiders have come with the springtide and left with the snow, like a bloody tide. I think too many of us have died—"

"My people have died, too," she said. "My mother died during an attack on our village when I was only seven. The Doriani burned our houses to the ground. Those cattle they couldn't drive away with them they left slaughtered in the pastures. Beloved, it's past time the slaughter stopped."

"But I can't do it, Eliade," he said. "No more than can you."

"Your brother," she said. "My father. Both are men of honor. Together, they might accomplish what we two cannot."

"And the raiding?" he said. "Can your father stop the raiding and the killing?"

She looked away. "Men come here from the old country . . . from the continent. There are always men here willing to go raiding with them. My father has never condoned it. Perhaps he can stop it."

"I wish it were so," he said quietly. "But I fear it can't be."

"You were led here for a purpose, beloved," she said. "Mayhaps this is the purpose."

"Mayhaps," he agreed, but he had no faith in his agreement.

She came into his arms again and kissed him. Once again, he lost himself in the wondrous merging of their bodies.

———

Donaugh awoke in the small chamber in the forest lodge. He turned over lazily and reached for Eliade. The place beside him in the bed was empty, but retained the warmth of another body. He opened his eyes and found the pillow next to his still imprinted with the shape of her head, but she was gone. Fresh snow mounded on the windowsill outside, and the room was chilly even with the fire blazing on the hearth.

His right arm moved without stiffness or pain beneath the thick padding of bandage, and his head felt perfectly clear for the first time since the attack by the raiders in the valley. He threw the covers back and sat up, and felt no dizziness as he looked around the room.

Eliade entered the room carrying a tray laden with cheese, bread, and steaming hot tea. She smiled when she saw him sitting on the side of the bed. He looked at her, then slowly sketched the sign for *soul*, and held out his cupped hands toward her.

"My soul lies cupped in the palm of your hand."

She crossed the room and set the tray down on the small table near the bed. Not smiling now, she stood before him and formed her hands into a cup to receive what he offered. Slowly, tenderly, as if she held something fragile and infinitely priceless, she closed her hands and pressed them against her heart.

"Your soul lies sheltered safe within my hands and my heart."

"For you," he said. "For you, Eliade, I will try . . . "

Tiernyn turned from the window as Ylana entered the room. He wore Kingmaker at his hip, his hand firmly grasping the hilt. The sword vibrated softly against his palm, transmitting power into his body.

"They're ready for you," she said.

She took his crimson cloak from a peg on the wall and held it up. He swung it about his shoulders, and she stepped forward to fasten the pin at his left shoulder. "Connor and the rest?" he asked.

"Waiting for you in the Great Hall."

Tiernyn nodded absently, his mind racing ahead to what he would say to the assembly of soldiers. Ylana fell into her accustomed place by his left shoulder as he left the room.

The five captains stood close to the hearth in the Great Hall. Tiernyn paused in the doorway, looking for a moment at each one in turn, assessing the man, counting over his strengths and weaknesses and how each could be used to best advantage.

Lluddor ap Vershad and Eryth ap Morfyn stood together, talking in low tones. Both had shown a remarkable ability to lead men and were fervent in their loyalty to Tiernyn and to Celi. Tiernyn thought their dedication was tinged with a desire to advance themselves, but the reason mattered little so long as they remained loyal.

Gordaidh of Dorian was the youngest grandson of Duke Blais of Dorian. Older by several years than any of the other captains, he was also the most difficult to read. He said little and preferred to spend most of his time with his men. A quiet, unboastful man, he had no wife, no children, and very few close friends. Tiernyn trusted him, but wasn't completely certain that he liked him.

Eachern of Mercia leaned against the stone wall of the hearth, his foot tapping impatiently on the polished tiles of the floor, a habitual gesture he seemed unaware of. A mercurial man of vastly differing and unpredictable moods, he led his company well and instilled a fierce loyalty in his men. His temper was nearly legend among the Companions. Quick to be roused to violent rage, he was just as swift to laugh and forgive. The one anger he could not let go, the anger that smoldered in his heart like a festering wound, was against the Saesnesi. In battle against them, he was a whirling storm of fury, and carried his men with him into the same rampage of battle-madness.

Connor of Wenydd stood a little apart from the others, his face in shadow, turned a little to one side in an unconscious effort to hide the scar that disfigured the left side of his face. The first of the Companions, Connor was also one of the most reliable—canny, capable, and competent. He led his company with efficiency and intelligence and was profoundly and unswervingly loyal. His loyalty might lie more with Donaugh than with the *Corrach*, Tiernyn thought, but he believed passionately in Tiernyn's cause. Tiernyn trusted him implicitly, perhaps the only one of the Companions to earn that honor.

Tiernyn entered the Great Hall, his cloak swirling about his legs. "Gentlemen," he said.

They turned to face him.

"Are your companies ready for me?"

Eachern answered for all of them. "They are, my lord *Corrach*."

"Then shall we go?"

The army had assembled in the practice field beyond the boundaries of the village. The five companies, each divided into five forces under a lieutenant, then further into five sections under a sectionmaster, stood at ease. The murmuring swell of voices gradually faded to silence as Tiernyn mounted a wooden dais on a slight rise.

Tiernyn paused, looking around at the sea of faces before him. They were mountain-born men of Skai and Wenydd, men of Mercia and Dorian who had left their grainfields and dairy herds, and men of Venia, toughened by the harsh life of fisher-folk or nomadic herdsmen. But they were all Companions of the *Corrach*, all men of Celi first before they were men of their home province, men who believed in him and his cause.

"Companions of the *Corrach*," Tiernyn cried. "Men of Celi. The time has come to take the fight to the Saesnesi. Are you with me?"

A roar of assent rose and washed against him like a giant ninth wave. Tiernyn smiled and raised his hand for silence.

"You all know my brother Donaugh has been taken by the Saesnesi. In five days, we have heard no word of him. I propose we go into the Saesnesi Shore and bring him back to these halls." He held up his hand again to forestall a reply. A few ragged cheers broke out, then died away. "Winter is upon us," he said, pitching his voice so that it carried well across the field. "The Cold Sea is now closed to the Saesnesi longships from Saesnes. Elesan will receive no reinforcements from the continent until the coming of spring. My father in Tyra strongly believes Saesnes will fall to Maedun this spring, or by summer at the latest. We must have the Saesnesi Shore secured before that, or face an invasion of not hundreds but thousands of Saesnesi fleeing Maedun invaders. If we have beaten Elesan back, if we control the Saesnesi Shore, they will have no place to land. Shall we take back the soil of Celi from the invaders?"

The roar of assent and approval was like a gale, physically battering against his body. He smiled and drew Kingmaker, brandishing it in the air above his head.

"Will you follow me, and will you follow Kingmaker?"

The men cheered wildly. A sea of hands rose, clutching swords and bows. Several voices at once cried out, "The *Corrach* and Kingmaker!" Section by section, the cry arose in a deep, rhythmic chant. "The *Corrach* and Kingmaker! The *Corrach* and Kingmaker!"

"Tomorrow," Tiernyn shouted above the uproar. "Tomorrow, Companions and friends, we invade the Saesnesi Shore. We will force Elesan to meet us, and we will defeat him!"

The cheering became a deafening roar as more than five thousand men cried their assent. Tiernyn saluted them with his sword, then turned and left the dais. Silently, the five captains wheeled as one man and followed him.

Connor fell into step with Tiernyn as they made their way

back through the gates into the courtyard. Lluddor and Eryth turned away toward the armory to begin their preparations, Eachern and Gordaidh following moments later. Connor remained with Tiernyn.

"Do you think we'll find Donaugh?" Connor asked quietly.

Tiernyn put his hand to Kingmaker's hilt. "He's out there somewhere, Connor," he said. "And he's alive. I'd know if he were dead. The sword would tell me."

"None of our spies could say where he is."

Tiernyn's mouth lengthened to a thin, grim line. "I intend to see my brother back here safely," he said, "or I intend to see the Saesnesi Shore laid waste from the River Lachlan to the sea, and the Saesnesi army destroyed at my feet. Make your men ready, Connor. We move tomorrow at dawn."

12

Donaugh awoke to utter darkness, covered in cold sweat. His head throbbed and pounded with each pulsebeat. No comforting glow of hearth or brazier broke the thick, smothering darkness. Dizziness swept over him in great waves, and he had to clutch the mattress beneath him as the bed swung and tilted crazily. The room was stiflingly hot, yet he shivered with an internal cold that threatened to freeze his heart in his chest. The air felt too thick to breathe, choking him as he tried to draw it into his straining lungs. He could not even cry out.

Desperately, he reached for Eliade, but the place beside him in the bed was empty and cold. Not even her scent remained as evidence she had been there when he went to sleep.

Why could he see no glow from the embers in the hearth or the brazier? He rubbed his eyes, but could not even see his hand before his face. Had he gone blind? Then he realized he could hear nothing. He clapped his hands together, but no sound penetrated the opaque darkness around him. In panic, he threw back the bedclothes and struggled to sit up. It was as if the air around him had turned to treacle.

He put his hands to his eyes and rubbed them again. Gradually, he became aware of a rushing sensation and realized it was his own blood pulsating in his veins. He staggered to his feet and blundered through the murky air. His outstretched hand rapped painfully into the rough, mortared stone of the fireplace, and he fell to his knees.

"Rhianna, help me," he cried, but could not hear the sound of his voice. "*Darlai,* Mother of All . . . "

Then, dimly, as if he looked through thick draperies, he saw the glow of the fire, each ember separate and distinct, flaring softly in its bed of ash and cinder. One ember seemed

to be brighter, more sharply delineated, than the others. Of its
own volition, his hand went out to it. He plucked it from its
place and held it cupped in the palm of his hand. Its heat dis-
pelled the frozen chill in his body, melted the ice around his
heart, yet did not scorch his hand. There was no pain, no sensation of burning.

He brought up his other hand and smoothed it across the
top of the ember. It felt as cool as the lustrous surface of a
cabochon gem beneath the pads of his fingers. It flared brightly
in his hand, and, as he stared down at it, he thought he saw the
tiny figures of men moving through the light—knots of men
locked together in mortal combat.

The ember grew brighter, and the room around Donaugh
shattered and spun. He was engulfed by the ember, swept up
and plunged into its dazzling heart.

It seemed to him that he stood on a hill overlooking a broad
glen. Below, two armies clashed amid the trampled and blood-
ied snow in an eerie and unnatural silence. For a moment,
Donaugh could not discern any details and saw only a struggling mass of men under a dull, overcast sky. Swords and ax
blades gleamed wetly red with blood, bright against the snow.

Near the center of the fighting, a banner streamed in the
wind, then snapped into focus. A red hart leapt across a green
field. The banner of the *Corrach*. Tiernyn's banner. Tiernyn
himself stood out sharply in his crimson cloak, Kingmaker
flashing and glittering in a deadly arc around him as he fought.

Under a bright red banner bearing a white boar, a tall blond
man fought valiantly with a short sword in one hand and a war
ax in the other. For an instant, Donaugh thought it was Elesan
himself, but then realized the man was too young. Aelric,
Eliade's brother. He bore a startling resemblance to her, and to
his father.

The battle raged back and forth across the floor of the glen
in swirling patterns that broke and re-formed, broke and re-

formed, time and time again. No sound reached Donaugh where he stood high above the conflict—no shouts or screams from the wounded or dying, no clash or clangor of steel meeting tempered steel. Men fought and died in an appalling, ghastly silence.

Unable to do more than watch, Donaugh stood tensely as the mass of men shifted and eddied below like moving water. Finally, it became evident that the Companions were gradually beating back the Saesnesi. Tiernyn spurred his horse forward, Kingmaker slicing through flesh and bone around him, and came face-to-face with Aelric. A Saesnesi ax blade bit deep into the forehead of Tiernyn's horse. He flung himself to the ground as the horse collapsed beneath him, and spun to face Aelric as Ylana leaned sideways and buried the edge of her sword in the neck of the man who had killed the horse.

Everything but the two leaders faded from Donaugh's field of vision. Kingmaker glowed with a light of its own under the gray sky, and Tiernyn moved with it as a dancer moves with a familiar and highly skilled partner. Aelric went to his knees under Tiernyn's onslaught. First his short sword fell to the ground, then his war ax. Blood burst from a deep wound in his arm, then from his hip. He let his arms fall to his sides and slumped down, his head bowed.

A sudden wave of dizziness swept over Donaugh. He closed his eyes briefly. When he opened them again, the scene below had changed.

Night had fallen. Campfires burned brightly amid neatly ordered clusters of tents. Beyond the camp, a huge fire burned, consuming the bodies of the Saesnesi dead. Burial parties worked silently to collect the bodies of the Celae dead.

Tiernyn stepped out of a large tent in the center of the camp, flanked by Ylana, Connor, Lluddor, Eryth, Gordaidh of Dorian, and Eachern of Mercia. Two tall guards dragged Aelric away from a group of prisoners and pulled him toward the spot where Tiernyn and his captains stood waiting. Aelric, his wounds hastily bandaged, drew himself up to his full height and shook off the hands of the guards. He strode alone to face Tiernyn.

Soldiers crowded around the two leaders. Donaugh could hear nothing, but he knew the soldiers were shouting by the way they gesticulated wildly. Tiernyn spoke to Aelric for a moment. Aelric folded his arms across his chest, then turned his head slightly and spit at Tiernyn's feet. Tiernyn stepped back, his face impassive and cold.

Eachern of Mercia leapt forward, the two guards with him. The guards seized Aelric's arms and wrestled him to a kneeling position. Donaugh lost sight of him as he disappeared behind the throng of Celae soldiers. Eachern drew his sword and raised it high, then looked toward Tiernyn. Tiernyn nodded almost imperceptibly. Eachern's sword sliced downward . . .

"No!" Donaugh shouted. He could not move. "By the gods, no!"

Even as the mass of Celae soldiers raised clenched fists in triumph, the flames of the campfires flared, leaping high into the air. The tents, the men, the glen all disappeared into a sea of flame. As Donaugh watched helplessly, the fire spread until it covered all of the Isle of Celi, consuming it until nothing was left but a vast, lifeless plain of ash.

Donaugh closed his hand on cold, gray, powdery ash. Behind him the sky framed by the window paled toward dawn. The wind picked up a skiff of snow, fine as the ash coating his palm, from the mounded drift on the window ledge, and swirled it through the tracery of barren vines climbing the outside wall. From the tips of the icicles that framed the top of the window, water dripped and carved scallops into the edges of the mound of snow. Donaugh climbed to his feet, stiff and sore as an ancient grandfather. He opened his hand and let the ash trail to the hearth.

All of Celi smothered in ash and cinder . . .

He shuddered. Was the vision of the present? Had Tiernyn's army met the Saesnesi army, and was Aelric now lying dead at Tiernyn's feet? Or was the vision a glimpse of the future?

Rhegar had said the future was not set in stone. Donaugh recognized the truth in the old man's words. If what he had seen was what *might* be, then, were the gods and goddesses with him, he had time to change it, to prevent the fire he had seen from consuming all of Celi.

He dusted the powdery ash from his hand and turned toward the bed.

Eliade lay curled in sleep, nearly lost among the heaped bedclothes. Her fine, pale hair lay tangled on the linen pillow and across one bare shoulder, gold against the ivory of her skin.

She came to him during the night, after all but the guards at the gates of the lodge slept, and always left before dawn. Donaugh misliked the deceit of meeting with Eliade like this, but could see no other way of their being together. He was afraid her father would kill her as well as him if he found them together like this, but the need of her was stronger than his fear. They would have to tell Elesan of their love soon.

He watched her sleep for a moment, his heart filled with the wonder of his love for her, and hers for him. But even as he watched her sleep, he knew he had to leave her.

He went to the bed and sat on the edge, careful not to disturb her. The renewed bond between them had strengthened his magic. It resonated along the link between them, its power a swelling chord pulsating through him with the rhythm of their combined heartbeats. His magic had more power now than he had ever dreamed of. How could he leave her now, when he had only just found her again?

She opened her eyes and looked up at him, then slowly reached up to put her hand to his cheek. Infinite sadness welled up in her eyes, but she smiled. He turned his head to kiss the palm of her hand, then took her into his arms. The power of his emotions, his need—his very words—thrummed along the threads that bound them together. His soul was hers, and hers was his. As long as he held her, words between them were superfluous, but he had no other way of expressing his thoughts. He had not yet enough practice in soul-to-soul communication. But soon, he knew . . . Soon he would not need to speak aloud to tell her what he felt.

"Eliade, I must go," he said, his cheek against the softness of her hair. She couldn't hear what he said, but he knew she understood him. "A Seeing came to me . . ." The vision of Celi reduced to a desert of ash swept before his eyes again and he shuddered. "Eliade, all my life I've believed that your people were my enemy, and that Celi must be rid of the threat your people held over us or we would perish. But that's not true. It's not true. We have to work together . . . A greater danger is coming, and if we—all of us, your people and mine—don't work together, we will all be overcome and swept away."

He told her about his vision, felt her tremble against him as he spoke about her brother's death. When he finished, she clung to him, her cheek pressed against his shoulder, and her grief swirled within him to mix with his own. Finally, he grasped her shoulders and held her away from him. He put one hand gently to her chin and turned her head so that she looked directly into his eyes. "Eliade, I once said I would be content with my life if all it held was service and duty, if no happiness. I was wrong. I want you with me always."

She lifted a handful of her hair and held it next to his, then pointed first to her eyes, then his. Her meaning was clear. He could not take a Saesnesi wife home to Dun Camus, and she could not bring a Celae husband into Elesan's household. She made the sign for *soul* and held out her cupped hands to him.

"*My soul is cupped within the palm of your hand.*"

He took her hands in his and pressed them against his breast. "*Your soul is sheltered safe within my hands and my heart.*" He kissed her, then got reluctantly to his feet. "And now, I must speak with your father."

Francia stepped back quickly and pulled the hem of her gown out of the way, fastidiously avoiding a spurt of blood that splashed to the floor by her feet. The woman on the bed moaned feebly as another contraction wracked her body. She was beyond any help the midwife could give, her pasty gray face and blue, bloodless lips foretelling the outcome of this birth. The child struggling to be born was too large for the birth canal and had already mortally damaged its mother. One of the attendant women soaked a rag in cool water and sponged off the dying woman's face, whispering soothing words to her.

Hakkar's second wife had fallen victim to the same sorcerer's curse his first wife succumbed to. No sorcerers' children came easily into this world. Five stillborn siblings marked the six years between Francia and Hakkar, and their mother, a strong woman, had nearly died producing Hakkar. The dying woman, although highborn and well connected, was obviously not strong enough to bear a sorcerer's child. Francia dismissed the woman from her mind and turned her attention back to the midwife.

The midwife was nearly as pale as the moribund mother, her lips pressed together in a thin, tense line as she tried to ease the child's head out of the birth canal. Every once in a while she glanced fearfully toward the door, as if expecting Hakkar to burst into the room, snarling with rage at the long delay.

Francia moved back until she stood behind the midwife, well out of the way, but able to watch unimpeded. The top of the child's head, crowned with thick, dark hair, was fully visible, but was unable to pass through the restricted space separating him from birth. The midwife's efforts seemed to be futile.

"Use the knife," Francia said at last. "You won't hurt Pila any worse, and you may save the child."

The midwife glanced up at her, then nodded. She took the small, razor-sharp knife from her belt and made a quick incision at the edge of the birth canal. The woman on the bed moaned softly, but hardly moved. The midwife slipped her fingers in around the top of the child's head, trying to get a grip on the slippery skin of the skull to ease the child out.

Francia watched. What a pity the midwife had no access to the ancient knowledge, the secrets lost so many generations ago. There once were women's spells and enchantments to help in just these situations. But that was before the men of Maedun decided women who had access to any magic whatsoever were too dangerous, too powerful. All books containing the knowledge were burned—as were some of the women who refused to give up the practice of their unique magic. The knowledge was eventually irretrievably lost.

Almost irretrievably lost, Francia amended under her breath. She smiled to herself. She had no idea who had secreted the proscribed books deep in the warren of passageways and small chambers beneath the manse, but she strongly suspected it must have been her great-grandmother, whose name was still synonymous with rebellion. Francia had found the books two years ago, shortly after the death of Hakkar's first wife. At first, she read them only for the fascination of reading something forbidden. The books contained more than just the small magics connected with home and hearth, the birthing of children and the winning of men's hearts. There were magics for revenge, magics for ridding oneself of rivals, magics for attaining power and influence. Enthralled and delighted, and very cautious, Francia tried several of them, and was astounded when they worked for her. Long, arduous hours of practice improved her abilities daily.

She had enough skill so that she could have helped Pila, had she wanted to—had Pila not taken her position as wife to Hakkar of Lake Vayle as an excuse to treat Francia with the same imperious contempt she treated her servants. Now Pila lay dying, and the child she bore would in all likelihood be stillborn. No pity stirred in Francia's heart. Pila had brought this down on her own head.

The midwife gave a startled gasp, then had to lunge forward to catch the slippery body of the child as it slithered all at once out of its mother. Its skin was mottled blue where it wasn't stained red with its mother's blood. The umbilical cord, hardly pulsing as the mother's life ebbed, had wrapped itself around the baby's neck. The midwife gently loosened it to free the child.

A boy, Francia noted with clinical detachment as the midwife held the child upside down to drain the fluid from its lungs. The child's head was badly misshapen from the birth canal, its features distorted to a travesty of a human face, and one of its legs appeared to be twisted. Even being a son, the incredibly ugly child would not please Hakkar.

The midwife patted the infant's back, encouraging it to breathe. For a long time, the child merely hung limp in her hands. Then finally, as if it drew the last of its mother's strength from her, it made a soft mewling sound.

"He lives," the midwife cried. "Praise be, he lives!"

Working quickly and expertly, she tied the umbilical cord, then used the sharp knife to sever the cord a few inches above the tie. One of the attendants stepped forward, holding a soft blanket that had been warmed by the fire. The midwife wrapped the child in the blanket, then wiped its face with a warm, damp cloth another woman handed her.

Francia looked at the child. Even now, she could see the faint outline of a hard, dark aura around the child's head—incipient magic inherited from its father. But the flame of life burned weakly within the tiny body, so feeble a breath of wind might smother it.

The blood smeared on the bed, on the floor, on the child itself, was blood shed in pain and fear, woman's blood, shed in woman's own unique pain. It had its own latent magic. Francia drew upon that power, felt it fill her as liquid fills a jar. She sent a thread of the magic out to the child, let it wrap itself around the frail spark of life. The spark flickered. Francia tightened the thread to a strangling pressure. The child's body spasmed and it wailed feebly in protest. The dark aura around its head flickered and was gone. The tiny spark flared brightly once, then died, completely extinguished.

The midwife cried out in fear, clutching the tiny body to her breast. Francia stepped forward and took it from her. She handed it to the woman who attended Pila and motioned her to place the dead child beside its dead mother.

"There was nothing you could do," she said to the midwife. "I won't let my brother harm you. Nothing could have saved the child."

The midwife nodded dumbly, then turned away to attend to preparing both the mother and child for burial.

Francia opened the door of the birthing chamber and stepped out into the corridor, unable to hide the small smile of triumph as she went to tell Hakkar that he had yet another still-born son.

13

Donaugh dressed quickly. His mind racing ahead to what he must say to Elesan, he barely noticed that his clothing had been cleaned and neatly darned until he fastened the right cuff of his shirtsleeve. The rent caused by the war ax was nearly invisible, mended with tiny, precise stitches. No sign remained of the bloodstains. He fingered the mend, achingly aware of the bond with Eliade and knowing that he must leave her, perhaps forever.

Something shimmered along the threads of the bond—an impression of a smile. *For us, beloved, no parting is forever . . .*

But one lifetime would seem forever without her.

Donaugh finished dressing and went to the door of the bedchamber. The door opened onto a long room furnished with cushioned benches and chairs. Embroidered tapestries and woven hangings covered the walls to keep out the chill of winter, and fires blazed on hearths at either end of the room. Two spinning wheels sat beside a large loom near a tall window that framed part of a formal garden outside. A gnarled, leafless apple tree stood against a stone wall, giving scant shelter to the dead stalks of flowers and herbs thrusting through the snow at the foot of the wall. Donaugh stared at the apple tree for a moment, remembering petals of apple blossoms sprinkled like pearls in pale gold hair. Then he turned away from the window and pulled the door closed behind him.

The room, obviously a women's dayroom, was empty but for Eliade. She came forward to meet him and touched his arm, smoothing the neatly mended rip in the sleeve of his shirt. He put his hand over hers and smiled down at her. She slipped her arms around his waist and pressed her cheek to his shoulder. He held her, his lips against the softness of her hair, breathing in the fragrance of herbs and apple blossoms. They stood like that for a moment before she stepped away. He traced a gentle finger down the line of her cheek, trying to memorize the exact shade of blue-gray of her eyes.

"Mayhaps someday," he said. "Mayhaps if this works out as we hope . . . "

She nodded, then took his hand.

The door of the day chamber opened onto a short corridor. A tall Saesnesi warrior stood on each side of the door. They stepped forward, blocking the way, hands on the hilts of their daggers, as Eliade led Donaugh out into the hall. She frowned and made an imperious gesture. The men moved aside, surprise showing on their faces. Eliade took Donaugh's arm to lead him down the corridor, and the men fell into step behind them.

The lodge was not as large as Donaugh expected. It was not more than a few paces to the end of the hallway. The room beyond was not large enough to be called a great hall, but it obviously served the same purpose. A woman cleared the remains of the morning meal from the long trestle table that stood against one wall. She looked up as Eliade and Donaugh entered, but went immediately back to her work, her face impassive. Eliade paid her no heed. She went directly to her father.

Elesan stood before the huge hearth, his back to the room, his posture one of abstracted thought as he studied the leaping flames. As Eliade put her hand on his arm, he turned to greet her, smiling down at her and making a quick sign of welcome. He caught sight of Donaugh, waiting in the middle of the room. One eyebrow rose in surprise, and his expression became carefully neutral.

"What are you doing here?" he demanded.

"I must speak with you, my lord Elesan," Donaugh said. "The lady Eliade was kind enough to bring me to you."

"I doubt very much you look upon me as your lord," Elesan said dryly. "Do not mock me with that title."

"I assure you, sir, I meant no disrespect," Donaugh said.

Elesan grunted noncommittally. "You're looking extremely well for a man who was dragged from the portals of death only five days ago," he said. He peered intently at Donaugh's temple, then frowned when he saw no sign of the head wound. In answer to the unspoken question, Donaugh unlaced the cuff at his right wrist and pushed up his sleeve. A thin, white scar marked the muscle of his upper arm, all that remained of the ax wound. Elesan tried to hide his startled reaction, but Donaugh saw it clearly in the sudden paling of the skin around his mouth as his lips tightened, and in the widening of his eyes. Elesan stepped back.

"So," he said evenly. "You truly do have magic."

"Aye," Donaugh said. "I have magic, although the Healing magic was not entirely my own."

"But it worked for you."

"Aye, it did. I am well. I must speak with you, sir." Donaugh glanced over his shoulder at the two guards, who stood stiffly alert in the doorway behind him. "Alone, if we might."

Elesan clasped his hands behind his back, his shrewd gaze measuring Donaugh. He nodded to the guards. They faded back into the shadows of the hallway. Elesan flicked his fingers toward the woman by the table. She picked up the last of the utensils and hurried toward a small door in the back of the room, giving Donaugh a searching, sidelong glance as she left.

"What would you say to me that my men cannot hear?" Elesan asked.

Donaugh took a deep breath and wished he had Tiernyn's gift for speech. But he had his own magic. It would have to serve. "Because of what I have been shown," he said, "I must leave here. Today. Now."

Elesan smiled sardonically. "You ask a lot," he said. "I have a messenger ready to send to your brother demanding ransom for you. Tell me why I must release you before the ransom is paid."

"Because we've so little time left," Donaugh said. "If we would save this island from destruction, we must work quickly."

Elesan stared at him, then laughed incredulously. "You expect my belief in such an obvious fabrication?" he said. He shook his head. "Surely a man of your talents can come up with a better story."

"I am completely serious, my lord Elesan," Donaugh said. "I don't know any other way to convince you except the simple truth. Had I my brother's gift of persuasion . . ." He made a helpless gesture. "You must believe me, Elesan. You *must*!"

Eliade left her father's side and crossed the room to stand beside Donaugh, lending her silent support. She took his hand in hers and faced Elesan calmly. Elesan's face darkened in anger. He put his hand to the haft of the dagger at his belt.

"What treachery is this, then?" he demanded. "What have you done to my daughter?"

Donaugh put his arm around Eliade's shoulders. "Your daughter has opened my eyes," he said quietly.

"If you've dishonored my daughter, I will kill you, Celae mongrel," Elesan snarled. He seized Eliade's wrist and tried to pull her away. She shrank back into the shelter of Donaugh's arm, shaking her head vehemently. Elesan released her wrist and stepped back, his face suffused with rage. He snatched the dagger from his belt and leapt forward.

Even as Elesan raised the dagger to strike, Donaugh pulled his magic to him. He caught a strand of power from the earth beneath him, another from the air around him. In his hands, they became shimmering gossamer filaments. He wove them quickly, adding more threads, until the air around his hands glowed and sparked with the growing power. Like a glistening cloak, the web of magic wrapped itself around Elesan, arrested his forward surge instantly. Elesan's eyes widened in fear. He struggled against the enfolding magic, his breathing rasping and labored, but he could not move or cry out.

"Don't struggle." Donaugh concentrated on holding the web of magic strong and steady. "The magic will hold stronger than iron chains. If you stop fighting it, the bonds will loosen. Will you listen to me now and hear me out? I ask no more than your attention."

Elesan went still. The glowing web dimmed but did not disappear. Elesan drew in a deep, shuddering breath, and some color returned to his face.

"I will listen," he said. "It would seem I have little choice."

Donaugh released the magic. Elesan staggered slightly, then went to the trestle table and collapsed into the carved and cushioned chair at the head of the table, his face strained and still pale. He scrubbed his hands over his cheeks and shook his head, then glanced up at Donaugh.

"I had not really believed in your magic," he said softly. "Not truly. Not until now."

Donaugh went to the table, his arm once again around Eliade's shoulders. He drew a chair for her, saw her comfortably seated, then sat down across the corner of the table from Elesan.

"Eliade is my love," Donaugh said simply. "She has always been my love, through all of time past, and will be for all of time to come. You may not approve, but you cannot gainsay our love. I tell you this to assure you there is nothing dishonorable in my feelings for her, nor hers for me."

Elesan looked at his daughter. Eliade met his gaze levelly, unsmiling. She put her hand over Donaugh's and traced a quick sign with her other hand. Elesan's lips tightened, but he nodded.

"So she tells me," he said. "Speak, then. I will listen."

"My lord Elesan, I told you that your daughter opened my eyes. I meant that fervently. She made me understand that she loves this island as much as I do." He held out his open hand to Elesan. "As much as you do."

Elesan inclined his head in acknowledgment. "Continue," he said quietly.

"There is a darkness spreading on the continent. You know this as well as I do."

Elesan made a gesture of distaste and contempt. "The Maedun," he said.

"Aye, the Maedun. Their darkness will come to Celi and will overwhelm all of us, Celae and Saesnesi alike, if we cannot settle our differences and work together. Already Falinor and Laringras are drowned in the darkness. Saesnes will fall soon. Mayhaps not this year, or even next year, but inevitably Isgard will follow Saesnes into darkness. And when the Maedun have all of the continent under their sway, they will look to us here on Celi." Donaugh made a fist and pounded gently on the table before him. "We will all go down before them just as surely as the continent if we cannot work together. They will strangle us as easily as you might wring the neck of a hen."

Elesan sat back, regarding Donaugh suspiciously. "This is a Celae trick," he said flatly. "My kinsman Baniff assures me that Saesnes is holding strong against the Maedun."

"Then Baniff is a blustering fool." Donaugh shook his head. "You can't help but know of the squabbles among his nobles. Saesnes is so torn by internal strife, it has no strength left. You are no fool yourself, Elesan. Surely you have informers in Baniff's court."

Surprise flickered briefly in Elesan's eyes. "You and your brother are better informed than we thought," he said.

"I offer you no tricks," Donaugh said. "If I am to persuade you, I can give you nothing but the truth. I had a Seeing, sir. I saw all of Celi covered in ash and cinder. It will happen if our two peoples continue to fight each other."

"You ask me to surrender to your brother?" Sarcasm tinged Elesan's voice and a bitter smile tilted one corner of his mouth. "And how long, do you think, would the men of the Summer Run allow me to remain Celwalda should I declare my intention to bend my knee to Tiernyn ap Kian?"

Frustration knotted in Donaugh's belly. He had never

before envied Tiernyn his gift of enchanting men with words. Desperately, he tried to organize his thoughts, searching for the one telling phrase that would convince Elesan.

"I would not ask you to surrender to my brother," he said. "Just as I would not ask Tiernyn to surrender to you. I'm not speaking of surrender. I would ask that you meet with Tiernyn, a meeting of equals, to discuss a settlement of our differences. A treaty, if you will."

Elesan gave a harsh, startled bark of incredulous laughter. "A treaty?" he repeated. "Do you say your brother's army would stand for talk of peace and a treaty between our two people?"

"Tiernyn's army follows him," Donaugh said. "They believe in him implicitly."

"Then your brother commands men's minds and hearts more surely than I do."

"Would you have us fight and kill each other until there is nothing left of this island but ash and cinder and bloody corpses?"

Elesan surged to his feet and made an impatient gesture. "You talk of ash and cinder . . ." His voice trailed off and he frowned, making a fist and beating it into his other palm. "How can I trust what you say?" he said. "You are Celae. We are sworn enemies . . ."

Donaugh drew in a deep breath. "I will show you what I saw," he said quietly. "If you won't believe what I say, believe what I show you."

The lines of power flowing in the earth beneath him, through the air around him, were thinner here than in Skai, more tenuous and fragile. He settled himself with an effort and began to gather power. He wasn't sure if he could do this, wasn't sure how to go about it, wasn't sure if it had ever been done before. He muttered a brief prayer to the *darlai* and to Rhianna of the Air for support and assistance. It he were to convince Elesan, it *had* to work.

He looked into the fire, concentrating on the power flowing around him in living streams. Sweat rolled down his forehead and into his eyes, stinging. As he had done at the shrine in Dun Eidon when he showed Tiernyn the king-shadow, he wove the power together. But this was infinitely more difficult. He must bring forth images stronger and sharper than mere shadows if Elesan were to believe him and help him.

Painfully, straining with the effort, he built pictures against the blaze of the hearth, brushstroke by agonized brushstroke. The battle scenes appeared before the flames, thin and nebulous as shadows, but recognizable and ghastly in their silence.

Donaugh bent his head, closed his eyes, concentrating to bring every nuance of his vision clearly to Elesan. His head throbbed and pounded, and his breath rasped like a file against the back of his throat, dry as sand and ash. Elesan watched silently. Only his tense breathing and the whitened knuckles of his fist on the polished wood of the table betrayed his tautly stretched nerves.

Donaugh faltered as he struggled to build the last of the vision in the air before the fire. The scene wavered as Eachern's soldiers pulled Aelric to the center of the ring of Celae soldiers, blurring and fading behind Donaugh's closed eyes. Eliade rose and placed her hands on his shoulders. The strength of the bond between them steadied him. He felt her tremble as she pressed against his back. Fighting for control of the power, he brought the last details of the scene to life. Again, Eachern's sword flashed down, and Aelric vanished behind the wall of Celae soldiers.

Elesan made a strangled sound in the back of his throat. He lurched to his feet, his hand reaching out to his son. But even as he did so, the fire rose up to consume the island. The images of blood and trampled snow vanished in the leaping flames. Ash and cinder . . .

Elesan cried out in anguish. "Enough," he shouted. "That's enough. I will watch no more."

Exhausted, Donaugh slumped in his chair. He released the

magic. The threads of power snapped, cracking like a whip, lashing him with pain as they sprang back into place in the earth and air. The images in the air crackled, then shattered like fragile glass. They flickered briefly, glinting in the firelight, then vanished.

Eliade went to her knees before Donaugh, reached up to cup his temples between her hands, her gaze searching his face anxiously. He covered her hands with his and tried to smile to tell her he was all right.

Elesan put out his hand, groping for the surface of the table for support, and lowered himself into his chair. He moved like an old man, slowly and painfully. For a long time, he didn't speak, his head bent, his eyes closed. Pain etched deep lines into his face. Finally, he looked up at Donaugh.

"Is that a true Seeing?" he asked hoarsely.

"You saw what I saw," Donaugh said.

Elesan drew in a deep, shuddering breath. He shouted something over his shoulder. The woman who had been clearing the table hurried into the room, carrying a decanter of wine and goblets. She set the goblets down before him, glancing nervously at Donaugh, and filled them from the decanter. Elesan made an impatient, dismissing gesture, and the woman left the room hastily. Elesan paid her no attention. He pushed one of the goblets toward Donaugh and took a deep draught from his own.

"Now you see why I must leave," Donaugh said. The wine had been heated and was redolent of sweet spices. It revived him, calmed the hard thudding of his heart against his ribs. "I would save your son, my lord Elesan. But more, I would save Celi. It seems that the fate of the two is intertwined—a wyrd my brother might have difficulty accepting."

Elesan sat quietly, head bowed, for a moment. Finally, he looked up. "I will speak with your brother," he said heavily. "If he will speak with me, tell him I will bargain in good faith for peace." He raised his goblet and drained it in one long swallow. "Can you save my son?"

"It seems I must," Donaugh said, smiling faintly. He looked at Eliade, who sat with her head bowed, pale and shaken, while tears coursed down her cheeks. "For Eliade if not for Celi . . . I must hurry, my lord Elesan. Even now, Tiernyn's army moves toward the River Lachlan."

Elesan looked up, startled. "You know this?"

"Aye. The same way I know your son will die if we don't stop them from executing him on the field."

Elesan's gray eyes narrowed in shrewd speculation. "My scouts only half an hour ago reported what you say is the truth," he said. "I will order you a horse. We shall leave as soon as possible."

"We?" Donaugh repeated.

"I will go with you." A sardonic smile twisted Elesan's lips. "Think of me as an escort to see you safe through my country."

"Or a guard?"

Elesan inclined his head. "Or a guard," he said. "If you prefer."

Eliade came out into the courtyard, wrapped in a cloak of thick, creamy wool. As a servant led two sturdy, shaggy ponies out of the stable, she clutched the cloak tighter about her and picked her way carefully across the muddy slush. Donaugh sensed her presence and took a moment to compose his face before he turned to her. He didn't want her to see the pain that leaving her stabbed into his heart.

He needn't have bothered. She looked up at him, then slowly raised her hand to cup his cheek in her palm. With the touch, the bond between them intensified. Her sadness mingled with his own grief. He wanted to take her into his arms but dared not before the servants and guards stationed around the courtyard. Instead, he let his soul reach out to her, enwrapped her with his love as surely as she folded her love around him.

"I will come back to you, Eliade," he said softly. "My life would be too gray and colorless without you."

"*We will be together again, beloved. Be very sure of that.*"

Drawing away from her hurt like tearing his heart from his body. The invisible filaments of their bond clung, then stretched and snapped as he stepped back. But the fragment of her soul he carried would always be with him, just as a portion of his soul would always be with her.

Elesan vaulted up onto the back of one of the ponies. "It's already midmorning," he said. "We must go."

Eliade smiled at Donaugh, then turned and walked back to the doorway. As she disappeared inside, Donaugh closed his eyes and murmured a silent prayer to all the seven gods and goddesses that she would remain safe, and that he and Elesan would be in time to save Aelric.

"We must go," Elesan repeated.

"Aye," Donaugh said. "We must." He swung up onto the second pony and gathered the reins. He put heels to the horse's flanks and turned its head toward the main gate.

14

Shortly before midmorning, the army reached the ford across the River Lachlan. Tiernyn called a halt to let the horses and men rest and to wait for the scout he had dispatched from Dun Camus shortly before dawn with orders to locate the Saesnesi army. Overhead, the clouds appeared misty and thin, turning the sky a wan, milky blue. The sun showed as a pale golden disk behind the nearly transparent cloud. The air was mild enough to turn the snow to thick, icy slush underfoot.

The men saw to their horses, giving them a small amount of grain and water and rubbing them down to keep them warm. The snow and slush made hard going for the horses. The Companions relied on their mounts as an extra weapon. Tiernyn didn't want them exhausted when they met the Saesnesi. There were no foot soldiers in wet boots to consider. He had brought only cavalry with him. Men on foot didn't have the speed he needed for this campaign.

Tiernyn attended his own horse, glancing up occasionally for any sign of the scout returning. Connor threw a blanket across his horse's back and joined Tiernyn and Ylana, blowing on his hands to warm them.

"He's late," he said, scanning the blurred horizon beyond the river.

"No, we're early," Tiernyn said. "We made better speed than I thought we would, even with the snow."

"He may not have found Elesan's army."

"It's possible," Tiernyn said. "But I doubt it. Elesan knows we're coming. He has his own spies and informers, and he understands well the use of them. He won't let us run roughshod through territory he regards as his. He'll have no choice but to bring the army out to try to stop us."

Ylana had been picking ice from the shoes on her horse's

front feet. She got the last of it, gave the horse an affectionate pat on the neck, and joined Tiernyn and Connor.

"The country gets rougher beyond those hills," she said. "I hope it's not too slippery. Even those spiked shoes on the horses could slide on icy rocks."

"There he is," Connor said, pointing.

A single rider appeared over the brow of a low hill on the other side of the river, a ghostly figure wrapped in a gray-white cloak on a dappled gray horse, nearly impossible to see against the background of snow and misty sky. They rode hard across the treacherous ground. Slush and snow flew in clumps and spray from under the flying hooves of the horse. Horse and rider splashed through the shallow water of the ford and drew to a skidding halt before Tiernyn. The scout flung himself from the saddle and went to one knee in the snow. One of the soldiers took the horse and led it away to be looked after.

"Get up, man," Tiernyn said. "You're already wet enough."

The scout got quickly to his feet and grinned at Tiernyn. "We rode hard and the snow is melting quickly," he said. "I've dry clothing enough in the saddle pack." He tried to wipe some of the mud and slush from his face, but succeeded only in smearing it.

"You found them?"

"Aye, my lord *Corrach*. They're not more than two leagues from here."

"How many men?"

"I'd estimate nearly a thousand to our own thousand, my lord."

"Is Elesan with them?"

"I didn't see him, my lord, but I did see his son, Aelric. He seemed to be in charge."

"Aelric?" Tiernyn nodded thoughtfully. "He's as canny as his father. But not as experienced. That may fall to our favor. Where are they?"

"If you have a map, my lord, I'll show you."

Tiernyn pulled his map from the saddle pack and spread it

against the back of the horse. The map was simply drawn, but accurate and reasonably detailed. The scout stepped closer and pointed.

"We're here," he said. He moved his finger to a spot depicting a range of low hills. "Right here the hills come together to form a narrow valley. The Saesnesi are setting up just beyond that. Probably hoping to catch us in an ambush. Were we to try to meet them there, they'd have us squeezed in that valley, and could pick us off like cattle coming through a branding chute."

Tiernyn studied the map, frowning. Finally, he smiled and nodded. "What are the hills like here?" he asked, pointing to an area half a league south of the narrow valley. "Steep or gentle?"

"Fairly steep," the scout said. "But not impossibly so. Better than to the north. Rocky there. A lot of broken scree."

"Could we take the army around here and catch the Saesnesi from the east? Behind them?"

The scout grinned. "You mean, catch them with their back to that gap and ambush them?" he asked. "Aye, my lord, we could. The valley's a bit of a box there, but the hills to the east are lower and not nearly so steep. We'd have the high ground if we could come around behind them like that."

Tiernyn folded his map and put it away. "Then that's what we'll do. Go put your dry clothing on, then come back here. You'll ride beside me to make sure we don't lose the way."

The scout grinned again. "Aye, my lord *Corrach*," he said. "I won't be but a moment."

Snow clogged the track through the forest, making the going treacherous and dangerous. Donaugh held his horse at an easy canter, clinging to it with knees and calves. The horse wore no saddle, just a thick pad of blanket strapped firmly across its back. Beside him, Elesan rode in silence, his face grim and set as he followed Donaugh's lead without question or comment. The horse Donaugh rode was not much more than a pony, far smaller than the warhorses bred from sleek and graceful stallions Connor had brought from the continent and crossed with the robust Doriani horses. It felt frail and meager under him, but Elesan assured him that the shaggy little beasts were sure-footed and had enough stamina to run leagues without tiring.

Donaugh glanced over his left shoulder at the sun. It was nearly midday. In his vision, he thought the light indicated that the time might be late afternoon. Tiernyn's army might already be in position in the battlefield. He was running out of time.

He cleared his mind and concentrated on the ties that bound him to his twin and to the sword he served no less than the sword itself served Tiernyn. The bond drew him along the track through the woods as surely as the Nail Star drew lodestone. They came to a fork in the track. Donaugh hesitated hardly an instant before turning his horse onto the track leading due north, out onto the rolling downsland beyond the forest.

Now the track sloped downward in a broad curve, following the flank of a low hill. A thick tangle of leafless bramble and dead bracken filled the hollow at the base of the hill. Donaugh didn't see the small stream until the horse was nearly upon it. He had no time to prepare the horse, or guide it.

The horse faltered indecisively beneath him, then gathered itself to jump the stream. It landed awkwardly on the opposite bank, its broad front feet skidding in the icy slush, its back feet half into the water. Scrabbling for purchase on the slippery surface, it lurched forward, throwing Donaugh sideways across its shoulder. Its feet went out from under it, and it sprawled to the ground.

Donaugh slid from the horse's back and tucked his head down as he threw himself clear of the tumbling horse. Instinctively, he tried to hold on to the reins, but the fall tore them from his hands. He landed heavily on his shoulder and arm, and rolled out of the way of the thrashing hooves.

Even as he climbed unsteadily to his feet, the horse was

already scrambling to get up. Elesan had drawn his horse to a skidding halt on the far side of the stream. He dismounted quickly, then leapt over the narrow thread of water and seized the reins of Donaugh's horse. It needed no restraint to prevent it running away, standing with its left rear foot raised from the ground, the hock swollen and bruised.

Elesan ran his hands down along the injured leg. "Lame," he said as Donaugh limped up to hold the horse's head. "He won't carry you farther, I fear."

Donaugh glanced at Elesan's horse. It stood calmly on the far side of the stream, its breath blowing in long, steamy banners from its nostrils. The horse was clearly incapable of carrying two. Despair clutched at Donaugh's chest, and he glanced up at the sun. Had the battle already begun?

"Is your magic sufficient to heal this horse?" Elesan asked.

Donaugh shook his head. "No," he said. "I haven't that skill."

Elesan frowned. "Surely it's a simple magic compared with the vision you showed me," he said. "Or with the Healing of your arm and the wound on your head."

"I wish it were so," Donaugh said. "Healing—any Healing, man or beast—takes a special magic. It wasn't I who Healed my arm. I can do nothing for the horse."

Elesan straightened up, his level gray gaze measuring Donaugh shrewdly. "I don't know you well enough, Donaugh ap Kian," he said softly. "I have no certain knowledge that you are an honorable man. I do, however, believe that the vision you showed me was a true one, and I must believe that my daughter would not give her love to a man with no honor. Take my horse. You have my word that when you send a messenger to me, I will meet with your brother to bargain in good faith for peace between our peoples."

He brought his horse across the stream and handed the reins to Donaugh. Donaugh took the reins, then turned to face Elesan.

"I will do my best to save your son, Elesan," he said quietly. He held out his right hand. "You have my hand on it, and my word."

Elesan hesitated, then reached out and took Donaugh's hand. For a moment, the two men stood silently, hands clasped. Then Elesan stepped away and Donaugh swung up onto the horse. Donaugh set heels to the horse's flanks and it leapt forward. When Donaugh glanced back over his shoulder, Elesan still stood in the middle of the track, erect as an oak tree, watching him.

The army crested the hill, and Tiernyn raised his arm to signal the halt. With the ease of long practice, the companies formed into a broad curve on the flank of the low hill. Directly behind Tiernyn, Connor's company assembled into precise ranks. Flanking them to the left, Eachern's company of mixed light cavalry and mounted bowmen took their places, mirrored on the right by Gordaidh's company. Out on the wings, lightly armed and ready to move against any vulnerable opening on the enemy's flank, Lluddor and Eryth deployed their companies in a loose, flexible formation. Tiernyn, with Ylana by his side, sat his horse in front of the army. Directly behind him, the Red Hart banner snapped and rippled on its standard, firmly anchored in a leather cup by the stirrup of the young soldier who held it with pride.

The wind had scoured most of the snow from the flat valley floor and left it drifted in mounds near the narrow defile at the eastern end. Tiernyn sat with his wrists crossed on the pommel of his saddle, studying the terrain below carefully. Aelric had chosen his ambush site well. The ground at the foot of the low hill was muddy with half-melted snow, but still afforded better footing for fighting men than the knee-deep snow in the defile. Had Tiernyn led the Celae army through that gap, he would have led them straight into a slaughter.

A marshy lake nearly filled the north end of the valley to Tiernyn's right. Between the ragged floes of ice, the dark glimmer of open water reflected the gray sky. Desiccated stalks supporting burst heads of bulrushes thrust up through the snow, surrounded by dry, brown reeds. A small, sluggish stream, narrow enough that a man could hurdle it in one easy leap, wound away from the lake and made its way down the valley, neatly dividing the valley floor into halves. Near the southern end of the valley where the marshy ground became more solid, tangles of brambles marked the course of the stream. A good place for an ambush, but not the best for a pitched battle.

Moving a thousand mounted men into position was difficult to do in secret, so Tiernyn was not surprised to find the Saesnesi waiting for them, their half-finished ambush abandoned. He could read little into the formation. The Saesnesi thronged together in an ever-shifting mass of men, flaxen hair blowing in the wind beneath metal helms. Only a few of them were mounted, racing their shaggy, sturdy little horses back and forth along the front lines, shouting and waving axes and swords. Aelric himself, mounted on a horse that surely must have been taken from a Celae soldier in a raid, sat quietly alone well in front of his army, studying Tiernyn with dispassionate appraisal and ignoring the tumult of his soldiers behind him.

The shouts of the Saesnesi soldiers reached Tiernyn faintly—vows, jeers and insults, exhortations, commands. Axes and sword blades waved above the swirling mass, catching the wan winter light, as the clamor rose to a ferocious crescendo. The wild, rhythmic drumming of ax blade against shield pounded in counterpoint to the shouts and cries. With careful, deliberate motions, Aelric looped his reins about the pommel of his saddle and drew a short sword and a war ax from scabbards at his sides. He lifted the sword in a brief salute to Tiernyn, then turned in his saddle to his men, his sword raised high. The sword blade flashed as he sliced it down and forward. He set heels to the flanks of the horse. Screaming, the Saesnesi surged ahead.

Tiernyn drew Kingmaker. As the first of the Saesnesi reached the small stream, he slashed the sword down and spurred his horse forward. The wild, eerie ululations of Celae war cries shattered the air, and the sound of thousands of hooves echoed like thunder up and down the valley.

The two hosts met in a rush, with a shock that seemed to splinter the very air.

Shortly after midafternoon, the borrowed horse began to flag noticeably beneath Donaugh, tired enough to become clumsy and careless about how it set its feet on the slushy, hazardous track. Reluctantly, Donaugh drew it down to a walk. Head drooping, sweat matting its shaggy coat, it gamely plodded on. It had all the heart and spirit he could ask of a mount; he wished only for more strength and stamina.

He was getting closer to Tiernyn's army. The clarity of the link he shared with his twin was sharper, more distinct. Two more hours, perhaps three, would see him to the valley he had seen in his vision. He glanced up at the sky. Cloud hid the sun, but he judged it two or three hours yet until sunset. He might reach Tiernyn in time to save Aelric, but it was chancy at best.

He felt the moment when the battle began. Some of Tiernyn's excitement and eager anticipation vibrated along the link, transmitting itself to Donaugh. He thought he could hear the strident blare of the battle, hear the men shouting and the clash and clangor of weapon meeting weapon. He tried to urge the horse faster, but it stumbled and only barely managed to catch its balance before it fell. It stopped in the middle of the track and flatly refused to move.

Donaugh slid from its back. The horse stood with its head down, its eyes glazed with fatigue. Donaugh led it off the track into a small brake of hawthorn. He stripped off the bridle, then unstrapped the folded blanket he had been using as a saddle, shook it out, and spread it over the horse's back, fastening it around the heaving chest to keep the horse warm as the sweat dried. It had carried him as far as it could without dying under him. One of Connor's warhorses could have done no more for him. He left it dully pawing at the snow for the grass hidden beneath it, and set out across the moor at an easy run.

At dusk, his lungs burning, his throat raw from gasping cold air, he saw the faint glow that indicated campfires ahead reflected on the low-hanging clouds. At least one more low hill separated him from Tiernyn's camp. In less than a quarter of an hour, it would be too dark to see his way clearly, and the ground was precarious underfoot, with small tussocks of grass and creeping brambles beneath the snow.

Several times, he stumbled and fell. Each time, Eliade's image before him, her face solemn and grave, gave him strength to pick himself up and continue running. And in the back of his mind, another image—flame and cinder and ash . . .

He reached the top of the hill overlooking the camp in full darkness. The scene spread below him was exactly as his vision showed him. Two guards seized Aelric's arms to drag him to the center of the circle of men where Tiernyn, with Ylana as always by his side, awaited him. Aelric shook off the guards and advanced alone, his head held proudly high, his shoulders straight.

Donaugh began to run, pain stitching his chest with every step. He was less than halfway down the slope, still nearly a furlong away, when Eachern drew his sword. Aelric knelt before him in the circle, but defiantly refused to bow his head, looking straight at Tiernyn.

Donaugh shouted, but the cheering of the soldiers drowned out his voice. Desperately, he reached for his magic, drew it to himself out of the earth and air about him. A stroke of wildfire streaked out of the dark sky, blazing and hissing and sizzling, until the snow-covered hills ran red and gold with its reflected color and light, and the sky seethed and boiled above. The bolt hit the ground behind Eachern and splashed like liquid, sending a dazzling spray of cold fire dancing and leaping around Tiernyn, Eachern, and Aelric. Eachern shouted in stark terror as the sword in his hand flared to brilliance, then bent and twisted as if it were made of tallow rather than good tempered steel. He flung it to the ground and stared at it in horror.

Stumbling and staggering, Donaugh pushed his way through the wall of soldiers stunned to silence.

"No," he cried. "No, you can't kill him. For the sake of Celi, hold!"

15

The wind had picked up and now blew directly out of the west.
Donaugh left the meeting room to find the clouds gone and
the sky a blaze of stars. He stood on the ramparts above the
gatehouse at Dun Camus, his hands on the cold granite of a
low crenellation. New snow mounded deep over the fields surrounding the village and lay thick as clotted cream on the
roofs of the houses and shops.

Torchlight blazed in the village to rival the stars, lighting
the taverns and the soldiers' quarters to festive brilliance.
Snatches of music and laughter carried faintly up from the village, where the soldiers celebrated the first decisive victory
over the Saesnesi army. Donaugh recognized the wild lilt of
the Skai pipes and the cheerful, breathy whistling of the odd
little Veniani bark flutes soaring above the pluck and strum of
a harp song. If the shouts of laughter were tinged with mayhaps too much wine and ale, the men had earned their right to
revelry.

To Donaugh's right, dark and heavily guarded, stood the
tower room where Aelric and four of his companions were
housed. Light glinted off the helm of one of the guards as he
shifted his weight from one foot to another. The guard leaned
on the spear he held clutched in both hands, his face turned
warily toward Donaugh.

Faster than the wildfire Donaugh called from the sky, word
had gone through the village how the *Corrach*'s brother had
appeared in a flash of flame out of the sky to prevent the execution of the Saesnesi leader. This even though Donaugh had
pushed his way past dozens of men to gain the center of the
circle of men where Tiernyn stood. There wasn't a man among
the Companions who had not seen Donaugh work some small
magic, but this was something beyond their experience.

Donaugh had to smile to himself as he acknowledged that this was how legends were born. He himself might well become a legend, but he would be only a small part of the songs and stories about Tiernyn. Tiernyn would be a man around whom legends arose as naturally as smoke rose from a fire. Very soon now, the night would come when the legends caught fire to blaze in men's hearts as long as bards sang ballads of mystery and bravery, and men told tales around winter fires.

Through the half-open door behind him, the voices of Tiernyn's captains rose and fell in argument. Eachern ap Gemedd's voice was alone now in its vehement demand for Aelric's immediate execution, while the others reasoned with him on the wisdom of having an important hostage. Tiernyn was noticeably silent. Donaugh had left him sitting back, Ylana standing behind his chair with her hand on his shoulder, listening. Both of them watched the others, waiting for the argument to die down before Tiernyn voiced his decision.

Donaugh knew his twin well. Tiernyn's decision had been made the moment Donaugh burst through the crowd of men in the field in the wake of the bolt of wildfire. Aelric was safe for as long as his value as a hostage held to Tiernyn's advantage. With Aelric safe, Celi also lay safe from the malignant and deadly flames of Donaugh's vision.

Aelric accepted his captivity with cold, taciturn dignity. Tiernyn had allowed him to send a message to Elesan, assuring his father of his safety. Donaugh desperately wanted to add his own message to Eliade to the messenger's pouch. But Eliade would know what he wished to say even without the words written on parchment before her.

Donaugh raised his eyes and looked eastward. Somewhere beyond the low hills smudged with tracts of black-green pine and leafless oak and birch, Eliade sat at her loom in a small lodge in a forest. His need to have her with him hollowed his belly and clawed at his heart.

"I'm trying, dear heart," he whispered. "If it can be done, we will do it."

He lifted his hands from the gritty stone and stared at the twin blotches of mottled, bloodless flesh across the heels of his palms. Rubbing them together to restore the circulation, he left the battlement and went back into the meeting room.

Eachern ap Gemedd's voice rose in protest as Donaugh entered. "There isn't one prince or duke in Celi who would countenance a treaty with the Saesnesi," he said. "You know that, Tiernyn. Why allow that barbarian murderer to live? I say you must execute him now and send his head back to his cursed father on a pike. Make an example of him to the rest of them."

"Victory tempered with mercy never harmed a warrior's reputation," Connor said mildly.

"What prince or duke would allow Tiernyn to bargain for a treaty?" Eachern repeated.

"Your father might," Donaugh said. "If he thought it would end the raiding on Mercia's farmlands and villages."

"My father would," Connor said. "And Tiernyn's brother."

"A wise *Corrach* might invite the dukes and princes to a Council at Dun Camus," Tiernyn said, with a ghost of a wink at Donaugh. "It wouldn't hurt to see who supports me and who doesn't."

Ylana straightened. "If you were High King," she said, "you would merely have to bid them come, and they would have to come."

"You do, after all, carry Kingmaker," Donaugh said quietly. "There's not one man or woman in all of Celi who doesn't know the legend and what it means."

"All the Companions would support your claim to the throne of High King, Tiernyn," Connor said. "With this army at your back, who would oppose you?" He looked at Eachern, one eyebrow cocked inquisitively. "Would you support his claim, Eachern?"

"Yes," Eachern said quickly. "Of course."

"Then we invite the princes and dukes to Dun Camus," Donaugh said. "And we watch to see who comes."

"And we see what sort of bargaining Elesan will do." Tiernyn glanced at Eachern. "Surely you agree that there can be no harm in holding Aelric hostage for the time being," he said.

Eachern scowled, but he nodded reluctantly. "You are *Corrach*, Tiernyn," he said. "I will accede to your wishes."

"Then you'll carry an invitation to your father to attend a Council here at Imbolc?" Tiernyn asked.

Eachern inclined his head, smiling sardonically. "I will, my lord *Corrach*. But I won't guarantee his attendance."

"You shall use your best persuasion," Tiernyn said. He grinned. "Which is considerable."

"I shall carry the invitation to my grandfather," Gordaidh said. "And be glad to. He'll attend if I have to drag him here."

"And I'll speak with my father," Connor said. "I think he'll take little persuasion if I can convince him there will be feasting and festivities. Imbolc is a bleak time, and any diversion is welcome."

Tiernyn laughed. "Dun Camus has never hosted a feast before. We shall have to put every effort into it. Eryth, will you attend upon Duke Morand of Brigland? Your task will be the more formidable one. Morand still grumbles about supporting the army."

Eryth grinned. "I think I can persuade him, my lord," he said.

"And I, my lord?" Lluddor asked. "What do you wish me to do?"

"You'll be in charge here at Dun Camus," Tiernyn said. "Donaugh and I will carry the invitation to Keylan in Skai. We will leave the day after tomorrow."

When they had all filed out, Tiernyn rose and went to the window. He looked out over the quiet courtyard for a moment, then turned to Donaugh.

"Will this work, Donaugh?" he asked quietly.

"Yes," Donaugh said. "Kingmaker will proclaim you at Imbolc. You will be High King of Celi before Vernal Equinox."

"High King . . ." Tiernyn's voice trailed off. He turned back to the window. "But only if the princes and dukes support me."

"And why wouldn't they?" Ylana asked. "Look how much you've done in the last two years. You've cut the Saesnesi raids to a small fraction of what they were. And you've defeated their army."

"Not yet," Donaugh said quietly. "We haven't defeated them yet. And there are more enemies out there than just the Saesnesi."

"The Maedun?" Tiernyn asked.

"Aye. The Maedun." Donaugh shivered as he remembered his vision. "Be very sure they're coming. We have so little time left. So very little time . . ."

Snow lay deep in the pass through the Spine of Celi. Struggling through drifts belly high to the horses slowed progress to a crawl. It took a full fortnight to reach the crossroads midway down the western slopes of the Spine, where Connor and his troop of soldiers parted company with Tiernyn and Donaugh to make his way to Wenydd. The day before the Midwinter Feast, Tiernyn led his soldiers up the road leading to the gates of Dun Eidon.

Keylan appeared at the head of the broad steps leading to the doors of the Great Hall, timing his arrival just as Tiernyn dismounted and casually tossed the reins of his horse to a servant. Looking up at his eldest brother, Donaugh noticed subtle changes in the two and a half years since he had seen Keylan. The Prince of Skai had not aged, but his face appeared more mature, the planes and hollows firmed and refined by the burden of responsibility. There was little of welcome or joy of reunion in his brown eyes and neutral expression.

Beside him, nearly as tall as he, Alys carried a large, ornate goblet which steamed gently in the cold air. Her raven-wing hair and blue eyes made a pleasing contrast to Keylan's brown eyes and red-gold hair. As Tiernyn and Donaugh mounted the steps, she stepped forward and dropped into a deep, graceful curtsey.

"The guest cup, my lords," she said, offering the cup to Tiernyn.

Tiernyn took the cup and thanked her. He drank deeply, then passed the cup to Donaugh. The hot mulled wine spread a welcome warmth through Donaugh's belly. He handed the cup back to Alys and smiled his thanks. Tiernyn stepped forward to greet Keylan.

"We have come home, my lord Prince," he said.

"So I see," Keylan replied. He looked through the courtyard gates at the men setting up camp near the practice field. "And you've come home with an army at your back."

Tiernyn smiled thinly. "Only a small portion of it," he said. "The rest are still at Dun Camus to keep the Saesnesi safely east of the River Lachlan. The Saesnesi have cause to respect that army."

"So I've heard." Keylan gestured toward the Great Hall. "Be welcome here," he said. "A meal is being prepared, and your rooms are ready for you."

Tiernyn paced the room restlessly, the hem of his houserobe swirling about his ankles. Keylan watched him, his face carefully neutral and impassive, and Donaugh watched Keylan. Keylan held his silence, waiting for Tiernyn to speak. Despite Keylan's outward calm, Donaugh noted the signs of tension in him—a knot of clenched muscle at the corner of his jaw, a constant tightening and relaxing of his fingers on the arms of his chair. He showed all the symptoms of a man wary and distrustful of his guests.

Apprehension stirred in Donaugh's belly. Was Lluddor's

desertion still gnawing at Keylan's spirit? Had Keylan gained enough sense of political expediency to put his personal feelings aside when it came to the good of Celi? Donaugh sat quietly in his chair, outwardly relaxed, but watchful and alert.

Tiernyn stopped pacing and turned to face his older brother. "You've read the message I brought with me," he said.

Keylan inclined his head in agreement, but said nothing.

"I know for many years there's been no love lost between the two of us," Tiernyn said. "I came to you in hopes that you would support me in this. You are Prince of Skai, and all Celi knows you as a man of strength and integrity."

Keylan glanced at Donaugh, then back to Tiernyn. "Arranging a truce with the Saesnesi in the Saesnesi Shore will be no mean task," he said. "You have generations of bitterness, anger, and hatred to overcome."

"I also have a hostage to ensure Elesan's cooperation," Tiernyn said. "And I have Elesan's word that he will bargain in good faith so long as Aelric remains unharmed. With your support and the support of Ryvern of Wenydd, Blais and Gemedd will follow. The four of you can persuade Morand of Brigland. But first, I must have your support."

Keylan studied Tiernyn, his face giving away nothing of what he was thinking. Finally, he nodded. "You have it," he said. "What else?"

"Your support for my claim to a throne."

Keylan sat straighter, his eyes narrowed. Tiernyn's eyes blazed with fierce intensity as they met Keylan's. The air between them seemed to stretch taut with tension, almost visible to Donaugh.

"A throne?" Keylan repeated flatly.

Tiernyn grinned suddenly. The smile transformed his face and he looked for a moment like a boy up to mischief. "Not the throne of Skai," he said. "Nor the throne of any other province." He became serious again. "You are Prince of Skai, Keylan, and you must remain so if we are to succeed."

"Then which throne are you claiming?"

Donaugh stirred in his chair and spoke for the first time. "Tiernyn will be High King of all Celi," he said quietly.

Keylan stared at him. "High King? He aspires to be High King?"

"No," Donaugh said. "He *will* be High King."

"They tell strange stories about your power, Donaugh," Keylan said. "Have you Seen this?"

"I have," Donaugh said. "He carries Kingmaker. You know what that means as well as he and I do. No matter what you answer now, Tiernyn will be High King of Celi, and he will be proclaimed so at Imbolc. Your support will only make it easier for him to deal with the Saesnesi as High King and not as merely *Corrach*."

"Celi has never had a High King . . ." Keylan's voice trailed off thoughtfully.

Donaugh smiled. "Then perhaps it's overdue. He can put an end to the Saesnesi raiding the rest of Celi."

Tiernyn began pacing again. "Make no mistake, Keylan," he said, his eyes blazing with fervor. "To accomplish this end, I will fight you and every other prince and duke in Celi. I would never take your throne, but I will make you swear fealty to me under threat of the sword if that's what it takes to bring peace to Celi and stop the Saesnesi from turning her into a slag heap of ashes and cinder."

"If you support us," Donaugh said, "then I believe Wenydd will follow. Blais of Dorian has already tentatively indicated he would support us. If you don't support us now, you should be aware that the army out there is well trained and eager, and they have but two loyalties. The first is to Tiernyn—and to me. The second is to Celi."

Keylan stared at him coldly. "Do you threaten me, Donaugh?"

"No. I merely inform you of the situation as it is."

Tiernyn stopped his restless pacing and threw himself into a chair. "In time the loyalty of the army will change," he said.

"In time, their first loyalty will be to a unified Celi, as it should be. But for now, a soldier can't be loyal to what is yet only a dream."

"Armies follow men," Keylan said, smiling sardonically. "We have all heard how well your army follows you, Tiernyn."

"You needn't give your answer now," Tiernyn said. "I'll give you all the time you need to think on it."

"You've set yourself an immense task," Keylan said. "I have difficulty believing that all the notoriously stubborn men of Celi could give loyalty to one man."

With no trace of conceit, Tiernyn said simply, "I am that man, Keylan." He reached up to touch the hilt of the sword behind his left shoulder. "Kingmaker decides, not I."

Keylan studied him carefully. Finally, he nodded. "I believe you might be," he said quietly. "Yes, I truly believe you might be."

"Father knew this when he took us to the Dance of Nemeara," Tiernyn said. He glanced at Donaugh. "Or he hoped it would be this way."

"For Celi, I will support you," Keylan said. "And for Father." He stood and stepped forward, his hand out. "I'm with you, then. Even if just for the amusement of watching you beat every other prince and duke on this island into submission, I'm with you."

Donaugh awoke before dawn on Midwinter morning. He dressed in the dark and slipped out of the palace, avoiding sleepy servants just beginning to stir in preparation for the day of feasting and celebration. Garlands of holly and cedar spilled down the walls of the Great Hall, casting faint shadows along the wall hangings and the polished tile of the floor. The Yule Log, gaily decorated with multicolored ribbons, sprigs of deep green and crimson holly, and twined with ivy and mistletoe, lay in the courtyard, ready to be dragged in amid music and laughter to signal the beginning of the celebration to welcome the waxing of the sun.

A skiff of new snow covered the track leading toward the shrine on the hill above the palace, glittering like a field of diamonds in the moonlight. Two sets of footprints marred the immaculate surface, close together, showing as shadowed depressions against the hard sparkle of the snow. Donaugh smiled to himself as he followed the tracks. No one had ever beaten Lameth and Shena to the shrine on the morning of a Feast Day.

Just below the shrine, the track divided. Donaugh took the path to the right, which led up the side of the mountain behind the shrine. Trees closed in around the narrow track. The air smelled of sea and the faint tang of cut cedar. Delicate traceries of bare boughs, oak, birch, and rowan, gleamed against the dark mass of pine and cedar. An owl glided by overhead with a muted rush of wings, and the snow squeaked and snapped crisply beneath Donaugh's boots. His breath came in long, white plumes that the gentle breeze frayed and shredded in seconds.

Well above the shrine, he rounded an outcropping of rock and the forest opened out into a wide clearing set in a hollow in the shoulder of the mountain. The seven standing stones of the Dance bulked tall and massive against the pristine clarity of the new snow. Pulling his cloak closer around him, Donaugh entered the circle. The sense of hushed stillness became more intense. He made obeisances to each of the stones in turn, then went to one knee before the seventh stone, head bowed.

He waited.

Cold seeped through the fabric of his breeks into his knee, then crept up his leg to chill his body. Still he waited. Nothing moved except the tattered mist of his breath on the breeze. No sound broke the silence. If the gods and goddesses were present, they were paying him no attention.

He raised his head and looked up at the *darlai* stone before him. It remained just a standing stone, carved by the hand of man, raised by music and magic, to represent the Mother of All. Her essence was not in it now.

The sky behind the shoulder of the mountain began to brighten with approaching dawn. Black leached out to midnight blue tinged with the barest hint of gold, and the stars faded, one by one, as the faint color spread. Donaugh climbed to his feet and brushed the snow from the knee of his breeks.

Someone said his name softly. Startled, Donaugh turned.

She stood between two of the stones, her face lit with laughter, wearing only the pale green gown she had worn when she said good-bye to him in the courtyard of Elesan's forest lodge. Her hair spilled over her shoulders, unmoving in the gentle wind. He held out his hand. Her feet left no imprint on the gleaming surface of the snow as she crossed the circle to him. The vague shape of the stones and the forest was faintly discernible through her body, but when she took his hand, her touch was warm and firm.

"I cannot stay long, beloved," she said. "I heard you calling me, so I came."

"Your brother is safe," he said. "And the princes and dukes will meet with your father to discuss a treaty. We have a good start."

She smiled, but said nothing.

"Eliade, you must come to me often. Once this treaty is in place, we will find a place where we can be together always."

"We will always be together, beloved," she said. "You know that."

He shook his head. "I mean now," he said. "I cannot bear the thought of being apart from you in this life, or any other."

She reached up to touch his face, drawing her finger down the line of his cheek to his jaw. Then she dropped her hand and held it to her belly. "Once this treaty is in place, our son will have a safe home to grow up in," she said. She stepped back from him and smiled.

"Our son? You're with child?"

"Your first son will be born between Lammas and Autumnal Equinox," she said. "A good time for a son to be born."

Soaring joy raced through him, and he laughed aloud. "A son," he said aloud, marveling at the wonder of the words. "We'll raise him together, beloved. When this war is settled . . ."

Her outline shimmered and began to waver. He tried to reach out to her, but his hands passed through her body as they might through a column of smoke. A moment later, he was alone in the center of the Dance. He turned again to face the *darlai* stone.

"Three sons for you, Donaugh Secondborn . . . " The *darlai's* words echoed faintly in his mind.

Donaugh made a deep obeisance to the stone, then turned and left the circle.

16

"We should have set the date for Beltane," Tiernyn *said as he* stood by the window of his workroom, looking out over the snowbound village. Twilight had finally emptied the practice fields and stilled the smoke rising from the forges. "It's too cold for traveling. No one will come."

A constant east wind scoured the moors, bringing with it some of the worst winter weather Donaugh could remember. The river had frozen from bank to bank, and the snow drifted deep against the east wall of Dun Camus. Hearthfires blazed day and night but did little to dispel the savage bite of the cold that crept into dwellings through every crack and gap. Frost grew thick on glazed windows, etching fantastic patterns along the glass.

Donaugh looked up from the worktable where he had been studying the map of the continent pinned to the wall behind the table. "Beltane is too late," he said. "Continue with the preparations. They will come."

Tiernyn glanced over his shoulder at Donaugh. "You're very certain," he said sourly.

Donaugh allowed a faint smile to touch his mouth. "Aye," he said. "As certain as I can be, at any rate."

"The Sight tells you?"

Donaugh shrugged. "Perhaps," he said. "Or perhaps Kingmaker himself tells me."

Tiernyn looked at the wall opposite the worktable. Kingmaker hung in its scabbard next to Tiernyn's and Donaugh's cloaks. In the wavering candlelight, the jewel in the pommel sent out occasional sparks that flashed against the stone. "The sword speaks to you?" Tiernyn asked.

Donaugh didn't bother to look at the sword. Its voice whispered softly in the back of his mind, always there to remind him of his purpose. "He speaks to me," he said.

Tiernyn turned and regarded his twin gravely. "Sometimes, Donaugh," he said slowly, "sometimes, now, you begin to frighten me. What happened to you while you were taken by the Saesnesi that increased your magic so much? You've changed, somehow."

Donaugh looked up, smiling. "Have I?"

"You know you have. You have power that I thought was only a thing of bards' tales, or legends men tell from the time before the Borlani tried to destroy all the magic in the world except their own."

"The Borlani are gone and their empire broken into its component countries again," Donaugh said. "Yet the magic lives on. It always will. And it will always be stronger in some men than in others."

"But so much power . . ." Tiernyn shook his head and turned back to the window. "Sometimes I wonder that one man can have so much power."

"My power works for you. It always has. You should be content with that."

"But still . . . "

"Tiernyn, your name will live on in legend and song when my name is but a whisper on the wind."

"And yet, it will be you who set me on a throne and placed a crown on my head," Tiernyn said quietly.

Donaugh laughed softly and shook his head. "No," he said. "It will be the people of Celi who do that. Not I."

"If, indeed, it happens."

"It will."

Tiernyn's eyebrows drew together above his eyes in a troubled frown. "Then why me?" he asked. "If you have such power, why not a crown and a throne for you instead?"

Donaugh smiled. "Because Kingmaker declared you the day we were born," he said. "In my hand, the sword wouldn't sing as he does for you. Nor would he fight fiercely for Celi as he does in your hand." He rose and went to the door, then paused, his hand on the latch. "You will see. At Imbolc, before all the princes and dukes of Celi, and before your army, Kingmaker will declare you again."

Tiernyn shivered visibly. "When you speak like that, your eyes go all blurred and black and your voice sounds as if it comes from somewhere beyond you," he said. "Sometimes, Donaugh, I feel as if I hardly know you anymore."

One of Donaugh's eyebrows twitched in a quizzical gesture. "Sometimes," he said slowly, "I hardly know myself. Good night, Tiernyn."

The weather broke a fortnight before Imbolc. A warm wind from the southwest began blowing across the downs just after midnight. By midmorning, the packed snow on the practice field and in the courtyard had turned to slush, then to mud. Huge floes of broken ice swirled in the river, and the water lapped at the rocks only an armlength below the foot of the great walls of Dun Camus as melting snow filled the rivercourse to the brim. The rays of the sun striking flesh or rock carried a faint but tangible warmth. Water dripped and splashed everywhere as icicles melted, and Dun Camus sang with the gurgle of running water. Within six days, only tired patches of grainy snow were left in areas of deep and abiding shade. Frost-killed grass lay brown and sodden in the practice field, sticky with churned mud.

The unseasonably warm weather showed no signs of changing when, three days before Imbolc, Blais of Dorian, his wife beside him, rode up the track leading to Dun Camus, with twenty of his thanes and their wives, and a troop of a hundred men behind him. With due ceremony, Tiernyn met Blais in the courtyard at the head of the steps leading to the Great Hall. Ylana offered the guest cup, first to Blais, then to each of his thanes in turn, while Tiernyn greeted the wives with small gifts.

When the cup had at last returned to Ylana, she curtsied

deeply to Blais. "You are most welcome here, my lord Duke," she said. "Our home is yours."

The old Duke, his hair and beard gleaming silver in the sunlight, bowed over Ylana's hand. "My grandson raves of your beauty, my lady," he said. "I felt I had to come to see for myself." He smiled at her. "And I see that he was not exaggerating."

Gemedd of Mercia and his wife arrived the next morning, accompanied by nearly thirty thanes, their wives, and a troop of eighty soldiers. Tiernyn and Ylana had no sooner offered them welcome than Morand of Brigland clattered into the courtyard with his retinue.

From the battlement outside his chambers, Donaugh watched the western downs and the track leading from the mountains. At sundown, there was still no sign of Keylan or Duke Ryvern.

Late in the afternoon of Imbolc Eve, Keylan, with Alys as always by his side, and Ryvern arrived together, their combined retinues filling the courtyard to overflowing. Donaugh left his chambers and descended to the Great Hall to greet his brother.

As the sun set, all the fires in the palace and in the village were left to die until there was nothing left but cold ashes in all the hearths. At midnight, all the men and women of Dun Camus met in the Great Hall, nobility and servant alike dressed in robes of coarse, gray homespun. The women carried large bowls made of unglazed earthenware, and the men carried small ash shovels and whisk brooms made from the last harvest's straw.

The priest and priestess from the shrine in the village, bound together as always to symbolize the male/female nature of the Duality, mounted the dais at the head of the hall and began to intone a prayer. As they finished, silence fell over the Great Hall. The priest and priestess raised their arms and smiled.

"Let the cleansing and renewal begin," they said.

In pairs, the men and women went to all the hearths in the palace. Donaugh found himself partnered with a young serving girl who smiled nervously and shyly as he swept the ashes from one of the cooking hearths in the kitchen and filled her bowl with the powdery ash.

Donaugh had always loved the quiet ritual of New Fire at Imbolc. While he drew water and scrubbed the hearth until it gleamed, he listened to the women singing as they walked out into the night with their bowls of ash to spread them along the riverbank. Their voices, high and clear, chimed in the night, filling it sweetly with music. He was reminded of Skai and how his mother's voice led the singing, while his father cheerfully scrubbed the hearths in the baking ovens, the most difficult to clean.

When Donaugh's hearth was clean, he returned to the Great Hall. Gradually it filled again as the men finished their cleansing tasks and the women returned from the river, their bowls empty now. The priest and priestess slowly circled the room, extinguishing the candles one by one as they went. As the last candle went out and darkness descended with a rush, an expectant hush fell over the room.

In the stillness, the priest's and priestess's voices seemed loud. "Let now the doors be thrown wide to welcome in any wandering gods of the night."

Donaugh carefully made his way through the crowd to the door of the Great Hall, then down the stairs to the palace gates. Tiernyn joined him, and they opened the massive gates wide. No lights at all showed in the village. Overhead, the moon and stars gave a faint illumination to the world.

People streamed out into the night, gathering the wood that had been stacked in readiness for the new fires. Laughter rang out, and snatches of song.

Donaugh carried new wood to the kitchen and carefully laid a new fire on the hearth he had scrubbed, then returned to the Great Hall. The darkness made it difficult to see. Muffled giggles and whispering made it clear that some were taking full advantage of the dark. Quiet descended again as the priest and priestess called for attention.

"Beodun, Father of Fires, hear us!" they cried from their place on the dais.

"Hear us, Father of Fires," Donaugh responded with the crowd.

"Father of Fires, bless this house with your New Fire, and bless the people herein. As the hearths are cleansed and made ready for your needfire, called from the heavens themselves, so cleanse the hearts and spirits of those gathered here. All praise to you, Beodun, Father of Fires."

"All praise to you, Father of Fires."

A rustle of movement shimmered through the Great Hall. Donaugh reached under his robe to bring out the special candle, made of beeswax from a wild hive. On the dais, the priest and priestess had already raised their candle.

"Send us your fire, Beodun," the priest and priestess cried in practiced unison.

Out of the dark came a bright arrow, a hissing lance of flame. The wick of the candle the priest and priestess held sputtered, then flared up brightly, casting flickering shadows across their faces, turning their gray robe red with reflected fire.

"Children of Beodun, share his gift with us," they said.

One after the other in a long file, the men and women in the hall stepped forward and touched their candles to the flame of the candle the priest and priestess held, until the Great Hall was ablaze with light. Ylana went to the hearth beside the dais and knelt, slowly reaching out with her candle to light the wood newly laid there. The flame caught immediately, a good omen, and a ripple of satisfaction shimmered around the room. The kindling crackled and popped, then smoke curled up and was swept up into the chimney.

New Fire had come to Dun Camus. The god's gift was accepted with gratitude.

Donaugh went to the kitchen to light the fire he had made. Music sounded in the Great Hall, then filled the whole house. Women laughed as the men formed and baked the flatcakes. The women brought the honey they had gathered from the wild hives during the summer for just this purpose. The men spread the cakes with honey and handed them around amid much good-natured laughter and bantering. Donaugh remembered his father teaching him how to form the cakes. His first had never been good and broke as he tried to lift them from the baking stones before the fire. He was gratified in a small way that the cakes he made now didn't break.

Dancing had already begun in the Great Hall when Donaugh returned. Keylan's bright red-gold hair stood out sharply among the dark gold and black hair in the Hall as he danced with Alys. Tiernyn and Ylana stood by the dais, greeting the thanes who had come with Keylan. Donaugh made his way across the crowded floor to stand beside them.

Keylan led Alys through the throng to stand before Tiernyn.

"It's Imbolc," Keylan said to Tiernyn. "As we cleanse everything for the New Fire, we should cleanse ourselves of all past bitterness. My support of you will be wholehearted in this, Tiernyn."

Tiernyn reached for Keylan's hand. "Thank you," he said simply.

The revelry continued until the sun rose, a confirmation of Beodun's gift of New Fire. At dawn, the celebrants retired to bed to sleep until midday, when the feasting would begin.

Toward evening, Donaugh began to feel a light, effervescent quivering in his chest. The sensation grew stronger as the sun set and the stars appeared in the clear sky. He was achingly aware of every thread of power that flowed in the air around him, through the ground beneath his feet. The air seemed alive with magic, and he was surprised that no one else seemed to notice how it fizzed and sparked around Dun Camus. It filled him as wine fills a goblet, until he could no longer stand being confined within walls.

The air outside was colder, crisp and clear. Overhead the stars burned fiercely against the black velvet of the sky. Donaugh made his way through the wide-flung gates of Dun Camus to the edge of the practice field. Around him, skeins of music and laughter from the main house and from the village wove through the glittering web of magic, intensifying the light, airy sensation in his body. He walked to a small rise and stood there, still as a stone, while the night flowed like water around him.

Rapt and captivated, Donaugh stared upward. He felt his soul break free of his body to run with the stars. Around him, the crystalline air chimed delicately, ethereal as a harp note heard across the green and misty distance of a Skai glen. The song of the sword resonated softly in his heart and spirit, growing in power and filling him with a sense of anticipation, buoyant and dazzling as a bubble in a wineglass.

The sword touched his mind imperatively, forcefully. Around him, the sounds of festivity faded until he stood in a silent bubble of air. The urgency Donaugh felt thrummed and vibrated along the link connecting him with Tiernyn.

He was barely conscious of people coming out into the night to fill the practice field. His magic tingled and throbbed through his body, leaving him breathless. When Tiernyn and Ylana came to stand beside him, he didn't move, watching the stars wheel slowly across the sky.

The stars blurred before Donaugh's eyes. He was barely conscious of the others as he looked up into the western sky. He hardly noticed the silence spread gradually throughout the practice field as, one after another, soldiers stopped their celebration to watch him, their attention riveted by his utter stillness. One by one, the pipes and flutes, the harps and gitterns, trailed off into silence as the soldiers moved forward to gather in a loose semicircle before Donaugh.

Keylan stepped forward to stand at Tiernyn's right shoulder, Ryvern of Wenydd beside him. Gemedd of Mercia stood with Blais of Dorian to Ryvern's right, Morand of Brigland beside Blais. Tiernyn's captains, Connor of Wenydd, Gordaidh of Dorian, Eachern of Mercia, Luddor ap Vershad, and Eryth ap Morfyn, arranged themselves behind Tiernyn. No one spoke.

As surely and insistently as a beckoning lover, the sword sang in Donaugh's soul. Even Tiernyn felt it because he stirred restlessly.

"What is it?" he asked quietly.

"It is now, Tiernyn," Donaugh said quietly. He kept his gaze on the stars. "Draw the sword. Draw Kingmaker. It is *now!*"

Tiernyn didn't question the command. Wordlessly, he drew the sword and glanced at Donaugh. As Kingmaker cleared the scabbard on Tiernyn's back, the blade flashed and flared to brilliance, and Donaugh raised his arms.

The shooting star burst into existence low on the western horizon, streaking across the sky from north to south. Behind it, a fiery trail of red and orange and yellow writhed and twisted, gossamer clouds in a silent wind. Kingmaker's polished blade caught the reflection of the Kingstar, spilling it around Tiernyn in a scintillating aura of gold and red, bathing him in light and color.

The star vanished. The radiance twisting around Tiernyn lingered for an instant, then faded. The darkness seemed more complete without the Kingstar. No sound broke the hush that hung heavy over Dun Camus. For several moments, not one man moved. Even the white, misty plumes of breath had stilled.

Then Keylan stepped forward resolutely. He dropped to one knee in the churned and muddy slush and drew his sword. Holding it across the palms of both hands, he offered it to Tiernyn. "I offer my sword and my life in service, my liege," he said quietly. "Truly, you have been proclaimed High King of all Celi."

He had no sooner finished speaking than Ryvern went to his knee beside him, his own sword offered in service and loyalty. "I, too," he said. "My life, my sword and my service, I offer to you as my King, and as High King of Celi."

Blais of Dorian was next to his knee, then Gemedd of Mercia. Morand of Brigland hesitated, but he, too, pledged fealty. Donaugh went to his own knee in the frost gray grass before Tiernyn.

"Kingmaker has declared you, my liege," he said quietly. "Will you accept the crown of Celi, and hold safe the island from all threats?"

Tiernyn's tongue came out to moisten his lips. His eyes wide and startled, he lowered the sword and stared at it in awe. The aura of color flashed and flared around the blade, and its song filled the night.

"Will you accept the crown?" Donaugh asked again.

Tiernyn nodded. He had to clear his throat before he could speak. "I will," he whispered. Then he raised the sword. "I will accept," he shouted. "For Celi, I will accept!"

Like a great wave moving along the shore, the ranks of soldiers fell to their knees. Raggedly at first, then gaining momentum and rhythm, the chant rose in the sparking cold of the night. "*The King! The King! The King!*"

Ylana, her face pale in the dim starlight, glanced at Donaugh. Her lips parted as if she would speak, but she remained silent. Donaugh studied her carefully. Three years of guarding Tiernyn's left in battle had changed her. She was no longer the impetuous, willful girl who had counseled Lluddor to desert Keylan. Donaugh stepped closer to her and touched her arm.

"He is King." His voice was low but carried over the tumult of the chanting soldiers. "And you, Ylana, shall be Queen, and your son King after him. Are you ready to accept a responsibility that will often be a burden?"

Her breath caught in her throat and she stared at him, her eyes wide. Again, her lips parted, but she said nothing. Instead, she nodded wordlessly, then moved closer to Tiernyn's left shoulder, head held proudly high.

17

Three days after Imbolc, the weather turned colder. Morning saw the grass gray with frost. Hoarfrost furred the bare tree branches, etching brilliantly white traceries against the hard blue of the sky. Donaugh left Dun Camus immediately after the morning meal, riding east toward the Saesnesi Shore. With him rode Connor of Wenydd and one of the Saesnesi prisoners, Devlyn Cynricson, who was cousin to Aelric and nephew to Elesan. Devlyn carried a message to Elesan in his saddle pack, sworn by Aelric to deliver it safely.

Connor led three of his specially bred warhorses, all of them laden with gifts for Elesan—saddles for the horses, jewels, furs, costly fabric. Donaugh hoped Elesan would accept them as they were meant—as gifts from a leader to a leader. He had worked hard to convince Tiernyn he must treat Elesan with the same courtesy and dignity he treated the other princes and dukes of Celi. Hostage or no hostage, Elesan would not allow himself to be condescended to. Nor would his pride allow him to accept gifts that he considered worth less than his position warranted.

Donaugh kept the pace easy to allow Devlyn to keep up. The Saesnesi was not used to riding with a saddle, nor was he accustomed to a horse as large as the warhorse Donaugh had given him. He rode in wary silence, casting hostile glances at Donaugh and Connor every so often, but he said nothing. His mistrust of the Celae hung around him like a haze, and Donaugh chose to ignore it. He rode in silence with his own thoughts.

At sunset, Donaugh called a halt only a league or two from the River Lachlan, which marked the boundary between Mercia and the Saesnesi Shore. He pitched the tent while Connor gathered wood and lit a fire. The wood was wet and made a sullen fire, barely sufficient to heat water for tea to drink with their meal of bread, cheese, and cold meat.

As they prepared to retire for the night, Donaugh called up a simple heat spell around the tent. Devlyn's eyes widened in shock as he entered the warmth of the tent. He withdrew into a far corner of the tent and hunched himself into his blanket, looking askance at Donaugh. With some amusement, Donaugh saw the fingers of Devlyn's right hand making the sign against evil.

In the morning, Devlyn continued alone. As he rode away from the camp, he glanced back over his shoulder once, his face carefully impassive. Then he put his heels to the horse's sides and set off eastward at a brisk walk, leading the three horses laden with gifts.

Connor watched him until horse and rider disappeared behind a low hill. He turned back to Donaugh, who sat before the fire waiting for the water to boil.

"Well, he's gone," he said. "That's probably the last we'll ever see of him."

Donaugh didn't look up. "He'll return," he said.

"And bring Elesan with him?" Connor's skepticism sounded plainly in his voice.

"Aye, he will," Donaugh said. "He gave his word."

Connor snorted derisively. "The word of a Saesnesi," he said.

Donaugh poured the water over the tea leaves and set the pot aside to steep. "Devlyn might not consider himself bound by an oath to you, or me, or even to Tiernyn," he said. "But he swore an oath to Aelric. A Saesnesi's oath to a kinsman is doubly binding and his oath to the Aethling, the Celwalda's son, is sacrosanct. He'll return, and he'll return with Elesan."

"You sound very sure."

Donaugh poured two cups of tea and offered one to Connor. Connor brushed the snow off a fallen log and sat, accepting the hot tea.

"We hold Aelric hostage," Donaugh said. "Elesan holds him as sacred as your father would hold you, were the situation reversed. Or my father would hold me, or Tiernyn, or any of his children."

Connor cradled the cup in both hands, frowning down into the fragrant tea as if he might read the future there. "It seems strange to think of a peace treaty with the Saesnesi."

"It won't stop the raids from the Saesnesi on the continent," Donaugh said. "But it will give them no safe landing in Celi." He looked across the low hills to the east, a vision of Eliade's face before him. "And it might save us fighting a two-front battle when the Maedun come."

"Are you so sure the Maedun will come to Celi?" Connor asked. "Across the Cold Sea? Maedun is a landlocked country. They have no ships, no seamen . . . "

Donaugh laughed without humor. "They've taken Falinor and Laringras. They will take Isgard and Saesnes. All of those countries are seafaring countries. Do you think the Maedun will find no ships or sailors who are willing to transport them across the Cold Sea?" He sipped at the tea, welcoming its warmth in his belly. "Make no mistake, Connor. The Maedun are coming. Perhaps not this year, or next. Perhaps not for ten years, or even longer. But they *are* coming. And unless we're prepared, they will grind us into ash and cinder under their feet. And whether we meet them, or our sons meet them, every man in Celi, including the Saesnesi, has to present them with a united front. Otherwise, there will be no more Celi—only a burnt and wasted island and none to remember what its name was, or to remember its glory and beauty."

Connor looked up and bit his lip. "Do you think it will be our sons who meet the Maedun?" he asked.

"No," Donaugh said. "It will be us." He got to his feet and looked again to the east. "It will be us," he repeated. "And the gods and goddesses willing, the Saesnesi under Elesan will meet them with us."

"If Elesan comes now."

"If he comes," Donaugh agreed. "If we can't arrange a treaty, then he may be attacking our rear while we're fighting a Maedun invasion. And Celi will go down into darkness with the rest of the continent."

Donaugh awoke suddenly, his heart hammering, his breath rasping painfully in his throat. Every sense cracklingly alert, his nerves stretched like harp wires, he listened intensely for a clue to the danger that had invaded his dreams. But no sound disturbed the stillness of the chill predawn silence.

He reached for his sword, then stayed his hand, remembering his dream.

. . . Blood pouring in thick, viscous streams down the walls of Dun Camus . . .

. . . Blood puddling at his feet as he stood helplessly frozen before the tight-fastened gates . . .

. . . And, far on the horizon to the east, the rising flames racing inexorably closer, consuming all in their path, leaving behind a wasteland of ash and cinder . . .

But whose blood had he seen?

Restlessly, he flung aside his blanket and got to his feet. The interior of the small tent was comfortably warm, but bitter cold met him as he stepped out into the faint, pearly light of dawn. He shivered and pulled his cloak around him, then bent to build up the fire.

He looked to the east and shivered again, but the fire on the horizon was only the sun rising behind a curtain of luminescent white cloud. Turning his back to the brightness, he busied himself heating the frozen slush of tea in the kettle. When it began to bubble, he poured himself a cup and cupped both hands around it, hunched forward, letting the steam curl up into his face.

Was the dream a Seeing? A warning?

But it hadn't the cohesiveness of a Seeing. It was only a jumble of vividly harsh images, unlike his vision of the battle in the marshy glen, or the execution of Aelric. Those were bright in their stark reality, living scenes moving before him as graphically distinct as if he were in their midst.

He wanted to dismiss the dreams as merely anxiety, or worry. Or something. If they were a warning, surely he would have been given more detail.

"Only a dream," he muttered into the steaming tea. "Just a dream, and nothing else . . . "

But he couldn't rid himself of the cold twist of dread wrapping his heart.

At midmorning, Elesan rode up to the small camp where Donaugh and Connor waited. He rode one of the warhorses Tiernyn had sent, signifying his acceptance of the gifts. A good sign, Donaugh thought. He was accompanied by a small force of seven men, Devlyn among them, coldly aloof, all of them richly dressed and displaying wrist- and armbands of intricately wrought gold. They wore short swords and double-bladed axes in leather scabbards on their belts, and their metal helms gleamed dully in the pale winter light beneath lowering clouds.

Donaugh rose from his place by the campfire to greet them. He searched Elesan's face, then the faces of his escort. Cold, ice blue eyes stared back at him. He saw nothing there but fierce pride and wary alertness. Instead of lessening his apprehension, the lack of expression on the Saesnesi faces intensified it. Could one of them be planning treachery and murder?

Elesan did not dismount. He sat his horse, his face impassive as he stared down at Donaugh.

"I have come," he said. "As I promised you."

"My brother is expecting you, my lord Elesan," Donaugh said, "together with his Council of the Princes and Dukes of Celi. He sent me and my companion, Connor ap Ryvern of Wenydd, to escort you safely to Dun Camus, where your son awaits you. There is to be feasting in your honor."

They made a strange procession as they cantered west toward Dun Camus. Elesan rode with Donaugh to his left and Connor to his right, looking at neither, but keeping his gaze straight ahead. He offered no conversation.

Donaugh hardly noticed the strained silence. He leaned forward tensely in his saddle, anticipating the first glimpse of Dun Camus, dreading it. Flashes of the dream blinked before him.

. . . Blood . . .

The sun rode low in the west when they topped the small rise half a league from Dun Camus. Smoke from the village chimneys rose straight up in the still air. No one moved among the houses; the streets were deserted as families and soldiers took their evening meal. The wide track leading up to the main gates of the stronghold lay clear and straight before them.

No blood stained the walls. The pale stone stood clean and bare. Donaugh let out his breath in a long, slow sigh. A dream, he thought. Only a dream born of anxiety . . .

He drew his horse to a walk as they approached the gates. They were less than fifty paces away when the gates opened wide to admit them.

Up on the walls, someone shouted, hurling a string of curses down on the approaching Saesnesi. Donaugh's head snapped up in shock. The figure of a man stood outlined against the darkening sky, his arms swinging as he flung something over the sill of the embrasure between two tall merlons. The man disappeared as the object flew down to land with a wet thud on the frozen mud of the track. It rolled, bouncing in the ruts, and came to rest at the feet of Donaugh's horse.

The horse snorted, startled, and reared, twisting as it plunged sideways on the precarious footing of the track. For a moment, Donaugh was too busy controlling the frightened horse to look at what had startled it.

"Sweet Piety," Connor said softly, his voice filled with dismayed awe. At the same moment, Elesan cried out in grief and horror.

All the dread and apprehension that had been simmering in Donaugh's chest since sunrise burst in a blinding flash of knowledge. Appalled, he turned and stared into the dead eyes of the head that lay before him on the track. Blood matted the fair hair; the slack jaw hung loose in the blank, expressionless face. There was no doubt that it was Aelric.

Elesan threw up his hand in an imperious gesture. The seven men of his escort, already drawing their swords, froze motionless but did not relax their grips on the hilts of their swords. Elesan dismounted and walked stiffly to the head of his son. Very slowly, he removed his cloak, then knelt in the frozen mud to wrap the cloak around the head. He straightened up, the head held cradled against his chest like a sleeping child, and turned to Donaugh.

"Is this how a Celae keeps his word?" he asked softly.

Donaugh's head swam with visions of blood dripping down the pristine walls of Dun Camus. His throat dry, his heart hammering against his ribs, he shook his head. "Elesan, I swear to you—"

Elesan's mouth drew down into a contemptuous line. "Do not perjure yourself before your gods, Enchanter," he said. "Your soul is already in mortal danger." He turned away. One of the Saesnesi nobles bent to take the cloak-wrapped head from him while he mounted his horse. He reached again for the bundle, and held it securely before him on the saddle. "This treachery means there can be no peace between our people now."

He wheeled his horse and set heels to its flanks. Followed by his seven companions, he galloped back along the track to the east. In moments, the gathering dark swallowed them up, and they were gone.

The tower staircase wound sharply to the right. Donaugh took the steps two at a time, the sound of his boots echoing hollowly around him. He was barely conscious of the sound of

Tiernyn's and Connor's footfalls on the treads behind him. His harsh breathing rasped in his throat as he ran up the stairs, but no hope stirred in his heart. Flame streamed back from the torch he held before him and the shadows twisted in a macabre dance on the curved stone walls around the stairs.

He came out onto the landing before the chamber where Aelric had been kept prisoner, and stopped so suddenly, Tiernyn nearly trod on his heel. The two guards lay crumpled on the rough wooden planking of the floor in front of the wide-flung door, eyes staring wide, blood from their slit throats puddled deep around their sprawled bodies.

The tower room stank of blood and death. Donaugh held the torch high to illuminate the terrible carnage. Four hacked corpses lay strewn around the chamber, blood pooling in congealing lakes on the woven matting, and splattered high on the walls. Only three heads lay amid the welter of severed limbs and torn torsos. Donaugh could not tell which parts belonged with which torso. A madman had been loosed in this room.

He closed his eyes and leaned against the doorjamb, sick with despair. Images of fire and ash and cinder swam before his mind's eye. His only hope for Celi's salvation lay dead before him. Everything he had worked for lay shattered beyond redemption in the charnel house of the tower chamber.

"Oh, my Eliade," he whispered.

Wearily, he pushed himself erect and turned. Five or six soldiers arrived, panting, on the landing. Pale and grim, Tiernyn wheeled about to meet them.

The squad leader caught his breath. "My lord, there was no sign of anyone on the battlements above the gatehouse," he said in a rush. "We found a trail of blood leading from this direction, but nothing else."

"I see," Tiernyn said. He gestured to the open door. "Gather a burial detail. These men are to be buried with full honors." He glanced down at the two guards and grimaced.

"Our men, too, of course. When all is ready, call me. I'll be in my workroom." He beckoned to Donaugh and Connor. "Gentlemen, with me, please."

Donaugh said nothing as he followed Tiernyn through the corridor to the small room above the gatehouse. Connor closed the door of the workroom behind them, then leaned back against it. Tiernyn walked behind his worktable and slumped into the chair. Donaugh went to the window and looked out at the brightly lit village. To the east, the stars burned fiercely in the sky above the low hills. He wondered if Elesan were out there, addressing his soldiers, planning the war to begin again with spring.

"This is a disaster," Donaugh said quietly.

Tiernyn rubbed his hand wearily across his eyes. "It certainly isn't an auspicious beginning to the reign of the first High King of Celi," he said.

Donaugh turned from the window, his face twisted with grief. "There still may be a chance to save ourselves," he said. "If we can show Elesan the murderer was punished, he may come back to the Council table."

Tiernyn kept his head down, his hands over his eyes. "It will be difficult to determine who the murderer is," he said indistinctly, his voice muffled by his hands.

Anger flared in Donaugh's belly. He folded his arms across his chest and watched his twin for a moment. Tiernyn did not look up to meet his eyes.

"You know as well as I who did this," Donaugh said, keeping his voice low and even only with an effort.

"How could I know? We have no witnesses. The guards I posted at the door were both killed along with the hostages."

A muscle jumped near the corner of Donaugh's jaw. His throat felt tight and raw as he spoke. "There is only one man who—"

"Enough, Donaugh." Tiernyn straightened up and dropped his hands to the table, slapping his palms down hard against the polished wood with a sound like the double cracking of a whip. "Connor, would you mind leaving us for a moment? Tell Ylana we will join her later in the Great Hall."

Connor glanced back and forth between Donaugh and Tiernyn. He nodded, then slipped out of the room, closing the door firmly behind himself.

Tiernyn rose to his feet and swung around to face Donaugh. "We will discuss this later," he said.

"By the gods, we will discuss it now," Donaugh said roughly. "You know as well as I do who slaughtered those men. I don't like it any more than you do that we'll have to execute one of our own men, a man who's been with us since the beginning. But for the sake of Celi—"

"It's for the sake of Celi that we will do nothing," Tiernyn interrupted. "I am to be High King of Celi, but I can't do it without the support of those men gathered down there in my Great Hall. The only man who supports me wholeheartedly in the question of negotiations with the Saesnesi is Keylan. Most of the others are skeptical, and some are positively hostile to the idea."

"If you don't punish the murderer, this island will go up in flame, and we will all be crushed, Celae and Saesnesi alike."

"Are you sure?" Tiernyn demanded. "It was a vision, Donaugh. Only a vision. Even Rhegar says the future isn't set in stone. Men's actions sway it and form it with our present."

"It was a true vision."

"Yet, you saw Aelric executed on the field of battle. He wasn't."

"Tiernyn—"

"You can't be sure what you saw was what must be." Tiernyn slammed his fist down onto the table. "Perhaps just the fact that Aelric didn't die on the battlefield that night was enough to change the fate you saw."

Donaugh took a deep breath and closed his eyes for a moment, consciously controlling his anger. "I am sure of what I saw," he said, each word sharp and distinct. "And I believe that if we take steps to show Elesan that we are men of honor, he will bargain for peace with us."

"All the princes and dukes of Celi are sitting right now in my Great Hall," Tiernyn said in a deadly calm voice. He gestured toward the door. "While you were gone these past days, only two subjects were discussed down there. My coronation at Vernal Equinox, and the wisdom of treating with the Saesnesi. Donaugh, you know I need the support of every man down there, especially now. Just how long do you suppose Gemedd is going to support me, or this army of ours, if we execute his oldest son for murder?" He ran his hand through his hair distractedly. "I know it was Eachern as well as you know it. But Eachern did it thinking he was avenging my honor for the insult Aelric offered me when he spit on my boot."

"So you will let him get away with murder," Donaugh said softly.

"For the sake of my kingdom, yes," Tiernyn said. "For the sake of holding this country together, I will turn a blind eye to the *execution* of four prisoners of war."

"And the guards? They were men of Celi—murdered where they stood for no other reason than they were discharging their duty—the duty you yourself set for them."

Tiernyn's lips tightened, but he said nothing.

"There is no honor in this," Donaugh said.

Tiernyn sat behind the table again. He leaned back in his chair and looked up at the ceiling for a moment before meeting Donaugh's eyes. "I will have direct or indirect command of every soldier in Celi after the Equinox," he said quietly. "We can protect our shores against raiders from across the Cold Sea, and we can mount a campaign that will crush Elesan's army. I know as well as you do that the Maedun will be looking toward Celi soon. But if we can overcome the Saesnesi, we will be ready for them."

Donaugh turned back to the window. He closed his eyes against a sudden vision of a black tide of men flooding out of the east, bringing fire and death with them.

"It won't be too late for us," Tiernyn said softly. "You'll see. We'll defeat Elesan, and the whole of Celi will be united when the Maedun come. I shall hold this island safe. I've pledged my life to that."

Donaugh glanced at him over his shoulder. "It *will* cost you your life, Tiernyn," he said quietly. "Aye, and mine, too," he added under his breath so Tiernyn could not hear him.

Tiernyn bit his lip. "Soon?" he asked.

Donaugh shook his head. "I don't know. But eventually."

Tiernyn smiled crookedly. "Well, a king's life is little enough to pay for the safety of his kingdom," he said. "Come. We must go back to the Great Hall. They'll be expecting us."

Donaugh paused at the door as he followed Tiernyn. His head rang with a sorrowful tone, like a harp chord in a minor key. He turned to look at Kingmaker hanging on the wall of the workroom.

A black stain marred the shoulder of the blade just below the hilt. Where before there had been only a small dull spot, now a blemish nearly as wide as Donaugh's thumb scarred the bright surface above the deeply etched runes.

18

Tiernyn ap Kian dav Leydon was crowned High King of Celi a fortnight after Vernal Equinox. The next morning, he married Ylana al Finn, his bheancoran. The feasting and celebrations continued for five days.

There were those who demurred the crowning was indecently soon after Tiernyn had been declared High King by the princes and dukes of Celi, but the fighting men of the country were pleased. The young High King had, for the first time in her history, pulled Celi together as one nation. Where no man of any of the provinces would have followed a prince or duke not his own, all were eager to offer their swords and their service to the High King. That the King had a powerful enchanter as advisor only increased the feeling that Celi's star was on the rise with that of its young King.

An air of high purpose infused the island. Even though the men of Skai and the men of Brigland still eyed each other askance, and the men of Dorian and the men of Mercia quite probably would never fully trust each other, they came together under the Red Hart banner of the High King, flying the banner of their own prince and duke beneath Tiernyn's banner. Each prince and duke, and several of the more powerful thanes of each province, had his own place at the Council Table in the new Council Hall being constructed adjacent to the Great Hall at Dun Camus.

With the ease of long practice, Donaugh withdrew quietly into the background, content to be seen only as Tiernyn's shadow. His work now lay behind the scenes, and he moved quietly into place.

Tiernyn's first decree as High King was that watchtowers were to be built to ring the coasts of Celi as they guarded the coasts of Skai and Wenydd. He sent Donaugh and Connor out to oversee the building of the watchtowers while he retired to the Council Table to discuss strategies with his newly formed Council.

The watchtowers were barely in place ten days after the Beltane Festival when word came from the continent that the Maedun had invaded Saesnes in a massive sweep to take the country. King Baniff's forces held out against the invaders for nearly a fortnight, but succumbed to the overwhelming numbers of Maedun aided by their warlocks, whose ability to turn any weapon back on the man who wielded it made the Maedun army nearly invincible. King Baniff died on the battlefield, mutilated by his own war ax. Baniff's son Marle tried valiantly to rally the demoralized Saesnesi army. He might have succeeded, but he, like his father, died with his own sword thrust through his heart.

As the Maedun army rampaged through Saesnes, the longships Kian had predicted would come left the Saesnesi coasts in swarms, fleeing before the invaders. Hundreds of them crossed the Cold Sea, some of them nearly swamped by their burdens of men, women, and children. Most fled with but the clothes on their backs and their weapons.

Elesan met the refugees as they beached their longships, and offered them shelter in return for fealty. The newcomers who accepted his offer swelled the ranks of his army. Some of the fleeing Saesnesi refused to swear fealty to Elesan and struck out on their own. Dorian and Mercia fell prey to fierce raids as the disaffected Saesnesi sought food and supplies.

Tiernyn mobilized his army to meet the onslaught, dividing it into forces under the captains. Each force acted independently, responding to raids all over the island. But Elesan refused to meet the Celae army. He fought a war of lightning raids and quick retreats. He organized his army into small raiding groups and struck in a dozen places at once, keeping Tiernyn's army busy racing from one trouble spot to the next.

One of the first men to fall to the raiders was Eachern of

Mercia. Tiernyn sent his body home to his father, draped with honor.

Ever after when he looked back on that summer, Donaugh likened the campaign against the Saesnesi to trying to dam up a flood. No matter how many times Tiernyn dispatched forces to meet raiders, there were always more behind them. Elesan kept his army moving like gadflies, striking at random throughout the island, refusing to be drawn into a pitched battle with Tiernyn's forces.

Twice during that first hectic summer, Donaugh made the journey to the Dance of Nemeara. On the night of the Summer Solstice, he stood sleepless before the *darlai* stone throughout the short night until the sun rose in a burst of splendor directly behind the center stone, framed by a massive trilithon. But if the gods and goddesses were present, they spoke not to him. Nor did Eliade join him even though her gentle presence filled his heart with her love. Bereft and alone, Donaugh left the Dance as the sun climbed above the imposing lintels of the trilithons and the capped menhirs of the inner circle.

When he returned on Lammas Eve, not even Myrddyn came to greet him. The Dance stood silent and empty, its magic stilled and subdued. Although the power of the place flowed around him like water, Donaugh could not conjure up a vision of Eliade. It was as if she had closed herself off from him, submerged in grief for her brother.

The stars wheeled slowly above him, silent and stately, as he stood before the *darlai* stone. He watched them progress in their majestic dance around the Nail Star, but no signs came to him. The Dance breathed softly around him, full of magic, but the stones remained only stones, and the center of the circle was empty but for him.

Autumnal Equinox approached, and the war raged on. Tiernyn had spent most of the summer in the field, living in a tent, constantly on the move. A fortnight before Autumnal Equinox,

Tiernyn called his captains together for a consultation. They were camped on the edge of the Dorian downs, only a league or two from the border of the Saesnesi Shore. Donaugh sat behind Tiernyn as the meeting went on.

Shortly before midday, he began to feel unsettled and jittery. Sitting still became difficult. He found himself listening inwardly for clues to his uneasiness, but nothing spoke to him. The tenuous link with Tiernyn's sword remained silent.

Something was wrong, but he could not tell what.

For the next two days, the restlessness grew worse. No tent was large enough to contain his undirected uneasiness. Barely suppressed nervous tension made a tight, uncomfortable knot under his rib cage and shivered down into his belly. He could not concentrate on what Tiernyn and the members of his Council were saying—their voices became merely an irritating buzz at the periphery of his consciousness. Finally, as evening fell on the third day, he realized he was distracting them with his preoccupation. He rose from his place and left the tent.

Autumn grew close, and the air was colder with the advent of sundown. Donaugh smelled a hint of frost in the crisp air as he swung his cloak about his shoulders, still pressed by the tight sense of urgency knotted in his chest. He set out across the camp, his aimless wandering taking him toward the edge of the oak forest.

A damp, chilly wind lifted the hem of his cloak and flapped it about his legs. As he approached a brake of hawthorn in the midst of the oaks, the urgency swelled to a crescendo, then suddenly subsided like an ebbing tide, leaving him hollow and empty. He put out a hand to steady himself. The rough bark of the tree felt dry and crusty beneath the pads of his fingers, devoid of life and resiliency. The living sap of the tree had drained away, leaving it brittle and arid, just as the lifeblood seemed to have drained from his heart.

His hand still pressed against the trunk of the tree, he twisted the magic from a thread of power in the air around him, then lifted his head.

"You can come out," he said, not raising his voice. "I've placed a masking spell. They can't see you from the camp. It's quite safe."

A man stepped out from the shadow of the hawthorns. He was tall, broad-shouldered, flaxen-haired. Donaugh had thought Elesan might send Devlyn, but he didn't know this man.

"My lord Elesan sends greetings," the Saesnesi said. "You have a son. He's called Aellegh."

Donaugh's heart gave a quick leap, then settled into a hard, slow rhythm. "Thank you," he said.

"There's more." The messenger's tone was flat and uninflected, as if he spoke by rote. "The lady Eliade—"

"When did she die?" Donaugh asked, his voice husky and raw.

The Saesnesi started visibly, then relaxed. "So you do have magic," he said softly.

"Aye, I do. When did she die?"

"An hour after the babe was born. Three days ago, shortly after midday."

When the cold chill had begun in his belly. Donaugh nodded. "I see," he said. "And the boy? What becomes of him?"

"Elesan will raise him as his son."

Donaugh nodded. "Yes. He needs an heir." Pain shot through his hands as his fingernails bit deeply into the palms of his hands. He made a conscious effort to relax his tightly balled fists. "Tell him I approve."

A sardonic smile twisted the messenger's mouth. "You have little to say in the decision," he said.

"That doesn't change the fact that Elesan's choice is the right one," Donaugh said. "Thank him for sending word to me."

The Saesnesi vanished back into the shadows with only a small rustle of dead leaves to mark his going. Donaugh let go of the masking spell. The magic effervesced for a moment as he released it, then was gone.

Spears of gold-and-red light radiated from the scattered fires of the camp, glinting like gems in sunlight through the tears in his eyes. Then, softly, gently, the wind brushed against his cheek. Its caress was warm and tender, like the touch of a living hand smoothing away his tears.

"Thank you for my son, beloved," he whispered into the night. The warm wind brushed his cheek once more, then was gone.

"Three sons for you, Donaugh Secondborn," he murmured, repeating the words of the *darlai*. "One your bitterest enemy . . . "

He remained in the shelter of the oaks, mourning the loss of the only woman he would ever love, and the loss of his son to the enemy.

Hakkar of Maedun burst into the chamber and strode to the bed, scattering the women before him like sparrows before a hawk. Francia straightened up and turned to face him. Her gown of brilliant emerald green was the only spot of color among the grays and browns of the gowns of the other women.

"Where is my son?" Hakkar demanded. "I want to see my son."

Francia glanced at the cradle near the bed. "Your son does well enough," she said. "But your wife is dying."

Hakkar spared no glance for the waxen pale figure lying on the bed. He pushed Francia aside and looked down into the cradle. The infant lay wrapped warmly in a blanket of rich, brown wool, awake, but quiet. Hakkar looked down into cloudy blue eyes that would soon be as dark brown as his own. The child's unwavering gaze seemed to hold his own, as if, even now, he understood the bond that would form between himself and his father.

"Horbad," Hakkar whispered. He reached out to touch the black fuzz crowning the infant's head.

Francia stepped forward and slapped his hand aside. "Don't

touch him," she said sharply. "He's far too young yet to forge a bond. If you even attempt it, you'll kill him."

Hakkar drew back and stared at her coldly. "I am not that stupid, in spite of the low opinion you hold of me," he said.

"My lord?" The midwife stepped forward, her head bowed.

"What do you want?" Hakkar said.

The midwife did not look up. "I fear the lady Mora has died."

Hakkar made an impatient gesture. "Then see to her," he said. "Do what must be done. Be very certain the chamber is ready for the child. It must be warm. If my son takes a chill, you will pay with your life."

The midwife bobbed a curtsy. "Yes, my lord."

"We must have a wet nurse," Francia said.

Hakkar stared at her coldly. "Well?"

"I understand one of the kitchen women was recently brought to bed with a child," Francia said. "She's young and healthy enough to serve well."

"Then see to it," Hakkar said. "Oh, and make sure her whelp is taken care of. I won't have my son competing with someone else's squalling brat for milk."

He looked down into the cradle again. The child was asleep. He turned on his heel and left the birthing chamber.

The fire on the hearth in his private quarters blazed brightly. As he entered, a servant finished replenishing the brazier and stood, hands clutched together across his belly, head bowed.

"Bring me mulled wine," Hakkar said. "Then get out of here." He held out his hand, waited until a goblet of hot wine was placed in it, then went to the window.

It had started snowing again. Ice lay thick on the surface of Lake Vayle, and the snow lay in mounds along the shore. Hakkar took a sip of the spicy wine and smiled thinly. It was the eve of the Midwinter Solstice—an auspicious time for his son to be born.

Three years ago, he had stood in this chamber, waiting,

only to hear the second woman had produced yet another still-born son. All those months of negotiating with Weigar to pro-cure Mora as his wife. Only a sorcerer's daughter was strong enough to bear a sorcerer's son. Hakkar's own mother had been the daughter of a sorcerer, and only the gods knew what she had cost his father. Mora had cost him the promise of revealing his secret to Weigar if the woman produced a son.

Hakkar smiled grimly. Weigar might not like the way he chose of revealing his secret. A graphic demonstration might be in order. Weigar definitely would not like the chosen method of demonstration, but a bargain was a bargain, and let no man say Hakkar of Lake Vayle did not keep his word.

But no matter. It had taken nearly three years, but now he had his son. In another five years, the child would be old enough to begin forging the bond. Already Hakkar could feel the magic strengthening in him. In ten years, he would be more powerful than his father was, more powerful than any other sorcerer in Maedun. Ten years was not long for a sor-cerer to wait—not when the reward was as sweet as the subju-gation of half a world. The Borlani had taken two centuries to extend their empire as far. Now the Borlani were gone. It was Maedun's turn. And more, it was Hakkar's turn.

Behind him, the door opened, but he did not turn. Francia snapped her fingers at the servant who hovered just outside the door. She received her goblet of wine, then came to stand beside Hakkar.

"So," she said. "You have your son."

"I have my son," he said. "And in ten years, Celi will be ours."

"And Isgard?" she asked. "Vanizen will be delighted you have your son. He wishes you to take Isgard for him."

"I will not waste myself on Isgard." He made a dismissive gesture. "Old Nordag's time is coming. He's nearly one hun-dred. His sorcery can't keep him alive much longer. When he dies and Nestin becomes Nordag, Vanizen will have his sor-cerer to tame Isgard."

Francia took a sip of the wine. "By the time we take Isgard, that Tyr's sons in Celi may have beaten back the Saesnesi. Who knows how strong they'll be when you're ready to invade Celi."

"It would be helpful if the Celae were still fighting the Saesnesi when I'm ready to take the island," he said. "But it won't matter. They can't stand before me."

She shrugged. "I've heard the young enchanter has powerful magic."

He turned and slapped the goblet out of her hand. "He is *not* an enchanter," he snarled. "He is a wizard, mayhaps. He may even be a powerful wizard, but he is *not* an enchanter."

She brushed the spilled wine delicately from the skirt of her gown, frowning at the stain. "Not the enchanter of the prophecy, mayhaps," she said evenly. "But still an enchanter, and a powerful one. Remember, it's from his line, the Tyr's line, the enchanter will come. Powerful magic does run in families."

Hakkar's hand closed around the goblet he held. The fragile silver crumpled under his fingers. "I will destroy him," he whispered. "I will destroy him, all his family, and every trace of magic on that accursed island."

"You will need a powerful weapon," she said.

He looked down at her. "You once told me you could bring the Prince of Skai, or any of his brothers, to his knees. Are you telling me you could be that weapon?"

"Mayhaps," she said. "But my price is high."

He laughed. "You overvalue yourself. The day will never come when I ask help of a woman."

"You may find yourself retracting those words, Hakkar," she said. "The one they call Tiernyn carries the same blade that killed our father. Remember that. That sword killed our father. It might yet kill you unless you have a strong weapon to use against it, and against the man who calls himself the High King of Celi."

She gathered her skirts and swept out of his chamber.

Hakkar put down the ruined goblet and stood by the window, his thick brows drawn together above the bridge of his aristocratic nose as he watched the snow fall from the swiftly darkening sky. Now that he had his son, the waiting would not be difficult. The time to bring Celi to its knees approached swiftly.

PART

3

High King

19

The wind whipped Torey's hair around her face and tugged at her light plaid as she stood on the promontory above the sea. Hundreds of feet below, foam-capped waves battered against the rocks, sending spume misting high enough to blow back against her like rain on the wind. The air smelled of salt from the living sea and of the new grass springing up in the protected rocky crevasses around her. The wind beating against her brought fresh color to her cheeks, but was blood-warm and felt soft as a loved one's caress. With the turning of the season, the winds blew from the southwest, bringing spring with them.

For the past fortnight, she had found herself drawn to this high vantage point beyond the walls of the Clanhold of Broche Rhuidh. On the far western horizon, the sea and sky blended in a misty blue haze. More than a hundred leagues beyond the wind-flayed promontory lay the Isle of Celi, invisible to her eyes, but clearly delineated in her imagination.

Torey lifted a hand and finger-combed the hair from her face. Nine years ago, she had left Celi two days after Beltane. Now another Beltane approached and she knew it was time to go home, to return to Dun Eidon. She had learned to love Tyra over the past years, learned to love the high, craggy tors and verdant glens, the tumbling rivers and still, placid lochs. But Tyra would never be home the way Skai and Celi were home. She found it easier now to understand her father and why he chose to return to his home even though he professed love for Skai and Celi.

Vernal Equinox brought a lessening of the spring storms that lashed the coast and whipped the Cold Sea into a boiling fury. Even though the sea appeared calmer now, a sudden storm could easily blow up out of nothing, driving an unwary ship onto the rocks and shoals that ringed the coast off Tyra and Isgard. Not until Beltane was the sea considered reasonably safe for ships to begin plying the trade routes up and down the coast and across the waters to Celi. When the first ship left the harbor below Broche Rhuidh, she would be on it. Going home.

They'd had no news from Celi since the winter storms closed the sea between the isle and the continent. Soon, with the coming of better weather, Tiernyn as High King would mobilize his army to continue the war against the Saesnesi that had dragged out for nearly seven years now. Surely this summer, or next summer, Tiernyn would be able to defeat the Saesnesi and finally free Celi of that threat.

She knew her father had serious misgivings about the ability of Isgard to hold out for very long if a sorcerer appeared to take charge of the invasion. Kian spoke of a Maedun general named Nordag, who was coming to the end of his span, and whose son was reputed to be a brilliant military strategist. If the son inherited his father's power upon the old general's death, Kian held out little hope that Isgard would long remain free. And once Isgard lay under Maedun rule, Kian was positive his old enemy Hakkar would come out of his seclusion to lead the assault on Celi.

Should that happen, Tiernyn would need her skills. She had to go home.

"Home," Torey whispered, her voice drowned by the booming rhythm of the waves and the gusty wind. "Home to Celi."

She missed it. She sorely missed the mountains and valleys of Skai. She missed her brothers, and she missed her friends.

An image of midnight hair and dazzling blue eyes flashed across her memory, and she smiled. Connor ap Ryvern of Wenydd was with Tiernyn and Donaugh. He had not been ignored by the bards and traveling minstrels who toured the noble landholdings on the continent. He figured prominently in their tales as the epitome of bravery, loyalty, and gallantry among the Companions of the King. She wondered what he thought of those songs and stories. Would he be pleased or exasperated?

Someone called her name behind her. She turned, coming out of her reverie with a start.

Fayden dav Garroch picked his way carefully up the steep slope past a clump of salt-bitten rock maple clinging tenaciously to the broken soil by a tumble of broken boulders. The wind fluttered his kilt around his knees and rippled the fabric of his plaid as he stepped across the uneven ground. His hair, dark as polished oak, hung free to his shoulders except for a heavy braid by his left temple. Blown by the wind, the single ruby on a fine gold chain dangling from his left ear tangled with the braid. Preoccupied with his footing, he raised one hand to unsnarl the earring, tucking the braid back behind his ear. The gesture was useless; the wind freed the braid only seconds later to snag with the earring again.

It always startled Torey at first to see the color of his hair. Nearly everyone she knew in Tyra had hair like her father's, red-gold or bright red. She had to smile when she remembered how long it had taken to become accustomed to seeing so many people with hair that color after Skai, where only her father, Keylan, and she had red hair. Now it was commonplace, and Fayden's dark hair was the anomaly. He laughingly claimed his hair wasn't his fault. It came directly from his twice-great-grandfather, who had passed the hair color to both his daughters, one of whom was Fayden's great-grandmother, the other of whom was mother to Rhodri, the Clan Laird, who also had dark hair.

"You're up early," he said as he reached her.

"So are you," she said. "When did you get home?"

"Late last night," Fayden said. "Tavis brought the company home for a rest. Just half a fortnight, then we return. We've had a right lively time along the border lately, ye ken."

"I've heard the Maedun are bringing more soldiers to the strongholds along there," she said. "Was there any fighting?"

He shrugged. "Not really." He grinned. "But the Maedun and the Isgardians are glowering at each other fiercely across that border, and there have been a few energetic skirmishes here and there. We saw a warlock or two among the soldiers."

"But no sorcerer yet?"

He made a face. "Sorcerers," he repeated. "Nasty business, they are. No. None yet, but rumors are flying thicker than ants to spilled honey. Tavis trusts the Ephir of Isgard no further than Rhodri does. Like his father, he wouldna put it past the conniving fox to barter the country for his life and a place to run to at the first sign of a sorcerer leading the army."

"But where could he run to?" Torey asked. "The Maedun have Falinor and Laringras and Saesnes, too."

"Aye, well, that's the thing, no? There's only Tyra, and if he betrays his own army and the Tyrs with them, it's no exactly a warm welcome awaiting him here." He grinned again. "Rhodri would bundle him into a sack and drop him into the sea right about here." He gestured to the edge of the cliff only a pace or two beyond their feet.

Torey gave him a quick smile in agreement, then said, "Fayden, I've decided to go home."

His face went blank for a moment. "Home?" he repeated. "But this is home."

Torey shook her head. "Home to Skai," she said softly.

He reached out and took her hand, pressing it to his chest. "But I had hoped that we'd say our betrothal vows this Beltane."

Gently, Torey freed her hand. "I'm sorry," she said. "I meant what I said last Beltane when I told you your heart could find no shelter in my hands or heart. I'm sorry."

He smiled wryly. "A man can hope a woman might change her mind," he said.

"Please," she said. "Don't . . . I haven't changed my mind."

"I can still hope," he said. "Or could until you said you had to leave. When will you go?"

"I've known for a while now that it was time to go home. I'm going to leave soon after Beltane."

Fayden let his hands drop to his sides. "I canna change your mind for ye, then?"

"I'm sorry," she said again. "Believe me, Fayden, I'm very sorry. I have to go home. My brothers are going to need me."

"But why now?" he asked, his brow furrowing in bewilderment. "Why just when I thought I might have a chance . . ." His voice trailed off as she put her hand on his arm.

"I don't know," she said. She could find no words to explain to him the urgency that had brought her to this promontory so often during the past fortnight. It was more than just the impression that she had to go home. She had the feeling that soon she would be needed there, that events were in motion that would make her presence in Skai or in Celi imperative. Something was in the wind and she *must* be there when it happened.

"I don't know," she said again. "But I must go. Mayhaps it's my *wyrd* calling me at last, Fayden."

He looked at her for a long time, his smoke gray eyes peering deep into her brown-gold eyes. Finally, he nodded reluctantly. He was a Tyr. He understood fate. "Then you must go," he said softly. "May I wish you a safe journey and a swift return?"

She reached up and kissed his cheek. "Thank you."

"When will you leave?"

"As soon after Beltane as I can book passage on a ship."

He smiled crookedly. "Then I might look forward to sharing heather wine with you Beltane Eve?"

"Mayhaps." She laughed. "Mayhaps, indeed."

The blacksmith's arm gleamed with sweat as he brought his hammer down for the last time on the glowing blade. He wrapped a scrap of leather around the long, hiltless tang and lifted the sword from the surface of the battered anvil, turning to Hakkar.

"It's ready now for final quenching," he said.

Hakkar took the half-finished sword, still glowing dull orange from the forge, and beckoned to the two Somber Riders who stood just outside the door of the smithy. They stooped and, between them, dragged a bound man from the ground at their feet.

The prisoner was Celae. He slumped between the soldiers, his legs unable to support his weight. His head lolled against his shoulder, his dirty and matted dark gold hair falling into his eyes. As Hakkar stepped forward, the man opened golden brown eyes and stared in horror at the blazing metal in Hakkar's hand.

"Horbad," Hakkar said quietly. "Come here."

His son, only two seasons past his sixth Name Day, and straight and slim as a sword himself, stepped from the shadows behind the Somber Riders. "Yes, Father?" he asked, his voice a clear treble.

"Stand beside me. We forge our bond now. Are you ready?"

"Oh, yes, Father." The child laughed in delight and skipped into his place. He leaned forward avidly, watching the Celae prisoner, his black eyes dancing with anticipation.

"Hold him straighter," Hakkar said to the two Somber Riders.

One of the soldiers gripped the Celae's hair and yanked his head back as the two of them pulled him into an erect standing position. The prisoner moaned as Hakkar stepped forward, then screamed in agony as the tip of the orange-hot blade touched his groin.

Grunting with effort, Hakkar forced the blade upward, through the skin and muscle of the Celae's abdomen, up through his chest, into his heart. The sizzle and crackle of scorching blood filled the forge, and steam rose from the ruptured body.

The Celae prisoner spasmed in the soldiers' hands. His head snapped back, his neck rigid. His eyes bulged, and his throat distended as his scream trailed off into death. Then his head fell limply forward until his chin rested slackly on his chest, his body held erect as much by the blade impaling him as by the soldiers' hands.

Slowly, Hakkar withdrew the sword. The blade now appeared to be made of black glass or obsidian, gleaming wetly in the hot light of the smithy. Holding the sword in his right hand, Hakkar turned and placed his left hand on Horbad's head.

The bonding was instantaneous. The magic stored in Hakkar since the death of his father burst forth, flashing and flaring around him in a black mist laced with twisting ropes of red-and-orange fire. The force of it knocked him to the beaten earth floor, writhing in agony and ecstasy together as it aligned itself to his will. He cried out as his body convulsed and shook. His hair stood on end. He clutched his son to him, both of them rolling on the packed dirt of the floor of the smithy, as the magic tied them irreversibly together.

Triumph and elation surged through Hakkar's body. He *felt* the presence of his son, felt the boy's own ecstasy, as the power flared around them. Brilliant flashes of light seared his eyes behind his closed lids, sparking red and orange. The tide of his blood flowed powerfully, then ebbed in a strong current. Chills and fever alternated in his belly, and he clutched the boy to him.

When finally it was over, Hakkar climbed shakily to his feet. Horbad lay in a heap, curled in a puddle of blood near the door of the shed. Hakkar bent and picked the boy up, set him on his feet, brushed back the sodden black hair from the pale forehead.

"Horbad?" he asked, a tremor quivering in his voice.

The boy opened his eyes. Hakkar saw the reflection of his own power there. The boy smiled tremulously, but his fear eased visibly as he looked up at his father. "Is it over?" he asked.

"Yes. We are one now. You are my true son."

The boy nodded. "I'm glad, Father," he said quietly, with a gravity beyond his years.

The sword no longer glowed, quenched by the Celae's blood, but it was still too hot to touch. Hakkar laid it gently on the rim of the forge. He looked up at the blacksmith. He had forgotten the man was there.

"Finish this now," he told the blacksmith. "I want the hilt engraved with silver in the pattern I showed you."

The blacksmith bowed, his face impassive. "Yes, Lord Hakkar," he said. "It will be finished within the fortnight."

Hakkar glanced out of the smithy door, westward toward the coast and the sea, where Celi lay beyond the horizon. He put his arm around Horbad's shoulders. "Look west, son," he said softly. "Soon we'll be leaving here to take Celi for Vanizen." He smiled. "And for us. Oh, yes. For ourselves."

Cold air poured in through the open window, but Francia hardly noticed. Icy mist hung in tendrils over Lake Vayle, penetrating the courtyard below where the boy Horbad played with a carved wooden sword. Unconsciously, Francia's fingers moved restlessly, pleating and repleating the fabric of the skirt of her gown, her other hand pressed to her bare throat.

Ice coated the cobbles of the courtyard, making them treacherously slippery, but Horbad seemed to have no difficulty with his footing as he battled imaginary enemies with the wooden sword. Even from the room where she watched, Francia could see the concentration in the childish face, and a determination beyond his years.

Francia narrowed her eyes and cocked her head to one side. Yes, there definitely was a faint, black aura around the child. Magic. Horbad now had magic—magic he could finally wield at will rather than instinctively—far stronger than it had been at his birth. But even then, his innate magic had been too strong for the strangling thread she had spun for him. He had shrugged it aside as a petulant child might push aside a mildly restraining hand. Then he had opened his eyes and stared at her, steadily and bluntly, almost as if he were aware of what she had tried. She shuddered.

The boy paused in his play and turned slowly to stare up at the window where she stood. At this distance, his face was unreadable, his eyes opaque and expressionless. He held her gaze for a moment, then went back to his game. Francia stepped back from the window, fingers clutched in the fabric of her skirt, and swallowed hard.

Hakkar's familiar tread sounded on the polished wood of the floor behind her. Carefully, Francia composed her face and turned to greet him.

Hakkar glanced through the window, checking to see what she was watching. He smiled coldly at her.

"A handsome boy, Horbad," he said.

There was something different about her brother, something she couldn't quite place for a moment. Then she realized that today, Hakkar reminded her of their father. His *presence* was more forceful, more physically overwhelming than it had been before. Understanding came in a rush, and she stepped back in surprise.

"You've bonded with him already," Francia said.

"Two days ago," Hakkar said. "It was an . . . exhilarating experience. For both of us."

Francia shrugged. "He's only six. You were lucky you didn't kill him."

"I was five when Father and I bonded," he said. "Horbad is as strong as I was."

She started to turn away from him. He caught her arm and swung her back to face him. That cold, hard smile was back in place. "You didn't count on him being so strong, did you, dear sister?" he said softly. "Did you think me unaware of the petty magic you've been playing with? If you had harmed Horbad, you'd be dead now, and before you died, you'd know father's secret."

The blood drained from her head and she swayed dizzily. "You wouldn't *dare* kill me," she whispered.

"Would I not?"

She struggled to regain her composure and pulled her arm away from his hand. Carefully, she straightened her skirt, arranging the heavy folds meticulously to give herself time to think. Her hands shook, but she had not the strength to steady them. "I've done nothing wrong," she said, not looking at him, a tremor in her voice.

He stepped closer, forcing her to step back against the wall beside the open window. He raised his hand and held it, palm out, inches from her face. Tendrils of black mist curled from his fingers, wrapped themselves around her throat. She couldn't cry out, couldn't breathe. Her vision swam and her knees buckled, unable to hold her weight.

At the last moment, Hakkar closed his fist. The black mist vanished. Francia drew in a long, sobbing breath, her hands pressed to the wall behind her for support.

"You know what happens to women who use magic," he said softly. He reached out and caressed her cheek, smiling. His smile reminded her of the teeth of a wolf. "Is there a reason why I shouldn't take you to Vanizen and denounce you?"

She stared at him, unable to speak. She shook her head.

"Or, perhaps you can be of service to me."

She put her hand to her throat. Where the black mist had touched, the skin was sore and blistered. "What would you have me do?" she asked hoarsely.

"You have always claimed you could bring the Prince of Skai or any other man to his knees," he said, his voice like silk against velvet. "I will let you do this for me. It might make my taking of Celi all the easier and save my strength for holding the island."

"And if I succeed? What reward will you give me?"

He smiled again. His fingers trailed down her cheek and traced the inflamed area around her throat. "Your reward?" he asked. "Why, your reward, dear sister, will be your life."

Francia bent her head. She stepped aside quickly. The touch of his fingers on her skin nauseated her. His fingers were colder than the ice-rimed stones outside the window.

"You have a bargain," she said. Gathering her skirts, she left the room quickly, aware that she fled from him, but unable to stop her undignified retreat.

20

The corridor was dark, lit only by a few guttering torches.
Francia clutched her robe around her and closed the door of
her chamber quietly behind her. She stood for a moment,
listening, but heard no sound of footsteps in the passageway.

Silently as a shadow, she hurried along the hall, keeping to
the edges by the walls. She reached the small door in the
tower without seeing a guard or a servant. The door opened
without a creak or whisper, and closed just as quietly behind
her.

The narrow stairway was blacker than a moonless night,
but she needed no light. She had been this way often enough
that she knew it by heart, every step, every twist and turn in
the passageway at the bottom.

Running her hand lightly along the damp stone wall, she
hurried across the uneven, crumbling floor. Four doors, five,
six . . . She paused before the seventh door and took a deep
breath before taking a key from the pocket of her robe.
The key turned in the lock with a faint *click*. She pushed
the door open and entered the small chamber. Her hand
went unerringly to the candlestick on the small table by the
door.

Francia concentrated, then touched the candle wick. A
tiny flame leapt from her fingertip and the candle blazed up
in the thick darkness of the small room. Francia smiled. It
had worked at the first try this time. Her magic was growing stronger, more reliable. While Hakkar had been gnash-
ing his teeth in anger and frustration, and setting all his
hopes on one day siring a son, then waiting impatiently for
the boy to grow old enough, and strong enough, to bond
with, Francia spent the time nurturing her own magic and

cultivating it like a delicate plant in her herb garden. Her way produced tangible results. It was a pity that Hakkar's last wife had finally produced a strong and healthy son. If not for that, Francia thought it likely that her magic might someday have outstripped his. Even yet, she might someday equal him.

He thought her magic *petty*, did he? He would learn just how powerful a woman's *petty* magic could be.

The bare stone walls, devoid of any hangings to dispel the chill, gleamed with a thin film of moisture in the light. The odor of mildew and pale, damp-slick fungus floated in the air. Francia's nose wrinkled in distaste at the sickly scent. She set the candle on a small triangular table just inside the door. Her shadow spilled across the damp, bare stone floor before her as she quietly approached the narrow cot, the only other furnishing in the cell.

The child lay huddled on the thin straw mattress, his fair hair spilling across the coarse woolen blanket. A faint golden glow surrounded him, visible only when she gathered her magic and looked at him in a certain way.

Perfect. He was perfect.

She had searched for a long time before she found what she needed. The child of a slave woman, he was simple, but he was gifted with that special loving innocence that only some simple children had. The strongest magic could be achieved only from innocence betrayed in blood.

Francia let her shawl drop to her feet, then slipped out of her robe. It puddled at her feet and she stepped over it. She stooped over the cot and put her hand to the child's brow. He sat up, almond-shaped eyes blinking vaguely in the dim light, slack mouth trying to form a smile. He reached up trustingly to put his arms about her neck as she picked him up. She sat on the cot and cradled him in her lap. His skin felt warm and smooth and soft against hers. He made contented, unintelligible sounds and smiled at her again as he cuddled against her.

Even as she drew the slender dagger, he smiled. She traced a line down the inside of his arm with the tip of the blade. Blood, black-red in the candlelight, welled up and spilled down to stain his chest and belly, then her arm and thighs. He stared, first at the blood, then at her, in confusion. He whimpered, but did not try to pull away.

Not until she thrust the tip of the dagger up under his thumbnail did he begin to scream. His fear blossomed in a red burst around him. Fear turned to terror as she twisted the blade, holding the struggling child tightly with her free arm. Slowly and lovingly, she began to slice off his fingers, one by one.

Presently, his screams became only hoarse, whistling sobs as his voice deserted him, strained beyond use. But his terror remained, fluttering between them like a wounded sparrow. Francia chanted the words of power until at last his depleted body went limp and still in her arms, and his blood soaked her from her hair to her bare feet.

Francia stood up, discarding the child's body. She ignored it as it fell in a heap on the floor by her feet. Power coursed through her, vibrating along her nerves and sinews. She felt light enough to float on the air like thistledown, potent enough to pluck the stars from the skies and use them as candles.

She smeared the child's blood over her face, tasting its salt on her lips, while she cried out the incantation. Her hair was matted and sticky under her hands as she rubbed in the blood as if it were delicately scented soap. She massaged the blood into her body, chanting out the words of the spell quickly, her eyes closed. Her skin tingled as a dark red mist formed and molded itself against her, seeping into her skin like water into thirsty ground.

When finally the spell was finished and the mist gone, Francia drooped with exhaustion. She gathered up her robe and her cloak, pulling them around her with slow, weary movements. Turning to leave the room, she spared no glance for the crumpled body by the cot. She blew out the candle and locked the door behind her.

No one saw her as she made her way quickly through the dark corridors of the fortress manse. As she entered her own chambers, she kicked the nearest of her women awake and ordered hot water brought for a bath.

Finally scrubbed clean, she stepped out of the porcelain tub and turned to the silvered mirror. Facing her was a slender woman with the blue-black hair and brilliant blue eyes of a Celae, skin faintly sun-touched to a pale gold. Gone were the aristocratic hawk nose and high cheekbones. Instead, a rounded, pretty face peered back at her, the tip-tilted nose dusted with a dainty spray of freckles.

Francia laughed and ran her hands down her sides, over her hips. "Now you will be mine, Tiernyn of Celi," she whispered. "Mine to do with as I will. What a surprise for my dear brother when he finally stirs from this rotting pile of stones and finds me ruling Celi from your bed." She turned to admire the back of her body in the mirror. "Hakkar will find I'm not so easily dismissed after all, won't he?"

The twin Beltane fires had crumbled to embers overnight. In the early dawn light, the young men and women of the Clanhold of Broche Rhuidh vied with each other to build them up again. Lower down in the glen, the children began gathering the beasts and flocks of geese to drive them up to the clearing.

Her skirts kilted up around her knees, Torey ran across the clearing with an armload of wood. The fire the men had rebuilt blazed higher than the women's fire. She threw the wood onto the fire, then turned to gather another load, laughing as she dodged past other hurrying women. Already she could hear the excited shouts and laughter of the children as they drove the beasts toward the clearing. Both fires must be burning brightly as the cattle and horses, the swine and sheep, even the geese and chickens, passed between them to ensure an increase over the coming year.

Landen, Rhodri's second son, found her in the forest on the flank of the mountain above the clearing. She straightened up as he stepped out of the shadow of a clump of willow. The sight of his face, grim and set, extinguished her laughter as water smothers a fire. She dropped the wood she carried, then quickly went to Landen.

"There's news," he said. "We're needed."

She followed him quickly down the track to the Clanhold. "What is it?" she asked. "What's wrong?"

"I don't know. My father just said that news was coming and sent me to fetch you. He said to hurry."

The family had assembled on the steps of the Great Hall. Rhodri, the Clan Laird, stood with his wife Linnet. His eldest son, Brychan, stood with his wife and their two sons. Landen took his place behind his father. Kian stood to his uncle's left, with Kerri by his side. Torey hurriedly unkilted her skirts and combed her fingers through her hair as she ran up the steps to take her place beside Kerri. She groped for Kerri's hand and gripped it tightly.

Torey bent her head toward her mother. "What is it?" she whispered.

"Tavis is coming home," Kerri said softly.

A troop of horsemen rode through the gates of the Clanhold. Fayden dav Garroch rode alone at the head of the troop. Torey's breath caught in her throat. Many of the men bore healing wounds. Fayden himself wore a bandage around his thigh, just visible below the hem of his kilt.

But where was Tavis? Torey searched frantically through the column, but saw no sign of him. She glanced at Rhodri. He stood stiff and erect, his hands clenched into fists at his sides, his face pale and set. Her heart tightened in grief, and the backs of her eyes stung with tears she could not shed before the returning men. She understood; she knew where Tavis was.

Fayden dismounted and handed the reins of his horse to a servant. He unfastened a long bundle from behind the saddle and held it cradled gently in his arms. Torey closed her eyes against threatening tears. What Fayden carried was Tavis's plaid, rolled into a long parcel. Tavis's sword was fastened to the bundle by two thick, silver cords, one at each end, and by a wide leather belt in the middle. Hidden within the folds of the plaid, wrapped in a carefully folded envelope of oiled parchment, lay Tavis's heart, his braid circling it and his blue topaz earring beside it.

Holding the heart bundle in his arms, Fayden mounted the steps. He stopped in front of Rhodri and held out the bundle. Rhodri took it, his face pale but composed.

"I have seen your youngest son home, Rhodri dav Medroch, Laird of Glen Borden and Broche Rhuidh," Fayden said, his voice low, the effort to keep it steady plain on his face. "I have seen my kinsman and my captain home to his Clanhold, as I so swore to him when he died in my arms. I wish it duly noted that I have discharged my obligation as his liegeman in this duty."

Rhodri's eyes flicked to the bundle he held, and, for the briefest moment, his pain flared in their gray depths. He looked back to Fayden. "You have my acknowledgment of my debt in this matter," he said.

Fayden dropped to his knee on the granite step, his head bent. "I bring other dire news, my lord," he said.

"See first to your men and your own wounds," Rhodri said. "Then come to my private chambers. There will be wine to ease your telling of the news." He turned and made his way into the Great Hall. One by one, the others followed him.

Torey remained on the step, her hand still clutched in Kerri's. Gently, Kerri disengaged her hand. "Go with Fayden to see to the wounded," she said softly. "I'll stay to watch Rhodri and make sure he's all right."

Torey nodded and hurried after Fayden.

———

The infirmary was tucked into a corner at the end of the barracks, a long, narrow room with tall windows to let in light and air. Torey found Fayden there, hovering anxiously over a priestess who was attending to an arrow wound in a young soldier's shoulder. Fayden's face was gray with strain and fatigue. The skin of his cheeks appeared to sag with it, and lines Torey couldn't remember seeing before cut deeply into his forehead and bracketed his mouth. He limped painfully as he moved to assure himself another of his men was receiving proper attention.

Torey caught his arm and pulled him to a bench by a window. He protested but had little strength to resist as she made him sit down.

"Stay there," she said firmly. "Are any of the men badly wounded?"

"Just Malkam," he said. He closed his eyes and leaned back against the wall. "The lad with the arrow wound. We lost five more men on the journey home."

"They've been seen properly home?"

He nodded wearily, not bothering to open his eyes. "Aye, they have. Tavis was the last." Sudden wetness gleamed along his eyelashes. He raised his hand leadenly to brush away the tears.

"I'll be back in a moment," Torey said. "You stay here and rest for a while."

The priestess had already removed the iron arrow point from young Malkam's shoulder when Torey knelt beside the pallet. The priestess rinsed her hands in a bowl of water and witch hazel.

"It's good you're here, Lady Torey," she said. "The wound is fevered and would have killed him, I fear. I've cleaned it as best I can."

"Thank you." Torey put her hands to the wound and smiled at the young soldier as he stared, wide-eyed, up at her. "I won't hurt you," she said softly. She gathered strength from the flows of power swirling in the air around her, in the earth beneath her knees. Slowly, the wound in the young soldier's shoulder drew together and closed. He gaped at the shiny pink scar tissue. Before he could say anything, Torey put her hand to his forehead and gave him sleep. He needed it to recover his strength.

"If you need me again, I'll be tending to Fayden," she told the priestess.

The priestess drew a blanket over Malkam and tucked it under his chin. "Thank you, my lady," she said.

Fayden hadn't moved. Torey went to her knees beside the bench and pushed back the hem of his kilt. The bandage around his thigh was dirty, and crusted with a yellowish red discharge. She pushed the hem of his kilt higher. Red streaks clawed up from beneath the bandage, reaching up his thigh toward his groin. She made a distasteful face as she unwound the bandage to expose the raw, ugly wound. The cut was deep, but Fayden was lucky. The sword blade had just missed the large vessel in his thigh. The wound needed cleaning before she attempted to heal it.

Before she could ask, a young priest set a bowl of warm water steeped with herbs beside her and handed her one of the clean cloths he carried. She smiled her thanks and turned back to her work.

"What news do you bring?" she asked Fayden to distract him from the pain her probing caused.

"Isgard has fallen," he said, his voice rasping in his throat. "A sorcerer named Nordag . . . "

He winced as she touched the raw flesh at the edge of the wound. The young priest handed Torey a small, sharp knife, still hot from the candle flame. She bent forward to see better, then cleanly sliced through the crusty scab. The wound burst open, and thick, greenish pus flooded out over her hands and Fayden's leg. The hot, sickly-sweet odor of putrefaction rose sharply from the wound. The priest worked quickly and competently with a wet cloth, swabbing the discharge away from the wound. Torey washed her hands before resuming her ministrations.

"What happened?" she asked. She ignored the reek of infection coming from the wound. "You said a sorcerer was there?"

Fayden turned his head away, gagging at the stench, his eyes closed tight. His face lost what little color it had. He grimaced, teeth clenched tightly to prevent himself from crying out in pain. It was a moment or two before he could continue speaking.

"The Isgardians could handle the warlocks simply by burning them out." His voice sounded raw and breathless. Torey glanced up at him, but he nodded at her to go on with her work. "Throw enough poor bastards at them and they end up looking like shed snakeskins. But the sorcerer . . . Gods help us, Torey, they swept through us like a scythe through grain. We couldna stand against them."

"Blood magic?" she asked, reaching for a clean knife. The dead flesh around the edges of the wound had to be cut away before she could begin to Heal it. She nodded to the young priest, who stepped forward and flooded the wound with water infused with willow bark and chalery leaf. "What happened?" She mopped at the wound with a clean cloth and continued with the knife, trying to be gentle.

"Blood magic," he repeated bitterly. "Aye, it must have been. We couldna move. It was like . . ." He caught his breath and winced again, his mouth twisting as he bit his lip against crying out.

She didn't look up, frowning in concentration as she worked. "It was like?" she prompted him.

"It was as if we'd been trapped in sand," he said. "We couldna move. The Maedun Somber Riders cut us down where we stood, and we couldna lift a hand to save ourselves. I watched as one of them killed Tavis. All the gods help me, Torey, I couldna move to help him. Then I got this."

He nodded toward his thigh. "I fell, and they rode right over me. I fancy they thought I was dead. And the rest of us, too, because they didna come back to finish us off."

"Somber Riders?" she repeated, working as quickly and gently as she could.

"Aye, that's what they call themselves. Their uniforms are all black, ye ken." He shivered. "And their swords are black metal, too." He managed a wry smile. "And verra sharp. Once they were gone, we found we could move again. I gathered the men who were left alive, and we attended to our dead." Again, the wetness seeped through his eyelashes. "So many dead . . ."

She put aside the soiled cloth and looked critically at the wound. The flesh burned hot against her palms as she put her hands against it, but it was clean and free from dead tissue. Slowly, she gathered the strength again and willed it into him. The red streaks climbing his thigh faded, then the edges of the wound began to draw together. Gradually, healthy flesh replaced the torn muscle and skin. Moments later, nothing was left but a long scar. Torey removed her hands and rinsed them in a fresh bowl of water provided by the young priest, then sat back on her heels and looked up at Fayden.

Some of the color had returned to his face, but the deeply etched lines had not smoothed out. He opened his eyes and managed a smile as he glanced down at his thigh.

"There was a time when I'd've been more gleeful to have you touching me there," he said with a ghost of his former grin.

She put her hand to his forehead. It was cool and dry beneath her palm. "I should give you sleep to regain your strength, but Rhodri needs to hear your news."

He made a face. "Aye, he does. Have we given him time enough to arrange for Tavis's homecoming?"

She nodded. "I believe so. When you're finished talking with me, I want you to find your bed and sleep." As the corners of his mouth lifted in a smile, she added, "Alone, Fayden. Ye've not the strength to be romping with a woman. Not yet."

He struggled to his feet and smiled. "Aye, not yet," he agreed. "I'd best find Rhodri, then."

21

Dark clouds hung low over the crags of Tyra the day Torey took ship for Celi. To the west, streaks of blue sky gleamed between bands of frayed cloud, giving the promise of better weather at sea. The ship's master had watched the west all morning, waiting for the first sign of a break in the weather before sending the mate to gather the passengers huddling around the fire in the small inn, out of the rain.

The master gave Torey his arm as she made her way up the narrow gangplank. "I'll no be promising ye a smooth trip, my lady," he said to her as he guided her along the deck cluttered with cargo secured by heavy rope nets. Above their heads, the pennons atop the tall masts snapped and popped in the stiff breeze. Beyond the harbor, whitecaps flickered and danced on the gray-green swells. Occasionally, a small twist of spume broke free to writhe briefly above the sea before the wind shredded it to blown mist. "But it will surely be a swift one."

He opened the door to her cabin and bowed her in. "If ye be needin' anything, my lady, the steward will be more than happy to provide it. Let's hope the voyage isna too rough."

Torey smiled. "Thank you," she said. "I'm a fair sailor, though. I haven't been ill aboard ship since I was a small child."

The master sketched a quick bow, then turned away, shouting for the deckhands to slip the lines as he left the narrow passage. Torey's baggage was already stowed in the tiny cabin, which was barely large enough to hold the bunk and a small chest with two drawers supporting a clamped-down basin and ewer for wash water. A small porthole opened onto the deck, giving her a view of the edge of the harbor and the open sea. She opened the porthole, letting in the sound of the rhythmic chant of the men singing as they worked the windlass to raise the anchor. The rattle of the anchor chain echoed the cadence of the chantey as the anchor came ponderously out of the sea.

As she was unpacking the few things she would need on the voyage, a small commotion broke out on the deck. The clanking of the anchor windlass stopped momentarily, and the rumble of the gangplank being dropped back onto the deck took its place. Torey looked to the porthole in time to see the figure of a woman, cloaked and cowled against the wind, hurry past on the deck, accompanied by the mate. Moments later, a cabin door down the passageway opened, then closed.

The windlass clattered and clanked again to the rhythm of the sailors' chanting. The ship creaked as the wind caught the canvas and bellied it out with a loud *crack*, and the ship slipped eagerly away from the pier.

As predicted by the master, the voyage was far from smooth. Once beyond the shelter of the harbor, the ship plunged and rolled as the wind swung around gradually to blow from the southeast. It was a warm wind, but the following sea did not make for a comfortable voyage. Torey spent most of the first day on deck, enjoying the brisk and lively motion of the ship, but saw nothing of her fellow passengers on deck. Only two or three turned up for the evening meal served in the master's cabin. She never saw the mysterious woman who had come aboard late. When she casually questioned the master, he informed her that the woman had booked passage to Gwachir on the Dorian coast, and appeared to be Celae, although she spoke with a slight accent, possibly Borlani.

Torey caught another glimpse of the woman when the ship docked in Gwachir late in the evening of the second day. Again cloaked and cowled in midnight blue, the woman left the ship on the arm of the mate, a darker shadow amid the flickering shadows on the pier. She disappeared into a carriage, and Torey dismissed her from her thoughts.

Torey left the ship with the leather pouch of letters her father had given her to see delivered to Tiernyn in Dun Camus. A carriage took her to the garrison commander, who received her with the respect due to the sister of the High King. He summoned a courier immediately to take the dispatches she carried and speed them on their way to Dun Camus. Refusing the offer of a bed for the night, Torey went back to her waiting carriage. As the driver flicked the traces to start the horses moving, Torey saw a woman slip around a corner by the garrison commander's house. The woman was gone before Torey could get a good look at her, but she was sure it was the woman who had just left the ship in the harbor.

On the afternoon of the next day, Torey saw what she had been waiting breathlessly for. The mountains of first Wenydd, then Skai appeared on the horizon, climbing into the sky as the ship made its way around the south coast of Celi. Her heart beat a little faster as she stood near the bow watching the land slipping past. Hawsers thick as her wrist lay coiled neatly near the windlass that raised the anchor. She seated herself on one coil and hardly moved as the ship rounded the Pointers and began picking its way past the rocky shoals of the west coast. When finally she saw the familiar shapes of the crags around the Ceg, she felt she could have left the ship and floated over the calm, blue water to the pier at the head of the deep, narrow inlet.

Home! The word rang in her head as she stood clinging to the rail, breathing in the well-remembered scents. The air was redolent of cedar and pine, curing leather and woodsmoke, all threaded through with the perfume of the wildflowers rioting along the slopes of the mountains and the smell of seaweed crisping on the shingle in the sun. And over it was a faint, indefinable tang that was unmistakably the scent of home. She was home.

———

Donaugh leaned back in his chair and wearily massaged the bridge of his nose with his thumb and forefinger. Piles of daily dispatches from the watchtowers ringing the isle cluttered the surface of the table before him. For the last several days, all had been remarkably alike. Each one reported the sighting of Saesnesi longships off the coast, mostly a single longship, and never more than two. But no reports had come in of raids.

He reached for another pile of dispatches from scouts stationed along the border of the Saesnesi Shore. They, too, reported little or no activity. The Saesnesi still remained in their winter strongholds.

Something was wrong. Spring planting was nearly done. It was long past the time when the raids usually began. Frowning, Donaugh gathered the papers and looked through the east window. The first stars of the evening glimmered above the low hills.

"What are you up to, Elesan, you old fox?" he murmured. He rose, still carrying the sheaf of papers, and went to the hearth. A log broke with a loud *pop*, sending a small constellation of sparks up the chimney. The embers glowed brightly, but no visions formed there for him. It was frustrating, but the Seeings still came to him on their own terms and in their own time. Well, even Rhegar could not always control what he Saw or when he Saw it, and Rheghar's gift of the Sight was far stronger than his own. Donaugh gave up. He left his workroom to make his way to Tiernyn's.

Tiernyn was at his worktable when Donaugh entered, surrounded by his own pile of papers. Ylana sat curled on a cushioned bench by the window, her sword across her lap as she cleaned and oiled it. Kingmaker hung on its peg on the wall behind her, its freshly oiled plain leather scabbard gleaming in the last light of day streaming through the window. The leather scabbard hid the stain on the blade above the runes.

"Are you still working, too?" Tiernyn asked. He pushed himself back in his chair and stretched like a cat.

"I thought you might be interested in this," Donaugh said. He seated himself and looked through the papers in his hand. Tiernyn rested his elbows on the arms of his chair and propped his feet on the edge of the table as he listened to Donaugh. When Donaugh finished speaking, Tiernyn remained silent, frowning, staring thoughtfully at the far wall.

"You're right," he said finally. "Elesan is up to something. Where were all those longships going?"

Donaugh shuffled through his papers again. "No reports from any watchtowers of a gathering," he said. "But there are a few places along the coast—offshore islands, mostly—that aren't under observation from any watchtower. They might be hiding there."

"Surprise raids?" Ylana asked from her bench. "Dozens of them, coordinated to try to hit us in too many places at once?"

"That could be," Tiernyn said. He frowned and tapped a forefinger contemplatively against his lips. "Or that's what he wants us to think."

"Yet the scouts report no activity along the border," Donaugh said. "It might be that Elesan is trying to get us to break up the army into small detachments and send them out against expected raids."

"And then hit us from an entirely unexpected direction when our strength is depleted? That sounds like the old fox." Tiernyn sat up. His feet hit the floor with a soft double thud. "Ylana, send someone to fetch Connor here. Tell him I need him for a special scouting mission."

Ylana put aside her sword and left the room quickly. Tiernyn looked back at Donaugh.

"If anyone can ferret out what's going on out there, Connor can," he said.

———

Francia hated the voyage to Celi. With only a brief respite when the ship docked in Tyra, she was ill from the time she set foot on board the ship at Honandun to the moment she disembarked in Gwachir. Only by constant use of her magic could she keep the nausea at bay. That left little to maintain the semblance of being a Celae woman. Fortunately, the weather remained windy and chilly, and wrapping herself closely in her cloak caused no excess curiosity.

She found an inn away from the waterfront in Gwachir and took a room. The inn was a good one, frequented by a well-dressed and refined clientele. The landlord was discreet and made no comment when faced with a woman traveling alone. She had encountered the same noncommittal acceptance in Isgard. It drove home the fact that she had left Maedun far behind. No wellborn Maedun woman would dare travel without at least two well-armed men to protect her. Francia found herself caught halfway between envy for the freedom of Celae women and contempt for their flagrant lack of restraint or modesty.

She awoke in the morning to find that her spell had worn off. The aristocratic Maedun face in her mirror dismayed her. The spell should have been simple to maintain, even in sleep. Had fighting the shipboard illness used up too much of the power gained from the slave child?

Listening inwardly, she tested the strength of her magic. No, it was not depleted any more than she might have expected. There should have been more than enough to maintain the spell.

She called forth the magic again. The face in the mirror before her wavered and began to take on the semblance of the Celae woman she wished to be. But she could not complete the spell.

Startled, she let go of the spell and stared into the mirror. The grotesque, half-Celae face shimmered and became her own again. She drew more deeply on her magic and tried again. This time it worked. Once the spell was in place, it took a little more effort than normal to maintain it. She would have to remember that, and she would have to find a way of replenishing her power more often than she had originally planned.

Was there something in the air of Celi that weakened her power? Something in the land itself? If so, she wondered if it might also affect Hakkar's magic. And if Hakkar's magic was weakened by this island, might there be some way she could turn that to her own advantage while Hakkar floundered around wondering why his magic was not working as he thought it should?

She smiled at her reflection. Her Uncle Vanizen might be Maedun down to his ugly feet, but he was a coldly pragmatic man. If *she* could deliver Celi to him rather than Hakkar—if she could prove herself as strong as Hakkar—Vanizen might be persuaded to let her hold the island as Lady Protector.

Francia left her room and descended to the common room to break her fast and to inquire about hiring an escort to take her to the High King.

Walking into the solar at Dun Eidon gave Torey a sudden, disconcerting sense of being thrown back in time. It had not changed since the last time she had been there, when Keylan and Alys were married seven years ago. Cernos of the Forest still squinted above the carved chest. The same tasseled and embroidered cushions still padded the benches and chairs. It appeared that Alys had added nothing to change the look of the comfortable room.

Keylan, though, had changed since Torey had last seen him. The responsibilities he bore had settled around him like a cloak. Warmth and humor still lurked at the corners of his mouth and in his eyes, but he was quieter now and more measured in his speech and movements, and less impulsive. He bore a startling resemblance to Kian in the way he handled himself and how he spoke.

Of course, fatherhood might have something to do with that, Torey thought in amusement as she watched her brother with his daughters. Rowana was just turned four, a bright, sunny little creature with a gamine smile and the ability to dart through her parents' hands with dazzling agility and quicksilver grace. The baby, Merlaina—called Merly for love, as Alys put it—was in the first throes of experimentation with the wonders of walking by herself. Both girls looked exactly like Alys, and it was plainly evident that Keylan adored them and was in turn adored. Torey promptly fell in love with both girls.

Keylan seated himself in the chair that had once been Kian's. Merly clambered into his lap and watched Torey with shy curiosity from the shelter of her father's arms.

"You've timed your arrival well." Keylan shifted Merly to a more comfortable position on his lap and brushed a strand of hair from her forehead. "We've just got word that the passes are open. We were planning to leave for Dun Camus tomorrow for the spring Council meeting."

"You'll come with us, of course," Alys said. "You must be anxious to see Tiernyn and Donaugh again, too."

Torey nodded, then laughed. "I was going to ride up to Dun Camus from Gwachir, but I wanted to see home first," she said. "If I'd known you were going to go there, I'd have waited. But yes, of course I'll go with you."

A tall young woman entered the room, and nodded pleasantly to Torey. She wore trews and a tunic, her dark gold hair caught back in a heavy braid that fell to her waist. Her heavy, dark gold eyebrows made a straight line above her golden brown eyes. Something about her was familiar, but Torey could not place her.

"Letessa al Morfyn, my lady," the girl said. "Do you remember me?"

Torey rose and hugged the girl in delight. "Of course I do," she said. "You look like your brother, Eryth. You've grown." She hadn't seen Letessa since the girl was only a child of eight. Now a tall fifteen, she had turned into a lovely woman. "Well, of course you have," Torey said, laughing. "It's been nearly ten years!"

"You haven't changed much, my lady," Letessa said. "Excuse me. I have work to do." She smiled at Torey, then scooped Merly from Keylan's lap. Merly went to her, laughing. Letessa held out her hand to Rowana, who ran to take it. "Time for dinner, loves," she said as she took the children from the room.

"She's good with them," Alys said as Letessa left. She sighed. "She has more patience with them than I seem to. And I know she'll look after them well while we're in Dun Camus."

"Letessa still hasn't declared whom she'll serve?" Torey asked.

Alys shook her head. "No. For a while last summer she and Ralf ap Ryvern of Wenydd were seeing quite a lot of each other, and we thought she might declare for him."

"The Dukes of Wenydd have never had bheancorans," Torey said. "I suppose there's no reason for them not to. But I take it nothing came of it?"

"No. Nothing. She's better than I am with a sword. It's odd to have a bheancoran her age who hasn't declared yet." She smiled at Keylan. "Perhaps when we have our son, she'll declare." She turned to Torey. "Now, tell us all the news from Tyra and the continent."

22

Francia presented herself at Dun Camus as a healer skilled in the ancient Borlani arts of herbal healing, and was welcomed. The army of a fighting king was always in need of skilled healers, and she knew enough of the art to pass. Her books had taught her more than just magical skills.

She was pleased enough to find her lodgings airy and reasonably spacious. As a guest in a Maedun stronghouse, she would have received far less pleasant accommodations. The room in the guest wing of Dun Camus was comfortably furnished. Fires in both the hearth and a black iron brazier held back the damp chill of an island spring. The single window, narrow but adequate, was glazed with thick, rippled glass. It kept out the drizzle, but distorted the view from the window.

The window opened out onto a small garden, ringed by a low wall. The servant who had shown her to her room demonstrated how to open the window so she could step out into the garden when she wished some air.

A man came from the stable, leading two of the biggest horses Francia had ever seen. He was neatly groomed, clean, and well dressed in woolen trews and tunic of dark blue and green. Even the servants here were treated like guests, it seemed. No servant in Maedun would be allowed to wear such fine clothing. Nor would they move with such confidence and self-assurance. The servants in Dun Camus badly needed lessons in humility and proper reverence for their betters.

Two people, a man and a woman, left the Great Hall and mounted the horses. The man was tall and slender, his dark blond hair falling to his shoulders. The woman was nearly as tall, but with hair as black as a crow's wing. She exchanged a few words with the servant, who grinned, then stepped back. As the mounted man and woman readied the horses to leave, the servant sketched a bow that would have earned him twenty lashes for insolence in Maedun.

"Who is that?" Francia asked, gesturing toward the couple.

"Why, the King and Queen, of course, my lady," the servant said. "King Tiernyn and Queen Ylana."

Francia studied them carefully. The Queen did not wear a gown, but an open-necked shirt and breeks, covered by a thigh-length tunic. The fabric of the clothing was fine, expensive linen and light wool, and rich embroidery banded the hem, armholes, and neckline of the tunic. It horrified Francia to see a woman wearing man's clothing almost as much as it outraged her to see a woman carrying a sword.

She managed to hide her distaste and shock at seeing a woman who not only openly carried a man's weapon, but carried it with the casual ease of long practice. She studied the woman carefully and decided she herself in her Celae semblance was far prettier than this warrior woman. Men preferred beautiful women in their beds. It made them feel more like heroes. She thought that this unwomanly sword-wielder would offer no real competition once Francia found her way into the King's bed.

But first, she had to accomplish that.

The servingwoman bustled back into the chamber and wrestled Francia's baggage into a neat row along one wall. "Will you need help unpacking, my lady?" she asked.

"None, thank you," Francia said curtly.

The servant curtsied briefly. "Then I'll leave you, dearie." Francia's lips tightened at the unwarranted endearment, but the servant either didn't see her distaste, or blithely ignored it. "You'll be called when the meal is ready." The woman started for the door, then turned and smiled. "It's nice to have another woman healer here. We can always use a good healer."

Best to act as if she were used to this cavalier treatment,

Francia thought. She inclined her head graciously. "Thank you," she said. "I welcome the opportunity to serve the King."

During the first five days after her arrival, Francia saw the King only twice, both times from a distance. She was unable to speak with him at all. As a resident, she had free run of the lower floor of the main house. The second and third levels contained the King's private quarters, including his workroom, and chambers for guests. Access to the upper floors was by invitation only, and Francia had no plausible reason to be invited to the King's own quarters. At least, she thought with a predatory smile, not yet . . .

She spent her time becoming familiar with the main house and the infirmary, which was located at the far end of the barracks wing, and exploring the village. As the court of a king, Dun Camus was almost a travesty. It had none of the pomp and ceremony she expected to find in the headquarters of a king. Her Uncle Vanizen would have sneered, then laughed at a king's palace that contained nothing even approximating a throne room and was completely barren of courtiers. A king should stand out splendidly from his subjects. He should *look* regal and act as important as he was. As far as she could tell, the King acted more like the general of an army than a king. In truth, Dun Camus was more like an army camp than the seat of power of a king.

The Isle of Celi itself was very different from Maedun, Francia quickly discovered. She sensed the presence of magic all around her, both in the air and in the ground. Streams of power flowed everywhere around her, but when she tried to use it, she found she couldn't.

All that magic, and she couldn't use it. Every time she tried, she *felt* the threads between her fingers, but they twisted away from her uselessly and dissolved back into the air or the ground. It seemed it was not so much that she *couldn't* use the magic, but that it *would not allow* her to use it. Not only could she not use the magic, it seemed to inhibit her own power. Her father had learned how to "steal" Celae magic and make it work for him. If she had her father's secret, perhaps she could have made it work for her, too. She had to work harder to make any of her spells work here, and it was worse at Dun Camus than it had been in Gwachir. The only relief to her frustration was knowing that if the inherent magic worked against her, it would work against Hakkar, too.

At midmorning on the sixth day, she was just leaving the infirmary on an errand for one of the priestesses who was caring for the sick, when a troop of riders clattered into the courtyard. Francia paused to watch.

The man leading the troop of soldiers was tall and broad-shouldered. His hair glowed bright red-gold in the sun, and a golden torc glinted at his throat. Francia's heart gave an odd little lurch in her chest. For a moment, she thought she was looking at her father's murderer. How many times had she heard Hakkar describe the man who had killed their father? She always knew she would recognize him instantly.

The man in the courtyard dismounted and reached up to help the first of the two women who had come with him. One of the women wore a sword across her back, exactly as the Queen wore a sword. The other wore a gown with a divided skirt for riding, and had red hair nearly the same color as the man's.

Francia realized that the man was too young to be Red Kian of Skai. His eldest son, then. The one called Keylan, elder brother to the King. The red-haired woman would be the young sister. Francia had yet to see the youngest brother, the enchanter whose reputation had spread even to the continent.

The King himself came out of the Great Hall and ran lightly down the steps to greet his brother, his blue cloak swirling around him. Except for the glint of gold at his wrist, he was dressed as plainly as the officers of his army. He came alone, without his Queen. Francia had heard that they had both ridden out yesterday for Dorian. It would seem that the King had returned without her, despite the twittering of the servants that said the two were all but inseparable.

The red-haired woman threw herself into the King's arms, and he picked her up and swung her around, both of them laughing. He greeted the dark-haired woman more formally, then the four of them went up the steps together. Francia waited until they were inside, then hurried to complete her errand.

The chambers Donaugh showed her to were large and airy, looking out onto a landscaped terrace above the courtyard. Torey waited until the servants had brought in her baggage, then flung her arms about Donaugh's neck. He held her in a firm embrace, then kissed her forehead.

"Oh, Donaugh, it's so good to see you again," she said. "I've missed you terribly."

"We missed you, too, Littlest," Donaugh said. "I'm sorry Tiernyn isn't here to greet you. He and Ylana are with Blais of Dorian right now, poring over plans for a string of fortifications along the south coast. They left the day before yesterday, but he should be back late tomorrow morning."

She took his hand and led him to a bench by the window. "Sit and talk with me. We've got so much catching up to do. I want to know everything."

"All of it?" Donaugh laughed. "This could take awhile."

"We've time enough, don't we?"

"I always have time for you."

As he told her about the events of the past years, Torey found herself studying Donaugh. He had changed even more than Keylan had. Worry or responsibility had etched fine lines in his face, around his eyes and around the corners of his mouth. The fires she had always sensed in him now seemed to burn closer to the surface. In certain lights, his skin appeared almost translucent, and she wondered if he might be ill. But when she hugged him again as an excuse to use her Healing gift, she found nothing wrong, and she blushed when he gave her a knowing grin as she let him go.

"Your magic is stronger," Torey said.

"Aye," Donaugh said. He smiled, then grimaced. "I only hope it's strong enough."

"The Maedun?"

Donaugh nodded. "But first we have to take care of the Saesnesi. It's been a long campaign there." He grinned and changed the subject. "With luck, Connor will be back within the next day or so. He's been out on a scouting mission. I'm sure you'll be as happy to see him as he will be to see you."

Torey gave him her most serene smile. If he was expecting her to blush, she wanted him to know that she, too, had grown up and changed in the last six years. "It will be nice to see him again," she said. She laughed. "I wonder if he's still as beautiful as I remember?"

The corridors were deserted when Francia left her room that night. She clutched her houserobe around her as she hurried across the Great Hall. It was empty. Even the servants had separate sleeping places on this island, a luxury that certainly wouldn't be wasted on any Maedun servant. She saw no signs of movement as she ran quickly and lightly up the stairway leading to the second floor.

Only a few torches lit the passageway beyond the landing. She paused, trying to remember the one time she had seen the King mounting these stairs. Had he turned left or right at the top?

Right, she thought. Resolutely, she turned and crept down the corridor. The first door was a workroom, as was the second. She opened the third door just wide enough to catch a glimpse of the interior of the room. The sky-blue cloak she had seen the King wearing when he greeted his brother and sister lay across a chair by the hearth. The gleam of the embers cast deep, purple shadows through the folds of the fabric.

Francia glanced both ways along the corridor to make sure no one was about, then let herself into the room. Gliding silently across the room, she went to the half-open door to the sleeping chamber. The man in the bed lay deeply asleep, his back to the door. Moonlight flowed through the window, highlighting the dark gold hair spread on the white pillow. She could see nothing of his darkly shadowed face.

For a moment, she stood in the doorway, gathering her magic about her. But she was unable to penetrate his sleep to conjure up a vision of his dreams. Annoyed by her lack of success, she pulled her magic around her again. This should be a simple spell, but nothing on this accursed isle was as easy as it should be. Mayhaps she needed to find another innocent to renew and augment her powers.

Her third attempt succeeded. A nebulous vision formed in the air above the bed—a tall woman with hair like moonlight and sunlight spun together, and eyes as gray as woodsmoke.

Francia nearly laughed aloud. What would the sword-wielding Celae wench say if she knew her man dreamed of another woman? And dreamed with such tenderness, such love and longing?

"Sleep deeper, my King," she whispered. A tendril of black mist threaded from her fingers. It drifted silently across the room and coiled itself about the King's head. She crossed the room and stood above him. Closer now, she could make out his features. Sleep erased the small lines from his forehead and around his mouth.

The image of the blond woman wavered as Francia lay down on the bed beside the King. He moved restlessly, startling her. With her spell binding his sleep, he should not have been able to move at all unless she willed it. She tightened her control and he subsided into stillness.

Slowly, with great care, she insinuated herself into his dream, transforming her dream-self into the image of the blond woman. Her magic faltered again as the dream-woman herself resisted. Startled and momentarily frightened, Francia withdrew. But a dream-image could not harm her, and she would let nothing get in her way, not when she was this near to accomplishing her first objective. This had to be done now, while the Queen was away and the King was alone. Francia concentrated on strengthening her magic.

The woman faded as Francia moved more forcefully into the King's dream. Slowly, she drew him to her until their physical bodies coupled as their dream-images did. All her strength was taken up by the effort to hold the false image at the same time as she ensured his seed took root in her womb. She had no strength left to enjoy the act, or to bind the King to her with the intense physical need she must instill in him.

Pleasure would wait, she thought as she held him in her arms and smiled into the darkness. The overwhelming need of her would also wait until next time. The important thing right now was the son she must bear him.

When it was done and finished, she slipped from the bed and groped in the dark for her discarded robe. The moon no longer poured light through the window. A troubled frown marked the King's forehead, but he did not awaken. Francia put her hand to his brow, but had no strength left to deepen the spell. Exhausted and depleted, her magic shredding around her like blown mist, she fled down the corridor, back to her own room.

In the dark, she lay on her bed, hand pressed against her belly, where now the King's only son grew. She smiled to herself.

"I carry your only son, Tiernyn of Celi," she whispered. She laughed softly. If she had been able to ensure for so long that none of Hakkar's wives bore live children, how much easier would it be to make sure that the Celae sword-wielder remained barren? The King would find that his need of her, Francia, was far greater than his need for a simple female warrior.

The next time she and the King came together, he would be bound completely to her. His will would be submerged in hers, and he would make no move at all without her implicit consent. He might wear the crown and rule Celi, but she would rule him.

More of the odd reports from the watchtowers had come into Donaugh's workroom by messenger over the last few days. As he read them, Donaugh could almost see a strange procession of longships scurrying up and down the coasts. But none of them had a destination; none of them had a purpose. None of this made any sense at all. Not unless the ship movements really were decoys, a diversion to draw attention to the south and away from an attack from an entirely unexpected direction.

Donaugh put the reports aside and rubbed his temples wearily. His head ached. His sleep had not been restful, and he had been tired and irritable all day. He had dreamed last night, but he could not remember the dream, which was unusual. Upon waking, he felt troubled and faintly apprehensive, as if he had dreamed of danger but was unable to determine where it would come from, and there was a faint but unmistakable trace of depleted magic in his chamber. Not his magic. This magic had a tinge of something odd, almost putrescence, to it. If it happened again, it would bear some investigation.

When he had time. And time was one thing he had so very little of right now.

The sound of a troop of horsemen entering the courtyard brought him to the window. Below his window, Connor flung himself from his horse and ran to the door of the Great Hall, taking the steps two and three at a time. Donaugh gathered up his sheaf of papers and hurried down the corridor to Tiernyn's workroom.

"Connor's back," Donaugh said as he entered.

Tiernyn looked up, but before he could reply, Connor burst into the room, his face lit with excitement. The door slammed behind him, and Connor grinned widely.

"We've got him," he announced gleefully. "After all these years of chasing that old wolf the length and breadth of this island, we've finally got him!"

Connor went to the wall map and pointed to the confluence of the Camus and Wysg rivers, several leagues northwest of Dun Camus. "Right here." He stabbed his finger against the parchment. "We found him here. It looks as if he's been spiriting his men out of the Saesnesi Shore and bringing them here in small groups. They've been coming at night, when it's easier to steal past our scouts along the border. I'd say he's getting ready to spring a surprise raid on Dun Camus itself within the next few days."

Tiernyn went to the map, frowning thoughtfully. "Surprise is right," he said. "We certainly wouldn't expect them to come from the west." He traced a route down along the river. "If they come southeast, this is the easiest way," he said. "They'll want to move quickly if they think to take us by surprise." He moved his finger down the map to a steep-sided valley. "Right here," he said. "Brae Drill. If we meet them here, we can turn the surprise back on them. It's the best place along here to ambush them. What do you think, Donaugh?"

Donaugh studied the map. The markings on the map indicated marshy land to the east of the rivercourse. Firmer land lay to the west, but it was rough and barren country, and the whole area was only sparsely populated. Elesan had chosen his gathering point well. The lack of farmers or herdsmen in the area made accidental discovery unlikely.

"I agree," Donaugh said. "But I think Elesan might have already thought about an ambush there. In that case, he might bring his army around this way." He traced another route, skirting Brae Drill to the east and returning to the river valley farther south. "In either event, if we were to deploy the army along here"—he circled an area between the two routes—"we can send out scouts both ways and move quickly enough to intercept him." He looked at Connor. "How many men does he have with him now?"

"It was hard to tell," Connor said. "They've made cold-camp. No fires, and it was dark most of the time we lay on the top of the hill watching small troops of men come in. But I'd say that he has well over a thousand men there now. Perhaps two thousand."

Tiernyn nodded, studying the map. "Most of our men are still out for the spring sowing," he said. "This morning, we had three thousand men here at Dun Camus, but eight hundred of them are bowmen." He rubbed one eyebrow, then frowned again. "I say Elesan will bring his men through Brae Drill. It's nearly a full day faster than this other route, and he knows he needs to rely on speed if he wants to catch us by surprise. Hard to do once that many men begin moving . . ." He smiled grimly. "You have to admire the old wolf. With all those reports of longships running up and down the coast, this is the last place we should expect an attack to come from."

"If we're to set up a proper ambush, we'll have to deploy the archers well in advance," Connor said. "And under good cover. If we guess wrong, by the time we know we made a mistake, it'll be far too late to bring the archers across to surprise Elesan."

"But which way will he come?" Tiernyn asked, more to himself than the others. "East of the rivercourse? Or down the valley?" He studied the map intently for a moment, then turned to Donaugh. "What do you say, Donaugh? The moors, or Brae Drill?"

Donaugh glanced at Kingmaker, hanging in its accustomed place on the wall of the workroom. The song of the sword echoed at the edge of his consciousness. As he listened, a note of urgency threaded through the soft harmonics. Certain now, Donaugh turned back to the map.

"Brae Drill," he said. "Elesan will come through Brae Drill."

"Aye," Tiernyn said. "Brae Drill. Call the captains to the Council Room. We haven't much time."

23

Torey found Connor down by the paddock, beyond the town, watching the spring crop of foals frisking in the lush grass. He stood with one foot propped on the lowest rail, arms resting on the top rail, his chin down on his interlaced fingers. The black hair she remembered so well shimmered with blue highlights in the watery light. He stood with his back to her. His shoulders appeared broader than she remembered. He wasn't quite so slender and willowy as he had been. Nine years were more than enough to turn a boy into a man, and it was definitely a man—and a warrior at that—not a boy, who stood watching the horses.

Mindful of the wet grass, Torey kilted her skirts a bit higher and picked her way around the puddles toward the paddock. She paused before she reached him.

"Connor?"

Startled, he turned to face her, his foot still poised on the bottom rail. She wasn't prepared for the scar that disfigured his face, running from just beneath his right eyebrow across his cheek to the corner of his mouth. Her stomach lurched, but she got herself in hand immediately. A sword cut, obviously, but cleanly healed. And when he smiled, as he did as soon as he recognized her, the scar tipped the corner of his mouth up at a decidedly rakish angle. The smile, at least, was easily as devastating as she remembered it being.

He gave an odd little bow, not removing his foot from the rail. "My lady Torey," he said.

"My lady," she repeated. "How very formal you've become, my lord Connor."

"You are, after all, the sister of my King," he said gravely, but laughter danced in his eyes. That, too, had not changed in nine years.

She said a rude word, then blushed when he laughed aloud. Her wet shoes squelched in the grass as she went to the fence. One of the foals eyed her warily, trying to decide if she were friend or foe, then came cautiously forward on its comically long legs to nudge at her hand. Its glossy hide was almost the same color as Connor's hair. Torey stroked its neck, and it blinked at her.

"Oh, you're a beauty, you are, young lady," she said. The foal condescended to let her stroke it for a moment or two, then bounded away to find its mother. "They're all beauties, Connor. Your reputation as a horse breeder has spread even to Tyra."

He looked out over the paddock, smiling as he watched the horses. "Well, it's something I'm good at," he said. "One of the few things."

She arched an eyebrow at him. "I've heard otherwise," she said. "Surely you've heard some of the songs and stories the bards and minstrels are spreading around. They're quite popular in Tyra."

Unexpectedly, he blushed scarlet, then laughed self-consciously. "You mustn't go about believing everything you hear," he said. "Especially from bards and minstrels, who are notorious for their scandalous embellishment of the truth."

"I choose to believe there is always some truth behind even the most outrageous story," she said. "Even about Connor Catfoot." She climbed nimbly up to sit on the top rail next to where he stood. He was taller than she remembered. When he turned sideways and leaned one elbow on the rail, his face was nearly level with her shoulder.

"I heard this morning you'd come home," he said. His eyes were still the bluest blue she'd ever seen. "I almost wish you'd stayed in Tyra."

She searched his face for signs of bitterness or enmity, but found no trace of anything but perhaps regret. "Is this any welcome for me, Connor?" she asked softly.

He reached out and captured her hand. "You are well come

home, Torey al Kian," he said. "What I meant was that this is a poor time for your coming."

"No," she said. "This is the best time for me to come home."

"There's a battle coming," he said.

"I know. I've been watching the soldiers. I know enough to recognize an army preparing for war."

He turned her hand in his and traced a small circle just above her knuckles. "We ride out tomorrow morning to meet the Saesnesi," he said. "This could be the opportunity we've been seeking for nearly ten years. A decisive, final victory."

"That's why I came home, Connor," she said quietly. "I have to be here when that happens. I'm a Healer. I'll be needed."

"Aye, I'm afraid you will be," he said. "I'd rather you stayed where you'd be safe, but I know you won't." He looked up at her and smiled crookedly. "If I survive that battle, I will have something to say to you."

She hesitated. "Why don't you say it now?"

"Do you remember what I said when you left?"

She smiled. "You kissed me and startled me right down to my shoes," she said. "Then you said you'd be here when I returned."

He gave her a mocking little bow. "And so I am, as you see."

He stepped around to face her and put his hands to her waist. She reached for his shoulders for balance. He was very close. She could see precisely how each separate hair sprang crisply from his scalp to fall in waves to his shoulders. His eyebrows were the same dense black as his hair, but his eyelashes were paler, nearly brown. The faintest suggestion of a dimple hovered near the undamaged corner of his mouth.

"But were you aware that my father has been suggesting to your father since you were born what a fine match you and I would make?" he asked. The dimple deepened with the laughter lighting his eyes.

She caught her breath. "My father said nothing of that to me."

"He wouldn't, though, would he?" he said. "Your father told my father that you, being his daughter, and more, being your mother's daughter, would most certainly not take kindly to anyone picking out a husband for you. He said you would just as certainly decide for yourself."

"He was right," she said somewhat breathlessly.

"Stubborn yrSkai woman," he said, but the expression in his eyes did not match his words.

"Don't wait until after the battle," she said. "Tell me now, Connor, so you'll know my answer. So you can carry it with you onto the field."

He reached up and gently brushed the back of his fingers down her cheek. "Torey al Kian," he said gravely, "my soul is cupped in the palm of your hand."

"Connor ap Ryvern, your soul is sheltered safe within my hands and my heart." She would have added, "It always has been." But he had pulled her off the fence and into his arms, and was kissing her before she had the chance.

Tiernyn had built his army for speed. His cavalry and mounted bowmen could reach any place on the island in a matter of days, and his foot soldiers could force march faster and farther than any army since the Borlani had pulled their legions back to an embattled Borlan and abandoned their far-flung empire. But even the swiftest and strongest army needed support, and when the fighting started, it needed its healers.

The infirmary was caught in a whirlwind of preparations when Torey got there. The priests and priestesses from the shrine were in the midst of packing boxes of bandages and medicines, going about the business with grim and practiced efficiency. Besides Torey, there were three others with a Gift for Healing among the healers. One of them, the High Priest from the shrine, was too old to make the arduous trek behind the army, and would stay to attend to the infirmary while the army was gone.

Torey rolled up her sleeves and went to work with the packing. The light, two-wheeled carts stood ready outside the infirmary in the courtyard, waiting to be loaded with supplies and the field hospital tents used when there were no buildings near the battle site that could be used to shelter the wounded.

By the time the packing was finished and the last cart ready to go in the morning, it was past midnight. Gradually, the infirmary emptied as, one by one or in small groups, the healers left. The priests and priestesses left together to return to the shrine, to pray for guidance and success. The others made their way back to their rooms in the west wing of the main house, or to homes in the town.

Torey was among the last to leave. She walked out into a night lit by a moon and stars scudding through broken clouds. The air still smelled of rain and damp, and a fitful wind snapped at the standards above the gatehouse. Torey hoped for drier weather in the morning but admitted to herself that it wasn't likely. Spring in Celi was usually wet, interspersed with a few truly glorious days borrowed from midsummer. She could wish for one of those days tomorrow, but she wouldn't count on it.

Behind her, the barracks were quiet and dark as the soldiers slept. In the town, Torey knew women lay wakeful beside their men, wondering if they would come home again after the battle, or if their children would be orphans by dawn of the next day.

Torey rubbed her temples tiredly. The least Rhianna of the Air might grant the Celae army would be a dry day. Wet, slippery grass or greasy mud made for treacherous footing for both men and horses. Men would fall to the Saesnesi swords and war axes, but Torey hoped there might be no needless deaths or injuries due to falls. Broken limbs were—

She put her hand over her eyes and shook her head in wry amusement at the trivial direction her thoughts had taken.

Tomorrow, men would be horribly wounded, or die, and she stood in the dark tonight, worrying about broken limbs and sprained joints. It was time to find her bed. She was too tired to think rationally.

The last light in the infirmary went out. A woman, cloaked and cowled against the damp night air, slipped out of the darkened door and made her way across the courtyard, carrying a small lamp. She passed within a few feet of where Torey stood hidden in the shadow of the porch overhang. The cowl slipped and the woman paused for a moment to adjust it. The light from the lamp she carried reflected from dark blue eyes. She hurried up the steps to the Great Hall and vanished through the door.

Torey frowned. She had seen that woman before somewhere, she was certain of it. But where? A pennon snapped overhead in a gust of wind, making a sound like a ship's sails bellying out to the wind. Startled, Torey shook her head and stared at the main doors of the Great Hall. It could have been the woman from the ship. This woman held her cloak around her in the same manner, and she moved with the same quick grace.

Intrigued, Torey started across the courtyard, then stopped as the glow of a lamp appeared in a window of the guest wing. Framed in the rippled glass, the woman from the ship removed her cloak and stepped forward to the window. She was tall and slender, her black hair fell over her shoulder, bound in a heavy plait braided with a bright ribbon. As the woman reached up to draw the draperies together, Torey thought she saw her outline waver. An odd, dark shadow shimmered around her head for an instant. Then the draperies closed and she was gone.

Torey stood rooted in the courtyard. Surely the wavering outline of the woman was only a trick of the flawed glass. But that dark shadow . . . Torey shivered, remembering Kian's stories of Maedun sorcery.

A Maedun woman at Dun Camus? Surely not, Torey told herself firmly. A trick of the light and the rippled glass, and a mind that was overtired and misinterpreting what the eyes saw. And certainly no Maedun woman ever had blue eyes.

She climbed the steps and crossed the Great Hall to the staircase, still denying what she had seen. She needed sleep, that was all. But she went to bed resolving to find out more about the woman.

24

Two hours after midday, Tiernyn halted his army beneath the southern face of Creighail Na Drill. Donaugh dismounted and wiped the misty drizzle from his face as he looked up at the rocky crag. The tor thrust upward from the flat valley floor, its crown shrouded in mist and cloud. While it was nowhere near as high as the crags and peaks of Skai or Wenydd, its very isolation in the rolling moor surrounding it gave it a brooding grandeur. Scrub thornbush and ragged tatters of heather grew sparsely on the lower slope facing the river, only partly covering the barren, rocky crag.

The tor stood with its foot in the wide gravel strand where the Camus made a sweeping bend around it. The valley narrowed below it from over a league to barely a bowshot in width. On the west bank, opposite Creighail Na Drill, where the river undercut the stony clay bank, low cliffs rose to three times the height of a man.

The gravel on the broad strand was fine and level. Firm footing for both horses and men, Donaugh thought, studying it. He saw no large, loose stones that a horse might stumble over, or that might roll treacherously beneath foot or hoof.

"A good place for an ambush," Connor murmured beside him.

Donaugh nodded, still studying the terrain. "If Elesan comes this way, it is."

"He'll come," Connor said with firm conviction. "You said it yourself. Going around to the east of Creighail Na Drill would take him most of an extra day. He needs to keep his traveling time as brief as possible and hope he won't be seen. He'll take the risk because he has to. When he comes, it will be through here. Brae Drill."

The Veniani bowmen began climbing the flank of the tor.

Their dull green and brown cloaks stood out sharply against the gray-white of the sky. In moments, as each man found a clump of heather, or a scant thicket of thornbush, or even a small boulder, they faded into the hillside as effectively as if Donaugh had placed a masking spell. Their ability to vanish into the ground like that never failed to amaze and bemuse Donaugh. The Veniani had no need of his powers of enchantment; they had their own, which served them well.

Connor nodded in satisfaction as the last of the bowmen melted into invisibility. "Now we wait," he said.

They waited, a whole army hidden from the narrow defile by a small rise in the river valley.

Donaugh and Connor lay together on their bellies at the top of the rise, watching the entrance to the narrow valley. The cold ate its way into Donaugh's belly and chest, but he didn't move. As the day wore on, the clouds lifted and the drizzle stopped. Donaugh breathed a small prayer of thanks to Rhianna of the Air, who governed the clouds and the winds. Without the drizzle, the ground would not be so slippery underfoot.

The cry of a rock falcon rose from the flank of the tor.

"They're coming!" Donaugh whispered. "Get my horse. I'll give the signal after the bowmen have fired."

Connor gripped Donaugh's shoulder briefly and gave him a hard, fierce grin. He sprang to his feet and raced back down the slope for the horses.

Donaugh glanced over his shoulder. Tiernyn and Ylana had already mounted their horses, both of them leaning forward tensely, watching the flank of the tor. Behind them, men mounted quickly, soothing restive horses so that no uneasy whickering would warn the approaching Saesnesi.

The Saesnesi poured into the enclosure of Brae Drill in no particular formation that Donaugh could discern, rank after rank of blond warriors, iron helms gleaming dully beneath the cloud. In a living river of men, they flooded through the cleft, round shields slung over their shoulders, short swords and war axes at their belts. They moved in that league-defeating trot the Saesnesi could maintain tirelessly for hours, the tread of their booted feet on the sandy gravel strand like the muted rumble of distant thunder.

Donaugh looked for Elesan and found him on the left flank of the throng, riding one of the sturdy, shaggy little horses. The gray light gleamed on the gold decorations on his iron helm and the gold rings banding his arms. As Donaugh watched, Elesan drew the horse to a stop and shaded his eyes with his hand to scan the hills around the valley.

Donaugh held his breath. Then, as one man, the Veniani bowmen on the flank of Creighail Na Drill rose and fired their bows. The air rang with the music of their bowstrings. The hushed, whispering voices of the arrows in flight reminded Donaugh of wind in the rushes along a shore.

Fully one man in ten of the Saesnesi fell under the first deadly shower. Confusion and consternation exploded among the survivors. While the invaders were still milling about, uncertain of where the attack came from, the Veniani fired again, and more of the blond warriors fell to the gravel strand.

Shouting orders, Elesan spurred his horse and raced around the left flank of the massed Saesnesi to the front rank, holding his shield above his head. Slowly at first, then with more alacrity, his men raised their shields. Most of the third volley of arrows from the bowmen sank harmlessly into wood and leather.

Donaugh leapt to his feet and waved to Tiernyn. Seconds later, the army surged forward, swerving to pass Donaugh as a stream parts around a rock. Connor drew his horse to a halt beside him, holding the reins of Donaugh's horse.

"Hurry!" Connor cried. He curbed his prancing horse while Donaugh threw himself into his saddle.

The battle was shockingly brief and bloody.

The Celae fell upon the Saesnesi like an avalanche pouring down the slope of Creighail Na Drill. In the forefront of his cavalry, Tiernyn hurled himself down the slope, Kingmaker flashing as he swung its shining blade. With Ylana to his left and Keylan and Alys to his right, he forged to the center of the mass of Saesnesi.

Donaugh had no memory of drawing his sword as he spurred his horse after Connor. The roar of combat filled his ears. In the narrow valley, the muddled confusion of struggling men burst apart into knots of savage conflict, then into individual battles, man against man. Already, the sand was sodden with blood. In the center, where the fighting was fiercest, Tiernyn laid about him with Kingmaker, his horse lunging and dancing beneath him.

The Celae gradually but inexorably pushed the Saesnesi back toward the river. To either side of Donaugh as he strove to reach Tiernyn's side, men fell and died. Donaugh spun his horse and chopped at a Saesnesi soldier who leapt at Connor's back, and seconds later, Connor's blade took the arm from another Saesnesi reaching for Donaugh.

Donaugh glanced to his left just in time to see Elesan on his small horse launch himself through the brawling mass of men and horses, and fling himself at Tiernyn. The blade of his war ax bit deep into the muscle of Tiernyn's left arm, and both men tumbled to the ground together.

Ylana screamed, but could not break free of the knot of Saesnesi surrounding her. Keylan and Alys plunged through the flailing mass to her side. Donaugh spurred his horse toward the struggling leaders even as Ylana, Keylan, and Alys fought to help Tiernyn. Before Donaugh could reach Tiernyn, Connor hurled himself from his horse onto Elesan's back. Connor threw his arm around Elesan's throat and pressed the blade of his dagger into the notch between Elesan's neck and shoulder.

"Yield or die!" Connor shouted.

Donaugh leapt from his horse and flung himself down beside his brother. Blood spurted from Tiernyn's arm. Quickly, Donaugh ripped the sleeve from his own arm and bound it tightly over Tiernyn's wound. Ylana dropped from her saddle to her knees beside Tiernyn.

"I'm all right," Tiernyn said faintly. "Help me onto my horse."

Someone screamed. Donaugh looked up. A boy charged across the churned and bloody sand, a dagger in his hand held ready to thrust. Donaugh spun around and lunged. His outstretched arm snagged the boy around the waist and yanked him from his feet. With his other hand, Donaugh grabbed the boy's fist, still tightly clenched around the haft of the dagger, and held the blade harmlessly extended to one side. The boy struggled fiercely. He dropped the dagger and tried to twist out of Donaugh's grip, but Donaugh held him firmly. The child was no more than six or seven years old, but strong as a flailing mountain cat. His head knocked painfully against Donaugh's chin. Donaugh pulled the boy back against him, smothering the boy's struggles against his own body. He seized the boy's dagger and thrust it into his own belt, well out of the way.

Elesan looked up at Donaugh, ignoring Connor's dagger at his throat. "Don't hurt the child," he said. "He was only trying to protect me. He's my page. He followed the army against my word."

"Do you yield then, Elesan?" Donaugh asked.

Elesan closed his eyes as Connor loosened his grip. He drew in a deep breath, then nodded. "I yield," he whispered. "I am sorely weary of this war."

"Then call to your men to surrender," Tiernyn said. He held himself erect only by clinging to Ylana's shoulder. His face, drained of all color, was nearly gray in the clouded light. "We will honor their surrender. They will be treated fairly."

Elesan climbed wearily to his feet. He shouted to his army in his own language. One by one, then in droves, the Saesnesi dropped their weapons and surrendered to the Celae, and silence descended on the gravel strand of Brae Drill.

Donaugh looked down at the boy he still held. Defiance and

anger warred with fear on the young face that was so like his mother's that Donaugh's heart contracted painfully in his chest. He released the child and set him gently onto his feet.

"Go to your grandfather, Aellegh," he said quietly. "The war is over, and you will be safe. I will stand surety for it."

Torey placed her hand on Tiernyn's forehead and gave him sleep, then gently pulled the blanket up to cover his arm and shoulder. The wound had been a bad one, and Tiernyn's stubborn refusal to rest had not helped it. Right up to the moment he nearly fainted from loss of blood at Torey's feet, he denied the wound was anything more than just a scratch. When he stumbled and nearly fell, Connor, Donaugh, and Keylan had forced him to his tent and all but held him down while Torey cleaned the wound, then Healed it. It was, fortunately, a clean slice and Healed quickly, leaving only a thin scar. Tiernyn was lucky the ax had not taken his arm. The blade had cut clear to the bone.

"Will he be all right?" Ylana knelt on the other side of the pallet, hands on her knees, knuckles white on her clenched fists. Worry and fatigue lined her pale face. Blood matted her black hair above her left temple. More blood trickled down her cheek, dried to a shiny brown.

"He's sleeping," Torey said. "When he awakes, he'll have some of his strength back. But he's lost a lot of blood. He'll have to rest for a while before he's fully recovered.

Ylana smiled wearily. "Rest," she said, shaking her head. "You know what it's like trying to make any son of Kian ap Leydon do something he doesn't want to do."

Torey's hair had straggled onto her sweaty forehead and stuck. It itched. She lifted a hand and pushed it back, trying to tuck it back into its combs. She smiled back at Ylana. "That's true," she said. "But in this case, he'll be trying to outstubborn both of his brothers *and* his sister. One of us, he might defeat, but certainly not all three of us together." She got to her feet.

"You'd better come with me and let me look at that cut on your head."

Ylana touched the matted hair and grimaced. "This really is just a scratch," she said. "It doesn't even hurt anymore."

"Just the same, it needs cleaning and a bandage."

As they entered the hospital tent, the woman Torey had seen on the ship rose from her place beside a wounded soldier. In the uncertain light, Torey thought she could see a misty shadow clinging around the woman, cloaking her in darkness. The woman gathered up her medicine box and hurried out of the tent, barely glancing at them as she passed.

Torey turned to watch her. "Who is that?" she asked.

Ylana glanced over her shoulder. "The woman who just left? Her name's Francia. She's been trained as a Borlani herbal healer, I understand. She came to Dun Camus about a fortnight ago. I've heard she'd lived in Borlan since she was a child."

The woman had vanished into the night. A sudden, hard chill gripped Torey's chest. She hurried across the tent to the pallet where the soldier Francia had been attending lay. Nausea spasmed in Torey's belly as she looked down and realized the man was dead.

"Tiernyn," she whispered. She spun and ran back to Ylana. "Don't let her touch Tiernyn," she gasped. "I've got to find Donaugh. Don't let that woman get near Tiernyn."

The camp lay quiet in the still night. A crescent moon shone through a layer of thin cloud, looking hazy and furred in the dark sky. Francia clutched her box of medicines closer to her and drew in a deep breath. The renewed power moved within her, stirring her belly to breathless excitement. Her hands were no longer slippery with blood, but she still felt its hot, sensual flow moving against her skin.

The young soldier was no innocent child, and the letting of his blood had caused him little pain in his unconsciousness, but he provided a surge of renewal to her power. And there had been that one moment when he opened his eyes and realized what she had done in opening his wound wider, in slitting the large vessel in his groin. In those few seconds of stark terror, she had felt the power flow into her as wine pours into a goblet and fills it to overflowing. Trembling with the ecstasy of it, she let the last of his gushing blood flow through her fingers. When he was dead, she washed her hands in the basin beside him, dried them on a small towel, then gathered up her medicine box and her bag of herbs.

She looked back over her shoulder as she stood in the shadow of the tent, but the Queen and the King's sister had gone in. Neither of them had more than glanced her way.

Francia made her way through the neat rows of tents toward the pavilion where the King lay. Only the sentries were still awake, pacing off their appointed posts around the perimeter of the camp. Nearby, more sentries ringed the tent where the Saesnesi leaders lay. The rest of the Saesnesi prisoners, heavily guarded, were penned in a hastily constructed stockade just beyond the camp by the river.

She paused for a moment, regretfully watching the prisoners' tent. The Saesnesi leader had a child with him, a young boy. Unfortunately, the child was uninjured. She had been given no excuse to approach him. He would have been so much better than the young soldier for her purposes. But no matter. After tonight, she would have no trouble finding what she needed. As the King's mistress, she could command what she wanted, and none could gainsay her.

No one challenged her as she moved quickly through the camp. The sight of healers going from tent to tent to tend the less severely wounded was a common one. She reached the King's tent and waited as one of the guards stepped forward to intercept her.

"The lady Torey sent me to make sure the King sleeps well," she said. She held up her box of medicines so he could see it. "She sent wine and poppy if he seemed restless."

The guard stepped aside to let her pass.

A brazier glowed near the center of the tent. Beyond it, the King lay on a raised pallet, covered by a thickly woven blanket. Surprised, Francia saw he was alone. No servants attended him, and the Queen was with his sister, probably having her own wound attended to.

Francia set the box down on the ground and went slowly to the King's pallet. In the faint light cast by the brazier, he was still pale. He slept deeply in the aftermath of the Healing his sister had performed. Of the ax wound in his arm, only a faint scar remained. A goblet of watered wine stood on a small table beside the bed. It didn't look as if it had been touched.

She went to her knees beside the pallet, smiling to herself. Weakened as he was by both the wound and the Healing, and the exhaustion of the battle itself, he could offer no resistance to her spell. He was hers, now. Hers for as long as she wished to keep him at her side the same way she might keep a dog she was fond of.

She gathered her magic about her, drawing extra strength from the blood of the soldier she had killed. A black mist formed at her fingertips, hovering in the air. Slowly, she reached out to touch the King's forehead.

Something sharp pricked against the skin of her throat. Light flashed off the blade of a dagger.

"Touch him, and you die," the Queen said softly.

The black mist stretching from Francia's fingers lashed like a whip toward the Queen. But before Francia could transform the magic from a controlling spell into a weapon, a man's hand closed tightly around her wrist. She jerked her head around, then cried out in shock as she stared directly into the King's face, his golden brown eyes lit from behind with the fire of magic. The same magic she had felt in the air and the ground.

Not the King, she realized too late. The King still lay asleep behind her. This was the younger brother, the enchanter. And he could use the magic of this accursed isle.

He spun it about her in a dense web, cutting her off from her own power. Then, even as she stared into his eyes, it was as if her whole body was turned inside out. Nausea churned in her belly, and a light brighter than the sun seemed to burst in her head. It burned with a searing cold flame. Her own magic shriveled before its light and power, then charred to ash and fell away. The sense of emptiness and loss overwhelmed her, horrified her, terrifying in its strength.

"No," she whispered. Then she fainted.

In the hot, shadowed darkness, Donaugh fought a grimly silent battle. Dregs of the woman's magic scuttled like huge, vile spiders as they fled the bright lance of his power. Doggedly, he hunted down each hideous fragment and impaled it on the point of his magic. Even as he destroyed them with the light of air and earth magic, they turned on him with unexpected strength, reaching out to wrap tendrils of black around his throat. But the searing brightness of his own magic scorched them to flakes of ash.

When finally, the last of the blood magic was cauterized and rendered harmless, Donaugh sat back on his heels. Sweat streamed from his forehead and down into his eyes. His chest ached, and his belly churned with nausea. Torey handed him a cool, damp cloth, and he wiped away the sweat gratefully.

"Is it gone?" Tiernyn asked groggily from his pallet.

"Yes." Donaugh shuddered. "I've never known anything as vile."

The Maedun woman lay in restless, uneasy sleep on a rug on the ground, her face twisted in rage and loss. Donaugh nodded to Torey. She put her hand to the woman's forehead and removed the gift of sleep.

Eyes as black as the shadows in the room glittered in the woman's pale face as she awoke. She surged up off the pallet, clawed fingernails reaching for Donaugh's eyes. But he was ready for her. He caught her wrists in his hands and forced her

back down to the pallet. She struggled violently, legs thrashing. One knee slammed painfully into his upper arm.

"Stop it," he said firmly. "I'll have you bound like a common criminal if you continue this."

The woman subsided, but the glitter of rage in her eyes
remained.

"Now, you'll tell us who you are and why you're here,"
Donaugh said. "We'll have the truth from you."

She spit in his face. Calmly, he wiped his cheek on his
sleeve, then turned to Torey. "Fetch the guards," he said.
"Have them take her out and execute her now."

Torey knelt behind the woman, who couldn't see her startled expression. She glanced at the woman, then at Donaugh.
Before she could move, Ylana stepped forward.

"I'll kill her myself," she said.

The woman stopped struggling and lay quietly on the pallet. "You can't kill me," she said clearly. "I carry the King's
child."

25

Donaugh walked out into the misty chill of the night and breathed deeply of the clean, fresh air. Dealing with the Maedun woman had left him with a headache severe enough to blur his vision. His magic reacting against hers, he supposed. His father had spoken of the stench blood magic left in the air, but Donaugh had never before encountered it. He devoutly wished never to meet it again, either.

Getting the truth from her had been a long and arduous process. Even with only a few burned-out scraps of her magic left, she had still managed a strong resistance to the truth spells. But her story explained the disturbing dream he'd had before leaving Dun Camus. Knowing he'd lain with her, albeit under a spell, chilled Donaugh to the heart.

The woman's magic was startlingly powerful—powerful enough so that he remembered little of her coming to him in his dreams. A most troubling concept, that. If Hakkar's sister possessed such strong magic, how much more powerful would he be, being born with the full potential of his father?

That hardly bore thinking about right now. But Donaugh would have to think about it soon. And think hard, he knew.

If any good had come out of this incident, it was that the brush with blood magic taught him how devastating it could be. He would not underestimate Hakkar's abilities when the time came. And another useful thing was that he now thought he might have an idea how to overcome the blood magic after the brush with Francia's magic. Gentle Tyadda magic could not be used to kill, but it was the magic of earth and air, magic of the light. And light overcame and banished darkness, provided the light was bright enough, and the darkness not all-encompassing.

He looked back into the tent, his own tent that he had

given up to hold the woman. Francia lay stilled by the spell of sleep Torey had placed. She wore her own face now. Donaugh could not deny it was a most beautiful face, but the traces of the black mist of blood magic still drifting around her made her beauty sinister rather than enticing or alluring. She lay with one hand to her belly, as if protecting the child she carried.

Donaugh had no intention of disabusing her of the notion that she carried Tiernyn's child. Even though her pregnancy was the only reason she was not on her way back to Maedun and the doubtful mercies of her brother—indeed the only reason she still lived at all—Donaugh had few illusions as to how long Francia would continue to carry the child had she realized he was the father and not Tiernyn.

This child he would not lose to an enemy. This child he intended to claim and raise, even if he had to raise him as the King's bastard rather than as his own. If the child inherited magic from both parents, he would need much help in reconciling the two incompatible powers. Donaugh was the only person who could help the child in this.

Pain pounded behind his eyes. He rubbed his temples wearily. He thought he could still smell the dregs of the magic Francia had tried to use on him. For a moment, his belly clenched with nausea. He took a deep breath and his head cleared. He still needed to speak with Tiernyn before he found his way to his bed.

Torey left the tent and came to his side. She, too, drooped with fatigue. Donaugh remembered belatedly that she had spent most of the day using her Gift for Healing. If anything, she would be more tired than he.

"She'll sleep all night now," Torey said. "I'll stay here to guard her. She can't do anything now that you've stripped her of her magic."

He reached out and stroked her cheek. "You're exhausted," he said. "Go to bed. I'll have one of the priestesses keep watch over the woman. That will be enough."

"You're tired, too," she said. She smiled. "And I probably can't trust you to take a Healer's advice and find your own bed, can I?"

"As a matter of fact, you can," he said. "As soon as I've spoken with Tiernyn."

"Of course," she agreed gravely, then smiled in resignation. "That could mean hours, though." She reached up to kiss his cheek. "Good night, Donaugh."

Donaugh caught a glimpse of a man lurking in the shadows beyond the tent. He smiled at Torey. "I believe you have an escort waiting to see you safely back to your quarters," he said. "Good night, Buttercup." He raised his voice slightly. "Good night, Connor. Take good care of my sister."

Connor's chuckle floated on the air behind Donaugh as he turned away for Tiernyn's tent.

Donaugh paused in the dark as he came to the tent where Elesan and his captains lay. Guards ringed the tent, alert and watchful for all it was well past midnight. Lamplight glowed softly within the tent. As Donaugh watched, a shadow flickered briefly on the canvas as a man moved between the light and the wall. Donaugh wanted to go in, but what could he say to Elesan? What could he say to the boy who attended his grandfather as a page, whose eyes, soft gray as his mother's, had regarded Donaugh so flatly and appraisingly after the battle? Donaugh had seen no signs of fear in those wary young eyes, but neither had he seen any indication of recognition or even curiosity. It seemed obvious that Elesan had told the boy nothing. Aellegh could not know who his father was.

"Oh, Eliade," he whispered. "What's to become of our son?" He longed to speak with Aellegh, but knew he could not. Not yet. Perhaps not ever.

Reluctantly, he turned away and continued the short journey to Tiernyn's tent.

Tiernyn sat on the edge of his bed, alone in the tent except for Ylana, who lay curled in sleep behind him. He held

Kingmaker across his knees, abstractedly tracing the deeply etched runes with one finger as he looked into the distance at his own thoughts. Donaugh could not read the runes on the blade—no man could read the runes on a sword not his own—but he knew what they said. **Take up the Strength of Celi**. Between them, Tiernyn and Kingmaker had proved the strength of Celi to be sufficient to overcome the Saesnesi after all these generations. The first part of the task set for man and sword had been accomplished and was complete. There yet remained the question of the Maedun.

Donaugh waited for a moment after letting the door flap fall shut behind him, but Tiernyn didn't speak. Not until Donaugh took a seat on a low, cushioned stool did he look up.

"So, we have survived this far," he said.

Donaugh smiled. "A good sign," he said.

A brief smile flitted across Tiernyn's face. "A good sign, indeed," he said. "I must admit, though, I had my doubts of it when I faced Elesan and his war ax nearly took my arm." He looked down at Kingmaker again, and traced the outline of the stain above the runes. "But the sword didn't let me down. Not this time."

Donaugh said nothing. The stain was glaringly obvious against the polished metal of the blade.

Tiernyn sheathed the sword and put it gently aside. "Mayhaps I've learned some wisdom after all these years." He smiled, bemused, and shook his head. "One can hope, at any rate." He got up and went to the table, where a flask of wine and a tray of goblets stood. He poured two cups and handed one to Donaugh. "Now I'll prevail upon your wisdom and your vision of the future. Whatever shall I do with Elesan?"

Donaugh nodded toward the door, indicating the army camped without. "They're going to demand you execute him," he said quietly. "They'll clamor for his death."

"But you won't."

"No. I won't. And you understand why."

Tiernyn rubbed his eyes. "If I execute him, the chances are excellent that in ten years, or even less, I'll be facing his grandson across a battlefield."

Donaugh nodded. "That's a fair assumption."

Tiernyn gave a grunt of humorless laughter. "And even if I were the type of king who slaughtered children, I would not dare to touch that particular boy. Not knowing that I'd have to go through you first."

"Where would you stop the slaughter, Tiernyn?" Donaugh asked. "Elesan has other kinsmen, and they, too, have children."

"Aye, there's that about it, too." Tiernyn sipped at his wine, frowning thoughtfully. "Have you spoken with the boy?"

"No." Donaugh shook his head. "There's no point to it. Aellegh doesn't know he's my son."

"No. But you know, and I know. And so, for that matter, does Elesan."

"What will you do?"

"I've thought about little else since the battle." Tiernyn made an irritable, helpless gesture. "Why couldn't the old wolf simply have died there on the battlefield? It would have made all this much simpler."

Donaugh grinned. "Talk to Connor about that. He's the one who captured Elesan after pulling him off you."

"It bears a severe talking to," Tiernyn said. "Well, I think I've come to an answer. I'll deal with Elesan in the morning."

"Will you tell me what you intend to do?"

Tiernyn drained his goblet and placed it carefully back on the table. "I think not," he said slowly. "You know I value your counsel, but I think this is one decision I must make on my own."

Donaugh glanced at the sword, but it was quiescent. Only a faint echo of its music and magic lilted in Donaugh's mind. Whatever Tiernyn's decision, the sword was not allowing Donaugh to learn it from its song. He got to his feet.

"In the morning, then," he said. "Sleep well, my lord King."

Tiernyn grimaced. "I will sleep this night as well as you will, I think."

Just before dawn, Torey awoke to a gentle touch on her cheek. She sat up on the pallet to see Connor kneeling beside her. He had lit a candle and the light cast dark, wavering shadows across his face. He looked haggard and drawn, his mouth pulled down into a grim line, the flesh beneath his eyes like bruises against his skin. A jolt of fear kicked in Torey's chest.

"What is it?" she asked.

"We found Ralf," he said. "He's dead."

Sudden tears sprang to Torey's eyes. Connor had always idolized his elder brother. The news shattered the small, faint hope they had been clinging to. She reached out instinctively to him. He came to her and she held him like a child in the private darkness of the small tent.

"Oh, Connor, I'm so sorry," she said, knowing the words to be hopelessly inadequate.

"We have him ready to take home now," he said wearily, his breath moving warmly against her skin. "I'll leave as soon as Tiernyn has dealt with Elesan and the Saesnesi."

She drew him down onto the pallet beside her, put her hand gently to the back of his head as he buried his face in the hollow of her shoulder. Hot tears fell on the bare skin of her throat. She called on her Gift for Healing and reached into him to touch the festering grief. It was a wound she could not Heal, but she could give him the gift of sleep to ease the pain temporarily. When he awoke, the grief would still be with him, but it would no longer be a blade to flay his soul.

———

The morning dawned cloudy and cool. Tendrils of mist trailed along the crowns of the hills to either side of the valley as Torey emerged from her tent. A bright, pearlescent glow marked the sun's place behind the clouds above the hills, and the air was completely still. No breath of breeze stirred the young leaves of willow and silverleaf maple along the stream, or rippled in the newly green grass.

All the soldiers were up and moving, preparing to break camp and return to Dun Camus. At the far end of the valley, beyond the rise that hid the battlefield, black smoke from the Saesnesi funeral pyre rose straight and smooth into the gray sky. On the hillside behind Torey, the burial parties finished raising the last cairns over the Celae dead.

Connor came out of the tent, his cloak of dark Wenydd green clasped at his shoulder by a stag-head brooch. He carried her cloak with him and stepped behind her to drape it over her shoulders. She turned and smiled her thanks. The air was chilly enough to warrant wearing the cloak.

He looked better this morning. Grief and loss still clouded his eyes and shadowed his face, but his color was back to normal and he stood as straight as always. Weariness no longer weighted him down. While he slept, acceptance of his brother's death had filled him, and while he yet grieved, the sense of purpose imparted by the duty of taking Ralf's body home to Wenydd sustained him.

A young officer left Tiernyn's tent and hurried to the tent where Elesan and his officers were being held. Another, right behind the first, ran for the stockade beyond the camp.

"Tiernyn must be ready," Connor said. He bent to kiss Torey quickly. "I must go then."

Torey found a place on the hillside where she could watch unimpeded. The Saesnesi prisoners straggled out of the stockade, closely guarded by Celae soldiers with swords held ready and bows nocked with arrows. When they were assembled on the bank of the river, more guards brought Elesan and his captains from their tent. The boy Aellegh, Elesan's page, stood stiffly to his grandfather's left, a pace behind him. His fine blond hair fell about his face in soft waves, gleaming in the watery light.

Something about how the boy moved caught Torey's attention. A familiarity in how he held his head, the attitude of his body at rest. He stood in profile to her, the soft, childish lines of his face defined sharply and clearly against the background of the misty green hills. The Saesnesi were considered men at fourteen, she knew, trained in weaponry since they could walk. This child could not yet be eight years old, but already, he was becoming a warrior. Someday soon, he would make a formidable foe—or ally.

The child shook his hair back out of his eyes and looked up at his grandfather. Elesan bent his head and spoke a word or two to the boy. Reassurance? Torey couldn't tell. But the child stepped closer to Elesan, his shoulders straight, and for a moment, Torey thought of Donaugh standing beside Tiernyn.

Before she should pursue that fancy to any conclusion, a flurry of motion by Tiernyn's tent took her attention from Aellegh. Dressed in his court regalia, Tiernyn stepped out onto the trampled grass. His scarlet cloak, trimmed with fur and gold-thread embroidery, swirled around him, and the light caught the soft gleam of the gold crown about his brow. Kingmaker rose from its sheath behind his left shoulder. To his left, Ylana also wore scarlet and gold, a golden diadem binding back her dark hair. To Tiernyn's right, Donaugh wore his blue, and under it, he was as plainly dressed as Connor, who stood beside him. Keylan moved to stand at Ylana's left, Alys beside him. Behind them, the Captains of the Companions took their places in silence.

Torey thought the river valley might overflow with men as the Celae army gathered in the space between the camp and the stockade. They left a wide lane between Tiernyn and Elesan. Even from the hillside where she stood, Torey felt the tension hanging in the air above the gathering. It was palpable as heat from an oven—a live and savage thing, waiting to be released. The army waited in ominous and expectant silence as Tiernyn began the short march to where Elesan awaited him by the stream, his own army behind him.

For a moment that stretched taut in its eternity, the two leaders faced each other. Torey's clenched fists ached as she waited for something—she didn't know what—to break the tension.

Then Elesan went slowly to one knee before Tiernyn. But his body remained stiffly erect, his head proudly raised. Defiantly, he stared straight into Tiernyn's eyes.

"You have beaten me, Tiernyn of Celi," he announced clearly. "But you have not defeated me."

Tiernyn made no move. He stood returning Elesan's gaze, his arms folded across his chest, his stance relaxed and easy. Finally, a small, tight smile tilted up the corners of his mouth.

"To defeat you, Elesan, Celwalda of the Saesnesi Shore, I fear I would have to kill you."

"Aye, King. You would."

"I prefer a different way." Tiernyn raised his voice. "We are both men of Celi. For five generations have your people lived in the East, and for five generations have our people fought bitterly and died at each other's hands. This day it ends. In this place, it will stop forever."

Tiernyn's unique magic flared around him, carrying to all who heard his voice. Torey found herself leaning forward eagerly, captured by her brother's ringing tones. Breathlessly, she watched the tableau spread below her. Not a man moved; every face she saw was turned toward Tiernyn, lips parted in rapt attention. Even the Saesnesi appeared captivated, riveted by Tiernyn's speech.

Tiernyn stepped forward and held out his hand to Elesan. "Swear fealty to me, Elesan, Celwalda of the Saesnesi, and to you and your descendants forever will I grant the Summer Run so that you might live there and flourish for the rest of your days, and our people might live in peace and understanding each with the other. Swear fealty to me, Elesan, Celwalda of the Summer Run, and your title of Celwalda will be as the title of duke or prince in Celi, and you will rule your province as each duke or prince rules his, subject only to my rights and laws as King of Celi. Pledge fealty to me, and I will stand surety for the safety of the Summer Run as I stand surety for all of this island."

Again, the moment stretched like a bowstring as Elesan looked up at Tiernyn. Just when Torey thought she must scream with the strain of waiting, Elesan climbed to his feet. He reached out his hand to Donaugh.

"Lend me your dagger, Enchanter," he said.

Unhesitatingly, Donaugh unsheathed his dagger and placed the haft in Elesan's outstretched hand. Elesan looked again at Tiernyn. Tiernyn's shoulders straightened, and he dropped his hands to his sides.

Elesan bent back his left hand, his heart hand, stretching the skin of his wrist taut across the bones so that the veins showed clearly. Then, slowly and deliberately, still looking at Tiernyn, he used the point of the dagger to open the veins. Dark blood welled up in a flood and splashed to the ground at Tiernyn's feet.

The symbolism was ancient and explicit. Elesan offered his life's blood to nourish the soil Tiernyn ruled. Tiernyn could accept Elesan as an ally and vassal and stanch the flow of blood, or he could deny the offer and let him bleed to death. The choice was his. Elesan kept his gaze on Tiernyn's eyes, level, steady and outwardly calm. Tiernyn nodded.

"Bind your wound," he said quietly. "I accept your service." He took the scarf from his throat and handed it to Elesan.

Elesan wrapped the scarf tightly around his wrist, stopping the flow of blood. He went slowly to one knee and bowed his head. "My lord," he said clearly. "My sword and my life I pledge to your service, from now until the last days." He rose and turned to the Saesnesi gathered behind him.

"Bear witness," he cried. "I give in honor to this man what he could not take by force of arms. My life and my loyalty I give to him, and my sons to his sons, until the last days."

"My lord Celwalda," Tiernyn said. "You may take your people home."

26

*Imbolc had come and gone, and still the winter dragged on inter-*minably. Heavy in the last season of her bearing, Francia felt bloated and distended to grotesqueness. The face in her mirror was puffy and swollen, as were her fingers and ankles. Her feet constantly pained her when she walked, or even stood, and she was always cold.

The house was little more than a hunting lodge, set high among the mountains in Skai, but it was furnished comfortably enough, and there was always plenty of wood for the fires in the hearths. She could not bear to look out the windows, though. In one direction, the chillingly high mountains stretched to infinity, and in the other, the land fell away sharply to the dizzying depths of a valley far below the foot of the garden. While the sheer distance down to the floor of the valley below made her shiver in distaste, the overwhelming bulk of the mountains filled her with terror. They seemed to weigh down on her, crowding around her, sullen and vengeful in their solidity.

The enchanter himself had brought her to this prison high in the mountains to await the birth of the child. He had ignored all her demands to speak with the King, saying only that the King had absolutely no wish to speak with her, now or ever.

"Has he then no care or concern for his son?" she asked.

"That," the enchanter said calmly, "he will see to in due course." Then he had bundled her ignominiously into a carriage to begin the horrid journey into the mountains. But no carriage could manage the steep track up from the valley to the lodge. She had completed the trek on horseback like a common trollop.

He had left her with servants to attend her—a woman to

work in the kitchen and to keep the place clean and tidy, a man to work in the gardens, look after the animals, and provide firewood. But they watched her. They both watched her all the time. Constantly. Incessantly. They never stopped. Even as she sat in her own rooms by the fire, she could feel them watching her the same way she felt the weight of the mountains around her. She was sure the combination would drive her to madness.

The air around the small lodge was thick with the threads of magic she had first sensed in Gwachir. They ran like rivers through the ground beneath her feet, swirled around her in the air when she moved. The enchanter had woven those threads into something that held her in this ridiculous house. Like a curtain around the walls of the garden, it held her back. She could go anywhere within the walls, but she could not leave the compound. The one time she had attempted to walk through the gate, that curtain had stopped her. As impenetrable as stone, it gave her no pain to touch it, but it filled her with such revulsion, she could not bear it.

Her own magic had deserted her. Even the simple spells she had learned first were useless here. She didn't know if it was the magic in the air around her inhibiting her power, or if the enchanter had truly stripped her of all her magic in that one horrifying moment when he had looked into her eyes.

Her magic might return if she went back to Maedun. But going back to Maedun meant facing Hakkar, and that she would not do. Not now. Not knowing how dismally she had failed. If he allowed her to live at all, he would make her life hardly worth living. She would not crawl to him, begging forgiveness. She *could* not.

She ran her hands over her swollen belly. The child within kicked strongly against her palm. If she had any power left, it was here, with this child, the son of a king. The child was a tool, a weapon, the only weapon she had. That she would not be allowed to keep it with her, that it would be taken from her as soon as it was born, she had no doubts at all. The enchanter had as much as assured her of that. But the child was hers, after all, and if the magic bred true, she could bind him to her as securely as Hakkar bound his son to him. Surely she still had that mother's magic in her.

It was almost worth the humiliation at the hands of that accursed enchanter to see the Queen's face when she heard Francia say the child she carried was the King's. The Queen shot an angry glance at the King, who was then awake but still groggy. The King, of course, protested, but Francia merely laughed.

"Do you not remember, my King?" she asked. "I came to you when you slept, and you welcomed me to your bed. And now, I carry your son." She glanced at the Queen, then smiled demurely. "Shall I tell the Queen of whom you dreamed that night, my lord King?"

But the Enchanter had cut her off then, allowed her to say nothing more. He and his sister had taken her to his own tent, and the sister had done something to her to make her sleep.

"You will know who your enemy is, won't you, my son?" she crooned to her swollen belly. She caressed it again, smiling. "You are the King's eldest son—his only son. You will take revenge for the way your mother was treated."

If she could find some way to take the child with her when she returned to Maedun, Hakkar would certainly welcome a weapon like him. The child would be her safe passage back to Maedun. Delivering such a weapon, such a tool, into the hands of her brother would be her triumph.

The son of the King of Celi in Hakkar's hands . . . Francia smiled. Her son had a claim to the throne of Celi. Through the child, Hakkar could be more than just Lord Protector of Celi. As the child's nearest relative, he could be King. Certainly there would be no other male claimants to the throne once Hakkar was finished with this accursed island.

Her time grew nearer, but no plan for escape with the child presented itself. She certainly could not walk or ride away from the mountain lodge in her condition, even if she could get past the curtain of magic the enchanter had woven around the lodge. But after the child was born, it might be different. Even if one of the servants left the moment her labor started, the enchanter could not reach the lodge until several days after the child was born. By then, she would have her strength back, and her limber body. And once the man had gone to take the news to the enchanter, Francia could easily overcome the woman. Once free of the watchers, she might be able to escape. If a messenger could find a way through the net of enchantment, surely she could, too. The enchanter would not set a snare that could kill. He would never take the chance that he might accidentally kill the child she carried.

She would bide her time. A chance would come.

Drifted snow surrounded the small lodge, piled into deep mounds against the gates and in the small courtyard. Dark green pine and bare birch and aspen crowded close to the walls of the compound, offering some protection from the wind. Smoke rose from the chimneys, and icicles thick as a man's wrist hung from the slate roof. In the shadowed dusk, no welcoming light gleamed from the windows.

Torey dismounted and led her horse into the stable. A mule placidly munching fresh hay looked up, long ears twitching with vague curiosity. Torey unsaddled the mare, covered her with a blanket, and left her to share the meager warmth of the stable with the mule.

She had seen no sign of anyone coming to investigate her arrival. For a moment, she wondered if Francia was inside. But this late in her pregnancy, it was unlikely she was out in the snow. But where were Mag and Drust? Surely they had heard her ride in.

Mag sat alone before the hearth in the small main room of the lodge, her arms folded across her chest. She looked up as Torey entered, then sprang to her feet.

"Thank the goddess you've come, my lady," she said. She

gestured to the closed door behind her. "That one . . . Herself will have none of us right now. Won't let me near her. Screamed like a harridan at Drust, too. I think it's the baby, my lady."

Torey glanced at the door, then back at Mag. "Where's Drust?" she asked.

"In the kitchen. I set him to boiling water. The way he's cursing that woman, it'll be a wonder if he needs the fire to do it."

"I'll go in," Torey said. "I'll call you if I need you."

Mag sat down again and folded her arms across her chest. "You're welcome to her, my lady. I've had quite enough of herself for now. She throws things when she's angry, and she's been angry all day."

Torey pushed at the door. It opened to reveal a comfortable bedchamber. The air smelled of applewood from the embers of the fire in the hearth. More wood lay stacked neatly beside the hearth. The draperies around the bed were half-drawn, throwing deep shadows across the bed itself.

For a moment, Torey thought the room was deserted. The small table beside the hearth stood bare but for a broken ewer, mute evidence of a fit of temper. Water puddled around the feet of the table, and the iron stand holding an unlit lamp beside it.

Torey stooped on the hearth and put more wood on the fire, then lit a taper from the embers. The draft from the open door tore the flame into a ragged streamer. She cupped her hand around the taper and lit the lamp, then turned to push the door closed.

Light and shadow flowed swiftly around the room, wavering with the uncertain light of the lamp and the leaping flames on the hearth. Something moved on the bed. It sounded like a small animal scrabbling in straw.

Francia pulled herself into a sitting position on the bed. Her black hair and dark gown blended in with the shadows of the draperies, leaving her face as a pale oval floating in darkness. Her hair flew wildly around her face, her eyes little more than pools of darkness in her gaunt face, her mouth a twisted slash against her pale skin. She had lost all semblance of being Celae. Her dark gown hid her swollen belly in shadow. She stared blankly at Torey for a moment, then hunched over and wrapped her arms around her belly in pain.

"You're in labor," Torey said.

Francia laughed wildly. "You timed your arrival perfectly," she said, gasping. "You're just in time to watch me die, and the child along with me. Is that what you came for?"

Torey crossed the small room and went to her knees beside the rumpled bed. She opened the draperies wide to let in light and air. This close, the fever-bright glitter of Francia's eyes showed plainly. Torey reached out and put her hand to Francia's forehead. Beneath the palm of her hand, the skin was cool and dry. So the fever glitter was not illness—merely anger and fear.

Francia pulled back angrily and slapped her hand away. "Don't touch me," she snarled.

"I came to make sure you lived," Torey said. "You and the child both."

Francia's harsh laugh ended in a gasping sob. "Did the King send you?" she demanded. "Is he so anxious to claim his bastard?"

Torey got up and went to the tall wardrobe chest by the window. She found a light bedgown and brought it to the bed. "Get undressed and into this," she said, her tone matter-of-fact and crisp. "We can't deliver the child while you're wearing that gown. It will get in the way. Can you do it yourself, or do you need help?"

Francia snatched up the bedgown and glared at Torey. Torey shrugged, then went to the hearth to build up the fire. Behind her, Francia cried out in pain once more, but when Torey turned, she saw Francia had changed into the bedgown and was lying down on the bed.

She went to the door to call Mag, but Francia struggled to a sitting position again.

"No," she cried. "No, don't call that woman in here."

"We're going to need her," Torey said.

"No," Francia said again. "I refuse to be in the same room with that hag and her evil blue eyes. She watches me as a snake watches a bird. I'd rather die than have her here while I birth this King's bastard."

Torey's palm itched with the sudden desire to slap the woman. She clenched it into a fist and placed it firmly on her knee. If not for the child, and what the child meant to Donaugh, she would not have come. But it wasn't in her to refuse him. He so seldom asked anything of her. Putting up with this harridan was the least she could do for him.

"You won't die," she said, keeping her voice brisk to mask her dislike. "And neither will the child. I'll make sure of that."

Francia laughed harshly, then gasped as another contraction wracked her body. "Is the King so worried about the only son he's ever likely to have?" Sweat beaded her forehead and upper lip. She licked at the sweat above her mouth and closed her eyes. "But will the baby be safe? Can you be sure that sword-wielding wench won't have him poisoned because he wasn't born to her?"

"The baby's father will see he's raised properly." Torey put her hand to Francia's belly. "The child will be safe."

Francia writhed with another contraction. Beneath Torey's hand, the vibrant pulse of life that was the baby quivered with an odd mixture of impatience, fear, and eagerness. Francia's own smoldering hatred throbbed above it, but Torey found no sense of anything amiss. The child was healthy, Francia was healthy, and the birthing process advanced normally. "Try to relax," she told Francia. "Don't fight the contractions. If you relax, it will go easier with you, and with the child."

Just before the sun rose, Torey delivered the child. His hair was already long, and black as his mother's. He didn't cry as she held him head down to drain his lungs of fluid, but he breathed, quickly turning a healthy pink. As she wrapped him in a warm blanket and placed him into a cradle, he watched her. Cloudy blue eyes stared up at her, eyes that would soon be as dark as Francia's.

For a moment, as the first light of dawn streamed in through the window, Torey thought she saw a faint black shadow hovering about the child's head. But when she bent over the cradle with a candle to look closer, the child's eyes closed in sleep, and she saw no trace of the mist. If it had been there, it was now gone.

"You poor little thing," Torey murmured. She glanced at Francia, who was also asleep, then reached down and gently stroked the child's cheek. It was soft and tender as any infant's skin, and the child was like any other child. He could not be held responsible for who or what his mother was. "Your father will look after you, Mikal," she said softly. "He'll help you all he can."

Donaugh was alone in his workroom when the messenger arrived. Drust had ridden hard for four days to reach him, and the leagues had marked him. His clothing was stained and dusty, his cloak ragged from catching on bushes and trees. He refused the wine Donaugh offered and went to one knee.

"My lord, the woman has gone," Drust said. "Mag and I awoke four days ago to find her bed empty, and no trace of her in the house or around the compound."

Donaugh looked out the window, turning his pen end for end in his hands. The trees wore a blush of green with the coming of spring. He could not see the mountains, but his mind's eye pictured the landhold deep in the Spine of Celi where the child Mikal was fostered with a trusted family. Francia could not find the child there. The child was safe.

"The spell I wove about the lodge decayed sooner than I expected," he said. He turned back to Drust. "I don't blame you, Drust. Neither you nor Mag. You served me well, and you'll be rewarded. The lodge and its lands are yours now, in freehold. I'm grateful for your help."

"Thank you, my lord," Drust said, bowing his head in gratitude. "Mag and I would serve you for nothing more than the honor of doing it." He glanced up. "And the woman?"

Donaugh shook his head. "I fear we've not heard the last of her," he said. "But the child will be safe from her."

PART

4

Enchanter

27

Torey stood in the bow of the ship, her hair blowing about her face, watching the rugged tors and crags of Tyra draw nearer on the horizon. Connor's arms drew her comfortably closer to him, her back pressed against his chest and belly. She leaned her head back until it rested on his shoulder. He bent his head so that his cheek lay pressed against her temple.

"It looks a bit like Wenydd or Skai," he said into her ear.

"I thought the same thing when I first saw it all those years ago," she said. "This doesn't feel like coming home, but it's good to see Tyra again."

"Will your father meet us at the harbor?"

She laughed. "Are you nervous?"

He slid one hand down and pressed it to the fabric of her skirt over her belly. She put both her hands over his, smiling as she thought of his child growing there.

"Well," he said, laughter bubbling in his voice, "you must admit it's just a bit late to ask his permission to marry his daughter."

"He'll give us his blessing," she said. "And he'll be pleased to know that the succession of Wenydd is assured."

He bent his head closer to hers, and his arms tightened momentarily around her. She knew he was thinking of his brother Ralf, who lay in the crypts behind the shrine of Dun Clennadd in Wenydd. Connor himself had brought his brother home after the Battle of Brae Drill only a little more than two years ago.

It had been a strange two years. This year for the first time in generations, spring did not bring a flood of Saesnesi raids. Men prepared the fields for sowing, then watched the grain ripen toward harvest without the necessity of keeping weapons to hand. In the cities of Gwachir on the south coast and Clendonan on the Tiderace, Celae and Saesnesi traded together, sat side by side in the taverns and inns. Elesan himself and several of his thanes attended the Council meetings at Dun Camus. The atmosphere was always strained and tense, but no trouble worth noting had broken out. But Torey had seen one thing that gave her hope—two children playing knucklebones together outside a shop while their mothers purchased bread. One child fair-haired and gray-eyed, the other black-haired and blue-eyed, laughing as they took turns snatching the knucklebones out of the dust of the entranceway. Children like that were the foundation of a strong, united Celi.

And as always, the Celae watched the eastern sea for the first signs of invasion from the continent. But this year, the Saesnesi watched with them, and the ships they looked for were not longships.

The dead were buried and mourned. The living mended themselves and got on with the business of life.

Torey reached up and put her hand to Connor's cheek, his fleeting sorrow sharp in her own heart. He turned his head to kiss her palm.

"Wenydd's succession is assured," he said. "But Kian will fret because Celi's isn't yet. Nor is Skai's."

She laughed softly. "Alys is with child again," she said. "This one is a son. My Healer's Gift tells me that much. I told her before we left. And Ylana told me she would be pregnant by the time we came home again." She thought briefly of the small boy she had last seen taking his first hesitant steps, leaving the safety of his nurse's arms for the lovingly outstretched arms of his foster mother. Mikal was a perfectly normal child in all respects. She had watched him closely during her brief visit to Dun Llewen, but she had seen no trace of the black mist about his head. Eryth ap Morfyn's wife Ganieda obviously loved the boy as much as she loved her own son and daughter.

Torey shivered softly. Connor's arms tightened around her.

"What is it?" he asked.

"I was thinking of the children," she said. "What will happen to them if the Maedun invade Celi?"

"We'll protect them," he said. "We'll protect them the same way our parents protected us from Saesnesi raiders." He stepped away and caught her hand. "We'll be in the harbor soon. Come back to the cabin. We have to gather our things."

She laughed and reached up to kiss his cheek. "And tomorrow night, I'll show you what Lammas in Tyra is like. I think you'll enjoy it."

He grinned. "I will, will I?"

"Well, you do like heather ale, don't you?" she asked innocently.

Ylana stood by the window, the dark blue velvet of her bedgown blending with the darkening sky beyond the glass. None of her women attended her. She was alone in the room. Only half a dozen candles burned in the chamber and the shadows leapt and flickered in the dim light. She did not turn from the window as Donaugh entered the chamber.

"You sent for me, my lady?" he asked softly.

"You used to call me Ylana," she said. "My lady is too formal between us, Donaugh."

"If you wish," he said. "Ylana, then."

"They've almost finished laying the wood for the Lammas Fire," she said. "See? Up there in the oak grove. Ever since I was a child, I've always loved the Fire Feasts best of all. Haven't you?"

He crossed the room to stand beside her. Small lights flickered on the crest of the low hill beyond the shrine at the edge of the town, winking through the trees. He watched them for a moment, then looked down at her.

Her features had firmed with maturity. She was a lovely woman, but responsibility had taken the last of the girlish softness from her face. Glints of premature silver streaked her hair above her left temple. She didn't laugh as easily as she once used to, and her smile was no longer the carefree grin of a young girl. Between them, a deep friendship had arisen over the years. She trusted him, and he trusted her.

"How may I serve you, Ylana?" he asked.

She turned, her robe swirling about her, and crossed the room to a small table flanked by two comfortable chairs before the hearth. The table held a crystal decanter of wine and two gold and crystal goblets. She poured wine into the goblets and held one out to him. A small tremor shivered the surface of the wine. He said nothing as he took the goblet from her and raised the cup to his mouth, barely wetting his lips. She drained her cup, then refilled it. As she began to raise it to her mouth, he caught her hand.

"Ylana . . ." he said gently.

She turned from him and set the goblet too carefully back onto the table, then leaned both hands on the edge of the table and stood with her back to him, head bowed. Her unbound hair spilled forward across her cheeks in a gleaming river of black silk.

"Donaugh, I need your help," she said quietly. "I desperately need your help, but I don't know how to ask for it."

"You know you need only ask," he said. "Anything I can do for you, I shall."

"I may ask for more than you're willing to give," she said. "Or are able to."

He said nothing, merely waiting.

She went back to the window and stood like a carved image for a long moment, her arms stiffly at her sides. Finally, she turned to look at him, her eyes shadowed and widened.

"Donaugh, I must have a child," she said.

He set down his goblet. "Ylana, my magic can't work that way," he said. "I'm not a woodwitch who can conjure up a fertility charm."

"Nor am I asking for one," she said. "It would do me no good."

"Then what are you asking for?"

She gestured toward the chairs by the hearth. "Come sit with me for a moment."

He followed her across the room and sat down. The fire threw red glints into her hair and put color into her cheeks. She looked like a girl again. She sat quietly for a moment, looking into the fire, her expression remote as she gathered her thoughts. He waited patiently, allowing her the time she needed.

"Tiernyn is a good king," she said at last. "His soldiers will follow him anywhere. All the princes and dukes pay ungrudging homage to him now. Even the Saesnesi."

Again, he merely waited.

"It's been nearly two years since Brae Drill. People are beginning to wonder why I'm not with child yet." She looked up at him and smiled wanly. "While we were campaigning against the Saesnesi, it didn't matter so much. No one expected a bheancoran to become pregnant while there were battles to be fought. But now . . . "

"But now?" he asked.

She got to her feet and paced restlessly. "This is retribution, isn't it?" she said, her voice harsh. "The sword—that accursed sword—is exacting payment for what I did in persuading Lluddor ap Vershad to desert Keylan and follow Tiernyn." She whirled to face Donaugh. The hem of her sleeve caught the goblet and overturned it. Crimson wine flooded across the table and splashed onto the floor by her feet. She ignored it. "But he must have an heir, Donaugh. He must. And soon, if all we've worked for isn't to go for naught . . . "

"Ylana, calm yourself. The fact that you've no children yet isn't retribution. Believe me."

"Then what is it?" she demanded.

"I don't know." He took her arm and led her back to her chair. She sat reluctantly, then leaned forward, arms crossed over her belly as if in pain. "Calm yourself." He righted the overturned goblet and poured wine for her. She straightened as he placed the goblet into her hand. "Tell me."

She took a sip of the wine, then put the goblet down. "It's been suggested by a few members of the Royal Council that Tiernyn put me aside since it appears I might be barren." A hint of moisture misted her eyelashes.

"Tiernyn would never do that."

She looked down at her hands, knotted together on her lap, the knuckles white. "No, he would never do that," she said. "He loves me as much as I love him. Donaugh, the problem isn't with me. It's with him."

"With Tiernyn?"

"His seed isn't strong enough to take root." She raised a hand to forestall his reply. "I have some magic. I know. Remember the wound he took the day we rode into Mercia and rescued Eachern?" She smiled bitterly. "The day Lluddor showed up and rescued us in turn?"

"I remember."

"I think it was that wound." She got up and began pacing restlessly. "I'm frightened, Donaugh. The Celae won't follow an impotent king. You know as well as I do all the stories about maimed kings and maimed lands." She paused and looked at him. "And don't mention Mikal to me. I know the truth of him just as surely as you do, even if Tiernyn doesn't."

"I wasn't about to bring up the subject," he said calmly, his expression sardonic.

"Tomorrow is Lammas Eve," she said. "Donaugh, I must give Tiernyn a child come Beltane. I must."

"If you're not looking for a fertility charm, what *do* you want?"

"I think you know," she said softly.

"Ylana, I . . . "

"Donaugh, you must sire the child," she said in a rush. "Tonight. Now. That way, after Tiernyn and I come together at the Lammas Fire to celebrate the first fruits of the harvest, everyone will think the child was conceived there, and know it to be lucky and blessed."

He looked at her, pain in his heart. "Ylana, I can't." He had not been with a woman willingly since Eliade. He wanted no woman in her place. Ylana was powerfully attractive, but he felt no desire for her. He loved her the same way he loved his sister Torey.

"If you sired the child, no one could ever say the child wasn't Tiernyn's. It would have his blood as surely as you and he share the same blood." She sank to her knees before his chair and put both her hands over his on the arm of the chair. "Donaugh, you must. If not for me and for Tiernyn, then for Celi. There must be an heir. A legitimate heir, not the son of that accursed Maedun woman."

"And if we make a daughter?" he asked sardonically. "What then?"

"It will be a son," she said. "You have enough of the Healer's arts to assure that."

"Ylana, no . . ." He shook his head. "It would be like betraying Tiernyn. He's my brother, and you're my brother's wife. I can't . . ."

"It wouldn't be a betrayal of Tiernyn," she said softly. "How could it be when all we're doing is ensuring the succession of his kingdom. You're my only hope, Donaugh. I've nowhere else to turn."

He looked down at her. The *darlai's* words once again echoed in his mind. "*And one son will seed a line of kings forward to the time when these stones will crumble back to dust . . .*" He could not deny the fate the *darlai* had placed upon him. Nor the responsibility.

He rose slowly to his feet and held out his hand to her. "Come, then," he whispered.

Torey awoke in the night, shivering with the cold sweat soaking through her thin bedgown and into the bed linen. Her mouth felt dry as ashes and thirst raged in her throat. Temples pounding, she struggled to sit up, then leaned forward, cradling her head in her hands. The chill passed and the fire of fever consumed her body. Connor lay sprawled on his belly beside her, unmoving in profound slumber.

She staggered out of bed, pulling at the neck of her bedgown to let the crisp night air cool her body. The rugs on the floor caught at her feet as she stumbled to the door and wrenched it open. Beneath her bare feet, the polished tile of the corridor felt like ice. Pain clutched at her belly, and fear for the child stabbed through her.

It wasn't her husband she needed now. He had no help for her in this. Her mother . . . She had to find her mother. Kerri would know what to do. Only Kerri could soothe this fever.

The throbbing pain in her temples increased. Dizzy and nearly blinded by the red haze of pain, Torey did not notice she had passed the doorway to her parents' chambers. When she became aware of her surroundings again, she was outside the Clanhold, out of the courtyard and halfway up the hill to the small Dance of stones above the shrine.

"No," she moaned, struggling to turn back to the promise of comfort and safety held in her mother's chamber.

But someone or something else commanded her body, drew her inexorably up the grassy slope of the hill, into the midst of the stone Dance. She reached out a trembling hand to steady herself against the gleaming stone pillar in the center of the Dance. The full moon transformed the Dance into a place of washed silver and sharp, black shadows. There was magic here. Strong magic. It beat against her mind like the pain and fever beat against her body.

The shivering began in her belly, then quickly spread to the rest of her body until she would have fallen had she not clung tightly to the pillar. Fever burned in her until she felt she must surely turn to ash and drift away on the gentle breeze blowing toward the sea. The fever and the moonlight played tricks on her eyes. She thought she could see the figures of men and women carved in relief into the tall stones of the Dance; carved with such clarity and precision, the figures seemed alive. Startled at first, then frightened, she realized they were men and women, and she recognized them. Rhianna of the Air, her long, moon-silvered hair floating like a veil about her body. Cernos of the Forest, with the tall rack of stately antlers rising from his brow. Adriel of the Waters, carrying her enchanted ewer. Gerieg of the Crags, with the mighty hammer he used to smite the crags and shake the ground, spilling great landslips down the crags. Beodun of the Fires, carrying in one hand the lamp of benevolent fire and in the other, the lightning bolt of wildfire. Sandor of the Plain, his hair blowing like prairie grass around his face. And the *darlai*, the Spirit of the Land, the Mother of All, smiling at her with compassion and tenderness.

Torey slipped to her knees and pressed her forehead against the cool, smooth basalt of the pillar, closing her eyes. A moth-wing touch of air brushed her cheek, lifted the wet hair from her sweat-dampened forehead, soothing her fever, easing the pounding ache in her temples.

Rhianna stepped from her place in the circle, her hand extended. "I have a Gift for you, my child," she said softly.

"No," Torey said, shaking her head painfully. "I don't want it."

"But you must take it."

Torey raised her head and found a small stone clutched tightly in her hand. Around her, the stone columns stood silent and still in the moonlight.

Slowly, reluctantly, she opened her hand. The stone was the size and shape of a plover's egg, smooth and warm to the touch. As she looked down at it, she realized it was a crystal, faceted like a gem and clear as water. It collected the light of the moon until it filled and overflowed onto the palm of her hand like quicksilver. Fascinated, she found she could look deep into it, down into its heart. Tiny figures moved within it. Then the world tipped and tilted crazily, and she fell into the crystal.

———

Saesnesi raiders poured out from between the trees, a flood of tall men, hair flaxen blond under horned helmets. The early morning sun flashed off war axes and sword blades. They came with no warning, catching the people of the village by surprise. Men, women, and children fled in terror before them, running for the safety of the palace. The raiders hewed down the weak and the slow. Flame blossomed in thatched roofs, pale and shimmering in the bright sunlight.

The gates of the palace burst open as the yrSkai soldiers surged out to meet the raiders. Impeded by the panicked villagers, the horsemen broke into small groups, dodging men and women carrying children.

Ignoring the confusion, the raiders charged into the midst of the mounted soldiers, ax blades flashing. The two forces met in a tangle of men and horses.

The bright hair of the Prince of Skai shone like a beacon in the midst of the fighting, but it was Letessa al Morfyn who guarded his left side. His sword flashed and glittered as he swung it. Raiders fell to either side of him, some to the blade, some to the slashing hooves of his horse. One of the Saesnesi leapt over the bodies of the dead, ax chopping toward Keylan's belly.

Jorddyn ap Tiernyn, fighting by Keylan's right, spun his horse and hacked at the raider. The Saesnesi went down. Keylan gave Jorddyn a hard, fierce grin, then pivoted his horse to meet another attack.

The fighting ended suddenly as the last knot of raiders fell to the swords of the defenders. Keylan shouted orders to Jorddyn, then spurred his horse down the slope toward the lambing pens beyond the practice field. He brought the horse to a skidding stop, setting it back on its haunches, and flung himself to the ground. Five bodies, all women, lay near the perimeter fence. He went to them, one by one. At the last, all the tension drained from his body, and he sagged to his knees beside the woman.

Slowly, he reached out and turned Alys over, then drew her into his arms, cradling her against his chest. Pain etched into his face as he bent his head to press his cheek against her hair. As Keylan knelt there, two soldiers came forward, each bearing the body of a child. Mutely, they stood before Keylan, grief distorting their features. Keylan looked at his daughters, then buried his face in his wife's hair. Wracking sobs shook his body.

Letessa dismounted, leaving her horse beside Keylan's, and went to his side. He looked up at her, tears flowing freely from his eyes. She said nothing, but put her hand to his shoulder, her own tears running down her cheeks.

After a long time, Keylan raised his head. Pain and grief ravaged his face and stole the life from his eyes. Still cradling the body of his wife in his arms, Keylan climbed stiffly and painfully to his feet. He carried her as easily as he might carry a child. Letessa caught the reins of both horses and followed him back to the palace.

Torey's field of vision widened above the bloody scene of slaughter, and penetrated into the forest beyond the place where the raiders had first appeared. Deep in the shadows she saw the men who had led the raiders. Men dressed in black, hair and eyes as black as their clothing, blended with the shadows, and melted back through the trees toward the rugged coastline beyond the mouth of the Ceg.

The crystal in Torey's hand shivered and crumbled to dust. The gentle breeze lifted it and spilled it into a small, sparkling cloud around her hand. The cloud vanished, but left her hand glittering with traces of the powder. She wiped her palm against her thigh, leaving a small, bright smear on the thin fabric of her bedgown. She tried to rub away the tears and left another smudge of brightness on her cheek.

The moon had set. Around her, the Dance of stones was cold and silent and dark. Using the pedestal for support, she pulled herself to her feet and stumbled between two of the stones, away from the circle, tears blurring her vision.

She had no memory of walking back to the Clanhold, no memory of making her way back to her bedchamber. She fell asleep, exhausted and still crying.

She awoke in the morning curled in the warm circle of Connor's arms. Her head ached mildly, and a fragmented memory of a dream swirled briefly in her mind, then was gone.

A dream?

She raised her right hand, fingers spread, and stared at it. The lines on the palm of her hand still contained traces of the sparkling powder. She shuddered and rubbed her hand hard against the bed linen.

28

The nursery at Dun Llewen was large and airy, the slate floor covered in rugs. A fire burned in the hearth to ease the chill of a cool, wet day. Eryth ap Morfyn's son, a boy of nearly four, sat in one corner, quietly playing with his miniature army, moving the carved wooden men and horses around a field drawn on the slate. Eryth's two-year-old daughter played by herself with a corn doll near the hearth, surrounded by brightly colored wooden beads as big as a man's fist. Young Mikal rode a hobbyhorse around the room, his face intent as he waved a small wooden sword.

Donaugh stood hidden in the nurse's alcove, watching Mikal. At just over a year and a half, the boy was sturdy and strong. His black hair and black Maedun eyes made a startling contrast to Eryth's two fair-haired, blue-eyed children. Quick and intelligent, Mikal already showed signs of the deft grace of a born swordsman, and he clamored for a pony of his own like the one Eryth's son rode. Ganieda, Eryth's wife, called the boy determined. He usually got what he wanted.

Mikal grew tired of his hobbyhorse and wooden sword. He dropped them in the middle of the room and went to the hearth, where Alida played happily with her dolls and beads. He stood watching her for a moment, then reached down and snatched two red beads from her as she tried to string them on a braided cord. For a moment, she sat in shocked silence, then scrambled to her feet.

"Mine," she said firmly, and grabbed the beads back.

When Mikal tried to seize them, she struck out at him and pushed him away, then turned her back on him and sat on the hearth rug again. The boy retreated and stood watching her, his eyes narrowed, a frown drawing the heavy black brows together above his dark eyes. Alida got to her feet, the string of beads dangling from her hands. Mikal looked around carefully. For a moment, his gaze lingered on the nurse, whose back was turned as she folded clothing to place into a chest near the window.

Something dark shimmered around Mikal's head. Even from the alcove, Donaugh felt the cold chill of Maedun magic. The hairs along his arms rose and his skin crept. He began to move even as Mikal rushed forward, his arms extended, clearly intending to push Alida into the fire on the hearth. Before Mikal could touch the girl, Donaugh swept the boy up into his arms.

Startled, Mikal stiffened. He pushed at Donaugh's chest, struggling to escape. Donaugh thought he had caught up a whirlwind. Mikal struggled, small arms and legs thrashing wildly, raining blows on Donaugh's head and throat. He screamed in protest. When Donaugh searched for signs of the blood magic, he found the mist gone from around Mikal's head, lost in the blind anger. He held the boy tightly to contain his struggling.

"Mikal, stop it," he said, his voice quiet but firm.

The boy paid no attention to him, screaming and thrashing wildly in his attempt to free himself. Donaugh took both the small hands into one of his to restrain the child.

"Mikal, I said stop it. Now."

Mikal stopped struggling and glared at Donaugh. For a moment, those black eyes stared into Donaugh's, flaring with rage. Then, as the child recognized him, the fury vanished. No trace remained of the faint darkness around the black hair.

The boy laughed in delight. Donaugh closed his eyes as the child's soft cheek pressed against his and the small, chubby arms closed around his neck. He hadn't wanted to believe Torey when she told him about the black shimmer about Mikal's head shortly after the child was born. In all the times he'd visited Dun Llewen Landhold to see Mikal, Donaugh had not seen it. Not until now. Nor had the child ever shown any sign at all of having inherited the potential to use Celae magic.

Donaugh sat on a padded bench on the other side of the hearth and held Mikal on his knee. He put his hand up to cup the back of Mikal's head, despair wrenching at his heart. If this son wasn't to be lost to him, too, he desperately needed to find a way to combat the influence of Francia's blood in the child. Mikal was far too young to survive the same magical quenching Donaugh had used on Francia. Unless Donaugh could find a way to strip away the potential for blood magic while Mikal was still very young, it might be too late.

"You mustn't ever try to hurt Alida again, Mikal," Donaugh said quietly, his voice calm despite the torment churning in his heart.

Mikal leaned back in his arms and looked up into his eyes. The child was simply a child again, sunny-natured and bright. He reached up to play with the brooch in the shape of a Skai falcon at Donaugh's shoulder, fascinated by the bright gleam of the gold and the glitter of the sapphire eyes.

"Mine?" he asked.

"No," Donaugh said. "Mine. Someday, you'll have one of your own. I promise."

Eryth burst into the room, out of breath and pale. "Donaugh, come quickly," he called. "News from Dun Eidon."

Donaugh set Mikal down and hurried to the door. "What happened?" he demanded.

"Saesnesi raiders at Dun Eidon," Eryth said. "A messenger just arrived. My sister Letessa sent him because she thought you might be here."

A cold fist of shock clenched in Donaugh's gut. He stared at Eryth. "Saesnesi raiders? She's sure?"

"She said so." Eryth made a helpless gesture. "We've all seen enough of Saesnesi raiders to know what they look like."

"When?"

"Five days ago. The messenger says Alys and the children are dead, and Keylan is preparing to ride east with two hun-

dred men. Letessa believes he means to ride into the Summer
Run to take vengeance."

"Then he may already be on his way. Get the horses ready.
We ride for Dun Camus now. We have to stop him."

Eryth looked into the nursery at his two children. His face
hardened. "Keylan has a right for revenge," he said softly.

"Aye, he does," Donaugh said. "But he has no right to
plunge Celi into war again."

From her vantage point high on the flank of the mountain,
Torey saw the dust cloud moving on the road long before she
saw the horse and rider. No one but a courier bearing an urgent
message would force his mount to such a reckless pace in the
heat of the late summer afternoon. A knot of cold foreboding
closed around her heart. She got to her feet and shaded her
eyes with her hand, trying to get a better look at the rider.

The dust raised by the flying hooves obscured both horse
and rider, but she thought she recognized the uniform the man
wore. Foreboding turned to dread. The courier was yrSkai, one
of Keylan's men.

Vivid images flashed before her eyes. Saesnesi helmets
glinting in the sun. Keylan's red hair gleaming like a beacon.
The red of Alys's blood soaking into her hair and gown. Two
small girls limp and dead in the arms of grief-stricken soldiers.

"No," she whispered, unaware she spoke aloud. "Oh, no.
Please."

Her knees gave way as a wave of dizziness washed over
her. The basket containing the herbs she had been gathering
fell from her nerveless fingers, spilling its contents at her feet.
She sat abruptly in the soft, lush grass. The rider vanished
around a bend in the track, leaving only thin, trailing wisps of
brown dust to mark his passage.

Still dizzy, her temples pounding, Torey scrambled to her
feet and began to run. She had wandered too far from the
Clanhold. She would never reach it before the rider, even

going straight over the shoulder of the mountain rather than the long way around by the road.

Soft purple heather caught at the hem of her gown. She heard the fabric rip as she tore it free, hardly pausing in her headlong rush, sobbing with effort as she ran. Then she tripped and fell sprawling into the grass, and remembered the child she carried. She got to her feet, listening inwardly, frightened now for the child as well. The child had suffered no harm in the fall, but Torey slowed her pace, walking as quickly as she dared.

There was no sign of either the messenger or his horse when she staggered into the courtyard. She paused for a moment to catch her breath as she looked around, then gathered up her skirts and ran up the wide stone steps leading to the Great Hall.

One of the servingwomen was refilling the lamps on the long table, humming to herself, as Torey burst into the room. She looked up in astonishment as Torey seized her arm.

"My lady Torey," she cried. "Why, whatever happened—"

"The messenger," Torey gasped. "Just come. Where is he?"

"Why, in your father's solar—"

Torey was running again before the woman finished speaking. Up the curving staircase, down the long, cool corridor. Then, before she reached the door of the solar, she paused. She did not want to go in there, and she did not want to hear the news the courier bore from Skai. She put her hands to her face. The dust caked on her sweaty forehead and cheeks felt gritty beneath her fingers. She lifted the tattered hem of her gown to wipe her face, then tried to arrange her snarled hair with her fingers into some semblance of order. Finally, with no more excuses to delay, she pushed open the door.

Kian stood in the center of the room, holding Kerri, his head bent over hers as she wept against his chest. On a stool near the window, the white-faced, grimy young courier sat, helplessly clutching a goblet of wine. Dust motes danced in a shaft of light falling across the young man's leg, forming a

nimbus of gold around the curve of his knee. The blue of his
tunic and trews reflected upward onto his face and made him
appear haggard and worn.

Torey's heart beat so hard against her ribs, she wondered
why they could not hear it. She took one step into the room,
arms stiff at her sides.

"Father?" she asked, her voice scratchy and raw.

Kian looked up at her across Kerri's bowed head. Torey
saw the grief and pain etched into his face and suddenly knew
what he would look like as an old man.

"What news?" she asked. Her dry mouth made the words
difficult to frame. "Is it Keylan?"

"Raiders at Dun Eidon." Kian's voice rasped in the utter
stillness of the room. "Keylan still lives."

"But Alys is dead," Torey whispered. "And the child she
carried. And Rowana and Merly . . ." Sick and dizzy, she put
out a hand, reaching for support. The wall felt cool and firm
beneath her fingers, the only solid anchor she had. "I saw it,"
she murmured. "I saw it half a fortnight ago. Up there. In the
Dance." Her hand slipped against the rough stone of the wall
as her knees betrayed her again. Before she could fall to the
floor, Kian was beside her, his strong, comforting arms around
her, offering protection and safety.

"I saw it," Torey repeated. She sobbed, holding on to her
father desperately. She feared she would fly to pieces if she let
go. "I should have told you. You might have warned them."

Kerri came to her quickly, smoothed back the tangled hair
from her forehead. "It happened six days ago," she said.
"Torey, you saw what happened, not what would happen. Oh,
child. Child, the Sight isn't an easy gift, but the future is so
seldom given."

Torey clung to Kian, trembling violently. "I don't want it,"
she cried. "Oh, Mother, I don't want this gift."

"It was a harsh first Seeing." Kerri held a goblet to Torey's
lips. "Drink this," she ordered gently.

The watered wine tasted tart and clean. It calmed her, and

she was able to leave the shelter of Kian's arms without fear of collapsing. Kerri led her to a cushioned bench near the wide window and sat beside her. Torey gripped her mother's hand while Kian turned his attention back to the young courier.

"Why was there no warning?" he asked. "Where were the men in the watchtowers?"

The courier made a helpless gesture. "Their longships were found more than ten leagues south on the coast of Wenydd," he said. "On one of the offshore islands. My lord Jorddyn thinks they came ashore in coracles, under the cover of night, then came overland. They . . . My lord Jorddyn thinks they meant only to kill Prince Keylan and his family and destroy Dun Eidon. They didn't come for plunder."

Kian nodded. "Thank you," he said. "Go to the guardroom. There will be a meal there for you. And a place you may rest. I'll have a reply for you to take with you on your return." He crossed the room and sat by Torey, placing his hand gently on her forehead. "Are you all right?" he asked. "The child?"

"The baby is fine. Really." Torey cradled the small swelling of her belly and began to weep again. "Oh, Father. Poor Alys. Oh, poor Alys. And the children . . . Oh, gods, the children." She wiped the back of her hand across her eyes. "Alys was by the sheep pens and they killed her before she even saw them." Her tears came faster and she clung to Kerri. "What will Keylan do now? They loved each other so much."

"Keylan will carry on," Kian said softly. "As he must. As we all must."

Torey nodded but didn't look up.

"I've had more news this morning," Kian said. "Not good news, I'm afraid." He looked up as Connor entered the room, breathless and pale. "Come in, Connor. We've been waiting for you."

Connor went directly to Torey. She moved gratefully into the protective circle of his arms as he sat beside her on the bench.

"What news, my lord?" Connor asked.

"My old enemy Hakkar has left Lake Vayle," Kian said. "I believe it means he's preparing to invade Celi now. I was writing a letter to Tiernyn when Keylan's messenger came."

Torey sat up. "Father . . ." She looked at Kerri, then back to Kian. "In my Seeing. There were men leading the Saesnesi. Men dressed in black with black hair and black eyes. They hid in the forest and didn't show themselves at all."

Kian's eyebrows rose in surprise. "Saesnesi lead by Maedun?"

"Yes. I think so."

"Tiernyn must hear of this at once," Connor said. "We must return immediately."

Kian hesitated for a moment, then smiled. "I had hoped to keep you both here," he said quietly. Then, as Torey felt Connor stiffen in preparation to protest, Kian raised his hand to forestall an interruption. "If I could," he said. "To ensure you were both kept safe. But I know you must go."

Connor nodded, then looked thoughtfully at Torey.

"No," she said instantly. "Where you go, I go." She squeezed his hand. "I'll be needed, too."

The Isgardian port city of Honandun baked under the late summer sun. A fleet of a hundred ships lay at anchor, tied snugly to the long stone jetties in the deep harbor where the River Lachruch flowed into the Cold Sea. The waterfront swarmed with activity as stevedores sweated under the weight of crates and bundles of the provisions and supplies they loaded into the holds of the ships. Next to a long, low warehouse, a thousand horses fretted restlessly in spite of the heat, nervous and uneasy with the unfamiliar scents of the sea and city as they awaited their turn to be loaded into special compartments in the holds. In rows of hastily constructed barracks, an army of black-clad Somber Riders waited with the fatalistic patience of all soldiers.

Hakkar of Maedun stood before the window of the best

room in the best waterfront inn, ignoring the organized confusion below him. He lifted his gaze to the hill above the city, to the white stone elegance of what had once been the palace of the Ephir of Isgard. Now the graceful building housed Nordag, Lord Protector of Isgard. Visiting him to watch the launching of the invasion that would finally rid Maedun of the threat of the enchanter of the prophecy was Maegrun, second Lord Protector of Falinor.

A small, disdainful smile curled one corner of Hakkar's mouth. Maegrun was second Lord Protector of Falinor because Weigar, the first Lord Protector was gone—nearly seven years gone. Mysteriously disappeared. His son Walthor swore his father was dead, but was unable to produce a corpse. Indeed, he was unable to provide proof he now wielded his father's power.

He didn't, of course. Hakkar knew Weigar had been unable to pass his magic to Walthor as he died for the very logical reason that Weigar's power now resided in Hakkar himself.

Never would it be said that Hakkar of Lake Vayle, nephew of King Vanizen himself, did not keep his end of a bargain. Weigar, of course, was in no position to complain.

Slowly, Hakkar turned his attention westward. The sea rippled slate blue under a sky milky with heat-haze. Far to the northwest, the jumbled black towers of a thunderstorm rose ominously on the horizon, moving swiftly southeastward. Perhaps, he thought, this storm might end the heat wave and break the cycle of stifling, muggy heat and violent storms that had prevailed for the last five days. The ships were nearly ready to sail. Today would see the last of the provisions and supplies of invasion loaded. Only the men and horses remained ashore, waiting for the weather to clear. The ferocity of the daily thunderstorms was more than capable of scattering the fleet at the least, or shredding canvas sails and splintering tall, wooden masts at worst. As eager as Hakkar was to begin the subjugation of Celi, he was too wise to risk failure because of a storm.

The sky darkened as the storm moved inland. At the first flash of lightning, the penned horses snorted and danced on the verge of panic. The stablemasters moved carefully among the restive animals, soothing and calming them with words and touches.

Hakkar watched them for a moment or two, then looked west again. A curtain of rain obscured the horizon. Beyond that blurred horizon lay Celi. Within days, his lifelong obsession would be satisfied.

He turned from the window. Horbad lay already asleep on one of the beds. On the wall behind him hung the black sword in its ornate scabbard. Hakkar bent over his son and stroked the boy's head. Then he reached for the sword. As he drew it, a spurt of darkness spilled from the ebony tip. The room became darker as the sword's darkness swallowed the watery light.

"Your time is near," Hakkar murmured to the obsidian blade. "Within the fortnight, you will drink more Celae blood."

29

The sun had been gone for nearly an hour when Donaugh approached the gates of Dun Camus. The flagging horse stumbled into the courtyard and drew to an exhausted stop, head hanging, lathered flanks heaving. Donaugh flung himself from the saddle and tossed the reins to a waiting servant. He ran up the steps to the Great Hall, glancing upward. Tiernyn's banner flapped above the parapets. The tension in Donaugh's belly eased fractionally. Tiernyn was here.

Servants moved through the Great Hall, lighting candles and lamps, as Donaugh hurried across the tiled floor. Someone called his name from the top of the stairway leading to the private quarters. Torey leaned far out over the railing above the Great Hall, then turned to run toward the stairs.

They met at the first landing. She flung her arms around him, and he was surprised to discover she was trembling.

"I knew you'd come," she said. "Oh, Donaugh, there's trouble."

"I heard about the raid on Dun Eidon," he said. "I came as quickly as I could."

"Keylan's here," she said. "He—"

Hope leapt in Donaugh's heart. "Keylan's here?" he repeated. "He hasn't been into the Summer Run yet?"

She shook her head. "No, not yet. He's up there talking with Tiernyn."

He started to pull away from her, looking upward along the corridor to the doorway of Tiernyn's workroom. Torey clutched at his arm.

"I need to talk to you," she said breathlessly. "Please, Donaugh. It's important. It's about the raid at Dun Eidon."

He looked down at her. She was on the thin edge of

exhaustion, her eyes shadowed, her face gaunted. If she and Connor had braved the storms at sea to come back to speak with him, it must be important. Torey would not risk her child if it weren't.

Donaugh took her arm and escorted her up the stairway to his own workroom. Before he let her speak, he made sure she was comfortable with a goblet of watered wine.

"How long have you and Connor been back?" he asked.

"Only an hour or two," she said. "Donaugh, I had to come back to tell you. I had a Seeing in Broche Rhuidh. I *saw* the raid on Dun Eidon."

"You saw it?"

She nodded, looking down into her goblet and not at him. "In the Dance above the Clanhold. Probably on the same day it happened. I spoke with Letessa, and she says what I saw was exactly what happened." She swallowed back a sob. "It was too late to warn Keylan. I thought it was only a dream until the messenger came, and even then, I didn't want to believe it. I still don't. But I did see it."

He sat beside her. He took the goblet from her, set it on the chest, then took both her hands in his. She gripped his hands tightly, but hers still trembled. "Seeing isn't easy," he said gently. "But when you're given a gift by the gods, you can't help but use it."

"I know."

He touched her cheek gently. "It doesn't surprise me," he said. "Remember the night after the battle when you knew Francia was going to try to take Tiernyn? That was the first glimmer of the gift."

She looked up at him and smiled tremulously. "Donaugh, I had to tell you about this first, before I go to Tiernyn. Or to Keylan. In my Seeing, there were men in black with the Saesnesi who came to Dun Eidon. They stayed in the trees. Nobody saw them."

"Maedun?" he asked in sudden, certain knowledge.

"Yes, I think so. So does Father."

He nodded. It made more sense now. Elesan would not go back on his word, once given. Nor would he let any of his people violate his bond. The vast sensation of relief that flooded through Donaugh left him feeling weak. He got stiffly to his feet, still holding Torey's hands, and drew her up with him.

"Come, then," he said. "Tiernyn must know this."

His arm around Torey's shoulders, Donaugh left his chambers and hurried to Tiernyn's workroom. The torches in their sconces along the passageway flared brightly with the wind of their passing. Their intertwined shadows leapt and twisted ahead of them over the polished tile of the floor, growing and shrinking, advancing and dwindling as they passed the torches. He heard Keylan's voice raised in anger long before they reached the door of the workroom.

As Donaugh stepped into the room, Keylan slammed both fists down onto the gleaming wood of Tiernyn's worktable, leaning forward intensely. His face, pale and haggard in the flickering candlelight, was twisted into lines and planes of anger. Letessa al Morfyn sat huddled on a bench by the door, her eyes wide and shadowed as she watched Keylan. She winced at the sound of his hands hitting the table. Torey went quickly to sit beside her.

"My family is dead, Tiernyn," Keylan said, his voice low and dangerous. "Dead, do you hear? Alys, Rowana, Merly . . . Dead, all of them, and it was Saesnesi who murdered them. I demand retribution. If you don't send the army into the Saesnesi Shore, I'll take my own army in there—"

"No," Donaugh said quietly.

Keylan whirled about, his eyes blazing as he glared at Donaugh.

"No!" he repeated. "How dare you—"

"No," Donaugh said again. He crossed the room and stood at the opposite end of the table from Keylan. "I can't let you undo the work of ten years, Keylan."

Keylan closed the distance between them in two long strides. He seized the front of Donaugh's robe and yanked his youngest brother forward so that his face was mere inches from Donaugh's.

"My family is dead," Keylan said, each word as sharp and distinct as the crack of a whip. "My daughters, my wife, and my unborn son. Who are you to tell me—"

Donaugh reached up and gently unfastened Keylan's hands. He stepped back, then quickly raised his hand as Keylan started forward. "Don't make me use magic against you, Keylan," Donaugh said.

Keylan hesitated, then turned and stumbled to a chair at the other end of the table. He lowered himself into it, moving like a weary and ancient man.

Tiernyn rose. "You might tell *me* why I can't take the army into the Saesnesi Shore, Donaugh," he said quietly.

"We must keep our heads here," Donaugh said. "Suppose Gemedd came to you and accused Morand of Brigland of raiding his territory and killing his people. Would you immediately lead the army out to slaughter the Brigani?"

Tiernyn bit his lip. "No," he said thoughtfully. "I'd call them both together and find out what happened, of course."

"The men of the Summer Run are your subjects just as surely as are the men of Brigland, or Mercia," Donaugh said. "And Elesan is your liegeman as surely as is Morand or Gemedd."

"It was Saesnesi who came to Dun Eidon," Keylan said bitterly. "Don't you think I recognize Saesnesi when I see them?"

"I saw them, too," Letessa said from her corner. "They were Saesnesi, Donaugh. I swear."

"The men who raided Dun Eidon weren't from the Summer Run," Donaugh said.

"They were Saesnesi," Keylan cried. "Where else would they come from?"

"The continent," Donaugh said. "From Saesnes itself."

"Saesnes is part of Maedun's empire now," Tiernyn said.

"Yes," Donaugh said, glancing at him quickly. "Exactly."

Torey spoke for the first time. "They were from the continent," she said quietly. "And what's more, there were Maedun soldiers leading them. I saw them in the forest."

Keylan's head snapped up, and he stared at her. "You saw them?" he asked.

"In my vision." She looked down at her fists, knotted in her lap. "In the Seeing. I was in the Dance at Broche Rhuidh, but I saw them."

Tiernyn went to the window, his head bent, hands clasped behind his back. Finally, he turned back to face Donaugh and Keylan. "I'll call Elesan here and ask him."

"I want a Truth-Seer here," Keylan said. "I won't believe what he says without the blue flame. We've seen what the word of a Saesnesi means . . . "

"There will be a Truth-Seer present," Donaugh said.

Keylan got up from the chair so quickly, it skittered back across the polished floor, leaving scratches as it went. His anger and grief still twisted his face as he strode toward the door.

Letessa jumped up from her place by the window and started after him. He swept out his arm, thrusting her aside. She staggered back and dropped onto the bench again, huddled in upon herself, defeat and anguish in every line of her body.

Donaugh went to the window. No trace of dawn stained the eastern sky, but he thought he saw the flare of approaching fire.

"They're coming, Tiernyn," he said. "The gods and goddesses help us if we aren't ready."

"You think it will be soon, do you?" Tiernyn asked.

"Aye. Send a messenger in the morning to ask Elesan to attend you. But send other messengers to call in your Council and start making preparations for an invasion."

Torey found Letessa in the corridor near the door to Keylan's chambers. She stood with her arms crossed on the sill of a low window, looking out over the town and the river beyond. Silvery tracks of tears etched her cheeks, glistening in the torchlight. She looked defenseless and bereft, and so very young. With a shock, Torey realized Letessa was already two years older than she herself had been when she left Dun Eidon, and a year older than Ylana had been when she followed Tiernyn nearly thirteen years ago.

Torey smiled to herself. Was she becoming so old that a newly declared bheancoran looked like a child to her? She stepped forward and put her hand to Letessa's shoulder.

"Are you guarding his door?" she asked gently.

Startled, Letessa stiffened and turned quickly, eyes wide in the shadows. She shook her head, a self-deprecating smile touching her mouth. "Just standing here keeping company with my misery," she said in a vain attempt at humor. She closed her eyes, grief lining her face. "We bonded while he was holding Alys's body in his arms, Lady Torey. I felt it. But he refuses to admit the bond. He won't let me be his bheancoran. What am I to do? I'll die if he won't let me serve him."

Torey put her arm around the girl's shoulders. "Stay with him, Letessa," she said. "He's submerged in grief and anger now. He hasn't room for anything else. He'll accept you in the end."

Letessa managed a wan smile. "Is this another of your Seeings?" she asked.

Torey repressed a shudder. *Another Seeing.* She never wanted to have another in her life. She could live her life quite nicely without more of that.

"Mayhaps," she said at last. "Or mayhaps it's just a reflection of how well I know my brother."

Letessa glanced down the corridor at Keylan's firmly shut door. "I have no choice but to stay with him," she said in a resigned voice.

"You'd best get some rest," Torey said. "Tomorrow is likely to be a hectic day."

"Aye, so it might." Letessa looked at the closed door again, then turned and made her way to her own chamber.

Torey took her own advice and went to find Connor and her own bed.

Wrapped in a cloak of faded brown homespun, Francia pressed herself inconspicuously into a corner of the tavern. The door opened; she glanced up, her heart giving a small lurch in her chest. But it was another stranger.

She had seen Bryn ride back into Dun Camus with the rest of the enchanter's small escort. She had cultivated his acquaintance carefully, planned every step of the courtship until he was hers to command. He knew she always waited for him here in the tavern. He would come to her. In the three seasons since he had been employed as the enchanter's horsegroom, he always came to the tavern when he returned from one of the enchanter's mysterious visits. But no matter how persuasive she was, he would not tell her where they had been.

Francia touched the small bottle tucked into the bodice of her gown. Shame and fury knotted in her belly when she thought about how she had been reduced to begging a potion prepared by a common hedge witch. The enchanter would pay dearly for this humiliation.

The old woman had cackled cheerfully as she gave Francia the potion. "Just pour it into his ale, lovie," she said. "He'll tell you all you want to know. This will give you the truth about any other women he might be seeing. He'll declare his undying love for you . . . "

Francia certainly didn't want Bryn's undying love. All she

wanted to know was where the enchanter went when he left Dun Eidon two or three times a season and rode west. Discover where the enchanter went, and she would find Mikal.

The door opened again, and Bryn stepped into the tavern. He paused at the door to let his eyes become adjusted to the gloom, then slowly searched the tavern until he found her. She opened her arms to him as he slid onto a chair at the small table beside her. Her smile dazzled him, and he didn't see her reach around him to empty the vial into the flagon of ale the barmaid set down beside him.

Vague images of Eliade filled Donaugh's sleep. She stood in the center of the Dance of Nemeara, calling him urgently. But he was trapped in a matrix of dark magic beyond the circle of standing stones and could not break free. Eliade's summons became more insistent, but the harder Donaugh tried to break free from the ensnaring mesh, the stronger it held him.

The sky above the Dance flared with orange-and-red flames roiling through sooty black smoke. Thunder shook the ground, and the very stones trembled before it. The flames leapt higher, the black smoke lit by blue-white flashes of lightning. Helplessly, Donaugh watched as the flames reached down to engulf Eliade.

Soaked with sweat, Donaugh sat bolt upright in his bed, the echo of his own cry nearly drowned by the rumble of thunder outside his window. He looked out at a clear, star-scattered sky and realized it wasn't thunder he heard. It was the clatter of a hard-ridden horse arriving in the courtyard.

Donaugh met Tiernyn and Ylana at the head of the stairway. "This could be the news we've been dreading," Tiernyn said grimly. "Let's not keep the messenger waiting."

They descended the stairs together and found the messenger in the Great Hall. The young Tyr's clothing was spattered with dirt and stained by splashes of lather from the chest and sides of his horse. He flung himself to one knee before Tiernyn, pale and exhausted.

"My lord, your father sends word. The Maedun fleet is gathering even now in Honandun harbor. The invasion is on its way."

30

From all over the island, Tiernyn gathered his army. He reinforced all the coastal garrisons, and doubled the number of lookouts in the watchtowers circling the island. He sent scout troops out daily to patrol the coasts between the watchtowers, the riders lightly armed for speed, their horses the swiftest in Connor's herds. With Donaugh, Ylana, and Connor, he retired to his workroom to pore over the map of Celi as they tried to predict the most likely place for an invading army to land.

"They could come ashore anywhere," Tiernyn said grimly, running his finger along the deeply indented shoreline. "East here." He stabbed a finger at the open stretches of the Summer Run. "Or north here." His finger moved up to the barren flatlands near the Veniani mountains. "Or even south here along Dorian or Mercia." He glanced up at Donaugh. "What do you think?"

Donaugh listened inwardly, but Kingmaker didn't speak to him. None of the places on the map Tiernyn pointed out felt *right* as Brae Drill had felt right before the final battle with the Saesnesi. "I can't tell," he said.

"Then we'll have to rely on our watchtowers," Tiernyn said, clearly unhappy with the necessity. He glanced at Connor. "And the swiftness of your horses, Connor."

Donaugh left the preparations to Tiernyn and rode alone to the Dance of Nemeara. He entered the Dance as darkness fell. Framed by the massive trilithons, the fading glory of the sunset cast long, black shadows across the polished altar stone. The jet surface gleamed softly with reflected light, the colors changing subtly as the light faded and the shadows lengthened. The seven inner stones of the horseshoe, painted in alternating bands of blood red and deep black, seemed alive in the fey light, and they radiated a soft, welcoming peace. The air moved softly through the Dance, carrying the perfumes of fresh hay and Lammastide daisies plaited with the scent of the sea. Very faintly, the faraway cries of seabirds sounded sweetly, like chimes in the distance.

Donaugh had not been here since the Lammas Eve before Aellegh was born eight years ago, nor had the gods and goddesses spoken with him. Eliade had come to him in dreams, but they were simple dreams, not the awareness of her very real presence he had felt in the Dance at Dun Eidon. He came now to the Dance in supplication.

The sky faded to black velvet. Stars glimmered above the shoulder of Cloudbearer. Donaugh stood before the *darlai* stone, head bowed, waiting. The magic of the Dance flowed about him in living rivers, riffling his clothing and hair as if it were an ocean breeze, tingling along his skin and nerves and sinews like music.

Silence closed around him, broken only by the hushed whisper of wind in the tall grass beyond the circle. Just below the threshold of hearing, threads of music wove around the flows of magic, filling him with a light, airy effervescence. The heightened sense of hush quickened his breathing, made him feel as buoyant as thistledown, as insubstantial as the shadows rippling through the grass. The magic of the Dance surrounded him, palpable as a blanket, yet delicate as spider lace.

Donaugh gathered the magic around him and focused his mind on the Guardian of the Dance. Awareness of the living presence of the Dance quivered in his belly and sang through his body. It seemed to him that the air about him fizzed gently, sparking with thousands of tiny points of light just barely visible out of the corner of his eye.

The moon rose behind Cloudbearer, sending the shadows of the menhirs racing across the ground. Donaugh sensed a presence behind him, but did not turn. "Myrddyn, I come to you for help," he said quietly.

Myrddyn moved out of the shadows between the stones and stood on the opposite side of the altar. His hair and beard gleamed softly silver in the moonlight. Around him, the figures of the gods and goddesses stood quietly, their eyes fixed on Donaugh.

"You call with great strength, Donaugh Secondborn," Myrddyn said. "I am more accustomed to summoning rather than being summoned."

"I meant no disrespect, my lord Myrddyn."

The old man smiled. "I know that. I would not have come otherwise. We both serve the Sword. How may I serve you?"

"They come, Myrddyn," Donaugh said. "The Maedun are ready to take ship to come to Celi. How shall we stop them?"

"You have the means," Myrddyn said.

"Kingmaker is weakened," Donaugh said. "Will it be strong enough?"

"Who can say?" Myrddyn held out one hand, palm up. "I told your father the same thing, Donaugh Secondborn. Even to me, the future is not a scroll I may easily read. What men do day by day changes what might have been yesterday. What might be tomorrow will be changed by what you do, by what your brother does today. I cannot say if the Sword will be strong enough. Nor can I say if you will be strong enough. Or Tiernyn Firstborn."

Donaugh looked up at the *darlai*, who stood calm and silent behind Myrddyn. A small smile touched her mouth, but she said nothing to him. "We must meet Maedun magic with our own," Donaugh said. "Might I ask that my magic be strengthened enough to destroy them?"

Myrddyn laughed softly and shook his head. "Donaugh Secondborn, you know our magic may not be used to kill."

"Then how may we protect this island?"

"You have the means," Myrddyn said again. "Remember the night your brother acquired Kingmaker?"

"How could I forget?"

"Then you will remember what I said to you then. I had no

gift for you, but I told you that what you needed would be provided."

Donaugh held out his hands and looked down at them. Moonlight collected in them, then spilled away between his fingers, gently splashing into the grass by his feet. "I have nothing but gentle Tyadda magic," he said. "Nothing but the magic of this land to fight against magic that kills." He clenched his fists. "Is it enough?"

But when he looked up again, Myrddyn was gone, and the megaliths were merely standing stones again. Despair filling his chest, he sank to his knees before the altar stone, eyes closed. Visions rose before his eyes. Drifts of ash and cinder covering Celi from shore to shore, the land desiccated and dead.

Something brushed against his cheek. Startled, he straightened to find Eliade kneeling beside him. She smiled at him and reached out again to touch his face.

"Beloved, you must not despair," she said softly.

He reached for her. She felt solid and vitally alive in his arms, warm and vibrant against his chest. Her hair smelled of herbs and apple blossoms. He held her, unable to speak, and tears blurred his vision. He had not realized how sorely he missed her until he held her again against him. She was the other half of him, the part that made him complete and whole. As he held her, he wondered again how long he could bear her absence from his life.

"I cannot stay long, beloved," she said. "I came only to ask that you remember the night Tiernyn was proclaimed King." She eased herself gently from his embrace and stood.

He scrambled to his feet, but she was already fading. The air around her shimmered, and she was gone.

The gates of Dun Llewen Landhold stood open wide to the late afternoon sunshine. A steady stream of heavily laden oxcarts flowed into the courtyard under the watchful eyes of guards posted at the gates and on the parapets above the gatehouse. Men and women bearing baskets and bales of goods walked beside the carts, exchanging cheerful greetings with the guards. If the stronghold were laying in provisions for an expected long siege, the people didn't seem overly worried about it. The banner of the lord of Dun Llewen Landhold was conspicuously absent above the gatehouse. Gone to join the King, rumor in the marketplace said.

All across the countryside, rumors of invasion ran rife. As she journeyed from Dun Camus to the northern frontier of Skai, Francia heard them from innkeepers, farmers, merchants, soldiers, and alewives. Everyone had his own favorite rumor and imparted it with the solemnity of the sworn truth. The Saesnesi were loose upon the land again. The Maedun were coming from the continent. Some even said the Borlani were returning to reclaim their lost empire.

Francia believed the rumor of invasion by Maedun. Hakkar had already been making the first preparations when she had left Maedun over two years ago. Horbad, now nearly nine, would have grown stronger in his own magic, making Hakkar's magic that much more powerful.

She watched the procession of carts and people for a while from her place near the market stalls, then glanced over her shoulder at the massive bulk of Cloudbearer. The mountain filled the sky to the south, ponderous and overwhelming in its powerful presence. If the people of Dun Llewen were relying on their sacred mountain to save them, they were to be severely disappointed. Cloudbearer had not protected them from the Saesnesi raiders; it would not protect them from Hakkar's swarms of Somber Riders.

Time was running short for her. She had to ascertain that Mikal was here, and if he was, she had to get him out quickly. Before the first Somber Riders arrived. If she couldn't, he would surely die when the Riders took the stronghold. The Riders would have no compunctions about slaughtering the children of noble families, especially in this west country where magic ran so strongly in the blood of the people. But in the confusion behind the invading army, a farm woman with a child would hardly be noticed.

Casually, Francia moved out onto the track and fell into step with an elderly woman carrying two awkward bundles. "Let me help you there, grandmother," she said as she took one of the bundles. It was heavier than she thought, and she staggered beneath the load before she got it set securely on her hip.

The old woman smiled gratefully, her face creasing like old parchment. "Thank you, dearie," she said. "I haven't much worth saving, but it's all I have in this world. Lord Eryth is kind enough to offer shelter for them as needs it, and I'm not so young and agile as I once was."

"Is it Saesnesi coming against us again, do you think?" Francia asked as they approached the gate. She studiously kept her gaze upon the old woman, not looking at the guards. She didn't want them to see her dark eyes, unnaturally dark on this accursed isle.

The old woman greeted one of the guards by name, then looked back at Francia. "Saesnesi." She shrugged. "Maedun. Borlani. What does it matter? An enemy is an enemy. But the young King will take care of us. He always has. He carries Kingmaker, and the sword was made to protect Celi."

The courtyard teemed with people and animals. Once beyond the sight of the guards, Francia handed the bundle back to the old woman and turned to make her way along the wall of the main house toward the kitchens in the back.

She found the three children playing in the garden while their nurse dozed over her spinning in the shade of an apple tree. From the shaded green shelter of a clump of lilac bushes near the gate, Francia watched her son. He had grown into a sturdy child, as handsome as her brother, his uncle. She could see nothing of his father in him, unless it was the promise of grace in the young body. His hair and eyes were as dark as hers, as dark as Hakkar's. He chased his brightly colored ball around the grass, laughing in delight, and ignoring the other two children, intent on his game.

The nurse came awake suddenly, jerking erect. She looked quickly around for the children, then relaxed when she saw they were all playing quietly. For a moment, her hands moved busily at her spinning. The spindle gradually slowed as her head nodded drowsily again, then her chin fell forward onto her chest.

Mikal scooped up his ball and threw it into the air, laughing as it caught the sunlight. It fell onto the grass and rolled to within a few paces of where Francia stood. As the child ran across the garden toward it, she stepped out from behind the lilac bushes. Mikal drew to a stop and looked at her, unafraid but curious. Francia smiled.

"Would you like a bigger ball, Mikal?" she asked.

Mikal looked at his ball, then grinned at her and nodded.

She held out her hand. "Then come with me. I have a big gold ball that's just for you."

He glanced back over his shoulder at the sleeping nurse. Neither of the other children paid any attention to him, or to Francia. He grinned again, then ran forward to take her hand.

The fleet sailed from Honandun harbor with the evening tide. Sail after sail caught the wind and bellied out as the ships leaned hull down into the water. Their bow waves churned the water before them, and their masts blotted out the stars. In the lead ship, Hakkar stood on the quarterdeck beside the ship's master, his hands clasped behind him as he watched the western horizon. Beside him, Horbad leaned over the rail, fascinated by the rush of water past the steeply curved flank of the ship.

The master gestured toward the horizon, where the last of the sun's glow touched the lingering clouds with vivid pink and gold. "At dawn the day after the morrow, my lord General, Celi will lie there before you."

Horbad looked up, his face gleaming damply from the blown spume. "Do you think they know we're coming, Father?" he asked.

Hakkar smiled grimly. "I'm sure they do," he said. "It's difficult to move a fleet this size in secrecy. Remember that. Always assume your enemy knows what you're doing, then try to do something he won't expect to catch him off guard. The Celae will expect us to land on their eastern shore, closest to the continent."

Horbad nodded gravely. "That's why we're going to come around to the south shore, to that great bay," he said, reciting the lesson by rote.

Hakkar put his hand to his son's head. "You'll be an able general when you're grown, Horbad," he said. He looked ahead to the horizon again. "And an able Lord Protector of that troublesome island."

31

All along the south coast of Celi, the signal fires by the watchtow-
ers flared brightly, turning the dawn sky black with smoke.
Tiernyn led his army from Dun Camus, but far too late to save
the garrisons strung along the south of the Dorian downs. By
the time the Celae army arrived, the Maedun had a firm
foothold on the soil of Celi.

A solid line of black-clad riders faced Tiernyn's army.
Between the two forces lay a broad, flat meadow. The sun
glinted on black metal helms and drawn swords. Behind them
on the glittering water of the bay lay the ships, their masts rising like a forest against the sky.

Donaugh watched the ships, conscious of the slight weight
of the letter from Eryth's wife Ganieda in his belt pouch.
Mikal was gone, and Ganieda's two children said he had
been taken by a woman with black hair and very dark eyes.
That it was Francia, Donaugh had no doubts. He had immediately dispatched three men to search for her and the child, but
had little hope they would find her. He had no time now to
worry about Mikal, but the loss of the child preyed on his
mind.

Beside Donaugh, Keylan let out a long, slow breath. "All
those years," he said softly. "All those years we fought the
Saesnesi, I never really believed this day would come. I
thought the Saesnesi were our only real enemies." He
laughed, an odd mixture of astonishment and awe. "I was
wrong."

Donaugh said nothing. He tried to estimate the strength of
the Maedun across the valley. Rank upon rank of them lined
the gentle slope of the meadow. They seemed to stretch out
for half a league.

Keylan shook his head in amazement, looking at the

ordered black ranks. "Thousands of them," he murmured. "Look at them. There must be thousands of them."

Behind the massed invaders, the smoke from the sacked garrison stockade rose to stain the sky. The stench of burning and blood masked the scent of the sea on the gentle breeze.

"We'll die here today," Keylan said grimly. He reached behind his shoulder to make sure of Bane. "We'll die here, or they will." His lips drew back from his teeth in a bloodless grin that reminded Donaugh of a northern wolf. "I wonder if the men who led the raid on Dun Eidon are among those Riders. What say you, Donaugh?"

Letessa drew in a ragged breath, then edged her horse closer to him, her lips compressed into a thin line. All her attention was on him. She leaned forward in her saddle, every line of her body shouting her determination to stand by him, to protect his back and his left at all costs. For the first time, Donaugh noticed, Keylan didn't try to edge away from her. His full attention was on the Maedun; he seemed hardly to notice her.

Donaugh glanced at Keylan. His eldest brother all but vibrated with his overwhelming need to avenge his family. His face, gaunted and pale except for two splotches of hectic color on his cheeks, looked to be carved out of marble. "I don't know," Donaugh said. "Don't let the need for revenge make you careless, Keylan. Tiernyn needs you for Celi."

Keylan gave a harsh bark of laughter. "Celi needed my children, too, but the Maedun killed them."

Donaugh turned away and searched the ranks of mounted Somber Riders. The stark black-and-white banner of Hakkar of Lake Vayle blew languidly on the wind, but Donaugh was unable to tell if Hakkar himself was among the Somber Riders. Their ranks stood solid and firm. Except for the waving of the banners, nothing moved.

A well-disciplined army, he noted sourly. And a much more formidable foe for the Celae army than the Saesnesi, who fought with fierce abandon, but fought as a group of individuals, not as a unit. These Somber Riders would be a savage crucible to test the mettle of the Celae.

Here and there among the motionless Riders, Donaugh picked out the gray-cloaked warlocks. If the Somber Riders would test Tiernyn's army, these men—and Hakkar himself—would be Donaugh's own personal trial. Their blood magic killed. His own gentle Celae magic—Tyadda magic—would and could not. But might it meet blood magic and neutralize it? Donaugh had no way of telling until he had to try. He had succeeded in overpowering and containing Francia's magic, but comparing her magic to Hakkar's magic, or even to the warlocks' magic, was to compare a candle to a lightning bolt.

Tiernyn turned in his saddle and beckoned to Donaugh. As Donaugh urged his horse forward, Tiernyn led them out of earshot of the captains.

"They look menacing, don't they?" Tiernyn said softly.

Donaugh smiled without humor. "You could call them that," he agreed.

Tiernyn glanced over the army behind him. "Elesan is not here," he said. "All the princes and dukes answered my summons. All but Elesan." He held up his hand to forestall Donaugh's reply. "Nor did he reply to my request to appear before me to answer Keylan's accusations. It would seem you misjudged him, Donaugh."

"He swore fealty to you, Tiernyn. I can only judge him by what I know a Saesnesi's oath to be worth to him."

"I hope you're right," Tiernyn said. He looked out over the Maedun army arrayed on the other side of the shallow valley. They stood with utter stillness, more like figures carved from rock than living men. "Donaugh, will my kingdom survive this day?"

Donaugh paused before he answered. "My own Seeing tells me nothing," he said. "But I yet have little control over it. What I can tell you is that the night you received Kingmaker from Myrddyn, the *darlai* promised me a line of kings stretching from you forward until the time the Dance of Nemeara should crumble back to the earth."

Tiernyn smiled wryly. "Cold comfort, but comfort nonetheless." He sat for a moment, wrists crossed on the pommel before him, not looking at Donaugh. He watched the Somber Riders across the wide meadow. "Donaugh, the sword . . . Kingmaker . . ." He reached behind his shoulder to touch the leather-bound hilt. "You once warned me if I played the sword false, it would let me down when my need of it was greatest. And twice my foolish stubbornness stained the blade. All I can say is, I made the best decision I could at the time for the sake of Celi. Is today the day it will let me down?"

Donaugh glanced at the sword. Kingmaker's unique music sang in his head, fierce and defiant, but conveyed no message to him. He made a helpless gesture. "Tiernyn, how can I know?"

Tiernyn's laugh contained no mirth or humor. "An unfair question, to be sure. But I expect it's a king's prerogative to pose unfair questions once in a while."

He looked down at his hands knotted into fists on his reins, then cleared his throat. Donaugh straightened, his full attention on his twin. Tiernyn was about to reveal the real reason he had taken Donaugh apart from the knot of his captains.

"Ylana is with child," Tiernyn said quietly. "My son, she assures me with that maddening self-assurance of women." He paused, then continued in a carefully neutral tone. "Donaugh, I charge you as both my brother and as my liegeman by the oath you swore to me, to watch over Ylana. Should I not survive this day, you will be my son's regent until he's a man."

Donaugh studied the Maedun. When he spoke, his voice was as careful as Tiernyn's. "Should the child need a regent, I shall be honored to serve him."

Tiernyn nodded. "Thank you," he said simply. He turned his full attention to the Somber Riders. "They have at least a dozen warlocks with them. Can your magic contain them?"

"I hope so," Donaugh said quietly.

"Then that will be your part of this fight. Stay up here and give what help you can. We will pray it will be enough."

Between the space of one heartbeat and the next, the Maedun attacked. On some imperceptible signal, the Somber Riders drew their swords as one man. The horses leapt forward. In a sharply defined black line, the Riders swept down the gentle slope. They shouted no battle cries, no slogans. In an eerie, intense silence, they careered across the sea grass toward the waiting Celae army. The warlocks hung back, spread out behind the main body of Riders, their gray cloaks flapping wildly.

Gray carrion crows, Donaugh thought, and shuddered. He concentrated on the lines of power swirling in the air around him, flowing through the ground beneath his feet. They were tangible as linen threads in his hands, strong, malleable, and supple. He began weaving them into glowing, sparking nets.

Tiernyn drew Kingmaker and raised it high above his head. He held his men back as the precise ranks of black riders plunged into the meadow. As the range closed, he signaled to Connor. Connor kicked his horse into motion, galloping down the line of Celae horsemen to his company of Veniani bowmen.

Connor gave the signal. Eight hundred Veniani arrows sprang from the lethal little recurved bows, a flock of deadly birds rising to darken the sky. The rushing whisper of their passage hissed across the meadow.

Even as the arrows rose to their zenith, black threads of blood magic spun away from the hands of the warlocks. The arrows hesitated in mid-flight, then began to turn back toward Connor's company. Connor's voice came faintly to Donaugh.

"Shields!"

The Veniani raised their oblong shields and held them above their heads.

Donaugh flung his nets. They floated like gossamer on the air, billowing and glinting in the sunlight. As a spider wraps its prey, the nets found warlocks and enfolded them in shimmering brightness. Donaugh drew strength from the air around him and concentrated on his magic. The nets tightened as the warlocks struggled against the stricture. Two of them fell from their horses, thrashing on the ground.

Again, the arrows hesitated in the air. As the warlocks, enmeshed in the nets of Celae magic, strove to free themselves, the arrows fell harmlessly to the ground ahead of the charging Maedun and well clear of the Veniani bowmen huddling under their shields. Connor shouted for another volley, his voice nearly lost in the thunder of the Maedun charge.

Eight hundred bows sang like plucked harp strings. Once again, the arrows rose into the air, a deadly cloud that caught the light on polished, gleaming shafts. This time the arrows struck home, bursting the ordered ranks of Somber Riders. Tumbling horses and riders tangled the taut forward line and sundered the precise file. Tiernyn brought Kingmaker down in a swift slice, and the Celae poured down into the valley.

Donaugh remained on the crest of the hill. The fragile webs of magic enmeshing the warlocks weakened as they met the dark blood magic. Threads snapped, and the backlash of the shattered magic stung against Donaugh's skin in needles of burning pain. The effort of holding the nets together took more strength than he could draw from the flows of magic around him. He poured his own energy, his own vitality, into the nets, willing them to hold. His strength drained from him. Pain burned in his chest, in his belly, tearing at his guts. It took every ounce of his concentration to maintain the nets. He had none left to watch the battle to see how Tiernyn's army fared.

He became aware of a different smell in the air, the putrid reek of a charnel house, foul and fetid. It drowned out the noisome stench of the warlocks' stifled magic, swirling around him in a stinking cloud. He looked up.

From one of the ships anchored in the wide bay, a cloud of

black mist rose. Roiling like smoke, it wafted toward shore, moving against the wind, fingers of darkness writhing out of it. The dark cloud spread in tendrils, reaching for the warlocks. As it touched them, Donaugh's webs of magic first crazed like old crockery, then burst asunder. Bright glints of shattered magic sparked in the air, then vanished as the black mist withdrew to hover over the shoreline behind the battlefield.

Donaugh fell back, blinded and deafened by the exploded magic. He couldn't breathe; his heart hammered against his ribs as if bent on tearing itself loose. He slumped over the neck of his horse, gasping for breath. Knives of pain lanced through his chest and belly, and bright whorls of light spun behind his eyelids.

The black mist began to descend over the confused tangle of men and horses in the meadow.

Keylan urged his horse forward, plunging into the advancing line of black-clad Somber Riders, his company of yrSkai men behind him. The distinct threads of the bond tying Letessa to him tore at his guts, rousing both fury and twisting grief. It was so similar to the bond he had shared with Alys, yet so heart-wrenchingly different. He didn't want it, but he could no more stop it than he could prevent the tide from flowing into the Ceg. Even as he laid about himself with Bane, he was conscious of Letessa's presence at his left, conscious of her sword and her body between him and the swords of the Somber Riders he need not worry about because she was there.

Doggedly, he hurled himself forward, deeper into the black ranks, as if by the sheer driving force of his need for revenge he could find the men who had led the attack on Dun Eidon. Letessa kept pace with him, her sword rising and falling around her, gleaming with the blood of fallen Somber Riders. Her own anger, her own need for revenge, vibrated along the strands of the bond between them and merged with his.

His horse went down beneath him, blood gushing from its

half-severed neck. Keylan kicked free of the stirrups and flung himself clear as the horse tumbled to the ground. The grass beneath his feet was sodden with blood, and slippery. He stumbled, went to one knee, nearly dropped his sword.

Letessa screamed. He spun around, still on his knee. A Somber Rider bore down on him, black sword hewing the air toward his head. Even as Keylan raised Bane to defend himself he knew he would be long seconds too late. He could not bring Bane around soon enough. He knelt, watching his death rushing toward him, flashing with an obsidian glitter.

Shrieking incoherently, Letessa spurred her horse around. She leaned far out in her saddle, her sword swinging in a vicious backhand slice. The blade caught the Somber Rider just below the ribs. He flopped back bonelessly in the saddle, then fell with a jarring thud nearly at Keylan's knee. The riderless horse shied violently, then leapt clumsily over Keylan. One flying hoof grazed his shoulder, sending numbing pain down his arm.

He scrambled to his feet, tightening his grip on Bane, the sword held raised and ready as he looked for a horse. A knot of struggling men and horses swept across the field in front of him, and he dodged aside. When he looked around, he couldn't find Letessa. She was gone.

A riderless horse, eyes showing white in fear and confusion without the accustomed presence of a man upon its back, trotted toward him, head held high to prevent the reins from tripping it. Keylan seized the reins and swung himself into the saddle. He could not see Letessa in the chaotic shambles of the battle around him.

Someone cried out, pointing to the sky. Keylan looked up. A black mist moved like smoke above his head, then settled to engulf the struggling men. One by one, the Celae around him froze into stillness. Something that felt like a smothering blanket closed around him.

The air thickened with the foul, black mist. It wrapped itself in snaking tendrils around his throat, suffocating and strangling. Cold as lost hope, it fastened itself to his soul, draining his strength and will, replacing his lifeblood with its own chilling void. He coughed, choking and gagging on the loathsome stuff, tasting death against the back of his tongue. Fingers of mist closed around his heart, squeezing until each labored beat was agony.

He could hardly move. Raising Bane to slice at a Somber Rider took all the strength he had. He felt as if he had been detached from his body. As he looked around in stunned shock, he saw that only a few of the Celae were still moving. They were all men of Skai, the men who claimed Tyadda blood.

How very odd, Keylan thought in remote amazement. With a detached calm, he realized they were all going to die here on this meadow, but felt only a mild regret.

Restlessness seized Torey, drawing her away from the clustered carts of the Healers. She could barely make out the lone figure of a rider on the top of the rise above the battlefield, and recognized Donaugh by his blue cloak. A vivid aura of magic surrounded him, flaring brightly even in the late summer sunshine.

The healers' camp was far behind the battlefield, but she could hear the clash and clangor of weapon against weapon, and the screams and cries of men above the agonized shrieks of the horses. And over it all, the eager squawking of the flocks of ravens that turned the sky black. She squeezed her eyes shut and covered her ears with her hands.

How many times must she listen helplessly while everyone she loved battled for their lives? Connor was out there, and Tiernyn, and Donaugh, and Keylan. She could not bear it. She could not merely stand by and wait. Not this time.

She put her hand down to her belly. The child within had not yet quickened, but the bright pulse of life below her heart beat gently against the palm of her hand, warming it. Connor's son. Her son. How could she stand here, doing nothing, while her child's father fought and perhaps died?

Resolve firmed into action. She gathered her skirts and ran to the edge of the camp, where the horses were picketed. Without bothering with a saddle, she swung herself up onto the nearest horse and gathered in the hackamore rope. She bent forward across the neck of the horse and kicked it to a gallop.

It took only moments to reach the top of the grassy hill. Donaugh did not look around, even though he must have heard her approach. His face pale and stiff with the intensity of his concentration, he watched the battle below him. Torey drew her horse to a stop beside him, and cried out as she looked out over the torn and trampled meadow.

A thick black mist poured from one of the ships, settling over the struggling men and horses. One by one, the men of Celi froze into rigidity. Blood magic. Fayden had described it to her while she tended his wound the day he saw Tavis home, how it left Tavis's Tyran regiment helpless while the Maedun cut them down.

"No," she whispered.

Donaugh paid her no attention. He raised his hands, fists clenched, and threw back his head, the cords on his neck standing out like steel cables.

"Celi!" he shouted.

The air around Torey shivered, and the ground beneath her feet trembled as an immense explosion of thunder rent the air. Blue-white lightning flashed from a sky that had been clear only moments before. She slid from the horse, clinging to its mane to prevent herself from crumpling to the still-quivering ground. The sky darkened and a great wind battered against her, tearing at her clothing and hair as if it meant to pluck her from the ground and send her whirling through the choking air. Incredibly, the horse stood, calm and docile, paying little attention to the tumult while she stood with both arms around its neck, her face buried in its mane to escape the fury of the wind.

As suddenly as it had come, the wind died. The air no longer clogged her nose and throat, thick as dust. Dazed, Torey lifted her head and risked a look around. The black mist had disappeared.

So had Donaugh.

32

Clutching Mikal to her, Francia stumbled along the beach. Each breath she took stabbed into her side like a knife, and her raw throat rasped as if it had been scoured with pumice. The hem of her gown dragged in the wet sand, threatening to trip her with every step. Mikal clung to her, his face pressed tightly against her throat, dazed now by fear and exhaustion. Beyond the dunes to Francia's left, the sounds of the battle shivered the air.

Beyond a spur of sand and sea grass, the masts of Hakkar's invasion fleet rocked gently against the clear sky. There would be boats of some sort on the beach there, Francia hoped. A boat she could take to reach Hakkar's ship. If the men stationed by the boats would not take her out into the bay, she would row it herself. She would steal a boat, if she had to.

Her arms ached from carrying the child. He had seemed to grow heavier with each furlong along the beach, and the deep sand made it difficult to walk. But at least he wasn't screaming in terror anymore. If he had not represented her entry back into Hakkar's good graces, she would have abandoned him like an unwanted kitten long ago. His cries pierced her head until she wanted to scream with him.

She sank to her knees behind a clump of tall sea grass and peered through it at the curve of beach ahead. As she had expected, the shore was covered with boats and barges of all sizes. In dismay, she realized all of them were far too big to be handled by a woman alone, or even one or two men.

She put Mikal down on the sand and rubbed her arms, trying to restore the circulation. Her back ached, her feet hurt, and her head throbbed with pain. For a moment, she closed her eyes, wishing to have even the smallest part of her magic back. But it was gone, stripped away completely by that accursed enchanter. She could not even sense the lines of magic in the air and ground around her now, much less try to use them. Perhaps when she got back to Maedun . . . *If* she got back to Maedun . . .

Mikal whimpered. She looked down at him in distaste. His face was grimed and dirty, his dark hair matted. He stank. He looked nothing like the heir to a throne. When she got him back to Maedun, she was going to turn him over to a nurse and have as little to do with him as possible.

"Be quiet, child," she snapped. "Hold your tongue and stop that sniveling before I beat you." She turned back to her study of the shoreline ahead.

Mikal made an odd noise. Francia turned. He looked up, one grubby paw reaching toward the sky. He gurgled in delight, trying to reach something above his head. Involuntarily, she glanced upward. Her breath caught in her throat. A thick, black mist rolled across the sky above their heads, twisting and boiling like a storm cloud. She watched it for a moment, then looked back at the ships in the bay. The haze poured up from one ship on the far edge of the anchored flotilla.

Hakkar's ship. She marked it in her memory, then looked back at the beach, and finally found what she wanted. A small, two-man coracle lay pulled up onto the sand between a huge barge and a heavy wooden skiff. She was certain it had not been there a few minutes ago, but it was light enough and swift enough to be used by couriers running back and forth between Hakkar's ship and the army just beyond the dunes. It looked light and maneuverable. She thought she could handle it by herself.

She could see no sailors on the barge, no guards on the sand. But they would not be expecting someone to come up on the beached boats from the shoreside.

Francia watched for a few more minutes. A sudden rumble

of thunder startled her, and the accompanying flash of lightning nearly blinded her. A howling wind picked up sand and
grit, swirling it around them, stinging her eyes and face. Mikal
screamed in panic. She snatched him up and slapped him. "Be
quiet!" she cried.

She pressed him against her and pulled her tattered shawl
over her head to protect her face. The wind whipped the fabric
against her bare arms, howling in her ears like a soul in torment. Blinded and deafened, she couldn't hear Mikal's
screams of terror. The child clung to her, pushing his face hard
against her already-soiled bodice.

As suddenly as it had come, the wind died. When Francia
looked up again, the black mist was gone.

Donaugh struggled to breathe as the black mist closed about
his throat. He leaned forward, trying to see through the black
miasma. On the field below him, men of Celi fell to the black
swords of the Somber Riders, held frozen and defenseless
beneath the black sorcery cast by Hakkar of Maedun from his
ship in the bay.

Anger burst in Donaugh's chest. He raised his clenched
fists before him and threw back his head, straining to draw the
magic of his island around him. Crackling like lightning, the
flows of power writhed around him, seething through his body
and into his hands.

Voices swirled around him, whispering in his mind, tan-
gling with visions of tall swords standing among towering
menhirs. Myrddyn's voice murmured, *"I have no sword for
you, Donaugh Secondborn, but I think you will find your own
gift."* Donaugh heard what he had missed while he watched
Tiernyn with Kingmaker in the Dance all those years ago. The
subtle emphasis on Myrddyn's first word. *He* had no sword he
could give Donaugh. But might another have the gift of a
sword for him?

"Celi!" he shouted. "I have need now! Celi!"

A great wind swirled up around him, blinding him. The sky went dark; the world tumbled about him. The battlefield disappeared and an echoing void swallowed him. He cried out and covered his eyes with his hands to protect them from the surging tempest.

The wind died as suddenly as it had come. Silence and calm descended around him. When he took his hands from his eyes, the battlefield was gone.

He stood outside a low, wooden structure under a cloudless black sky. Trees crowded close around the small building, and a stream rippled and splashed only a few paces from the doorway. Age silvered the wood of the door and walls of the building, and burned-in brand marks scored the surface, some of them fresh and charred black, some weathered to pale, iridescent gold.

Magic swirled through the air, thick as honey. It sparked around him, flowing across his skin and along his nerves, through his bones and veins. Music sang in the trees and in the brook at his feet, chiming in the crags around him. Every breath he took was laden with it, and it filled him as wine fills a goblet.

Eight figures stood just inside the building, barely visible in the gloom, and behind them loomed the cold bulk of a forge, its fires stilled and dead. Above him, the sun, paled to a wan disk, sailed among a sea of stars, but cast no shadows across the beaten earth outside the forge.

On the walls of the smithy hung the tools of the smith's trade, worn but clean with constant use and care. A shining metal vat for water stood next to the anvil, empty now, and spare hammers in varying sizes lay on a block of wood that served as a table. The beaten earth floor had been swept clean, and water sprinkled to settle the dust.

One of the men inside the forge stepped forward. He wore a leather apron covering his chest and belly. His powerful arms, thick as a normal man's thigh, were bare and gleaming in the eerie light. Broad-shouldered and heavyset, he stood easily half an armlength taller than Donaugh. In one hand, he carried a square hammer, its handle polished like silk by years of use. Startled, Donaugh recognized Wyfydd Smith, and the song echoed in his head.

Armorer to gods and kings
Wyfydd's magic hammer rings . . .

"I can make no sword without the King's fire, Donaugh Secondborn," Wyfydd said, his voice deep as the pealing thunder. "Call me the fire for your sword."

Donaugh glanced at Beodun, Father of Fires. The god stood with his arms folded across his chest, his hands empty of the lamp of benevolent fire or the lightning bolt of wildfire. "Call my fire, Donaugh Secondborn," he said. "This is my gift to you for your sword."

Donaugh bowed and turned back to Wyfydd. "And the metal for the sword, my lord Smith?" he asked.

The smith's laughter pealed heartily around the smithy. "Gerieg will provide it for you. Call the fire quickly, for our time runs short."

Donaugh turned to face the west. Eliade's words whispered through his head. "*Remember the night Tiernyn was proclaimed King . . .*" His breath was too light for his chest to contain it. Buoyant and quivering, he drew on the magic, sent it lancing through the sky.

The Kingstar blazed across the western sky, leaving a fiery trail of incandescent haze behind it. It plunged down through the lesser stars, and its seething tail brushed across the upthrusting head of Cloudbearer. As the Kingstar passed, smoke and flame poured out of the top of the mountain, sending gouts of brilliant embers soaring into the black sky.

Straight as the flight of an arrow, the Kingstar slanted down through the sky, blinding in its brilliance, searing Donaugh's eyes as it flew past him. The air hissed and crackled to its passing. Behind it came a molten stream of gleaming metal, pouring from the smoking summit of Cloudbearer.

The forge exploded into flame. Light flared around the interior of the smithy, sending black shadows dancing along the silvered walls until the forge ran with brilliant color, red and gold and orange. Wyfydd reached high and pulled a bar of the sparking metal from the sky, whirling it above his head and then down into the molten heart of the forge fire.

The bar of metal from Cloudbearer lay in the fire, glowing brilliant white-orange with a life of its own. Using a pair of bright tongs, the smith pulled the metal from the Kingstar fire and laid it upon the anvil. The heat oiled the skin of the smith's bare shoulders and arms with a film of sweat. The muscles beneath the bronzed skin rippled and flowed as the hammer beat down on the glowing metal.

Slowly, slowly, the metal on the anvil began to take shape as the smith's hammer drew it out. When it lost its malleability as it cooled, the smith thrust it back into the fire. Time after time, the bar of metal flattened to a thin sheet beneath the hammer. The smith folded the sheet, pleating it into layers, and let the rhythmic beating of the hammer draw it out again in an endlessly repeated cycle. Behind him, against the wall of the smithy, a shadow smith built a shadow sword in vivid counterpoint.

Donaugh was aware of the changing shape of the shadows moving across the beaten earth of the floor, but time had no meaning here. Before his eyes, the sword began to take shape. Long after the graceful shape would have been sufficient for any ordinary sword, the smith continued to fold and draw out, fold and draw out. Strong and flexible, this blade would take and keep an edge no matter what it was required to cleave through.

The last part to be shaped was the tang, the point that would fit into the hilt. When it was done, the smith lifted the blade and held it above the oaken vat lined with bright metal.

Adriel of the Waters stepped forward and tilted her enchanted ewer. Water flowed over the golden lip and into the vat, bright and sparkling, clean and cold and sweet. When the vat was full, she stepped back. The smith plunged the glowing blade into the water. A cloud of steam rose, thick and fragrant, as the blade sizzled, then cooled. Behind him, in echo against the wall, a shadow smith quenched a shadow sword.

One by one, the gods and goddesses brought their gifts for the sword to add to the gifts of Beodun, Adriel, and Gerieg. Cernos stepped forward, one of the tines from his antlers in his hand. Wyfydd took it and bent it around the naked tang for a hilt, long enough to be used two-handed, light enough to be wielded with one hand. Rhianna wove her air magic into an intricate web of silver to embellish the glowing, translucent horn of the hilt. And last, Sandor of the Plains held forth a baldric and scabbard braided of tough prairie grasses, as lustrous and strong as gilded leather.

Wyfydd lifted the sword and presented it to the *darlai*. She stepped forward and ran her finger down the gleaming blade. On the wall behind her, the shadow of the sword leapt stark and clear, appearing as real as the sword itself. Sparks flew from beneath her finger and fire ran down the metal, etching runes into the blade. The music of magic swelled to a lilting crescendo.

Magic to the hilt he gave
With music did the blade engrave . . .

When the *darlai* stepped back, the runes blazed up, brilliant as the cut facets of a gem, and the words flared in the smoky light.

"Can you read them, Donaugh Secondborn?" she asked.

Donaugh bent forward and traced the shape of the runes

with his finger. Heat scorched his fingertip. "**I Am Blood and Bone of Celi.**"

"Then hold out your hands and accept the sword Heartfire, Donaugh Secondborn."

"Willingly, Lady." Donaugh lifted his hands and held them palms upward. The *darlai* stepped forward and placed the sword into his hands. Music burst around him, harp and bell and flute, singing in the air. The blade flashed and flared, brilliant gold and blue and green, the colors of the land.

On the wall, the shadow of the sword faded and disappeared.

"Soulshadow is not for you," the *darlai* said softly. "Go now and face your enemy, Donaugh Secondborn. Use our gift well."

"It will not leave my hand, Lady," Donaugh said. "I swear this."

"Then go to meet your enemy, my child. He awaits you."

Donaugh gripped the hilt of Heartfire in both hands. The sword balanced perfectly as he held it. The blade flashed, sending a bright flare of coruscating color around the smithy. He stepped through the door and raised the sword high.

"Hakkar of Maedun," he shouted into the fey darkness of the sky. "Come to me now! Meet me as your father met my father!"

The wind rose around Donaugh, gusting wildly. The smithy, the trees, and the stream faded and the tall, stark forms of the Dance of Nemeara took shape around him.

33

Gasping for air, Torey clung to the horse and watched the battle below. She could distinguish very little in the struggling mass of men and horses seething across the meadow. The stench of blood and burning mixed with something she couldn't identify at first, nauseating her.

Gradually, she realized she could pick out clear details in the chaos of the battle. At the edges of the conflict, men in gray sat their horses, faint black auras surrounding them.

Warlocks! And they had the ability to turn weapons back on the men who used them. In the meadow, Celae soldiers died by their own hands under the devastating spell.

A woman's voice spoke softly in her ear. "Look at the sunlight, child. Remember my gift."

Torey spun around, but nobody stood behind her. The woman's voice spoke again, and Torey recognized it. Rhianna of the Air, speaking in that same calm, quiet tone she had used the night in the Dance at the Clanhold.

"Look at the sunlight, child."

Torey held out her hands. Sunlight poured into them, warm and rich as precious oil. Its weight and substance moved against her fingers like threads that could be braided or woven . . .

Woven . . .

Torey's hands began moving of their own volition. The sunlight spun out to form golden strands, and she brought them together into an intricate pattern. The pattern expanded into a long oblong that hung in the air before her. Like a shield. Or a mirror.

Sudden understanding burst through Torey like sunshine through a rain cloud. Relief made her laugh as she left the first shield hanging in the air beside her and fashioned another, then another. When she had twelve of them, she flung them down the hill at the warlocks.

The bright shields moved swiftly, tracking straight as arrows through the air until each hovered before a warlock. Almost invisible in the clear air, they glinted softly like dust motes in a shaft of sunlight. Black threads of blood magic spun out from the warlocks' hands. Bright sparks shot from the mirrorlike shields as the black threads collided with the golden surface. The dark threads bounced back toward the warlocks.

One by one, the warlocks burst into flame.

Torey watched in horrified fascination as twelve columns of gray ash drifted away on the gentle breeze. The shields of woven sunlight shimmered for a moment, reflecting nothing but blowing ash, then dissolved and scattered like motes of dust.

A great cry of triumph rose from the throats of the men of Celi. With renewed ferocity, they attacked the Somber Riders.

The ground beneath her feet twisted and heaved. Torey cried out as a sudden smothering sensation gripped her. It felt as if she had been turned inside out. She screamed in terror and staggered, falling to her knees.

When she looked up, she knelt in the shadow of the Dance of Nemeara. Beyond the triple ring of standing stones, Donaugh and a man dressed in unrelieved black fought with murderous intensity.

Francia picked up Mikal, holding him tightly against her, and ran across the sand to the small coracle. Two paddles lay at the bottom across the fragile ribs. She placed Mikal near the bow and ran around to the stern, then glanced quickly around to make sure no one was watching. The small boat slid easily over the sand and into the water lapping gently against a line of gray-green slippery seaweed deposited by the ebbing tide. Shallow-drafted, the coracle floated immediately. She let go of the stern and scrambled aboard, groping in the bottom of the boat for one of the paddles. Kneeling in the middle of the boat, she tried dipping the paddle into the water.

For a few frantic moments, she thought she would not be able to move the boat out into the bay. Her first attempts with the paddle produced no results. Water splashed over the sides, soaking her, and the tiny coracle simply swung its bow around back to the shore. Sobbing with effort, she collapsed in frustration, nearly losing her grip on the handle of the paddle. Mikal wailed as water slopped over the sides and into his face.

Francia had always prided herself on her ability to think in tense situations. She took several deep breaths, forcibly calming herself, then looked at the paddle. She had watched men effortlessly skim these ridiculous little boats a hundred times across the surface of Lake Vayle in search of fish. They always sat near the rear of the boat. And they held the paddle differently.

She moved back toward the stern, and gripped the paddle as she had seen the men hold them. When she tried to imitate their movements, she found the little boat moved easily. After a few strokes, she discovered she was even able to steer it with reasonable accuracy.

The bay seemed endless. Each time she looked up, the shore looked a little farther away, but she couldn't tell if Hakkar's ship was any closer. Doggedly, she kept at it. She was approaching from an oblique angle, and would not have to pass too close to any other ship.

It startled her when she looked up and found the hull of Hakkar's ship looming above the little coracle. Hakkar's black-and-white standard flapped above the taffrail. Bringing the boat alongside the ship, she banged on the side of the hull with the paddle. A man's startled face peered over the rail at her.

"Bring us aboard instantly," Francia shouted at him.

The man hesitated. But Francia had spent her life commanding servants, and the sailor had spent his obeying commands. Francia's voice carried the unmistakable ring of authority. In moments, a rope ladder tumbled over the rail and two men scrambled down into the little boat to lift Francia and Mikal to the deck.

The ship's captain met her as one of the sailors lowered her to the deck, then handed Mikal to her. Francia held herself stiffly erect and gave the captain a haughty stare.

"Where is my brother?" she demanded. "Where is the Lord Hakkar? Take me to him immediately."

"I can't, my lady," the captain said, obviously nonplussed to find the sister of his commander, dirty and bedraggled, on his deck.

"You will do as you're told," Francia said coldly. "Where is he?"

The captain shook his head. "My lady, I don't know. He was on the quarterdeck, but he's vanished."

Blood flowed from a head wound into Keylan's eyes, but he couldn't stop to wipe it away. Somber Riders surrounded him, pressing him from all sides. Bane whirled in a glittering and deadly arc around him, its fierce song loud in his ears. Two of the Somber Riders fell, one to his sword and one to the sword of a man of Celi who fought his way through the tangle to Keylan's side.

Keylan hardly recognized Connor of Wenydd. The scar on Connor's cheek showed livid white against his skin, and blood matted his dark hair. Connor maneuvered his horse into place on Keylan's left side, pressing close for mutual protection.

"My thanks!" Keylan shouted above the pandemonium.

Connor laughed. "Torey would never forgive me—" He broke off and swung his sword in a wicked backhand slice. The edge of the blade swept a charging Somber Rider from his saddle. "—if I let you get yourself killed."

A man's voice rose above the tumult and confusion. "On the hill! Look!"

Keylan glanced over his shoulder. A line of men appeared on the crest of the hill behind the battlefield—men in horned helmets carrying short swords and war axes. Hundred upon hundreds of them, lining the brow of the hill.

"The Saesnesi," Connor shouted. "Elesan's brought his army."

"Aye," Keylan said. "But who will he attack?" He swung his horse around, finding a small island of relative calm in the midst of the carnage. Farther to his left, Tiernyn's banner, tattered now but still held high, fluttered in the gentle breeze. Tiernyn himself fought savagely, surrounded by a knot of his own men and Somber Riders.

Elesan himself led the Saesnesi, mounted on a black horse that could only have been one of Connor's warhorses. His sword and war ax hung sheathed by his side as he surveyed the field below him. For a moment, Keylan thought the Saesnesi Celwalda looked right into his eyes before his gaze moved on.

Mesmerized, Keylan stared at Elesan. What was the man thinking? What would he decide? Whom did he consider the greater enemy, the beleaguered Celae or the Maedun Somber Riders?

Slowly, deliberately, Elesan drew his sword and raised it high in the air. Keylan was certain Elesan watched Tiernyn as the King fought for his life. Then Elesan's sword sliced forward and down, and the Saesnesi began running down the slope into the valley. Even above the clangor and clatter of the battle around him, Keylan heard the roar of their battle cries.

Elesan, at the head of his army, plunged into the midst of the fighting, his sword in one hand, his ax in the other. The ax sliced out in a lethal arc and bit into the throat of a Somber Rider. The Maedun's head flew off, spouting blood in a bright arc.

Tiernyn raised his own sword high. "To me," he cried. "Men of Celi, to me!"

Keylan spurred his horse and leapt forward, Connor close beside him. "Celi!" he shouted. "For Celi and the King!"

34

They faced each other across a wide circle of grass starred with white, luminescent flowers, the air between them as charged with tension as the air just before a lightning strike. The sky glowed with a strange light that was neither dawn nor dusk, and cast no shadows. At Donaugh's back, stood the looming presence of the Dance. Behind Hakkar of Maedun spread a bleak vista of gray drifts of ash and cinder.

The sword in Donaugh's hands vibrated with urgency. The smooth, translucent horn of the hilt fitted his grip perfectly. Flaring light twisted around the blade, the runes glinting like gems. The sword's sweet, fierce song chimed around him and filled him with its soaring sense of power.

Hakkar was dressed in unrelieved black, his black hair and eyes blending with the shadows around him. He held his sword raised before him, its obsidian blade spilling darkness around it as a broken ewer spills water. It reminded Donaugh of a hole torn in the fabric of the world, trapping and swallowing all light.

"I misjudged you, hedge wizard," Hakkar said softly. "I had not thought you powerful enough to draw me here."

Donaugh flexed his hands around the hilt of Heartfire. "I think you'll find me as formidable a foe as your father found my father."

"I rather doubt that. But I shall not underestimate you again. You may be sure of that."

"You do me honor," Donaugh said.

"You and I will settle our quarrel here," Hakkar said. "And when I'm finished with you, I shall see to it that your brothers join you in death. I shall complete the task my father began, and your line will be ended."

Something moved within the darkness of the Dance

behind Donaugh. He stepped to the side, glancing quickly over his shoulder. A slender figure stepped out from the center of a trilithon, her silver-gilt hair flowing across her shoulders. For an instant, Donaugh thought it was Rhianna of the Air, then his heart leapt joyfully in his chest as he recognized Eliade. The air above her left shoulder shimmered, but he could discern no shape within the faint brightness. She said nothing, but her presence was sufficient. The threads of the bond he shared with her quivered with renewed strength. Donaugh turned quickly back to Hakkar.

"Then come and meet with Celae magic, sorcerer."

Hakkar plunged forward, body tense, the black sword in his hands describing a vicious and deadly arc through the fey light. Donaugh leapt back, bringing Heartfire up to meet the obsidian blade. The two swords met with the crash of cymbals, and bright sparks shot up into the air around them.

Donaugh let the sword take him deep into its own compelling rhythm. His magic sang in his veins and the sword sang with it. He watched only Hakkar, conscious of how the drifts of gray ash and the solid megaliths of the Dance changed places behind him. Eliade's presence behind him danced in sparks across his skin, her silver web of magic closing around him, stretching and flexing with his movements.

All his life, he had willingly assumed the role of Tiernyn's shadow. Now, for the first time, he allowed himself to be the light and cared not if he cast no shadow. Tiernyn had built a united kingdom on the island through his skill and unique talents, backed by Kingmaker. Now Donaugh would protect it with his own skill and talent. This task was his, and he embraced it passionately.

Bane shrieked as it bit through black armor and deep into the vitals of a Somber Rider. Keylan yanked back the sword and turned to meet another opponent. He found none. All around him, dazed Celae soldiers stared at each other, knee-deep in dead and dying.

Keylan went to one knee, surprised to find himself still alive. His hair and clothing were stiff with blood, his own and Maedun blood. Exhaustion closed around him like a mailed fist. For a moment, he knelt, head bowed, dragging in deep gulps of air.

Gradually, he became aware of something pulsing gently within his chest. He raised his head and looked around, wild hope springing into his heart. But Alys was dead, the bond between them severed forever by her death.

Letessa?

Keylan staggered to his feet, groping wearily for the scabbard on his back to sheathe Bane. Dead and dying covered the floor of the valley. The faint throb below his heart intensified as he looked toward the sea. He took two hesitant steps, then began to run, leaping over heaps of tangled bodies, dodging between men slowly gathering to celebrate the fact they still lived. Gasping for breath, almost sobbing with effort, he sped across the battlefield.

He found her sprawled half beneath her dead horse. Her dark gold hair had come loose from its braid and spilled across her face, stained with blood and dirt. Beneath the lank strands, her face was the color of chalk. For a moment he thought she was dead, then he saw that the hair lying across her mouth and nose moved slightly with the cadence of her breath. The wave of relief that swept through him dizzied him with its intensity.

He knelt beside her. She was covered in blood, as he was, but he could find no wounds to indicate the blood was hers. The carcass of the horse covered her body from the hips down. He put his shoulder against the bloating belly and heaved with all his strength. He managed to move the horse enough to pull Letessa from beneath it.

She opened her eyes and stared at him. She managed a smile. "You found me," she murmured.

"Of course," he said. "Are you all right?"

"I think my leg is broken," she said. "It hurts."

He gathered her into his arms and got to his feet. She put her arms around his neck and rested her head on his shoulder. He pressed his cheek to her hair, then made his way across the battlefield toward the camp of the healers.

On her knees, Torey clung to the rough bulk of the menhir. Above her head, the massive capstone blocked out fully half of the eerily glowing sky. The scent of trampled grass hung thick in the air, braided with the stench of burning and blood from the dunes of ash and cinder beyond the circle. She had no idea how she had come to this place, whether the Dance itself had called her, or if Donaugh's need had summoned her.

But this was why she had come back to Celi. She was about to meet her *wyrd*. She hoped only that she be equal to it.

A strange woman stood just beyond the arch of the trilithon where Torey crouched. Between the woman and Donaugh stretched a faint silver web. It might have been woven of spider silk, so fragile and delicate it looked. Power vibrated along the web, ebbing and flowing with the rhythm of Donaugh's battle with Hakkar, but the woman didn't move. Torey stared at her in astonishment. But if the gods and goddesses walked this Dance, surely the presence of Donaugh's lost love was no greater wonder.

The two men moved with the grace of dancers, sweeping back and forth and around the circle. Sparks flew as the blades met in thrust and parry, slash and riposte, first high, then low. Tirelessly, the men fought, first one attacking, then the other. The air rang with the fierce music of their weapons meeting.

The blades struck more sparks as they met, then parted. Blue and green and amber from Donaugh's sword twisting and braiding around sullen red and orange from Hakkar's blade, all rising into the uncanny glow of the sky. Flashes of color matching the sparks glinted off the silent megaliths, spilled brilliant runnels of color along the bleak, gray dunes of ash and cinder beyond the circle.

Slowly, slowly, Donaugh beat Hakkar back, pressing him inexorably toward the desiccated wasteland called forth by Maedun blood magic. Hakkar gave ground reluctantly, his face twisted into lines of strain as he struggled to stop Donaugh. Every inch Donaugh gained cost him more strength than he could replace, his determination reflected in the agony squeezing his eyes to narrowed slits, his mouth to a grim, bloodless line. Grace and fluid dexterity gave way to sheer, dogged, labored effort.

But he was winning.

Donaugh slipped in the sodden grass, lost his footing. He went to one knee. Hakkar leapt forward, shouting in triumph. His caliginous blade swept forward and down, spewing darkness as it moved. Off-balance, Donaugh tried to raise Heartfire. Hakkar's sword flashed beneath Donaugh's sword. The edge bit into Donaugh's arm, just above the wrist. The glowing sword spun off into the darkness, Donaugh's severed hand still clinging to it. Its shadow, cast by its own light, whirled across the grass, sharp and distinct as the sword itself. Hakkar reversed the swing of his sword and the tip of it sliced cleanly into the soft tissues below Donaugh's ribs.

Torey cried out as Donaugh fell back, blood pouring from the stump of his wrist and the wound in his side. Hakkar raised his sword for the killing blow.

Eliade made no sound. She plunged forward. Stooping low in a quick, graceful movement, she snatched up the shadow of the sword even as it spun past her. In her hand, it took on substance and weight, glowing with its own ghostly light. Without pausing, she thrust the shadow sword deep into Hakkar's side.

Hakkar's eyes widened in shock. He stumbled, groping with his left hand for the wound in his side. Eliade drew back

Soulshadow for another blow, but Hakkar's outline shimmered, grew transparent. As he vanished, so did the sword in her hands.

Horbad screamed.

Francia spun around, Mikal still clutched in her arms. She nearly dropped the child as Hakkar's sprawled body appeared where an instant before there had been nothing but empty deck. Blood poured from a deep gash in his side. The hand clutching the hilt of his black sword looked more like a talon than a human hand. His eyes, wide and blank, stared at nothing, but he still breathed.

"Horbad," he whispered hoarsely.

Horbad fell to his knees beside his father and grasped his hand. All traces of fear vanished from his face and he became calm and contained. Francia drew back in abhorrence as the boy smiled in anticipation.

"Are you dying then, Father?" he asked softly.

"Come closer . . ." Hakkar clutched at Horbad's shirt, pulling him down until the boy's face was within inches of his. "You must take my power, Horbad. Now . . . "

Francia dropped to her knees. The child she carried whimpered, struggling against her feebly. She had almost forgotten she still held Mikal. A last breath rattled in Hakkar's throat, and his hand fell limply from Horbad's shirt. Black mist rose thickly from his chest, tendrils reaching for Horbad's head.

The magic! Hakkar's magic passing to Horbad!

Mikal squirmed in her arms, protesting against the ferocity of her grip on him. Francia stared at him, then down at Hakkar's body. What if part of that magic should pass to her son?

She flung Mikal down on Hakkar's chest. The child screamed, thrashing wildly, but Francia held him down, glaring at Horbad. Horbad, lost in the ecstasy of the transfer, paid her no attention. Desperately, she shoved with her free hand at the boy, trying to push him away from his father. But her hand met an invisible barrier. She couldn't touch him.

The dark mist thickened. Horrified, she saw it pass right through Mikal's body and collect around Horbad's head and shoulders. It swirled for a moment, tongues of red and orange flickering dully within it, then shrank tighter around him. In seconds, it had disappeared.

Shaking, Francia picked Mikal up. Hakkar's blood smeared the child's face and hands, and he lay limp in her arms, his eyes wide and staring as he gasped for breath.

Horbad slowly climbed to his feet, then bent to wrest the hilt of the black sword from Hakkar's dead hand. The sword was almost as tall as he. Holding it in both hands, its point against the planking of the deck, he looked down at Francia, still on her knees beside Hakkar's body. He stared at her with Hakkar's cold gaze, his eyes like flat, brown stones.

"You have always wished me harm," he said quietly. "And you tried to steal my father's magic for that guttersnipe child. Why should I let you live now?"

A strange calm settled over Francia. She sat back on her heels and met his eyes. "Because I have a weapon here you will need." She held out the child in her arms. "This is the son of the King of Celi. Think of what a weapon and a tool he will make for you."

"I could kill you and easily keep him," Horbad said.

"True," she said. "But without Hakkar's powers, the invasion is lost. Look. Even now the Celae are winning the battle."

Horbad glanced over his shoulder. The truth of what she said was obvious, and he was no fool. He recognized it.

"Signal the ships," Francia said. "We must leave while we are still able, before the Celae bring in their own ships and trap us in this bay. There will be time enough for another invasion when your powers have matured and strengthened. And this child here will be your safe passage back to this island when next you come."

Doubt flickered in his eyes. Horbad might have his father's

powers, but he was still a child and lacked training. Francia pressed her advantage. "You are Hakkar now, Horbad. But you are still a child. You will need someone to guide your growing and help you train your powers. Whom would you rather trust with this, your aunt or another of Vanizen's sorcerers?" She smiled. "I am your nearest blood relative, and I stand high in Vanizen's favor. Let's call a truce between us and work together for Celi's downfall. We both have vengeance to take upon these people."

Horbad looked down at his father's body. It had shriveled to a dry, flaking husk, no longer human. Finally, he nodded.

"As you say, then," he said. "Tell the captain to weigh anchor."

Eliade went to her knees beside Donaugh. She pulled the girdle from her gown and bound it quickly around his wrist. The flow of blood from the wound slowed, then stopped. She put her arm beneath his shoulders and cradled his head in her lap, beckoning urgently to Torey. Torey scrambled out from the shelter of the trilithon. The grass around Donaugh was slippery with his blood, from wounds in his side and his thigh as well as from the severed wrist. Torey put her hands over her mouth and drew in a deep breath. Where should she start with the Healing? So many wounds . . .

Donaugh lay quietly, his eyes open but deeply shadowed. "The sword?" he whispered.

"Gone, beloved," Eliade said.

A grimace of pain twisted Donaugh's features. "I swore to the gods and goddesses the sword would not leave my hand."

"Aye, nor did it, beloved," Eliade said gently. "As they gave it to you, they took it back."

"And Hakkar?"

"Gone also, but with a sword wound in his heart."

Donaugh nodded and closed his eyes. "Then we have accomplished our purpose."

Torey reached out to put her hands to the wound in Donaugh's side. As she touched it, the child in her womb moved for the first time, a faint fluttering beneath her heart. A thread of joy mixed with the horror churning in her belly as she looked at Donaugh's injuries. The wound below his ribs could well prove mortal, as could blood loss from the missing hand.

Eliade looked up. "Can you save him, my lady?" she asked.

Donaugh reached up for her hand. "I would be with you, beloved," he whispered.

"You yet have work to do here," Eliade said gently. "Now you have met the Maedun blood magic, you know how to deal with it. I will be waiting for you when it's time. You know that."

Torey drew upon the strength of the Dance and poured the Healing power into Donaugh's body. Her own energy drained out of her and into him. Slowly, slowly, she felt the wound draw together, the torn tissues deep within knitting, restoring themselves. When finally she withdrew her hands, only a long scar remained.

She reached for his arm. But even as she touched him, the spark of life within him faltered. Beneath her fingers, his life ebbed and waned, then faded. Donaugh sagged back against Eliade's breast, his eyes closed, his face pale as chalk.

"No," Torey whispered. Then she shouted it out to the glowing sky. "*No!* I won't allow this!"

She gathered the power flowing through the air, seized it from the ground beneath her, and flung it into Donaugh. His body convulsed as the magic of the Dance smashed into him. The power flashed and flared around Torey, coiling in writhing, twisting ropes between her and Donaugh, spinning a web of potent force around them both. Coruscating color painted the looming megaliths of the Dance in brilliant shades of green and blue and pale amber, the colors of life, the colors of Celi itself. The child within her womb leapt as she willed life into her brother.

Then, even as she felt the fire within him kindle and blaze up again, her belly cramped. As the stump of Donaugh's wrist healed cleanly, the life of the child flowed out between Torey's thighs.

The Counter at the Scroll exchanged one life for another.

Epilogue

Donaugh stood on a promontory overlooking the Cold Sea.
A gold cuff encased the stump of his right arm, catching the
sun and reflecting bright glints back into Torey's eyes. The
battle at the Dance and the slow healing process after had
burned every ounce of excess flesh from his body and scattered streaks of silver in the dark gold of his hair. There was
something new in his face now, an austere *otherness* that had
not been there before. It gaunted his cheeks, etched lines into
his face to bracket his nose and mouth. The light of laughter
no longer lit his eyes as easily as it once had, and his smile,
rare now, contained a gentle awareness of how close beneath
the surface of joy lay grief. Torey put her hand to her flat
belly, now barren of the child who had quickened only
moments before it stilled forever. It was as if Donaugh had
glimpsed the Counter at the Scroll in that brief instant
between the time the spark of his own life faded and the life
flow of the child pulled him back. But Torey was unable to
tell whether he counted the bargain a fair one or not.

She was still unsure herself. The sacrifice of one unborn
child in exchange for the freedom of a country might be
counted as a small thing. But not by the mother of the child.
Nor by the uncle of the child, Donaugh's soft voice whispered
in her mind.

Connor put his arm around her shoulder and pulled her
tight against him. She put her head against his chest, still
watching Donaugh. He didn't move; he merely stood there
gazing to the east. She glanced over at Tiernyn and Ylana,
who stood to Donaugh's left. Tiernyn, too, had been marked
by the battle. But his scars were physical scars and would
eventually fade with time. Behind his left shoulder,
Kingmaker's hilt, bound in plain leather and adorned with

only a faceted crystal on the pommel, rose from its scabbard. Torey could not see the scar on the blade, but the sword had not let Tiernyn down. Ylana stood straight as a sword herself at Tiernyn's side. Her pregnancy swelled her belly beneath her gown. One hand rested on the rich curve below her breasts as she watched Donaugh.

Donaugh raised his left hand, palm out, and slowly swept it across the hazy line where sea met sky. At the far edge of vision, a gentle shimmer rose from the sea, almost like heat waves rising from sun-warmed cobblestones in summer. He stood for a moment, then turned to face Tiernyn.

"It's done," he said. "No Maedun ship can pass through the curtain of enchantment. It will remain in place for as long as I live, and as long as the man I train as my successor lives, and his successors, as well."

Tiernyn reached up to grip Donaugh's shoulder. "I have no words to thank you," he said. "I owe you a large debt, Donaugh."

"The *darlai* once promised me that I would be of service to my country and my King," Donaugh said. "I am content."

"Contentment you may have," Tiernyn said. "I wish I could give you happiness."

"Happiness was not promised." Donaugh smiled briefly, then went to Torey. He put his hand to her cheek, then bent slowly and kissed her forehead. "You will know happiness, Littlest," he said softly. "This I promise you."

He turned away and walked toward the horses waiting near a clump of hawthorn. Torey's breath caught in her throat. The faint, nebulous figure of a woman walked beside Donaugh, her bright silver-gilt hair gleaming in the sun.

Enter a New World

THE WESTERN KING • Ann Marston

BOOK TWO OF THE RUNE BLADE TRILOGY

Guarded by the tradition of the past and threatened by the danger of the present, a warrior — as beautiful as she is fierce — must struggle between two warring clans who were one people once.

Also available, *Kingmaker's Sword*

FORTRESS IN THE EYE OF TIME • C. J. Cherryh

THREE TIME HUGO-AWARD WINNING AUTHOR

Deep in an abandoned, shattered castle, an old man of the Old Magic mutters words almost forgotten. With the most wondrous of spells, he calls forth a Shaping, in the form of a young man to be sent east to right the wrongs of a long-forgotten wizard-war, and alter the destiny of a land.

THE HEDGE OF MIST • Patricia Kennealy-Morrison

THE FINAL VOLUME OF THE TALES OF ARTHUR TRILOGY

Morrison's amazing canvas of Keltia holds the great and epic themes of classic fantasy — Arthur, Gweniver, Morgan, Merlynn, the magic of Sidhe-folk, and the Sword from the Stone. Here, with Taliesin's voice and harp to tell of it, she forges a story with the timelessness of a once and future tale. *(Hardcover)*

Fantasy from HarperPrism

DRAGONCHARM
• Graham Edwards

IN THE EPIC TRADITION OF ANNE McCAFFREY'S PERN NOVELS

An ancient prophecy decreed that one day dragon would battle dragon, until none were left in the world. Now it is coming true.

EYE OF THE SERPENT
• Robert N. Charrette

SECOND OF THE AELWYN CHRONICLES

When a holy war breaks out, Yan, a mere apprentice mixing herbs in a backwater town, is called upon to create a spell that can save the land . . . and the life of his beloved Teletha.

Also available, *Timespell*

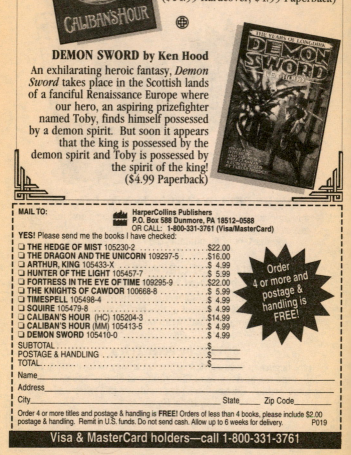